First Edition 2006.

The Clay Sanskrit Library is co-published by
New York University Press
and the JJC Foundation.

Further information about this volume
and the rest of the Clay Sanskrit Library
is available on the following websites:
www.claysanskritlibrary.com
www.nyupress.org.

ISBN-13: 978-0-8147-3183-3 (cloth : alk. paper)
ISBN-10: 0-8147-3183-x (cloth : alk. paper)

Artwork by Robert Beer.
Typeset in Adobe Garamond at 10.25 : 12.3+pt.
XML-development by Stuart Brown.
Editorial input from Dániel Balogh, Tomoyuki Kono,
Eszter Somogyi & Péter Szántó.
Printed in Great Britain by St Edmundsbury Press Ltd,
Bury St Edmunds, Suffolk, on acid-free paper.
Bound by Hunter & Foulis, Edinburgh, Scotland.

THE CLAY SANSKRIT LIBRARY
FOUNDED BY JOHN & JENNIFER CLAY

GENERAL EDITOR

RICHARD GOMBRICH

EDITED BY

ISABELLE ONIANS
SOMADEVA VASUDEVA

WWW.CLAYSANSKRITLIBRARY.COM
WWW.NYUPRESS.ORG

MAHĀBHĀRATA

BOOK FOUR

VIRĀṬA

TRANSLATED BY

KATHLEEN GARBUTT

NEW YORK UNIVERSITY PRESS
JJC FOUNDATION
2006

Library of Congress Cataloging-in-Publication Data
Mahābhārata. Virāṭaparva. English & Sanskrit.
Mahābhārata. Book four, Virāṭa /
translated by Kathleen Garbutt.
p. cm. – (The Clay Sanskrit library)
Epic poetry.
In English and Sanskrit (romanized) on facing pages;
includes translation from Sanskrit.
Includes bibliographical references and index.
ISBN-13: 978-0-8147-3183-3 (cloth : alk. paper)
ISBN-10: 0-8147-3183-x (cloth : alk. paper)
I. Garbutt, Kathleen. II. Title. III. Title: Virāṭa.
BL1138.242.V37E5 2006
294.5'92304521–dc22 2006032853

CONTENTS

SANSKRIT ALPHABETICAL ORDER

Vowels:	*a ā i ī u ū ṛ ṝ ḷ ḹ e ai o au ṃ ḥ*
Gutturals:	*k kh g gh ṅ*
Palatals:	*c ch j jh ñ*
Retroflex:	*ṭ ṭh ḍ ḍh ṇ*
Dentals:	*t th d dh n*
Labials:	*p ph b bh m*
Semivowels:	*y r l v*
Spirants:	*ś ṣ s h*

GUIDE TO SANSKRIT PRONUNCIATION

a	b*u*t
ā, â	f*a*ther
i	s*i*t
ī, î	f*ee*
u	p*u*t
ū, û	b*oo*
ṛ	vocalic *r*, American p*ur*dy or English p*re*tty
ṝ	lengthened *ṛ*
ḷ	vocalic *l*, ab*le*
e, ê, ē	m*a*de, esp. in Welsh pronunciation
ai	b*i*te
o, ô, ō	r*o*pe, esp. Welsh pronunciation; Italian s*o*lo
au	s*ou*nd
ṃ	*anusvāra* nasalizes the preceding vowel
ḥ	*visarga*, a voiceless aspiration (resembling English *h*), or like Scottish lo*ch*, or an aspiration with a faint echoing of the preceding vowel so that *taiḥ* is pronounced *taih*^{i}
k	lu*ck*
kh	blo*ckh*ead
g	*g*o
gh	bi*gh*ead
ṅ	a*n*ger
c	*ch*ill
ch	mat*chh*ead
j	*j*og
jh	aspirated *j*, he*dgeh*og
ñ	ca*ny*on
ṭ	retroflex *t*, *t*ry (with the tip of tongue turned up to touch the hard palate)
ṭh	same as the preceding but aspirated
ḍ	retroflex *d* (with the tip of tongue turned up to touch the hard palate)
ḍh	same as the preceding but aspirated
ṇ	retroflex *n* (with the tip

	of tongue turned up to touch the hard palate)
t	French *t*out
th	ten*t h*ook
d	*d*inner
dh	guil*dh*all
n	*n*ow
p	*p*ill
ph	u*ph*eaval
b	*b*efore
bh	a*bh*orrent
m	*m*ind
y	*y*es
r	trilled, resembling the Italian pronunciation of *r*
l	*l*inger
v	*w*ord
ś	*sh*ore
ṣ	retroflex *sh* (with the tip of the tongue turned up to touch the hard palate)
s	hi*ss*
h	*h*ood

CSL PUNCTUATION OF ENGLISH

The acute accent on Sanskrit words when they occur outside of the Sanskrit text itself, marks stress, e.g. Ramáyana. It is not part of traditional Sanskrit orthography, transliteration or transcription, but we supply it here to guide readers in the pronunciation of these unfamiliar words. Since no Sanskrit word is accented on the last syllable it is not necessary to accent disyllables, e.g. Rama.

The second CSL innovation designed to assist the reader in the pronunciation of lengthy unfamiliar words is to insert an unobtrusive middle dot between semantic word breaks in compound names (provided the word break does not fall on a vowel resulting from the fusion of two vowels), e.g. Maha·bhárata, but Ramáyana (not Rama·áyana). Our dot echoes the punctuating middle dot (·) found in the oldest surviving forms of written Indic, the Ashokan inscriptions of the third century BCE.

The deep layering of Sanskrit narrative has also dictated that we use quotation marks only to announce the beginning and end of every direct speech, and not at the beginning of every paragraph.

CSL PUNCTUATION OF SANSKRIT

The Sanskrit text is also punctuated, in accordance with the punctuation of the English translation. In mid-verse, the punctuation will not alter the *sandhi* or the scansion. Proper names are capitalized. Most Sanskrit metres have four "feet" *(pāda):* where possible we print the common *śloka* metre on two lines. In the Sanskrit text, we use French *Guillemets* (e.g. *«kva saṃcicīrṣuḥ?»*) instead of English quotation marks (e.g. "Where are you off to?") to avoid confusion with the apostrophes used for vowel elision in *sandhi*.

Sanskrit presents the learner with a challenge: *sandhi* ("euphonic combination"). *Sandhi* means that when two words are joined in connected speech or writing (which in Sanskrit reflects speech), the last letter (or even letters) of the first word often changes; compare the way we pronounce "the" in "the beginning" and "the end."

In Sanskrit the first letter of the second word may also change; and if both the last letter of the first word and the first letter of the second are vowels, they may fuse. This has a parallel in English: a nasal consonant is inserted between two vowels that would otherwise coalesce: "a pear" and "an apple." Sanskrit vowel fusion may produce ambiguity. The chart at the back of each book gives the full *sandhi* system.

Fortunately it is not necessary to know these changes in order to start reading Sanskrit. For that, what is important is to know the form of the second word without *sandhi* (pre-*sandhi*), so that it can be recognized or looked up in a dictionary. Therefore we are printing Sanskrit with a system of punctuation that will indicate, unambiguously, the original form of the second word, i.e., the form without *sandhi*. Such *sandhi* mostly concerns the fusion of two vowels.

In Sanskrit, vowels may be short or long and are written differently accordingly. We follow the general convention that a vowel with no mark above it is short. Other books mark a long vowel either with a bar called a macron (*ā*) or with a circumflex (*â*). Our system uses the macron, except that for initial vowels in *sandhi* we use a circumflex to indicate that originally the vowel was short, or the shorter of two possibilities (*e* rather than *ai*, *o* rather than *au*).

When we print initial *â*, before *sandhi* that vowel was	*a*
î or *ê*,	*i*
û or *ô*,	*u*
âi,	*e*
âu,	*o*

ā,	*ā* (i.e., the same)
ī,	*ī* (i.e., the same)
ū,	*ū* (i.e., the same)
ē,	*ī*
ō,	*ū*
āi,	*ai*
āu,	*au*

’, before *sandhi* there was a vowel *a*

FURTHER HELP WITH VOWEL SANDHI

When a final short vowel (*a, i* or *u*) has merged into a following vowel, we print ’ at the end of the word, and when a final long vowel (*ā, ī* or *ū*) has merged into a following vowel we print ” at the end of the word. The vast majority of these cases will concern a final *a* or *ā*.

Examples:

What before *sandhi* was *atra asti* is represented as *atr’ âsti*

atra āste	*atr’ āste*
kanyā asti	*kany” âsti*
kanyā āste	*kany” āste*
atra iti	*atr’ êti*
kanyā iti	*kany” êti*
kanyā īpsitā	*kany” ēpsitā*

Finally, three other points concerning the initial letter of the second word:

(1) A word that before *sandhi* begins with *ṛ* (vowel), after *sandhi* begins with *r* followed by a consonant: *yatha” rtu* represents pre-*sandhi yathā ṛtu*.

(2) When before *sandhi* the previous word ends in *t* and the following word begins with *ś*, after *sandhi* the last letter of the previous word is *c* and the following word begins with *ch*: *syāc chāstravit* represents pre-*sandhi syāt śāstravit*.

(3) Where a word begins with *h* and the previous word ends with a double consonant, this is our simplified spelling to show the pre-*sandhi*

form: *tad hasati* is commonly written as *tad dhasati*, but we write *tadd hasati* so that the original initial letter is obvious.

COMPOUNDS

We also punctuate the division of compounds (*samāsa*), simply by inserting a thin vertical line between words. There are words where the decision whether to regard them as compounds is arbitrary. Our principle has been to try to guide readers to the correct dictionary entries.

EXAMPLE

Where the Deva·nágari script reads:

कुम्भस्थली रक्षतु वो विकीर्णसिन्दूररेणुर्द्विरदाननस्य ।
प्रशान्तये विघ्नतमश्छटानां निष्ठ्यूतबालातपपल्लवेव ॥

Others would print:

kumbhasthalī rakṣatu vo vikīrṇasindūrareṇur dviradānanasya /
praśāntaye vighnatamaśchaṭānāṃ niṣṭhyūtabālātapapallaveva //

We print:

kumbha|sthalī rakṣatu vo vikīrṇa|sindūra|reṇur dvirad'|ānanasya
praśāntaye vighna|tamaś|chaṭānāṃ niṣṭhyūta|bāl'|ātapa|pallav" êva.

And in English:

"May Ganésha's domed forehead protect you! Streaked with vermilion dust, it seems to be emitting the spreading rays of the rising sun to pacify the teeming darkness of obstructions."

"Nava·sáhasanka and the Serpent Princess" I.3 by Padma·gupta

INTRODUCTION

'Viráta' (*Virāṭa/parvan*), the fourth book of the 'Maha·bhárata' (MBh), tells the story of the Pándavas' final year of exile, when they live disguised in the city of King Viráta. While they live incognito as Viráta's servants, Kíchaka, the Matsyan general, falls in love with Dráupadi, the Pándavas' wife, disguised as a hairdresser. Realizing that Viráta will not protect her, Dráupadi convinces Bhima to kill Kíchaka. Once he is dead, the Kíchaka kinsmen attempt to immolate Dráupadi on Kíchaka's funeral pyre, so once again Bhima comes to her rescue and kills the entire clan. Meanwhile, in their attempt to find the Pándavas, Dhrita·rashtra's spies discover that Kíchaka is dead and so the Kurus and the Tri·gartas launch an attack on Viráta. All the Pándavas, bar Árjuna, join Viráta's army and ride out to stop the Tri·gartan cattle rustlers. They do indeed defeat the Tri·gartas, but while they are engaged in battle Duryódhana and the Kurus take advantage of the undefended city to steal the rest of the cattle. As a result, Prince Úttara and Árjuna are forced to go out alone to win them back. This battle takes up a large part of the book. Though almost no blood is shed, Árjuna wins a convincing victory over the Kurus. At the end of the book Abhimányu is married to Viráta's daughter Uttará.

This book has been the subject of much debate. It has been shown to be a fairly late part of the 'Maha·bhárata,' though some of the most convincing evidence for this involves the hymn to Durga, which hardly proves that the entire book is a late addition. Regardless of when it was included in the epic, 'Viráta' proves to be a crucially important part of the 'Maha·bhárata.'

This thirteenth year acts as a microcosm of the twelve-year exile. Bhima tells us (MBh III.36.31) that twelve years can parallel twelve months, for example in the Veda. The thirteenth year acts as a buffer to close off the exile years and prepare for the next part of the epic, which should be peaceful but will inevitably turn to war, as the battle in this book demonstrates.

The points of interest that I shall discuss here are the "carnival" feel of 'Viráta,' the reasons for the Pándavas' choice of disguises, the book's use as a harbinger of the overall war to come and its inversion of the 'Bhágavad Gita' (*Bhagavad/gītā*).

'Viráta' as a Festival

While it is important not to overplay the importance of the "carnival" aspect of this book, it is undoubtedly there. 'Viráta' is filled with various kinds of humor, and the story itself involves a festival, a wedding and a city-wide victory celebration.

There are echoes of the Holi festival in this book, as van Buitenen (1980) has noted. This festival, which since ancient times celebrated Kama and fertility as a New Year revel, could perhaps underlie the book insofar as there is a generally festive feel and a hope for regeneration. The Pándavas spend this year waiting for a new beginning and phase in their life, but, on the other hand, the sexual license of Kama's festival is clearly not encouraged here. Sex is often in the air, but mostly unconsummated. Kíchaka's amorous advances bring him death, Árjuna's time spent living among women is entirely self-controlled and the book ends with a very proper wedding ceremony. The ideas of regeneration and new beginnings are more dominant, while sexual restraint is preferred to sexual license.

The city of Matsya itself is made the perfect setting for a book of humor, since its king, Viráta, is bumbling and incompetent. He offer his kingdom to every stranger he meets, falls into the Tri·gartans' trap by taking all his troops to battle, leaving no defensive force behind, and unquestioningly believes that his spoiled and untested son has managed to defeat an entire army single-handedly. When Kíchaka boasts to Dráupadi that he is the true ruler of the kingdom (MBh IV.14.42), it seems entirely plausible. Certainly the Tri·gartas believe it, which is why they attack.

The Pándavas themselves are all disguised in ridiculous ways. Here we see them as "tragic clowns," to use SHULMAN's (1985) phraseology. Yudhi·shthira disguises himself as a master gambler, and no one could deny the irony in that. Bhima is a cook, emphasizing his size in a new humorous light, displaying his enormous appetite, while his strength is now used to fight wild beasts for general entertainment. Nákula and Saha·deva take charge of Viráta's horses and cattle, respectively. Árjuna is undoubtedly the most ridiculously disguised son of Pandu. He presents himself as a eunuch, and one can just imagine how absurd he would look dressed as a woman. Indeed, even Viráta, who is portrayed as a simple-minded fool, immediately points out how unconvincing this costume is. The humor gets cruder, for Árjuna's chosen name as a eunuch is Brihan·nala, meaning "lady with a large reed." A great deal of the humor in this book is obvious and pantomime in character. For example, when Bhima lies in wait for Kíchaka, he pretends to be Dráupadi and compliments Kíchaka on his touch when he unwittingly caresses the son of Pandu (MBh IV.22.48). Then again, when Árjuna defeats the Kurus at the end of the last battle, he does not kill them, but instead settles for stealing their clothes, leaving them looking ridiculous and laughing at them just as they laughed when they saw him running around as a transvestite.

Pándavas' Disguises and Names

Apart from their humorous connotations, we may wonder why the Pándavas chose these particular disguises. Many suggestions have been offered. Árjuna's disguise as a eunuch is by far the most puzzling and so has garnered the most interest. The explanation offered by the 'Maha·bhárata' is that Úrvashi cursed him to live as a dancer among women because he rejected her (MBh III.46). However, there is undoubtedly more to it than that. Transvestism is a common motif, with everyone from Indra to Achilles (though some do not accept a common Indo-European heritage) doing it at some stage or another.

There is the view that the Pándavas' disguises still mirror their Dumezilian functions; so Yudhi·shthira is a brahmin, Bhima a warrior and the twins take *vaiśya* occupations. The problem here is, of course, Árjuna, though he is often an exception to the rule, fulfilling what Nick Allen calls the fourth function. However, even if we accept the "function" aspect, it does not entirely explain the exact occupations that the Pándavas undertake.

Hiltebeitel argues that the choices parallel Nala's disguise, since skill with dice, skill with horses and skill with cookery all feature as part of his charade, while his wife served as another queen's maid. Furthermore, Nala's ability to control fire and water are traits associated with the twins Nákula and Saha·deva. This leaves only Árjuna once again, but Hiltebeitel believes that he, too, can be accounted for since Damayánti says that Nala has become a eunuch to her (MBh III.77).

Other explanations for the choice of disguises rest primarily on the idea of inversion. The Pándavas have become the embodiment of all that a king should not be, Árjuna, for example, becoming the most literal embodiment of impotence, but this is a pattern we see time and time again. Indra is depicted as a "tragic clown," for example in the story of his brahminicide in 'Preparation for War' (*Udyoga/parvan*). In both these cases and in others, it is possible to see symbolism of ritualized separation—like a sacrificer's consecration. The text itself says that the Pándavas lived as though returning to the womb (MBh IV.13.12).

Though many suggestions have been offered, one should not necessarily accept that only one is right, but, rather, that all these varied theories are useful and not mutually exclusive. Much of the Sanskrit literature we still have today is highly complex and functions on many levels, so we should not underestimate how sophisticated 'Viráta' was intended to be.

Foreshadowing

It has been noted that 'Viráta' concludes the exile, neatly encapsulating the ideas of the Pándavas' fall from power, and prepares them for the future in terms of an initiation, but it also foreshadows the great war between the Kurus and the Pándavas which will follow. This foreshadowing can be found in the cattle rustling. Just as the Tri·garta brothers take an oath to protect Duryódhana in the real war, the Tri·gartas here tempt out the entire Matsyan army, leaving Duryódhana free to steal almost without risk. When Árjuna and Úttara drive out to face the full force of the Kuru army, the battle itself is clearly depicted as a rehearsal. It does not seem serious; in fact it becomes something of a spectator sport, since the gods gather in the skies above to watch. The showmanship of Árjuna's talents is on display here, just as Bhima's strength was paraded for entertainment earlier on. The Kuru heroes are humiliated and defeated in turn, though almost bloodlessly. The battle even has a suitably dramatic ending, almost designed for an audience: when the Kurus are stunned, Árjuna sends Úttara to collect all the heroes' clothes, so they are humiliated in a public fashion. These chapters certainly feel like a dress rehearsal, and, as for what they tell us of the plot to come, we see that when Árjuna shoots his final weapon it stuns all his enemies, except Bhishma, just as they will all die in the real war, except Bhishma, who will be merely incapacitated on a bed of arrows.

Once the battle is over, Abhimányu and Uttará marry, and after the real war is over their son Paríkshit carries on the race.

'Bhágavad Gita' Inversion

No one who has read the 'Bhágavad Gita' will fail to see similarities in the scene that takes place before the second and lengthier battle, when Árjuna tries to convince the reluctant Úttara that war is the only way. Once again the comic tone predominates.

Úttara runs off, and we watch with the Kurus as Árjuna chases him, his women's clothes and plaits flying in the wind. In the 'Bhágavad Gita' (6.24) Krishna begs Árjuna not to become a eunuch, but here it is that very figure of cowardice who proves to be the most manly. So 'Viráta' foreshadows the war to come but emphasizes humorous aspects at the expense of the philosophy. The lighthearted take on war which we find in this book is in stark contrast to the sense of horror and foreboding that permeates the next book, 'Preparation for War.'

Bibliography

Allen, Nick. 'Arjuna and the Second Function; a Dumezilian crux,' *Journal of the Royal Asiatic Society*, 3rd series, vol. 9, part 3, Nov. 1999.

Brockington, J.L. *The Sanskrit Epics*. Leiden: Brill, 1998.

Hiltebeitel, Alf. *Rethinking the Mahābhārata: A Reader's Guide to the Education of the Dharma King*. Chicago/London: University of Chicago Press, 2001.

Shulman, D.D. *The King and the Clown in South Indian Myth and Poetry*. Princeton: Princeton University Press, 1985.

van Buitenen, J.A.B. *The Mahābhārata: The Book of Virāṭa. The Book of the Effort*. Chicago: University of Chicago Press, 1980.

1–13
DISGUISES FOR VIRÁTA'S COURT

1.1 NĀRĀYAṆAṂ NAMAS|KṚTYA
Naraṃ c' âiva nar'|ôttamam
devīṃ Sarasvatīṃ c' âiva
tato «Jayam» udīrayet.

JANAMEJAYA uvāca:

kathaṃ Virāṭa|nagare mama pūrva|pitāmahāḥ
a|jñāta|vāsam uṣitā Duryodhana|bhay'|ârditāḥ?
pati|vratā mahā|bhāgā satataṃ brahma|vādinī
Draupadī ca kathaṃ, brahmann, a|jñātā duḥkhit" âvasat?

VAIŚAMPĀYANA uvāca:

yathā Virāṭa|nagare tava pūrva|pitāmahāḥ
a|jñāta|vāsam uṣitās tac chṛṇuṣva, nar'|âdhipa.
1.5 tathā sa tu varāl labdhvā Dharmād dharma|bhṛtāṃ varaḥ
gatv" āśramaṃ brāhmaṇebhya ācakhyau sarvam eva tat.
kathayitvā tu tat sarvaṃ brāhmaṇebhyo Yudhiṣṭhiraḥ
araṇī|sahitaṃ tasmai brāhmaṇāya nyavedayat.
tato Yudhiṣṭhiro rājā Dharma|putro mahā|manāḥ
saṃnivarty' ânujān sarvān iti h' ôvāca, Bhārata:
«dvā|daś' êmāni varṣāṇi rājya|viproṣitā vayam.
trayo|daśo 'yaṃ samprāptaḥ kṛcchrāt parama|dur|vasaḥ.
sa, sādhu Kaunteya, ito vāsam, Arjuna, rocaya
saṃvatsaram imaṃ yatra vasem' â|viditāḥ paraiḥ.»

ARJUNA uvāca:

1.10 tasy' âiva vara|dānena Dharmasya, manuj'|âdhipa,
a|jñātā vicariṣyāmo narāṇāṃ n' âtra saṃśayaḥ.
tatra vāsāya rāṣṭrāṇi kīrtayiṣyāmi kāni cit
ramaṇīyāni, guptāni. teṣāṃ kiñ cit sma rocaya.

Having paid homage to Naráyana, to Nara, the best 1.1
of men, and to the goddess Sarásvati, let the word
"Victory" be uttered.

JANAM·ÉJAYA said:

How did my ancestors, afflicted by fear of Duryódhana, pass their time undiscovered in Viráta's city? And how did the illustrious Dráupadi, who always refers to the Veda, devoted to her husbands, though grief-stricken, remain undiscovered, o brahmin?

VAISHAMPÁYANA said:

Hear, lord of men, how your ancestors passed their time
unrecognized in Viráta's city. When the greatest of virtuous 1.5
men had taken gifts from Dharma, he went to the hermitage and told the brahmins everything that had happened. When he had told the entire story to the brahmins, Yudhi·shthira presented the gathered drilling sticks to the brahmin.

Then high-minded King Yudhi·shthira, the son of Dharma, was sent back to his younger brothers, and said this, Bhárata:

"For twelve years we have been banished from our kingdom. The thirteenth miserable year, which will be the hardest to get through, has now arrived. So then, excellent Árjuna, son of Kuntí, choose a home for this year, where we may live undiscovered by our enemies."

ÁRJUNA said:

Due to Dharma's gift, king of men, there is no doubt 1.10
that we will wander among men without being recognized.
So I will run through some kingdoms that are pleasant and
secluded, as options for us to live in. Choose one.

santi ramyā jana|padā bahv|annāḥ paritaḥ Kurūn:
Pāñcālāś, Cedi|Matsyāś ca, Śūrasenāḥ, Paṭaccarāḥ,
Daśārṇā, nava|rāṣṭrāś ca Mallāḥ, Śālvā, Yugandharāḥ,
Kunti|rāṣṭraṃ ca vipulaṃ, Surāṣṭr'|Âvantayas tathā.
eteṣāṃ katamo, rājan, nivāsas tava rocate
yatra vatsyāmahe, rājan, saṃvatsaram imaṃ vayam?

YUDHIṢṬHIRA uvāca:

1.15 śrutam etan, mahā|bāho, yathā sa bhagavān prabhuḥ
abravīt sarva|bhūt'|ēśas, tat tathā, na tad anyathā.
avaśyaṃ tv eva vās'|ârthaṃ ramaṇīyaṃ, śivaṃ, sukham
sammantrya sahitaiḥ sarvair vastavyam a|kuto|bhayaiḥ.
Matsyo Virāṭo balavān, abhirakto 'tha Pāṇḍavān,
dharma|śīlo, vadānyaś ca, vṛddhaś ca satataṃ priyaḥ.
Virāṭa|nagare, tāta, saṃvatsaram imaṃ vayam
kurvantas tasya karmāṇi vihariṣyāma, Bhārata.
yāni yāni ca karmāṇi tasya śakṣyāmahe vayam
kartuṃ yo yat, sa tat karma bravītu, Kuru|nandanāḥ.

ARJUNA uvāca:

1.20 nara|deva, kathaṃ tasya rāṣṭre karma kariṣyasi?
Virāṭa|nagare, sādho, raṃsyase kena karmaṇā?
mṛdur, vadānyo, hrīmāṃś ca, dhārmikaḥ, satya|vikramaḥ,
rājaṃs, tvam āpadā kaṣṭaḥ! kiṃ kariṣyasi, Pāṇḍava?
na duḥkham ucitaṃ kiñ cid rājā veda yathā janaḥ
sa imām āpadaṃ prāpya kathaṃ ghorāṃ tariṣyasi?

There are agreeable and pleasant nations, rich in food all around the land of the Kurus: the Panchálas, the Chedi, the Matsyas, the people of Shura·sena, the Patáccharas, the people of Dashárna, the new Malla kingdom, the Shalvans, the Yugan·dharas, the extensive realm of Kunti, the Suráshtrans, or the Avántayas. So which of these places pleases you, my king, for us to spend this year, lord?

YUDHI·SHTHIRA said:

Long-armed man, what we heard is true. It will be just as the powerful, blessed lord of all creatures said, and not otherwise.* By all means let us all decide together on a pleasant, happy and auspicious place in which to live without fear from any quarter. 1.15

The old king of the Matsyas, Viráta, is mighty, munificent and virtuous in his conduct. Furthermore, he is devoted to the Pándavas and dear to all. So we will pass our time this year in Viráta's city, working in his service, Bhárata. So tell me, descendants of the Kurus, in what capacities will we each be able to serve the King of Matsya?

ÁRJUNA said:

Godlike man, what service will you perform for him in the kingdom? In what capacity will you dwell in Viráta's city, excellent man? You are tender, charitable, modest, virtuous and truly valiant, but alas for your misfortune, king! What will you do, Pándava? A king is unfamiliar with the misery normal to his people. How will you survive the terrible misfortune that has befallen you? 1.20

YUDHIṢṬHIRA uvāca:

śṛṇudhvaṃ yat kariṣyāmi karma vai, Kuru|nandanāḥ,
Virāṭam anusamprāpya rājānaṃ, puruṣa'|rṣabhāḥ.
sabhā|stāro bhaviṣyāmi tasya rājño mah"|ātmanaḥ
Kaṅko nāma dvi|jo bhūtvā mat'|âkṣaḥ, priya|devanaḥ.
1.25 vaidūryān, kāñcanān, dāntān phalair jyotī|rasaiḥ saha
kṛṣṇ'|âkṣāṃl, lohit'|âkṣāś ca nirvatsyāmi mano|ramān.
Virāṭa|rājaṃ ramayan s'|âmātyaṃ saha|bāndhavam,
na ca māṃ vetsyate kaś cit, toṣayiṣye ca taṃ nṛpam.
«āsaṃ Yudhiṣṭhirasy' âhaṃ purā prāṇa|samaḥ sakhā.»
iti vakṣyāmi rājānaṃ yadi māṃ so 'nuyokṣyate.
ity etad vo may" ākhyātaṃ vihariṣyāmy ahaṃ yathā.
Vṛkodara, Virāṭe tvaṃ raṃsyase kena hetunā?

BHĪMASENA uvāca:

2.1 PAURO|GAVO BRUVĀṆO 'haṃ Ballavo nāma, Bhārata,
upasthāsyāmi rājānaṃ Virāṭam, iti me matiḥ.
sūpān asya kariṣyāmi, kuśalo 'smi mahānase,
kṛta|pūrvāṇi yāny asya vyañjanāni su|śikṣitaiḥ,
tāny apy abhibhaviṣyāmi prītiṃ sañjanayann aham.
āhariṣyāmi dārūṇāṃ nicayān mahato 'pi ca.
tat prekṣya vipulaṃ karma rājā saṃyokṣyate sa mām.
a|mānuṣāṇi kurvānas tāni karmāṇi, Bhārata,
2.5 rājñas tasya pare preṣyā maṃsyante māṃ yathā nṛpam.
bhakṣy'|ânna|rasa|pānānāṃ bhaviṣyāmi tath" ēśvaraḥ.
dvipā vā balino, rājan, vṛṣabhā vā mahā|balāḥ
vinigrāhyā yadi mayā, nigrahīṣyāmi tān api.
ye ca ke cin niyotsyanti samājeṣu niyodhakāḥ,
tān ahaṃ hi niyotsyāmi ratiṃ tasya vivardhayan.

YUDHI·SHTHIRA said:

Listen to what I will do, bull-like descendants of the Kurus, once I have reached King Viráta. I will become "Kanka,"* a brahmin fond of gambling and reveling in dice, and I will be the high-hearted king's games-playing courtier.
I will set down cat's-eye gem, gold and ivory game pieces 1.25
on a gemstone gaming board, and cast beautiful black and red dice. I will entertain King Viráta along with ministers and relatives, and no one will recognize me as I amuse the king. If the king should question me, I shall say to him: "I was Yudhi·shthira's friend, as dear to him as life itself." So I will pass the time as I've told you, but by what means will you reside in Viráta's realm, Vrikódara?

BHIMA·SENA said:

My intention, Bhárata, is to announce myself to King 2.1
Viráta as a head chef, calling myself Bállava. I shall make curries and whatever dishes his highly trained cooks made in the past, since I am skilled in the kitchen. Moreover, I shall surpass them, for I am intent on favor.

I will carry heaped loads of harsh wood, even if they're huge. When he sees that monumental task, the king will be pleased with me, and when they see me perform supernatural feats, Bhárata, the other servants of his palace will 2.5
think of me as a king. I will be in charge of what food is to be eaten and what drink is to be drunk.

Or if powerful elephants and mighty bulls need restraining I will restrain even them, my king. I will fight whichever wrestlers will take me on in conflicts, putting an end to their fun, but I will not kill anyone who fights me. I will merely

na tv etān yudhyamānān vai haniṣyāmi kathañ cana;
tath" âitān pātayiṣyāmi, yathā yāsyanti na kṣayam.
«ārāliko, go|vikartā, sūpa|kartā, niyodhakaḥ
āsaṃ Yudhiṣṭirasy' âham, iti» vakṣyāmi pṛcchataḥ.
2.10 ātmānam ātmanā rakṣaṃś cariṣyāmi, viśām pate.
ity etat pratijānāmi, vihariṣyāmy ahaṃ yathā.

YUDHIṢṬHIRA uvāca:

yam Agnir brāhmaṇo bhūtvā samāgacchan nṛṇāṃ varam,
didhakṣuḥ Khāṇḍavaṃ dāvaṃ Dāśārha|sahitaṃ purā,
mahā|balaṃ mahā|bāhum a|jitaṃ Kuru|nandanam,
so 'yaṃ kiṃ karma Kaunteyaḥ kariṣyati Dhanañjayaḥ?
yo 'yam āsādya taṃ dāvaṃ tarpayām āsa Pāvakam,
vijity' âika|rathen' Êndraṃ, hatvā pannaga|rākṣasān,
Vāsukeḥ sarpa|rājasya svasāraṃ hṛtavāṃś ca yaḥ,
śreṣṭo yaḥ pratiyodhānāṃ so 'rjunaḥ kiṃ kariṣyati?
2.15 sūryaḥ pratapatāṃ śreṣṭho, dvi|padāṃ brāhmaṇo varaḥ,
āśīviṣaś ca sarpāṇāṃ, agnis tejasvināṃ varaḥ,
āyudhānāṃ varaṃ vajraṃ, kakudmī ca gavāṃ varaḥ,
hradānām udadhiḥ śreṣṭhaḥ, parjanyo varṣatāṃ varaḥ,
Dhṛtarāṣṭraś ca nāgānāṃ, hastiṣv Airāvaṇo varaḥ,
putraḥ priyāṇām adhiko, bhāryā ca suhṛdāṃ varā.
yath" âitāni viśiṣṭāni jātyāṃ jātyāṃ, Vṛkodara,
evaṃ yuvā Guḍākeśaḥ śreṣṭhaḥ sarva|dhanuṣmatām.

throw them down in such a way that they do not meet their end.

And when asked I will say, "I was Yudhi·shthira's cook, cow-slaughterer, sauce-maker and wrestler." This is the dis- 2.10
guise I will adopt to protect my identity, lord of the earth. So I am reborn, and will pass my time in this manner.

YUDHI·SHTHIRA said:

And what of that hero who was with Krishna when Agni, in brahmin form, eager to burn the Khándava forest, met him long ago? What of Dhanan·jaya, the son of Kuntí, the mighty descendant of the Kurus, that long-armed and invincible man—what will he do? What of the man who reached the forest and satisfied Agni, who vanquished Indra with a single chariot, who killed serpents and demons, and who seized the sister of Vásuki, the king of the *naga*s, taking her as his wife? That Árjuna who is the greatest of warriors, what will he do?

Just as the sun is the greatest of all blazing, celestial bodies, 2.15
the brahmin is the best of all bipeds, the cobra the greatest of all serpents, fire the most excellent of all things possessing brilliance, the thunderbolt the best of all weapons, the humped bull the best of all bovine creatures, the ocean the greatest of all masses of water, the rain cloud the best of the monsoon, Dhrita·rashtra the best of the *naga*s, Airávata the greatest of elephants; just as the son is superior to all beloved things and the wife the best of friends, so, just as it is with these distinct examples, each of their own type, so too the young Guda·kesha is the greatest of all bowmen, Vrikódara.

so 'yam Indrād an|avaro, Vāsudevān mahā|dyutiḥ
Gāṇḍīva|dhanvā Bībhatsuḥ śvet'|âśvaḥ kiṃ kariṣyati?
2.20 uṣitvā pañca varṣāṇi sahasr'|âkṣasya veśmani,
astra|yogaṃ samāsādya sva|vīryān mānuṣ'|âdbhutam,
divyāny astrāṇi c' āptāni deva|rūpeṇa bhāsvatā.
yaṃ manye dvā|daśaṃ Rudram, Ādityānāṃ trayo|daśam,
Vasūnāṃ navamaṃ manye,grahāṇāṃ daśamaṃ tathā,
yasya bāhū samau, dīrghau, jy"|āghāta|kaṭhina|tvacau,
dakṣiṇe c' âiva, savye ca gavām iva vahaḥ kṛtaḥ,
Himavān iva śailānāṃ, samudraḥ saritām iva,
tri|daśānāṃ yathā Śakro, Vasūnām iva havyavāṭ,
mṛgāṇām iva śārdūlo, Garuḍaḥ patatām iva
varaḥ sannahyamānānāṃ, so 'rjunaḥ kiṃ kariṣyati?

ARJUNA uvāca:

2.25 pratijñāṃ «ṣaṇḍhako 'sm'. îti» kariṣyāmi, mahī|pate.
jy"|āghātau hi mahāntau me, saṃvartuṃ, nṛpa, duṣ|karau.
valayaiś chādayiṣyāmi bāhū kiṇa|kṛtāv imau,
karṇayoḥ pratimucy' âhaṃ kuṇḍale jvalana|prabhe.
pinaddha|kambuḥ pāṇibhyāṃ, tṛtīyāṃ prakṛtiṃ gataḥ,
veṇī|kṛta|śirā, rājan, nāmnā c' âiva Bṛhannalā.

paṭhann ākhyāyikāś c' âiva strī|bhāvena punaḥ punaḥ
ramayiṣye mahī|pālam, anyāṃś c' ântaḥ|pure janān.
gītaṃ, nṛtyaṃ vicitraṃ ca, vāditraṃ vividhaṃ tathā
śikṣayiṣyāmy ahaṃ, rājan, Virāṭasya pura|striyaḥ.

What will glorious Bibhátsu do, he who is not inferior to Indra or Vasudéva himself, who carries the bow Gandíva, and has white horses? He dwelled for five years in the home 2.20
of Indra of a thousand eyes, attained the discipline of inhuman, supernatural weapons by his own strength and obtained divine arms by means of his luminous celestial form. I think of him as the twelfth Rudra, the thirteenth Adítya, and I regard him as the ninth Vasu and the tenth *graha*. His arms are long and equal, hardened by the strokes of the bowstring, and lumpy calluses have formed like the humps of bulls on both the left and right arm. He is like the Himálaya among mountains, the ocean among lakes, Shakra among heaven-dwellers, the fire among Vasus, a tiger among deer and Gáruda among creatures of flight. What will Árjuna, the best of warriors, do?

ÁRJUNA said:

I will claim that I am a eunuch, earth-king. My arms, 2.25
king, are scarred by the bowstring, large and difficult to conceal. I will cover my long, calloused arms with bracelets and fasten beautiful radiant earrings to my ears. So, with conch bracelets decked on my wrists, I will become a member of the third sex, and with a braid of hair falling down from my head, my king, I will call myself Brihan·nala—the large-reeded lady.

By living as a woman, I shall regularly entertain the king and others inside the palace's inner complex by giving short narrative recitals. I shall teach the women of Viráta's palace singing, my king, diverse dances and various musical instruments. I will hide myself, Kauntéya, through illusion, 2.30

2.30 prajānāṃ samudācāraṃ bahu|karma kṛtaṃ vadan,
chādayiṣyāmi, Kaunteya, māyay" ātmānam ātmanā.
«Yudhiṣṭhirasya gehe vai Draupadyāḥ paricārikā
uṣit" âsm', îti» vakṣyāmi pṛṣṭo rājñā ca, Pāṇḍava.
etena vidhinā channaḥ kṛtakena, yathā Nalaḥ,
vihariṣyāmi, rāj'|êndra, Virāṭa|bhavane sukham.

VAIŚAṂPĀYANA uvāca:

3.1 ITY EVAM UKTVĀ puruṣa|pravīras
tath" Ârjuno dharma|bhṛtāṃ variṣṭhaḥ
vākyaṃ, tath" âsau virarāma bhūyo.
nṛpo 'paraṃ bhrātaram ābabhāṣe.

YUDHIṢṬHIRA uvāca:

kiṃ tvaṃ, Nakula, kurvāṇas tatra, tāta, cariṣyasi
karma tat tvaṃ samācakṣva, rājye tasya mahī|pateḥ,
su|kumāraś ca, śūraś ca, darśanīyaḥ, sukh'|ôcitaḥ?

NAKULA uvāca:

aśva|bandho bhaviṣyāmi Virāṭa|nṛpater aham,
sarvathā jñāna|sampannaḥ, kuśalaḥ parirakṣaṇe.
Granthiko nāma nāmn" âhaṃ. karm' āitat su|priyaṃ mama.
kuśalo 'smy aśva|śikṣāyāṃ, tath" âiv' âśva|cikitsane,
priyāś ca satataṃ me 'śvāḥ, Kuru|rāja, yathā tava!
3.5 ye māṃ āmantrayiṣyanti Virāṭa|nagare janāḥ,
tebhya evaṃ pravakṣyāmi, vihariṣyāmy ahaṃ yathā:
«Pāṇḍavena purā, tāta, aśveṣv adhikṛtaḥ purā.»
Virāṭa|nagare channaś cariṣyāmi, mahī|pate.

entertaining them by telling tales of the heroic deeds of men.

Pándava, when the king asks me I will say, "I lived in Yudhi·shthira's palace as a servant girl to Dráupadi." Concealing myself by this method, just as Nala did,* I will spend my time happily in Viráta's palace, lord of kings.

VAISHAMPÁYANA said:

UPON SAYING THIS, Árjuna, the most excellent and fore- 3.1
most of virtuous men, came to the end of his speech, and the king again addressed another of his brothers.

YUDHI·SHTHIRA said:

What will you do? You are very tender, brave, handsome and used to luxury, Nákula, so tell me what service you will perform in the king's realm.

NÁKULA said:

I will be King Viráta's horse-keeper. I am wholly conversant with this field of knowledge, and skillful in caring for horses. I will go by the name of Gránthika. I really enjoy this task and I am skilled in training horses and equally so in curing them. I have always liked horses as much as you do, Kuru king!

This is how I will pass my time, and to whomever should 3.5
talk to me in Viráta's city I will say: "Previously, Pándava made me master of his horses." That is how I will act, hidden in Viráta's city, great king.

YUDHIṢṬHIRA uvāca:

Sahadeva, kathaṃ tasya samīpe vihariṣyasi?
kiṃ vā tvaṃ karma kurvāṇaḥ pracchanno vihariṣyasi?

SAHADEVA uvāca:

go|saṅkhyātā bhaviṣyāmi Virāṭasya mahī|pateḥ,
pratiṣeddhā ca, dogdhā ca, saṅkhyāne kuśalo gavām.
Tantipāla iti khyāto nāmn" âhaṃ viditas tv atha,
nipuṇaṃ ca cariṣyāmi. vyetu te mānaso jvaraḥ.
3.10 ahaṃ hi satataṃ goṣu bhavatā prahitaḥ purā.
tatra me kauśalaṃ sarvam avabuddhaṃ, viśām pate,
lakṣaṇaṃ, caritaṃ c' âpi gavāṃ, yac c' âpi maṅgalam.
tat sarvaṃ me su|viditam, anyac c' âpi, mahī|pate.
vṛṣabhān api jānāmi, rājan, pūjita|lakṣaṇān,
yeṣāṃ mūtram upāghrāya api vandhyā prasūyate.
so 'ham evaṃ cariṣyāmi, prītir atra hi me sadā.
na ca māṃ vetsyate kaś cit, toṣayiṣye ca pārthivam.

YUDHIṢṬHIRA uvāca:

iyaṃ hi naḥ priyā bhāryā prāṇebhyo 'pi garīyasī,
māt" êva paripālyā ca, pūjyā jyeṣṭh" êva ca svasā.
3.15 kena sma Draupadī Kṛṣṇā karmaṇā vicariṣyati?
na hi kiñ cid vijānāti karma kartuṃ yathā striyaḥ.
su|kumārī ca, bālā ca, rāja|putrī yaśasvinī,
pati|vratā, mahā|bhāgā, kathaṃ nu vicariṣyati?
mālya|gandhān, alaṅ|kārān, vastrāṇi vividhāni ca—
etāny ev' âbhijānāti yato jātā hi bhāminī.

YUDHI·SHTHIRA said:

Saha·deva, how will you spend your time in his proximity? What service will you perform to pass the time in disguise?

SAHA·DEVA said:

I will be King Viráta's cowherd, for I am skilled in milking and skilled in herding cattle. I will be called Tanti·pala by name, and since I am properly trained, I will conduct myself capably. Abandon the fever in your mind.

In the past, you yourself always put me in charge of your 3.10
cattle. I've learned thoroughly all about their health, lord of earth, their markings and even their behavior, as well as what makes them happy. Consider that I know all this very well, earth-lord. I also recognize bulls with the recommended markings, my king, the scent of whose urine can even cause a barren cow to produce young. I will always work happily. No one will recognize me, and furthermore I will please the king.

YUDHI·SHTHIRA said:

This is our dear wife, more precious to us than our lives, who should be cared for as a mother and honored as an
eldest sister. What task will Dráupadi Krishná undertake, 3.15
since she doesn't know how to perform any women's work? She is a very tender and powerful princess of wide fame, loyal to her husbands and illustrious, but how will she live? Garlands, perfumes, ornaments and various clothes—these are the only things that the passionate lady has known since she was born.

DRAUPADĪ uvāca:

sairandhryo rakṣitā loke bhujiṣyāḥ santi, Bhārata.
n' âivam anyāḥ striyo yānti, iti lokasya niścayaḥ.
s" âhaṃ bruvāṇā sairandhrī kuśalā keśa|karmaṇi.
«Yudhiṣṭhirasya gehe vai Draupadyāḥ paricārikā
uṣit" âsm', îti» vakṣyāmi pṛṣṭā rājñā ca, Bhārata.
3.20 ātma|guptā cariṣyāmi, yan māṃ tvaṃ paripṛcchasi,
Sudeṣṇāṃ pratyupasthāsye rāja|bhāryāṃ yaśasvinīm.
sā rakṣiṣyati māṃ prāptāṃ. mā bhūt te duḥkham īdṛśam.

YUDHIṢṬHIRA uvāca:

kalyāṇaṃ bhāṣase, Kṛṣṇe, kule jāt" âsi, bhāminī,
na pāpam abhijānāsi sādhvī, sādhu|vrate sthitā.
yathā na durhṛdaḥ pāpā bhavanti sukhinaḥ punaḥ,
kuryās tat tvaṃ hi, kalyāṇi, lakṣayeyur na te tathā.

YUDHIṢṬHIRA uvāca:

4.1 KARMĀṆY UKTĀNI yuṣmābhir yāni, tāni kariṣyatha,
mama c' âpi yathā|buddhi rucitāni viniścayāt.
puro|hito 'yam asmākam agni|hotrāṇi rakṣatu
sūda|paurogavaiḥ sārdhaṃ Drupadasya niveśane.
Indrasena|mukhāś c' ême rathān ādāya kevalān
yāntu Dvāravatīṃ śighram, iti me vartate matiḥ.
imāś ca nāryo Draupadyāḥ sarvāś ca paricārikāḥ
Pāñcālān' êva gacchantu sūda|paurogavaiḥ saha.
4.5 sarvair api ca vaktavyaṃ, «na prājñāyanta Pāṇḍavāḥ.
gatā hy asmān apāhāya sarve Dvaitavanād iti.»

DRÁUPADI said:

Bhárata, there are women in this world who are protected as menial servants and called *sairándhris*—independent maids*—but there is no such certainty concerning other women of the world. I will say I am a *sairándhri*, skilled in hairdressing. When asked by the king, I will say, "I lived in Yudhi·shthira's palace as Dráupadi's servant girl," Bhárata.
I will protect myself and do what you ask of me, and I will 3.20
serve Sudéshna, the king's illustrious wife. She will protect me once I have reached her, so do not be so miserable.

YUDHI·SHTHIRA said:

O Krishná, you speak excellently, but you were born into a good family, passionate lady, so you have no comprehension of sin. You are virtuous and engaged in observing strict vows. So don't allow wicked, sinful men to become happy again as they stare at you, because of the way you behave, lovely girl.

YUDHI·SHTHIRA said:

WELL, YOU SHALL undertake the jobs that you have de- 4.1
scribed. I, too, definitely find them attractive as far as I can judge. Let our family priest guard the Agni·hotra fires and enter Drúpada's dwelling with the cooks. Let Indra·sena and the men he leads go quickly to Dváravati, taking the empty chariots with them. This is my decision. Let all Dráupadi's servant girls go to the Panchálas, along with the cooks.
Everyone must say, "We do not know where the Pándavas 4.5
have gone. They all left us at Dvaita·vana."

VAIŚAMPĀYANA uvāca:

evaṃ te 'nyonyam āmantrya,
karmāṇy uktvā pṛthak pṛthak,
Dhaumyam āmantrayām āsuḥ,
sa ca tān mantram abravīt.

DHAUMYA uvāca:

vihitaṃ, Pāṇḍavāḥ, sarvaṃ brāhmaṇeṣu, suhṛtsu ca.
yāne, praharaṇe c' âiva tath" âiv' âgniṣu, Bhārata,
tvayā rakṣā vidhātavyā Kṛṣṇāyāḥ Phālgunena ca.
viditaṃ vo yathā sarvaṃ loka|vṛttim idaṃ tava,
vidite c' âpi vaktavyaṃ suhṛdbhir anurāgataḥ.
eṣa dharmaś ca, kāmaś ca, arthaś c' âiva sanātanaḥ
4.10 ato 'ham api vakṣyāmi, hetum atra nibodhata.
hant' êmāṃ rāja|vasatiṃ, rāja|putrā. bravīmy aham
yathā rāja|kulaṃ prāpya sarvān doṣāṃs tariṣyatha,
dur|vasaṃ c' âiva, Kauravya, jānatā rāja|veśmani
a|mānitair mānitair vā a|jñātaiḥ parivatsaram.
tataś catur|daśe varṣe cariṣyatha yathā sukham.
dṛṣṭa|dvāro labhed draṣṭuṃ rājasv eṣu na viśvaset.
tad ev' āsanam anvicched, yatra n' âbhipatet paraḥ.
yo na yānaṃ, na paryaṅkaṃ, na pīṭhaṃ, na gajaṃ, ratham
ārohet, «sammato 'sm' îti,» sa rāja|vasatiṃ vaset.
4.15 yatra yatr' âinam āsīnaṃ śaṅkeran duṣṭa|cāriṇaḥ,
na tatr' ôpaviśed yo vai, sa rāja|vasatiṃ vaset.

VAISHAMPÁYANA said:

Having consulted with each other in this manner, and told each other their jobs, each one in his turn, they consulted Dhaumya, and he gave them this advice:

DHAUMYA said:

Pándavas, everything that has been arranged for the brahmins, your friends, the chariots, weapons and fires is fine, Bhárata, but you and Phálguna must arrange Krishná's protection.

You two both know how this whole world works. Yet, even though you know, friends should repeat it out of affection.

It is known that law, desire and profit are eternal. For that 4.10
reason I will say this, so listen. Alas for living with a king, my princes! I will tell you how you will avoid all mistakes once you've reached the king's palace. O Káuravas, you must spend a full year in the king's palace, unrecognized by those who know you, who will either treat you honorably or not. Then, in the fourteenth year, you will live happily.

One should take the opportunity to see the king, once one has appeared at the gate, but one should not be confident in royal matters. Nor should one rush for a seat that another desires. He who would not climb onto the king's palanquin, couch, seat, elephant or chariot, while thinking to himself "I am highly honored," should live in a royal palace.

The man who would not sit down in a position that 4.15
causes evildoers to be alarmed should live in a royal palace.

na c' ânuśiṣyād rājānam a|pṛcchantaṃ kadā cana.
tūṣṇīṃ tv enam upāsīta, kāle samabhipūjayet.
asūyanti hi rājāno janān an|ṛta|vādinaḥ
tath" âiva c' âvamanyante mantriṇaṃ vādinaṃ mṛṣā.
n' âiṣāṃ dāreṣu kurvīta maitrīṃ prājñaḥ kadā cana,
antaḥpura|carā ye ca, dveṣṭi yān, a|hitāś ca ye.
vidite c' âsya kurvīta kāryāṇi su|laghūny api.
evaṃ vicarato rājñi na kṣatir jāyate kva cit.
4.20 gacchann api parāṃ bhūmim a|pṛṣṭo hy, a|niyojitaḥ,
jāty|andha iva manyeta maryādām anucintayan.
na hi putraṃ, na naptāraṃ, na bhrātaram, arin|damāḥ,
samatikrānta|maryādaṃ pūjayanti nar'|âdhipāḥ.
yatnāc c' ôpacared enam Agnivad, devavat tv iha.
an|ṛten' ôpacīrṇo hi hanyād eva na saṃśayaḥ.
yac ca bhart" ânuyuñjīta, tat tad ev' ânuvartayet;
pramādam, avalepaṃ ca, kopaṃ ca parivarjayet.
samarthanāsu sarvāsu hitaṃ ca, priyam eva ca
saṃvarṇayet tad ev' âsya priyād api hitaṃ bhavet.
4.25 anukūlo bhavec c' âsya sarv' ârtheṣu, kathāsu ca;
a|priyaṃ c' â|hitaṃ yat syāt, tad asmai n' ânuvarṇayet.
«n' âham asya priyo 'sm', îti» matvā seveta paṇḍitaḥ,
a|pramattaś ca satataṃ hitaṃ kuryāt, priyaṃ ca yat.

One should never lecture the king when unasked. Sitting beside him in silence, one should pay homage to the king at the appropriate time only. For kings are displeased with people who speak falsely, and equally they treat an eloquent minister who speaks uselessly with contempt.

The wise man should never conduct a close friendship with his wives, nor with the guardian of the women's apartments, nor with those who are hated and out of favor.

He should carry out even insignificant tasks with the full
knowledge of the king. If he conducts himself in this manner
while in the presence of the king, no harm will befall him.
Even upon reaching the highest position, when unasked and 4.20
uncommanded, he should think of himself as one who was
born blind, recalling the clear boundaries. Tamers of your
foes, kings do not even honor their son, nor their grandson
nor brother, if their boundaries are transgressed.

One should serve a king with effort, just as one serves
Agni and the gods in this world. He who is attended by
a deceitful man without a doubt puts him to death. One
should obey whatever one's master commands, and avoid
carelessness, pride and anger. In all deliberations one should
recommend what is beneficial and pleasant, and should do
this even if it should be beneficial rather than pleasant. One 4.25
should be well disposed to all the king's affairs and tales,
and not recommend to him something that is unpleasant
and disadvantageous. A wise man should serve him, thinking "I am not favored," and be careful to do whatever is advantageous and pleasing.

n' âsy' ân|iṣṭāni seveta, n' â|hitaiḥ saha saṃvadet,
sva|sthānān na vikampeta, sa rāja|vasatiṃ vaset.

dakṣiṇaṃ v" âtha, vāmaṃ vā pārśvam āsīta paṇḍitaḥ;
rakṣiṇāṃ hy ātta|śastrāṇāṃ sthānaṃ paścād vidhīyate.
nityaṃ hi pratiṣiddhaṃ tu purastād āsanaṃ mahat.
na ca saṃdarśane kiñ cit pravṛttam api sañjayet,
4.30 api hy etad daridrāṇāṃ vyalīka|sthānam uttamam.

na mṛṣ" âbhihitaṃ rājñāṃ manuṣyeṣu prakāśayet,
asūyanti hi rājāno narān anṛta|vādinaḥ.
tath" âiva c' âvamanyante narān paṇḍita|māninaḥ.
«śuro 'sm', îti» na dṛptaḥ syād, «buddhimān, iti» vā punaḥ;
priyam ev' ācaran rājñaḥ priyo bhavati bhogavān.

aiśvaryaṃ prāpya duṣ|prāpaṃ, priyaṃ prāpya ca rājataḥ
a|pramatto bhaved rājñaḥ priyeṣu ca, hiteṣu ca.
yasya kopo mahā|bādhaḥ, prasādaś ca mahā|phalaḥ,
kas tasya manas" âp' îcched an|arthaṃ prājña|saṃmataḥ?

4.35 na c' ôṣṭhau, na bhujau, jānū, na ca vākyaṃ samākṣipet.
sadā vātaṃ, ca vācaṃ ca, ṣṭhīvanaṃ c' ācarec chanaiḥ.
hāsya|vastuṣu c' ânyasya vartamāneṣu keṣu cit
n' âti|gāḍhaṃ prahṛṣyeta, na c' âpy unmattavadd haset.

The man who would not cultivate unpromising matters, who would not converse with the king's enemies and who would not shrink from his own position should dwell in a king's palace.

The wise man should sit either on the right or the left side of the king, but he should hesitate to sit behind him, for that is the space for armed guards. Sitting down in front of the king is always strictly prohibited. Let no one cling to the king when he happens to be engaged in his audience, for even if the audience is made up only of beggars, it is a 4.30
most improper position.

No one should reveal to men something the king has spoken falsely, for kings are displeased with those men who broadcast their lies. They also treat contemptuously those who think of themselves as wise men. One should not be arrogant, thinking "I am powerful," or, again, "I am intelligent." Instead, one will become dear to the king, and prosperous, by conducting oneself in a manner that is pleasing to the king.

Once one has obtained power and the favor of the king, which is hard to come by, one should be diligent in matters both pleasing and advantageous to the king. Which man, esteemed by the wise, would even mentally wish trouble on the man whose anger he knows is extremely damaging, yet whose graciousness is greatly rewarding?

No one should jerk their lips, arms or knees violently, 4.35
or shout. One should always pass wind, talk and spit with delicacy. Even in ridiculous situations or circumstances of any other kind, one should not be excessively cheerful nor laugh like a maniac. Nor should one behave with too much

na c' âti|dhairyeṇa cared, gurutāṃ hi vrajet tataḥ;
smitaṃ tu mṛdu|pūrveṇa darśayeta prasāda|jam.
lābhe na harṣayed yas tu, na vyathed yo 'vamānitaḥ,
a|saṃmūḍhaś ca yo nityaṃ, sa rāja|vasatiṃ vaset.

rājānaṃ, rāja|putraṃ vā saṃvarṇayati yaḥ sadā,
amātyaḥ paṇḍito bhūtvā sa ciraṃ tiṣṭhate priyaḥ.
4.40 pragṛhītaś ca yo 'mātyo, nigṛhītas tv a|kāraṇaiḥ
na nirvadati rājānaṃ, labhate saṃpadaṃ punaḥ.
pratyakṣaṃ ca parokṣaṃ ca guṇa|vādī vicakṣaṇaḥ
upajīvī bhaved rājño viṣaye c' âpi yo vaset.
amātyo hi balād bhoktuṃ rājānaṃ prārthayeta yaḥ,
na sa tiṣṭhec ciraṃ sthānaṃ, gacchec ca prāṇa|saṃśayam.

śreyaḥ sad" ātmano dṛṣṭvā paraṃ rājñā na saṃvadet,
viśeṣayec ca rājānaṃ yogya|bhūmiṣu sarvadā.

a|mlāno, balavān, śūraś, chāy' êv' ânugataḥ sadā,
satya|vādī, mṛdur, dāntaḥ, sa rāja|vasatiṃ vaset.

4.45 anyasmin preṣyamāṇe tu purastād yaḥ samutpatet,
«ahaṃ kiṃ karavāṇ'? îti,» sa rāja|vasatiṃ vaset.
āntare c' âiva, bāhye ca rājñā yaś c' âtha sarvadā
ādiṣṭo n' âiva kampeta, sa rāja|vasatiṃ vaset.
yo vai gṛhebhyaḥ pravasan priyāṇāṃ n' ânusaṃsmaret,
duḥkhena sukham anvicchet, sa rāja|vasatiṃ vaset.

composure and become solemn, but reveal a smile with tenderness instead, to show one's good humor. He who is always deliberate, and would not get excited by profit, nor waver when disrespected, is a man who should live in a king's palace.

He who always praises the king and the prince becomes a wise minister, and remains favored for a long time. The 4.40
minister who was previously promoted, and is now demoted with good reason, but does not speak badly of the king, receives glory once more. The man who happens to be dependent on the king, and the man who happens to live in his kingdom, praises his qualities both in his presence and absence if he is clever. The minister who is keen to forcibly exploit the king will not remain in his position for long, and he risks even his life.

No one who has constantly shown himself to be better, should agree that he is indeed superior to the king, nor should he completely overshadow the king in worldly practices.

The man who is bright, powerful, brave and follows his master unceasingly like a shadow, he who speaks truthfully and is gentle and controlled, should live in the king's palace.

The man who springs forward first when a task is com- 4.45
missioned, and says "I'll do it," should live in a king's palace. The man who does not tremble at the prospect, when given instruction either inside or outside the kingdom, should live in a king's palace. The man who does not remember his relatives when living away from home, and aims at happiness while in misery, should live in a king's palace.

sama|veṣaṃ na kurvīta, n' ôccaiḥ sannihito haset,
na mantraṃ bahu|dhā kuryād; evaṃ rājñaḥ priyo bhavet.
na karmaṇi niyuktaḥ san dhanaṃ kiñ cid api spṛśet,
prāpnoti hi haran dravyaṃ bandhanaṃ, yadi vā vadham.
4.50 yānaṃ, vastram, alaṅ|kāraṃ, yac c' ânyat samprayacchati,
tad eva dhārayen nityam, evaṃ priyataro bhavet.
evaṃ saṃyamya cittāni yatnataḥ, Pāṇḍu|nandanāḥ,
saṃvatsaram imaṃ, tāta, tathā|śīlā bubhūṣata.
atha sva|viṣayaṃ prāpya yathā|kāmaṃ kariṣyatha.

YUDHIṢṬHIRA uvāca:

anuśiṣṭāḥ sma, bhadraṃ te. n' âitad|vakt" âsti kaś cana,
Kuntīm ṛte mātaraṃ no, Viduraṃ vā mahā|matim.
yad ev' ân|antaraṃ kāryaṃ, tad bhavān kartum arhati
tāraṇāy' âsya duḥkhasya, prasthānāya, jayāya ca.

VAIŚAMPĀYANA uvāca:

evam uktas tato rājñā Dhaumyo 'tha dvija|sattamaḥ
akarod vidhivat sarvaṃ, prasthāne yad vidhīyate.
4.55 teṣāṃ samidhya tān agnīn mantravac ca juhāva saḥ
samṛddhi|vṛddhi|lābhāya, pṛthivī|vijayāya ca.
agnīn pradakṣiṇī|kṛtya, brāhmaṇāṃś ca tapo|dhanān,
Yājñasenīṃ puras|kṛtya ṣaḍ ev' âtha pravavrajuḥ.

One should not wear similar clothing, laugh excessively loudly or divulge a secret. This is how one becomes dear to the king. When undertaking tasks, one should not take any bribes, for if one takes money one suffers either incarceration or death. One should always use the carriage, clothes, 4.50
ornaments and other paraphernalia that he bestows, since it is by so doing that one becomes more favored.

So put effort into controlling your thoughts, descendants of Pandu, and strive for such conduct this year, my sons. Then, once you have regained your kingdom, do as you wish.

YUDHI·SHTHIRA said:

We have been fully instructed, bless you. There is no one to advise us except Kuntí, our mother, or highly intelligent Vídura. You ought to immediately perform the necessary tasks for our safe passage through this misery, for our journey and for our victory.

VAISHAMPÁYANA said:

Thus addressed by the king, Dhaumya, the most venerable of brahmins, then performed everything ordained for a journey according to the prescribed law. Lighting their fires, 4.55
and reciting mantras, he offered oblations for their profit and greater success and for their total victory over the earth. Once they had performed the rite of circling the fires and the brahmins, whose wealth lay in their asceticism, the six of them set out, putting Yajñaséni in the lead.

gateṣu teṣu vīreṣu Dhaumyo 'tha japatāṃ varaḥ
agni|hotrāṇy upādāya Pāñcālān abhyagacchata.
Indrasen'|ādayaś c' âiva yath" ôktāḥ prāpya Yādavān
rathān, aśvāṃś ca rakṣantaḥ sukham ūṣuḥ su|saṃvṛtāḥ.

VAIŚAMPĀYANA uvāca:

5.1 TE VĪRĀ BADDHA|nistriṃśās, tathā baddha|kalāpinaḥ,
baddha|godh"|âṅgulitrāṇāḥ Kālindīm abhito yayuḥ.
tatas taṃ dakṣiṇaṃ tīram anvagacchan padātayaḥ,
nivṛtta|vana|vāsā hi sva|rāṣṭraṃ prepsavas tadā,
vasanto giri|durgeṣu, vana|durgeṣu dhanvinaḥ.
vidhyanto mṛga|jātāni mah"|êṣv|āsā mahā|balāḥ
uttareṇa Daśārṇāṃs te, Pāñcālān dakṣiṇena ca,
antareṇa Yakṛllomān, Śūrasenāṃś ca Pāṇḍavāḥ
lubdhā bruvāṇā, Matsyasya viṣayaṃ prāviśan vanāt,
5.5 dhanvino baddha|nistriṃśā, vivarṇāḥ, śmaśru|dhāriṇaḥ.
tato jana|padam prāpya Kṛṣṇā rājānam abravīt:
«paśy', âika|padyo dṛśyante, kṣetrāṇi vividhāni ca.
vyaktaṃ dūre Virāṭasya rāja|dhānī bhaviṣyati.
vasām' êh' âparāṃ rātriṃ, balavān me pariśramaḥ.»

YUDHIṢṬHIRA uvāca:

Dhanañjaya, samudyamya Pāñcālīṃ vaha, Bhārata.
rāja|dhānyāṃ nivatsyāmo vimuktāś ca vanād itaḥ.

When those heroes had gone, Dhaumya, the best of ascetics who mutter prayers, took the sacred fires and set out for the Panchálas. Indra·sena and the others mentioned already guarded the chariots and horses, and passed the time happily, once they had reached the Yádavas.

VAISHAMPÁYANA said:

THE HEROES WENT toward the river Yámuna with swords fastened to them, and bound with their quivers and leather finger-guards. 5.1

Having previously lived in inaccessible hills and cut-off areas of forest, they were keen to regain their own kingdom, and so, abandoning their life living in the woods, those bowmen followed the south bank, going on foot. The great powerful archers, who had hunted deer, passed the land of the Dashárnas on the left and that of the Panchálas on the right, and near Yakril·loma and Shura·sena the Pándavas entered the land of the Matsyas from the forest, saying that
they were hunters, for the bowmen had swords strapped to 5.5
themselves, and were pale and bearded.

Then, having reached that realm, Krishná said to the king: "Look, we can see footpaths and various fields. King Viráta's capital will clearly still be far away. Let us stay here for the rest of the night, since I'm absolutely exhausted."

YUDHI·SHTHIRA said:

Dhanan·jaya Bhárata, pick up Pancháli and carry her. Once we are clear of the forest, we will reach the royal capital.

VAIŚAMPĀYANA uvāca:

tām ādāy' Ârjunas tūrṇaṃ Draupadīṃ gaja|rāḍ iva
saṃprāpya nagar'|âbhyāśam avatarayad Arjunaḥ.
sa rāja|dhānīṃ saṃprāpya Kaunteyo 'rjunam abravīt:
«kv' āyudhāni samāsajjya pravekṣyāṃaḥ puraṃ vayam?
5.10 s'|āyudhāś ca pravekṣyāmo vayaṃ, tāta, puraṃ yadi,
samudvegaṃ janasy' âsya kariṣyāmo, na saṃśayaḥ.
Gāṇḍīvaṃ ca mahad gāḍhaṃ loke ca viditaṃ nṛṇām.
tac ced āyudham ādāya gacchāmo nagaraṃ vayam,
kṣipram asmān vijānīyur manuṣyā, n' âtra saṃśayaḥ.
tato dvā|daśa varṣāṇi praveṣṭavyaṃ vane punaḥ
ekasminn api vijñāte, pratijñātaṃ hi nas tathā.»

ARJUNA uvāca:

iyaṃ kūṭe, manuṣy'|êndra, gahanā mahatī śamī,
bhīma|śākhā, dur|ārohā, śmaśānasya samīpataḥ.
na c' âpi vidyate kaś cin manuṣya,iti me matiḥ,
yo 'smān nidadhato draṣṭā bhavec chastrāṇi, Pāṇḍavāḥ.
5.15 utpathe hi vane jātā mṛga|vyāla|niṣevite,
samīpe ca śmaśānasya gahanasya viśeṣataḥ.
samādhāy' āyudhaṃ śamyāṃ gacchāmo nagaraṃ prati.
evam atra yathā|yogaṃ vihariṣyāṃa, Bhārata.

VAIŚAMPĀYANA uvāca:

evam uktvā sa rājānaṃ dharma|rājaṃ Yudhiṣṭhiram,
pracakrame nidhānāya śastrāṇāṃ, Bharata'|rṣabha.
yena devān manuṣyāṃś ca sarvāṃś c' âika|ratho 'jayat,
sphītān jana|padāṃś c' ânyān ajayat Kuru|puṅgavaḥ,

VAISHAMPÁYANA said:

Then Árjuna, like the king of elephants, quickly picked up Dráupadi, and when they reached the proximity of the city Árjuna put her down.

Once they arrived at the royal capital, the son of Kuntí said to Árjuna: "Where should we tie our weapons when we enter the city? For if we enter the city with our weapons 5.10
then doubtless we'll create great panic among the people. The great bow Gandíva is known to all men throughout the world, so if we go into the city carrying that weapon there is no doubt that people would soon recognize us. We would have to re-enter the forest again for another twelve years, as we promised, if even one of us is recognized."

ÁRJUNA said:

Lord of men, there is a massive, dense, formidably branched *shami* tree on the peak of that mountain, near the cemetery, which is hard to climb. There is no one who will notice us putting our weapons there, in my opinion, son of Pandu. For the tree has grown in a backwater of the 5.15
forest, infested with wild beasts and snakes, and is distinguished by being in the vicinity of that overgrown cemetery. So let's go to the city, having put our weapons in the *shami* tree. We will spend our time here diligently, Bhárata.

VAISHAMPÁYANA said:

Once he had said this to Yudhi·shthira, the king of righteousness, he prepared to deposit the weapons, bull-like Bharata. Partha took the bowstring off the great, loud-booming Gandíva: a cause of great fear and destroyer of accomplished armies, with which the bull of the Kurus

tad udāraṃ, mahā|ghoṣaṃ, saṃpanna|bala|sūdanam
apajyam akarot Pārtho Gāṇḍīvaṃ su|bhayaṃ|karam.
5.20 yena vīraḥ Kuru|kṣetram abhyarakṣat paran|tapaḥ,
amuñcad dhanuṣas tasya jyām akṣayyāṃ Yudhiṣṭhiraḥ.

Pāñcālān yena saṅgrāme Bhīmaseno 'jayat prabhuḥ,
pratyaṣedhad bahūn ekaḥ sapatnāṃś c' âiva dig|jaye,
niśamya yasya visphāraṃ vyadravanta raṇāt pare,
parvatasy' êva dīrṇasya visphoṭam, aśaner iva,
Saindhavaṃ yena rājānaṃ paryāmṛṣitavān atha,
jyā|pāśaṃ dhanuṣas tasya Bhīmaseno 'vatārayat.

ajayat paścimām āśāṃ dhanuṣā yena Pāṇḍavaḥ
Mādrī|putro mahā|bāhus, tāmr'|āsyo, mita|bhāṣitā,
5.25 tasya maurvīm apārkaṣac chūraḥ, saṃkrandano yudhi.
kule n' âsti samo rūpe yasy', êti Nakulaḥ smṛtaḥ.

dakṣiṇāṃ dakṣiṇ'|ācāro diśaṃ yen' âjayat prabhuḥ,
apajyam akarod vīraḥ Sahadevas tad āyudham.

khaḍgāṃś ca dīptān dīrghāṃś ca,
  kalāpāṃś ca mahā|dhanān,
vipāṭhān kṣura|dhārāṃś ca
  dhanurbhir nidadhuḥ saha.

ath' ânvaśāsan Nakulaṃ Kuntī|putro Yudhiṣṭhiraḥ:
«āruhy' êmāṃ Śamīṃ, vīra, dhanūṃṣy etāni nikṣipa.»
tām upāruhya Nakulo dhanūṃṣi nidadhe svayam,
yāni tasy" âvakāśāni dṛḍha|rūpāṇy amanyata,
5.30 yatra c' âpaśyata sa vai tiro|varṣāṇi varṣati,

conquered all gods and men alike, on a single chariot, and vanquished other flourishing nations.

Yudhi·shthira removed the undecaying string from the 5.20
bow with which that hero, the scorcher of his foe, defended the Kuru·kshetra.

Then Bhima·sena unfastened the string from the bow with which that powerful man defeated the Sáindhavan king* and defeated the Panchálas in battle, single-handedly opposing numerous enemies in his conquests stretching far and wide. When they heard the twang of that bowstring, like the cracking din of a mountain being torn asunder or like a thunderbolt, his inferior enemies ran from battle.

The red-complexioned and long-armed son of Pandu and Madri unfastened the string from the bow with which he defeated the western region.* He was a man of few words
but the brave man roared in battle. It was said of him that 5.25
there was no match for his beauty within his family, and so he was called Nákula.*

Then the hero warrior Saha·deva removed the string from the bow with which the excellent man, always upright in his conduct, subdued the southern areas.*

They laid down their long, splendid swords, their costly quivers and their large razor-edged arrows along with their bows.

Then Yudhi·shthira, the son of Kuntí, directed Nákula, "Hero, climb the *shami* tree and put those bows on it." So Nákula climbed the tree and he himself deposited the bows in the hollows of the tree, which he considered
sturdy-looking, and in a place where he saw that they were 5.30

tatra tāni dṛḍhaiḥ pāśaiḥ su|gāḍhaṃ paryabandhata.
śarīraṃ ca mṛtasy' âikaṃ samabadhnanta Pāṇḍavāḥ,
vivarjayiṣyanti narā dūrād eva Śamīm imām,
«ābaddhaṃ śavam atr', êti» gandham āghrāya pūtikam.
«aśīti|śata|varṣ' êyaṃ mātā na, iti» vādinaḥ,
«kula|dharmo 'yam asmākaṃ, pūrvair ācarito 'pi vā,
samāsajjy' âtha vṛkṣe 'sminn, iti» vai vyāharanti te,
ā go|pāl'|âvi|pālebhya ācakṣāṇāḥ paraṃ|tapāḥ.
ājagmur nagar' âbhyāśaṃ Pārthāḥ śatru|nibarhaṇāḥ.
5.35 «Jayo, Jayanto, Vijayo, Jayatseno, Jayadbalaḥ,»
iti guhyāni nāmāni cakre teṣāṃ Yudhiṣṭhiraḥ.
tato yathā pratijñābhiḥ prāviśan nagaraṃ mahat,
a|jñāta|caryāṃ vatsyanto rāṣṭre varṣaṃ trayo|daśam.

VAIŚAMPĀYANA uvāca:

6.1 VIRĀṬA|NAGARAṂ ramyaṃ gacchamāno Yudhiṣṭhiraḥ
astuvan manasā devīṃ Durgāṃ tri|bhuvan'|ēśvarīm;
Yaśodā|garbha|saṃbhūtāṃ, Nārāyaṇa|vara|priyām,
Nanda|gopa|kule jātāṃ, maṅgalyāṃ kula|vardhinīṃ;
Kaṃsa|vidrāvaṇa|karīm, Asurāṇāṃ kṣayaṃ|karīm;
śilātaṭa|vinikṣiptām ākāśaṃ prati gāminīm;
Vāsudevasya bhaginīṃ, divya|mālya|vibhūṣitām,
divy'|âmbara|dharām devīṃ, khaḍga|kheṭaka|dhāriṇīm;

protected from the rain, in case it rained. So it was that he tied them there tightly with firmly fastened knots.

The Pándavas tied up a dead body so that men would avoid that *shami* tree even from a distance. When they smelled the putrid odor, people said, "A corpse is hanging there." "It is our mother who is one hundred and eighty years old. We have fastened her to that tree according to our family tradition, practiced by our ancestors." This was the answer that the enemy-scorchers gave to the cowherds and shepherds.

Then the five foe-destroyering sons of Pritha approached
the city. Yudhi·shthira called them Jaya, Jayánta, Víjaya, 5.35
Jayat·sena and Jayad·bala, and so their real names were concealed in this trickery. Then they entered that great city, in accordance with the promises to live their thirteenth year unrecognized in a kingdom.

VAISHAMPÁYANA said:

AND AS YUDHI·SHTHIRA was on his way to Viráta's pleas- 6.1
ant city, he praised the goddess Durga in his mind. She is the mistress of the three worlds, born from the womb of Yashóda, fond of the boon of Naráyana, born in the lineage of the cowherd Nanda, an auspicious augmenter of the worshipper's family.

She is the one who made Kansa flee in terror and brings about the destruction of the *ásura*s. She is the one who ascended to the sky when thrown down onto a rocky slope. She is Vasudéva's sister, who appears with divine garlands, wearing heavenly garments, and she is the goddess who bears a sword and shield

6.5 bhār'|âvatarane puṇye ye smaranti sadā śivām,
tān vai tārayate pāpāt, paṅke gām iva dur|balām;
stotuṃ pracakrame bhūyo vividhaiḥ stotra|saṃbhavaiḥ
āmantrya darśan'|ākāṅkṣī rājā devīṃ sah'|ânujaḥ;
«namo 'stu, vara|de Kṛṣṇe, kumāri brahma|cāriṇi,
bāl'|ârka|sadṛś'|ākāre, pūrṇa|candra|nibh'|ānane,
catur|bhuje, catur|vakre, pīna|śroṇi|payodhare,
mayūra|piccha|valaye, keyūr'|âṅgada|dhāriṇi.
bhāsi, devi, yathā Padmā Nārāyaṇa|parigrahaḥ.
sva|rūpaṃ, brahma|caryaṃ ca viśadaṃ tava, khe|cari.
kṛṣṇa|cchavi|samā kṛṣṇā, Saṃkarṣaṇa|sam'|ānanā,
6.10 bibhrati vipulau bāhū Śakra|dhvaja|samucchrayau,
pātrī ca, paṅkajo, ghaṇṭī, strī viśuddhā ca yā bhuvi,
pāśaṃ, dhanur, mahā|cakraṃ, vividhāny āyudhāni ca.
kuṇḍalābhyāṃ su|pūrṇābhyāṃ karṇābhyāṃ ca vibhūṣitā,
candra|vispardhinā, devi, mukhena tvaṃ virājase,
mukuṭena vicitreṇa, keśa|bandhena śobhinā,
bhujaṅg'|ābhoga|vāsena, śroṇi|sūtreṇa rājatā,
vibhrājase c' ābaddhena bhogen' êv' êha Mandaraḥ.
dhvajena śikhi|picchānām ucchritena virājase,
kaumāraṃ vratam āsthāya tri|divaṃ pāvitaṃ tvayā.
6.15 tena tvaṃ stūyase, devi, tri|daśaiḥ pūjyase 'pi ca
trai|lokya|rakṣaṇ'|ârthāya, Mahiṣāsura|nāśini.

She always rescues men from evil, as though they were 6.5
weak cows in the mud, when they call her to mind as the kind giver of prosperity for the sacred removal of their burdens. She is the goddess whom the king and his brothers worshipped in the hope of seeing, determined to praise her with more and more various titles, deriving from hymns.

"Glory to you, granter of wishes, Princess Krishná, you who observe chastity, you whose appearance resembles the newly risen sun, and whose face is like the full moon, you who have four pairs of arms, four faces, you of the swelling hips and breasts, you with the bracelet of peacock feathers, wearing bangles on your upper arm. You shine, goddess, just like Padma, the wife of Naráyana. Your own form and rite of chastity are both beautifully pure, sky-going goddess. Dark
as the black weather, your face is like Sankárshana. You bear 6.10
long arms like raised banners to Indra. You are a completely pure woman, bearing a pot, a lotus, a bell, a noose, a bow, a massive discus and various other weapons.

You are adorned with shapely ears embellished with earrings. You are pure, goddess, with a face that emulates the moon, with a multicolored crown, and radiantly bound hair, with clothing made of the coils of a serpent, and the string around your hips, queen. You are luminous like the Mándara mountain bound with snakes. You are pure with your emblem of erect peacock feathers and heaven is puri-
fied by you as you stand by your vow of maidenhood. It is 6.15
because of this, goddess, that you are celebrated and honored by the gods for the sake of the protection of the three worlds, o Slayer of Mahishásura

prasannā me, sura|śreṣṭhe, dayāṃ kuru, śivā bhava.
jayā tvaṃ, vijayā c' âiva, saṃgrāme ca jaya|pradā.
mam' âpi vijayaṃ dehi vara|dā tvaṃ ca sāmpratam.
Vindhye c' âiva naga|śreṣṭhe tava sthānam hi śāśvatam,
Kāli, Kāli, mahā|Kāli, sīdhu|māṃsa|paśu|priye.
kṛt'|ânuyātrā bhūtais tvaṃ, varadā, kāma|cāriṇi.
bhār'|âvatāre ye ca tvāṃ saṃsmariṣyanti mānavāḥ,
praṇamanti ca ye tvāṃ hi prabhāte tu narā bhuvi,
na teṣāṃ dur|labhaṃ kiñ cit putrato, dhanato 'pi vā.
6.20 durgāt tārayase, Durge, tat tvaṃ Durgā smṛtā janaiḥ.
kāntāreṣv avasannānāṃ, magnānāṃ ca mah"|ârṇave,
dasyubhir vā niruddhānāṃ tvaṃ gatiḥ paramā nṛṇām.
jala|prataraṇe c' âiva, kāntāreṣv aṭavīṣu ca
ye smaranti, mahā|devi, na ca sīdanti te narāḥ.
tvaṃ kīrtiḥ, śrīr, dhṛtiḥ, siddhir,
hrīr, vidyā, santatir matiḥ,
sandhyā, rātriḥ, prabhā, nidrā,
jyotsnā, kāntiḥ, kṣamā, dayā.
nṛṇāṃ ca bandhanaṃ, mohaṃ,
putra|nāśaṃ, dhana|kṣayam,
vyādhiṃ, mṛtyuṃ, bhayaṃ c' âiva pūjitā nāśayiṣyasi.
so 'haṃ rājyāt paribhraṣṭaḥ śaraṇaṃ tvāṃ prapannavān.
6.25 praṇataś ca yathā mūrdhnā tava, devi sur'|ēśvari,
trāhi māṃ, padma|patr'|âkṣi, satye satyā bhavasva naḥ.
śaraṇaṃ bhava me, Durge, śaraṇye bhakta|vatsale.»

Best of the gods, be kindly disposed to me. Grant me your pity. Be gracious. You are victory, the prize of victory and the provider of victory in war. Grant me victory, and give me a boon suitable for the present circumstances. Your eternal home is on Vindhya, the greatest of mountains, o Kali, Kali, great Kali, fond of rum, meat and animal sacrifice! Your followers are made up of all living beings! You are the granter of boons, lady who travels where she pleases.

It is you whom men call to mind to relieve their burdens and you are she whom men bow to at dawn. For them nothing is difficult to attain: neither sons nor wealth. You 6.20
save men from afar, Durga, whether they're in the wilderness or drowning in the mighty sea, and it is for this reason that people call you Durga. You are the last refuge of men besieged by robbers, men crossing rivers, or men in forest wildernesses. Men who call you to mind, great goddess, do not sink into despair.

You are renown, you are prosperity, you are support, success, modesty, knowledge, continuity and intellect, morning and evening twilight, night, light, sleep, moonlight, beauty, patience and compassion.

On being worshipped you annihilate men's chains, folly, the loss of children, loss of wealth, disease, death and fear. So I, who have fallen from sovereignty, have come to you for protection. As I bow my head to you, o goddess, mistress of 6.25
the heavenly celestials, protect me, o lotus-petal-eyed lady, and be truth to those of us who live truthfully. Durga, be my protection, kind as you are to your worshippers who need protection."

evaṃ stutā hi sā devī darśayām āsa Pāṇḍavam,
upagamya tu rājānam idaṃ vacanam abravīt:

DEVY UVĀCA:

«śṛṇu, rājan mahā|bāho, madīyaṃ vacanaṃ, prabho.
bhaviṣyaty a|cirād eva saṃgrāme vijayas tava,
mama prasādān nirjitya hatvā Kaurava|vāhinīm.
rājyaṃ niṣkaṇṭakaṃ kṛtvā bhokṣyase medinīṃ punaḥ.
bhrātṛbhiḥ sahito, rājan, prītiṃ prāpsyasi puṣkalām.
6.30 mat|prasādāc ca te saukhyam, ārogyaṃ ca bhaviṣyati.
ye ca saṃkīrtayiṣyanti loke vigata|kalmaṣāḥ.
teṣāṃ tuṣṭā pradāsyāmi rājyam, āyur, vapuḥ, sutam.
pravāse, nagare c' âpi, saṃgrāme, śatru|saṃkaṭe,
aṭavyāṃ, durga|kāntāre, sāgare gahane, girau
ye smariṣyanti māṃ, rājan, yath" âhaṃ bhavatā smṛtā,
na teṣāṃ dur|labhaṃ kiñ cid asmil loke bhaviṣyati.
idaṃ stotra|varaṃ bhaktyā śṛṇuyād vā paṭheta vā,
tasya sarvāṇi kāryāṇi siddhiṃ yāsyanti, Pāṇḍavāḥ.
mat|prasādāc ca vaḥ sarvān Virāṭa|nagare sthitān
6.35 na prajñāsyanti Kuravo, narā vā tan|nivāsinaḥ.»
ity uktvā vara|dā devī Yudhiṣṭhiram arin|damam
rakṣāṃ kṛtvā ca Pāṇḍūnām tatr' âiv' ântaradhīyata.

And, thus praised, the goddess revealed herself to the son of Pandu, and, approaching the king, she spoke these words:

THE GODDESS said:

"Long-armed, powerful king, listen to what I have to say. Your victory in battle will come about soon, when you have conquered and slaughtered the Káuravan army by my favor. You will rule the earth again when you have made your kingdom golden. You and your brothers will obtain complete bliss, king. Through my favor, happiness and health 6.30
will be yours.

Those throughout the world who will glorify me will be freed from sin. To those with whom I am satisfied I will grant a kingdom, long life, beauty and a son. Regardless of whether they are in exile or in their home city, on the battlefield or in a truce with their enemies, in a forest or an impassable wilderness, on the ocean or an impenetrable mountain, those who call me to mind just as you have done, king, will find that nothing is hard to attain in this world. He who should listen to or recite this excellent hymn of praise with devotion will find success in all his undertakings, o Pándavas.

By my favor, when all of you are staying in Viráta's city,
no one will recognize you—not the Kurus' men nor those 6.35
who live there." When she had said this to enemy-taming Yudhi·shthira and given her protection to the Pándavas, the boon-giving goddess disappeared there and then.

VAIŚAMPĀYANA uvāca:

7.1 TATO VIRĀṬAM prathamaṃ Yudhiṣṭhiro
rājā sabhāyām upaviṣṭam āvrajat,
vaidūrya|rūpān pratimucya kāñcanān
akṣān sa kakṣe parigṛhya vāsasā.
nar'|âdhipo rāṣṭra|patiṃ yaśasvinaṃ
mahā|yaśāḥ Kaureva|vaṃśa|vardhanaḥ,
mah"|ânubhāvo nara|rāja|satkṛto
dur|āsadas, tīkṣṇa|viṣo yath" ôragaḥ,
balena rūpeṇa nara'|rṣabho mahān
a|pūrva|rūpeṇa yath" â|maras tathā,
mah"|âbhra|jālair iva saṃvṛto ravir,
yath" ânalo bhasma|vṛtaś ca vīryavān.
tam āpatantaṃ prasamīkṣya Pāṇḍavaṃ
Virāṭa|rāḍ indum iv' âbhra|saṃvṛtam,
samāgataṃ pūrṇa|śaśi|prabh"|ānanaṃ
mah"|ânubhāvaṃ na cireṇa dṛṣṭavān
7.5 mantri|dvijān, sūta|mukhān, viśas tathā,
ye c' âpi ke cit paritaḥ samāsate:
«praccha ko 'yaṃ prathamaṃ sameyivān,
nṛp'|ôpamo 'yaṃ samavekṣate sabhām.
sa tu dvijo 'yaṃ bhavitā nar'|ôttamaḥ,
patiḥ pṛthivyā, iti me mano|gatam,
na c' âsya dāso, na ratho, na kuñjaraḥ,
samīpato bhrājati c' âyam Indravat.
śarīra|liṅgair upa|sūcito hy ayaṃ
mūrdh'|âbhiṣikta, iti me mano|gatam.
samīpam āyāti ca me gata|vyatho
yathā gajas tāmarasīṃ mad'|ôtkaṭaḥ.»
vitarkayantaṃ tu nara'|rṣabhas tathā

VAISHAMPÁYANA said:

THEN, AS VIRÁTA was seated at his assembly,* King Yudhi·shthira entered, first fastening the golden and cat's-eye gem dice under his armpit, and holding on to his clothing. Approaching the celebrated king of his realm, the great-famed lord of men, the augmenter of the Kuru lineage, a man of dignified authority, of good repute, like a snake whose virulous poison is unparalleled, a strong-looking bull-like man, whose great beauty was unprecedented, as if a heavenly creature, was like the sun enveloped in clouds heavy with rain, or like a vigorous fire covered with ash. 7.1

Having examined the son of Pandu who had suddenly appeared at the assembly, like the moon covered in clouds, a man of dignified authority whose face shone like the full
moon, King Viráta immediately said to his twice-born ad- 7.5
visers, leading charioteers, vaishyas and others, who had also seen him and who were deliberating on all sides about who he was: "Ask who this man is who shines like a king and looks upon my court for the first time. My thoughts are that he is twice-born, the best of men, a king of the earth, but he has no slaves, or chariots or elephants, though he sparkles as if from the presence of Indra. My theory is that he is a king whose head has been consecrated as indicated by the marks on his body. Unanxious, he approaches my presence, like an elephant in rut approaches a lotus pond."

Yudhi·shthira, that bull among men, went up to Viráta as he was thus conjecturing, and said: "Supreme sovereign,

Yudhiṣṭhiro 'bhyetya Virāṭam abravīt:
«samrāḍ vijānātv iha jīvan'|ârthinaṃ
vinaṣṭa|sarva|svam upāgataṃ dvijam.
ih' âham icchāmi tav', ân|agh', ântike
vastuṃ yathā kāma|caras tathā, vibho.»
tam abravīt, «svāgatam ity» an|antaraṃ
rājā prahṛṣṭaḥ, pratisaṃgṛhāṇa ca.
7.10 taṃ rāja|siṃhaṃ pratigṛhya rājā
prīty" ātmanā c' âinam idaṃ babhāṣe,
«kāmena tāt' âbhivadāmy ahaṃ tvāṃ!
kasy' âsi rājño viṣayād ih' āgataḥ?
gotraṃ ca, nām' âpi ca śaṃsa tattvataḥ,
kiṃ c' âpi śilpaṃ tava vidyate kṛtam.»

YUDHIṢṬHIRA uvāca:
Yudhiṣṭhirasy' āsam ahaṃ purā sakhā.
Vaiyāghrapadyaḥ punar asmi vipraḥ
akṣān prayoktuṃ kuśalo 'smi devināṃ,
Kaṅk' êti nāmn" âsmi, Virāṭa, viśrutaḥ.

VIRĀṬA uvāca:
dadāmi te hanta varaṃ yam icchasi.
praśādhi Matsyān, vaśa|go hy ahaṃ tava.
priyāś ca dhūrtā mama devinaḥ sadā,
bhavāṃś ca, dev'|ôpama, rājyam arhati.

YUDHIṢṬHIRA uvāca:
prāpto vivādaḥ prathamaṃ, viśāṃ pate,
na vidyate kaṃ ca na Matsya hīnataḥ.
na me jitaḥ kaś cana dhārayed dhanaṃ.
varo mam' âiṣo 'stu tava prasāda|jaḥ.

know me as a brahmin whose entire property, my means for living, has been destroyed, and so has come here to this place. I want to live here in your proximity, faultless man, doing your bidding, my lord."

Then the king, delighted, immediately replied that he was welcome and should accept whatever post he wished for.
The king, having acquiesced to the lion among sovereigns, 7.10
spoke to him as follows, with a joyful mind: "I address you with love! From which king's realm have you come to this place? Tell me truthfully about your family, your name and what skill is known to you."

YUDHI·SHTHIRA said:

Previously I was a friend of Yudhi·shthira. I am a brahmin descended from Vyaghra·pad, skilled among gamblers at casting dice. My name is Kanka, heard of far and wide, Viráta.

VIRÁTA said:

Ah! I shall give you whatever boon you wish for. You rule the Matsyas, and I will be obedient to you. Even crafty gamblers are always dear to me, but you who are like a god deserve a kingdom.

YUDHI·SHTHIRA said:

The first favor I must be granted is that no gambling quarrels should arise between me and inferior people of Matsya, lord of earth, and, second, that a man I defeat should not keep back my winnings. Let this be the boon you grant me, by your favor.

VIRĀṬA uvāca:

7.15 hanyām avaśyaṃ yadi te ’|priyaṃ caret,
pravrājayeyaṃ viṣayād dvijāṃs tathā.
śṛṇvantu me jāna|padāḥ samāgatāḥ!
Kaṇko, yath” âhaṃ, viṣaye prabhus tathā.
samāna|yāno bhavit” âsi me sakhā,
prabhūta|vastro, bahu|pāna|bhojanaḥ.
paśyes tvam antaś ca bahiś ca sarvadā
kṛtaṃ ca te dvāram apāvṛtaṃ mayā.
ye tv” ânuvādeyur avṛtti|karśitā
brūyāś ca teṣāṃ vacanena māṃ sadā.
dāsyāmi sarvaṃ tad ahaṃ, na saṃśayo!
na te bhayaṃ vidyati sannidhau mama.

VAIŚAMPĀYANA uvāca:

evaṃ sa labdhvā tu varaṃ samāgamaṃ
Virāṭa|rājena nara’|rṣabhas tadā
uvāsa dhīraḥ param’|ârcitaḥ sukhī,
na c’ âpi kaś cic caritaṃ bubodha tat.

VAIŚAMPĀYANA uvāca:

8.1 ATH’ Â|PARO bhīma|balaḥ śriyā jvalann
upāyayau siṃha|vilāsa|vikramaḥ,
khajāṃ ca, darvī ca kareṇa dhārayann,
asiṃ ca kāl’|âṅgam a|kośam, a|vraṇam.
sa sūda|rūpaḥ parameṇa varcasā
ravir yathā lokam imaṃ prakāśayan,
sa kṛṣṇa|vāsā giri|rāja|sāravāṃś
taṃ Matsya|rājaṃ samupetya tasthivān.

VIRÁTA said:

I will definitely kill a man if he should act unpleasantly toward you, and if he is twice-born then I shall banish him from my realm. Let the people assembled here listen! Kanka is just as much lord in the kingdom as I am. 7.15

You will be my friend and travel in the same carriage as me. You will have plentiful clothing, and abundant food and drink. You shall look into everything, both internal and external affairs, and for you my door will always be open.

Always tell me in their own words what those who are thin from deprivation repeat to you, and I will give them everything. Have no doubt about that! You will have no fear while you stay with me.

VAISHAMPÁYANA said:

Having accepted this favor and an audience with King Viráta, the bull among men then lived resolutely and happily, most prominently honored, and no one discovered him as he lived in this guise.

VAISHAMPÁYANA said:

THEN ANOTHER MAN of dread strength, blazing with beauty, approached him with the stride of a playful lion, holding a spoon and a wooden ladle in his hand, as well as a dark-blue-bodied sword without scabbard or blemish. He had a cook's appearance, and he shone with his extraordinary brilliance like the sun over the world. Dressed in black, with the strength of the lord of the mountains, he approached the king of the Matsyas and stood before him. 8.1

taṃ prekṣya rājā ramayann upāgataṃ
tato 'bravīj jāna|padān samāgatān,
«siṃh'|ônnat'|âṃso 'yam atīva rūpavān
pradṛśyate ko nu vara'|rṣabho yuvā?
a|dṛṣṭa|pūrvaḥ puruṣo, ravir yathā,
vitarkayan n' âsya labhāmi niścayam.
tath" âsya cittaṃ hy api saṃvitarkayan
nara'|rṣabhasy' âsya na yāmi tattvataḥ.
8.5 dṛṣṭv" âiva c' âinaṃ tu vicārayāmy ahaṃ
gandharva|rājo, yadi vā puran|daraḥ.
jānīta ko 'yaṃ mama darśane sthito
yad īpsitaṃ tal labhatāṃ ca mā|ciram.»
Virāṭa|vākyena ca tena coditā
narā Virāṭasya su|śīghra|gāminaḥ
upetya Kaunteyam ath' âbruvaṃs tadā
yathā sa rāj" âvadat' Âcyut'|ânujam.
tato Virāṭaṃ samupetya Pāṇḍavas
tv a|dīna|rūpaṃ vacanaṃ mahā|manāḥ
uvāca: «sūdo 'smi, nar'|êndra, Ballavo.
bhajasva māṃ vyañjana|kāram uttamam!»

VIRĀṬA uvāca:

na sūdatāṃ, Ballava, śraddadhāmi te!
sahasra|netra|pratimo virājase;
śriyā ca rūpeṇa ca vikrameṇa ca
prabhāsase tvaṃ nṛ|varo nareṣv iva.

The king delightedly gazed at the man who had approached him and addressed his assembled subjects, saying: "Who is this fine bull-like young man who has appeared? Who is this spectacularly handsome man with prominent lion-like shoulders? I have never before seen a man so like the sun, and though I ponder the matter I cannot come to a conclusion about who he is. Even conjecturing, I cannot establish what this bull-like man's intention truly is. Seeing 8.5
such a man, I wonder whether he is the king of the *gandhárvas* or Indra, the sacker of cities. Find out who this man, who appears standing before me, really is, and let him take whatever he wants quickly."

Commanded by his orders, Viráta's men moved very quickly, and, approaching the son of Kuntí, they told Yudhi·shthira's younger brother what the king had said.

Then the high-minded son of Pandu approached Viráta and spoke these nobly formed words: "I am a cook, lord of men, Bállava by name. I make excellent dishes, so employ me!"

VIRÁTA said:

I do not believe your business is cooking, Bállava! You are radiant like the thousand-eyed god Indra. With your splendor, beauty and prowess, you shine like a king among men.

BHĪMA uvāca:

nar'|êndra, sūdaḥ paricārako 'smi te.
jānāmi sūpān prathamaṃ ca kevalān.
āsvāditā ye, nṛpate, pur" âbhavan
Yudhiṣṭhireṇ' âpi nṛpeṇa sarvaśaḥ,
8.10 balena tulyaś ca na vidyate mayā
niyuddha|śīlaś ca sad" âiva, pārthiva,
gajaiś ca siṃhaiś ca sameyivān aham
sadā kariṣyāmi tav', ân|agha, priyam.

VIRĀṬA uvāca:

dadāmi te, hanta, varān mahānase
tathā ca kuryāḥ kuśalaṃ hi bhāṣase.
na c' âiva manye tava karma yat samaṃ.
samudra|nemiṃ pṛthivīṃ tvam arhasi.
yathā hi kāmo bhavatas, tathā kṛtaṃ.
mahānase tvaṃ bhava me puras|kṛtaḥ.
narāś ca ye tatra samāhitāḥ purā
bhavāṃś ca teṣām adhipo mayā kṛtaḥ.

VAIŚAMPĀYANA uvāca:

tathā sa Bhīmo vihito mahānase
Virāṭa|rājño dayito 'bhavad dṛḍham.
uvāsa rājye, na ca taṃ pṛthag|jano
bubodha, tatr' ânucarāś ca ke cana.

VAIŚAṂPĀYANA uvāca:

9.1 TATAḤ KEŚĀN samutkṣipya vellit'|âgrān, a|ninditān,
kṛṣṇān, sūkṣmān, mṛdūn, dīrghān samudgrathya śuci|smitā,
jugūhe dakṣiṇe pārśve mṛdūn asita|locanā,
vāsaś ca paridhāy' âikaṃ Kṛṣṇā su|malinaṃ mahat.

BHIMA said:

Lord of kings, I am your cook and servant. My primary speciality is curries, king. King Yudhi·shthira always used to enjoy them in the past, king. Furthermore, you will not 8.10
find my equal in strength! Constantly practicing fighting, my king, by grappling with elephants and lions, I will always entertain you, sinless man.

VIRÁTA said:

Ah, well! I will grant your wishes in the kitchen, and you can do whatever task in which you claim to have expertise. However, I do not think that this task is equal to you. You rather deserve the earth encircled by the sea. But do as you wish, and be my foremost servant in the kitchen. You are appointed my head chef in charge of all men who were put there before.

VAISHAMPÁYANA said:

So Bhima, employed in the kitchen, became the sure favorite of King Viráta, and as he lived in the kingdom none of the common people or servants recognized him.

VAISHAMPÁYANA said:

THEN SWEET-SMILING, dark-eyed Krishná tied back her 9.1
long, soft, fine, black, faultless, curly-tipped hair, threw it over her right side and covered it. Her clothing consisted of a single large but very dirty garment.

kṛtvā veṣaṃ ca Sairandhryās tato vyacarad ārtavat.
tāṃ narāḥ paridhāvantīṃ striyaś ca samupādravan.
āpṛcchaṃś c' âiva tāṃ dṛṣṭvā: «kā tvaṃ, kiṃ ca cikīrṣasi?»
sā tān uvāca, rāj'|êndra, «Sairandhry aham ih' āgatā,
9.5 karma c' êcchāmi vai kartuṃ tasya, yo māṃ yuyukṣati.»
tasyā rūpeṇa, veṣeṇa, ślakṣṇayā ca tathā girā
na śraddadhata tāṃ dāsīm anna|hetor upasthitām.

Virāṭasya tu Kaikeyī bhāryā parama|sammatā
ālokayantī dadṛśe prāsādād Drupad'|ātmajām.
sā samīkṣya tathā|rūpām a|nāthām eka|vāsasam,
samāhūy' âbravīd, «bhadre, kā tvaṃ, kiṃ ca cikīrṣasi?»
sā tān uvāca, rāj'|êndra,
«sairandhry aham upāgatā,
karma c' êcchāmy ahaṃ kartuṃ
tasya, yo māṃ yuyukṣati.»

SUDEṢṆ" ôvāca:

n' âivaṃ|rūpā bhavanty evaṃ, yathā vadasi, bhāmini.
preṣayanti ca vai dāsīr dāsāṃś ca vividhān bahūn.
9.10 n' ôcca|gulphā, saṃhat'|ôrus, tri|gambhīrā, ṣaḍ|unnatā,
raktā pañcasu rakteṣu, haṃsa|gadgada|bhāṣiṇī,
su|keśī, su|stanī, śyāmā, pīna|śroṇi|payodharā.

So, once she had adopted the guise of a *sairándhri*, she rambled about as if in pain, and men and women rushed toward her as she roamed about, and asked her: "Who are you and what do you want?" She replied to them, lord of
kings, saying, "I am a *sairándhri* who has come here, and I 9.5
want to work for whomever will employ me." But because of her beauty and clothes and tender speech they did not believe that she was a slave who had come for food.

But Kaikéyi, the daughter of King Kékaya, Viráta's chief and most highly honored wife, saw the daughter of Drúpada as she looked about from her terrace, and, examining the beautiful, unprotected woman dressed only in a single garment, she called her near and said, "Beautiful girl, who are you, and what do you want to do?" So she answered, lord of kings, saying, "I have come here as a *sairándhri* and I want to work for whomever will employ me."

SUDÉSHNA said:

Beautiful woman, those possessed of your beauty are never what you claim to be, but rather they command many various male and female slaves of that sort.

Your ankles are not prominent, your thighs touch and you 9.10
are deep-voiced, deep-naveled and deep of character. You are endowed with the six prominent parts of the body; your big toes, bust, hips, back and sides, toenails and palms are all well developed, you are crimson in the five crimson areas of the palms, the soles of the feet and face, and you speak stutteringly, like a goose. You have lustrous hair, shapely breasts, are dark in complexion, and have swelling breasts and hips.

tena ten' âiva sampannā Kāśmīr' îva turaṅgamī;
arāla|pakṣma|nayanā, bimb'|ôṣṭhī, tanu|madhyamā,
kambu|grīvā, gūḍha|śirā, pūrṇa|candra|nibh'ānanā,
śārad'|ôtpala|patr'|âkṣyā, śārad'|ôtpala|gandhayā,
śārad'|ôtpala|sevinyā rūpeṇa sadṛśī Śriyā.
kā tvaṃ, brūhi yathā, bhadre! n' âsi dāsī kathañ cana.
Yakṣī vā, yadi vā devī, gandharvī yadi v" âpsarāḥ?
9.15 deva|kanyā, bhujaṅgī vā, nagarasy' âtha devatā?
vidyādharī, kinnarī vā, yadi vā Rohiṇī svayam?
Alambuṣā, Miśrakeśī, Puṇḍarīk", âtha Mālinī,
Indrāṇī, Vāruṇī vā tvaṃ? Tvaṣṭur dhātuḥ, Prajāpateḥ?
devyo deveṣu vikhyātās tāsāṃ tvaṃ katamā, śubhe?

DRAUPADY uvāca:

n' âsmi devī, na gandharvī, n' âsurī, na ca rākṣasī.
sairandhrī tu bhujiṣy" âsmi. satyam etad bravīmi te.
keśān jānāmy ahaṃ kartuṃ, piṃṣe sādhu vilepanam.
mallik"|ôtpala|padmānāṃ, campakānāṃ tathā, śubhe,
grathayiṣye vicitrāś ca srajaḥ parama|sobhanāh.
ārādhayaṃ Satyabhāmāṃ Kṛṣṇasya mahiṣīṃ priyām,
9.20 Kṛṣṇāṃ ca bhāryāṃ Pāṇḍūnāṃ, kurūṇām eka|sundarīm.
tatra tatra carāmy evaṃ labhamānā su|bhojanam,
vāsāṃsi yāvanti labhe, tāvat tāvad rame tathā.
‹Mālin" îty› eva me nāma svayaṃ devī cakāra sā.
s" âham ady' āgatā, devi Sudeṣṇe, tvan|niveśanam.

Like a Kashmiri mare you are endowed with various attributes. Your eyelashes are curled, your lips are red, your waist is slender, the lines of your neck are like those of a conch shell, your veins are invisible, your face is like the full moon, your eyes are like the petals of autumn lotuses, you are as fragrant as the autumn lotus, and in your beauty you are like Shri who resides in the autumn lotus.

Tell me who you are, beautiful girl! You are no slave. Are
you a *yakshi*, or a goddess, a *gandhárvi*, or an *ápsaras*? Are 9.15
you the daughter of a god, a female serpent, or the guardian goddess of a city? Are you a *vidya·dhari* or *kínnari*, or are you Róhini in person? Are you Alámbusha, Mishra·keshi, Pundaríka, or Málini, or the wife of Indra or Váruna? Are you Tvashtri's wife or Praja·pati's? Which of the goddesses celebrated among the celestial ones are you, beautiful girl?

DRÁUPADI said:

I am no goddess, *gandhárvi*, *ásuri* or *rákshasi*. I am an independent *sairándhri*. I am telling you the truth.

I know how to dress hair, and I will pound unguents well for anointing, I will string the most lovely and varied garlands, beautiful lady, of jasmine, blue lotuses, day lotuses and *chámpakas*.

I served Satya·bhama, the first and favored queen of Krishna, and also Krishná, the wife of the Pándavas and the 9.20
sole beauty of the Kurus. I wander here and there obtaining good food and clothes, and for as long as I can do this I stay there. The lady Dráupadi herself gave me the name Málini. So now I have come to your home, Queen Sudéshna.

SUDEṢṆ" ôvāca:

mūrdhni tvāṃ vāsayeyaṃ vai saṃśayo me na vidyate,
no ced iha tu rājā tvāṃ gacchet sarveṇa cetasā.
striyo rāja|kule yāś ca, yāś c' êmā mama veśmani,
prasaktās tvāṃ nirīkṣante; pumāṃsaṃ kaṃ na mohayeḥ?
vṛkṣāṃś c' âvasthitān paśya ya ime mama veśmani,
te 'pi tvāṃ sannamant' îva; pumāṃsaṃ kaṃ na mohayeḥ?
9.25 rājā Virāṭaḥ, su|śroṇi, dṛṣṭvā vapur a|mānuṣam,
vihāya māṃ, var'|ārohe, tvāṃ gacchet sarva|cetasā.
yaṃ hi tvam, an|avady'|âṅgi taral'|āyata|locane,
prasaktam abhivīkṣethāḥ, sa kāma|vaśa|go bhavet.
yaś ca tvām satataṃ paśyet puruṣaś, cāru|hāsini,
evaṃ, sarv'|ânavady'|âṅgi, sa c' ânaṅga|vaśo bhavet.
adhyārohed yathā vṛkṣān vadhāy' âiv' ātmano naraḥ,
rāja|veśmani te, su|bhru, gṛhe tu syāt tathā mama.
yathā ca karkaṭī garbham ādhatte mṛtyum ātmanaḥ,
tathā|vidham ahaṃ manye vāsaṃ tava, śuci|smite.

DRAUPADY uvāca:

9.30 n' âsmi labhyā Virāṭena, na c' ânyena kadā cana.
gandharvāḥ patayo mahyaṃ yuvānaḥ pañca, bhāmini,
putrā gandharva|rājasya mahā|sattvasya kasya cit
rakṣanti te ca māṃ nityaṃ. duḥkh'|ācārā tathā hy aham!

SUDÉSHNA said:

I have no doubt that I would keep you with it on my own head, were it not that the king would turn to you with his whole heart. The women in the royal palace and those in my apartment observe you and are fixated, so which man would not become stupefied? See how even the trees planted in my apartments bow before you, so which man would not become stupefied?

Beautiful-hipped lady, when King Viráta sees your oth- 9.25
erworldly beauty he will overlook me and turn to you with his whole heart, shapely-hipped girl. Any man at whom you gaze lovingly, faultless-limbed and large, trembling-eyed lady, would be a slave to love. Any man who stares endlessly at you, entirely faultless-bodied and sweet-smiling girl, would become a slave to his desire.

Just as a man climbs trees for his own destruction, so that would be my fate, too, with you in the royal apartments and palace, beautiful-browed girl. Just as the female crab conceives for her destruction, so I believe I will bring about my own destruction by giving you a home, sweet-smiling girl.

DRÁUPADI said:

I cannot be taken by Viráta or any other person, lovely 9.30
lady, for my five youthful *gandhárva* husbands, the sons of a great noble *gandhárva* king, always protect me. I am difficult to tamper with!

yo me na dadyād ucchiṣṭaṃ, na ca pādau pradhāvayet,
prīṇeraṃs tena vāsena gandharvāḥ patayo mama.
yo hi māṃ puruṣo gṛddhyed yath" ânyāḥ prākṛtāḥ striyaḥ,
tām eva nivased rātriṃ, praviśya ca parāṃ tanum.
na c' âpy ahaṃ cālayituṃ śakyā kena cid, aṅgane,
duḥkha|śīlā hi gandharvās, te ca me balava|priyāḥ
9.35 pracchannāś c' âpi rakṣanti te māṃ nityaṃ, śuci|smite.

SUDEṢṆ" ôvāca:

evaṃ tvām vāsayiṣyāmi yathā tvaṃ, nandin', îcchasi,
na ca pādau na c' ôcchiṣṭaṃ sprakṣyasi tvaṃ kathañ cana.

VAIŚAṂPĀYANA uvāca:

evaṃ Kṛṣṇā Virāṭasya bhāryayā parisāntvitā
uvāsa nagare tasmin pati|dharmavatī satī.
na c' âināṃ veda tatr' ânyas tattvena, Janamejaya.

VAIŚAṂPĀYANA uvāca:

10.1 SAHADEVO 'PI gopānāṃ kṛtvā veṣam an|uttamam
bhāṣāṃ c' âiṣāṃ samāsthāya Virāṭam upayād atha,
goṣṭham āsādya tiṣṭhantaṃ bhavanasya samīpataḥ.
rāj" âtha dṛṣṭvā puruṣān prāhiṇoj jāta|vismayaḥ,
tam āyāntam abhiprekṣya bhrājamānaṃ nara'|rṣabham.
samupasthāya vai rājā papraccha Kuru|nandanam:
«kasya vā tvaṃ? kuto vā tvaṃ? kiṃ vā tvaṃ tu cikīrṣasi?
na hi me dṛṣṭa|pūrvas tvaṃ. tattvaṃ brūhi, nara'|rṣabha.»

My *gandhárva* husbands are pleased with a house where they would not give me their leftovers to eat and where they would not make me wash their feet. The man who should seize me as if I were a common woman would spend that short night as his last, once it was begun.

No one can interfere with me, lady of well-rounded limbs, because those beloved but bad-tempered and mighty *gandhárvas* always protect me even when hidden, sweet- 9.35
smiling lady.

SUDÉSHNA said:

Thus, my daughter, I will take you in as you wish, and you won't have to eat any leftovers or touch anyone's feet.

VAISHAMPÁYANA said:

Soothed by Viráta's wife, excellent Krishná lived in that city, always devoted to her husbands, and no one else there knew who she really was, Janam·éjaya.

VAISHAMPÁYANA said:

THEN, WHEN Saha·deva had put together an excellent 10.1
cowherd disguise, he approached Viráta, talking in a cowherd's accent, and went up to the cattle pen, which stood in the vicinity of the palace. When the king saw that shining bull-like man approach, he was amazed and commanded his men to bring him forward.

When he had approached, the king asked the descendant of Kuru: "Whom do you belong to? Where are you from? Or what do you want? I haven't seen you before, so tell me truthfully, bull-like man."

10.5 saṃprāpya rājānam amitra|tāpanaṃ
tato 'bravīn megha|mah"|āugha|niḥsvanaḥ:
«vaiśyo 'smi, nāmn" âham Ariṣṭanemir.
go|saṅkhya āsaṃ Kuru|puṅgavānām.
vastuṃ tvay' îcchāmi viśāṃ, variṣṭha,
tān rāja|siṃhān na hi vedmi Pārthān.
na śakyate jīvitum apy a|karmaṇā,
na ca tvad|anyo mama rocate nṛpaḥ.»

VIRĀṬA uvāca:

tvaṃ brāhmaṇo yadi vā kṣatriyo 'si,
samudra|nem'|īśvara|rūpavān asi.
ācakṣva me tattvam, amitra|karśana.
na vaiśya|karma tvayi vidyate kṣamam.
kasy' âsi rājño viṣayād ih' āgataḥ?
kiṃ v" âpi śilpaṃ tava vidyate kṛtam?
kathaṃ tvam asmāsu nivatsyase sadā?
vadasva, kiṃ c' âpi tav' êha vetanam.

SAHADEVA uvāca:

Pañcānāṃ Pāṇḍu|putrāṇāṃ jyeṣṭho bhrātā Yudhiṣṭhiraḥ.
tasy' âṣṭa|śata|sāhasrā gavāṃ vargāḥ śataṃ śatam,
10.10 apare śata|sāhasrā dvis, tāvantas tathā pare.
teṣāṃ go|saṅkhya āsaṃ vai, Tantipāl' êti māṃ viduḥ.
bhūtaṃ, bhavyaṃ, bhaviṣyaṃ ca,
yac ca saṅkhyā|gataṃ gavām,
na me 'sty a|viditaṃ kiñ cit
samantād daśa|yojanam.
guṇāḥ su|viditā hy āsan mama tasya mah"|ātmanaḥ,
āsīc ca sa mayā tuṣṭaḥ Kuru|rājo Yudhiṣṭhiraḥ.

Once he reached the king, the tormentor of his enemies, he spoke to him in a roar like that of a strong-currented cloud: "I am a vaishya called Aríshta·nemi. I was the cowherd of the Kuru heroes, and I want to live in your community, best of men, for I do not know where those lion-like royal sons of Pritha are. It is not possible to live without a job, and in my opinion no other king is as splendid as you." 10.5

VIRÁTA said:

You are either a brahmin or a kshatriya, for you look like a lord of earth, encircled by the sea. Speak to me truthfully, tormentor of your enemies. A vaishya's work does not seem to befit you. From which kingdom's territory have you come to this place? What skill do you have? Tell me how you will live among us forever, and what your salary here will be.

SAHA·DEVA said:

Yudhi·shthira, the eldest brother of the five sons of Pandu, had divisions of one hundred and eight thousand,
ten thousand, a hundred thousand, and lastly two hundred 10.10
thousand cattle. I was their cowherd, and they knew me as Tanti·pala.

There is nothing that I do not know about the past, present and future number count of cattle from the neighboring ninety miles. Yudhi·shthira, the high-souled king of the Kurus, was well aware of my talents, and he was pleased with me.

kṣipraṃ ca gāvo bahulā bhavanti,
na tāsu rogo bhavat' îha kaś cana,
tais tair upāyair viditaṃ mam' âitad.
etāni śilpāni mayi sthitāni.
ṛṣabhāṃś c' âpi jānāmi, rājan, pūjita|lakṣaṇān
yeṣāṃ mūtram upāghrāya api vandhyā prasūyate.

VIRĀṬA uvāca:

10.15 śataṃ sahasrāṇi samāhitāni
sa|varṇa|varṇasya vimiśritān guṇaiḥ
paśūn sa|pālān bhavate dadāmy aham.
tvad|āśrayā me paśavo bhavantv iha.

VAIŚAṂPĀYANA uvāca:

tathā sa rājño '|vidito, viśām pate,
uvāsa tatr' âiva sukhaṃ nar'|ôttamaḥ.
na c' âinam anye 'pi viduḥ kathañ cana.
prādāc ca tasmai bharaṇaṃ yath" ēpsitam.

VAIŚAṂPĀYANA uvāca:

11.1 ATH' ÂPARO 'dṛśyata rūpa|sampadā
strīṇām alaṅ|kāra|dharo bṛhat pumān,
prākāra|vapre pratimucya kuṇḍale
dīrghe ca kambū parihāṭake śubhe.
bahūṃś ca dīrghāṃś ca vikīrya mūrdhajān
mahā|bhujo vāraṇa|tulya|vikramaḥ
gatena bhūmiṃ pratikampayaṃs tadā
Virāṭam āsādya sabhā|samīpataḥ.

I know by what means your cattle will soon multiply, and no disease will befall them for my skills are well established. King, I also recognize bulls with auspicious markings, the smell of whose urine can even cause barren cows to conceive.

VIRÁTA said:

I have one hundred thousand altogether, mixed with sub- 10.15
divisions of every color. I'm handing over the cattle and their herdsmen to you. My cattle are now reliant on you.

VAISHAMPÁYANA said:

Then the best of men lived there happily, unknown to the king, o lord of earth. No one else recognized him, and he earned the wages he hoped for.

VAISHAMPÁYANA said:

THEN YET ANOTHER handsome man of enormous propor- 11.1
tion appeared, wearing women's ornaments. He had decked himself with dangly earrings, which on him resembled fortified rampart walls, and beautiful gilt conch-shell bracelets. The long-armed person whose stride was like that of an elephant shook out his long and plentiful hair. Making the earth tremble with his approach, he came up to Viráta in the presence of his assembly.

tam prekṣya rāj" ôpagataṃ sabhā|tale
vyājāt praticchannam ari|pramāthinam
virājamānaṃ paramena varcasā
sutaṃ Mahendrasya gaj'|êndra|vikramam,
sarvān apṛcchac ca sabh"|ânucāriṇaḥ:
«kuto 'yam āyāti? purā na me śrutaḥ.»
na c' âinam ūcur viditaṃ tadā narāḥ.
sa|vismayaṃ vākyam idaṃ nṛpo 'bravīt:
11.5 «sattv'|ôpapannaḥ puruṣo 'mar'|ôpamaḥ
śyāmo, yuvā, vāraṇa|yūthap'|ôpamaḥ,
āmucya kambū parihāṭake śubhe,
vimucya veṇīm, apinahya kuṇḍale.
sragvī, su|keśaḥ, paridhāya c' ânyathā
śusobha dhanvī kavacī sarī yathā
āruhya yānaṃ paridhāvatāṃ bhavān.
sutaiḥ samo me bhava vā mayā samaḥ
vṛddho hy ahaṃ vai parihāra|kāmaḥ
sarvān Matsyāṃs tarasā pālayasva.
‹n' âivaṃ|vidhāḥ klība|rūpā bhavanti
kathañ can', êti› pratibhāti me manaḥ.»

ARJUNA uvāca:

gāyāmi, nṛtyāmy, atha vādayāmi.
bhadro 'smi nṛtye, kuśalo 'smi gīte.
tvam Uttarāyai pradiśasva māṃ svayaṃ,
bhavāmi devyā, nara|deva, nartakaḥ.
idaṃ tu rūpaṃ mama yena, kiṃ tava,
prakīrtayitvā bhṛśa|śoka|vardhanam?
Bṛhannalāṃ māṃ, nara|deva, viddhi
sutaṃ sutām vā pitṛ|mātṛ|varjitām.

Seeing great Indra's son, the abuser of his foes, enter the assembly hall with the stride of a mighty elephant, concealed by his disguise, but shining with his conspicuous brilliance, the king asked all his attendants in the court: "Where has this man come from? For I have not heard of him before."

When the men then replied that they had no idea who this newcomer may be, the king spoke in wonder: "You 11.5
are a godlike man endowed with true power. Dark-skinned youth that you are, with your hair tied in a braid and decked with beautiful gilt conch-shell bracelets and earrings, you resemble the leader of a herd of elephants. Alternatively, you are like one of those who drive about riding a chariot; a shining garlanded creature with beautiful hair and a retinue, bearing armor and carrying a bow and arrow. Become my sons' equal or even mine, for I am old and eager to resign. So rule over all the Matsyas. To my mind it seems that a person with an appearance such as this bears no resemblance to a eunuch at all!"

ÁRJUNA said:

I sing, dance and play instruments. I am a gifted dancer and an expert singer. Assign me to your own Uttará, and I will be the princess's dance tutor, lord of men. What will be the result of your forcing me to explain my form, other than greatly increasing my grief? Know me, god among men, as Brihan·nala—the large-reeded lady—a son or daughter without a mother and father.

VIRĀṬA uvāca:

11.10 dadāmi te, hanta, varaṃ, Bṛhannale,
sutāṃ ca me nartaya, yāś ca tādṛśīḥ.
idaṃ tu te karma samaṃ na me mataṃ.
samudra|nemiṃ pṛthivīṃ tvam arhasi.

VAIŚAṂPĀYANA said:

Bṛhannalāṃ tām abhivīkṣya Matsya|rāṭ
kalāsu, nṛtyeṣu, tath" âiva vādite,
saṃmantrya rājā vividhaiḥ sva|mantribhiḥ,
parīkṣya c' âinaṃ pramadābhir āśu vai,
a|puṃstvam apy asya niśamya ca sthiraṃ
tataḥ kumārī|puram utsasarja tam.
sa śikṣayām āsa ca gīta|vāditaṃ
sutām Virāṭasya Dhanañjayaḥ prabhuḥ,
sakhīś ca tasyāḥ, paricārikās tathā,
priyaś ca tāsāṃ sa babhūva Pāṇḍavaḥ.
tathā sa satreṇa Dhanañjayo vasan,
priyāṇi kurvan saha tābhir ātmavān,
tathā ca taṃ tatra na jajñire janā
bahiś|carā v" âpy, atha c' ântare|carāḥ.

VAIŚAṂPĀYANA uvāca:

12.1 ATH' ĀPARO 'dṛśyata Pāṇḍavaḥ prabhur,
Virāṭa|rājaṃ tarasā sameyivān.
tam āpatantaṃ dadṛśe pṛthag|jano
vimuktam abhrād iva sūrya|maṇḍalam.

VIRÁTA said:

Very well, I will grant your wish, Brihan·nala. Teach my daughter and those like her to dance. But in my opinion this task does not seem equal to you, for you deserve the earth encompassed by the ocean. 11.10

VAISHAMPÁYANA said:

Then, once the king of the Matsyas had examined Brihan·nala in the tone of his songs and in dances and similarly in the playing of musical instruments, he consulted with his various ministers. Then, quickly having had an examination made by wanton women as to whether he was really a eunuch, and finding that his lack of manhood was a permanent condition, the king then let him loose on the royal women's quarters.

So it was that the mighty Dhanan·jaya taught Viráta's daughter and her friends and attendants to sing and play musical instruments, and the son of Pandu became dear to them. Self-controlled Dhanan·jaya lived there in disguise, enjoying their company, but neither the people outside nor even those inside that place recognized him.

VAISHAMPÁYANA said:

THEN ANOTHER mighty Pándavan appeared, approaching King Viráta with speed. To the people of the land he appeared to be flying toward them like the sphere of the sun escaping from clouds. 12.1

sa vai hayān aikṣata tāṃs tatas tataḥ,
samīkṣamāṇaṃ sa dadarśa Matsya|rāṭ.
tato 'bravīt tān anugān nar'|ēśvaraḥ:
«kuto 'yam āyāti naro 'mar'|ôpamaḥ?
svayaṃ hayān īkṣati māmakān dṛḍhaṃ
dhruvaṃ haya|jño bhavitā vicakṣaṇaḥ.
praveśyatām eṣa samīpam āśu me.
vibhāti vīro hi yath" â|maras tathā.»
abhyetya rājānam amitra|h" âbravīj:
«jayo 'stu te, pārthiva, bhadram astu vaḥ.
hayeṣu yukto, nṛpa, saṃmataḥ sadā,
tav' âśva|sūto nipuṇo bhavāmy aham.»

VIRĀṬA uvāca:

12.5 dadāmi yānāni, dhanaṃ, niveśanaṃ.
mam' âśva|sūto bhavituṃ tvam arhasi.
kuto 'si, kasy' âsi, kathaṃ tvam āgataḥ?
prabrūhi śilpaṃ tava vidyate ca yat.

NAKULA uvāca:

Pañcānāṃ Pāṇḍu|putrāṇāṃ jyeṣṭho bhrātā Yudhiṣṭhiraḥ,
ten' âham aśveṣu purā niyuktaḥ, śatru|karśana.
aśvānāṃ prakṛtiṃ vedmi, vinayaṃ c' âpi sarvaśaḥ,
duṣṭānāṃ pratipattiṃ ca, kṛtsnaṃ c' âiva cikitsitam.
na kātaraṃ syān mama jātu vāhanaṃ,
na me 'sti duṣṭā vaḍavā, kuto hayāḥ.
janas tu māṃ āha, sa c' âpi Pāṇḍavo
Yudhiṣṭhiro, Granthikam eva nāmataḥ.

VIRĀṬA uvāca:

yad asti kiñ cin mama vāji|vāhanaṃ
tad astu sarvaṃ tvad|adhīnam adya vai,

He noticed the horses around and about, but when the king of the Matsyas saw him inspecting them the lord of men quickly said to his followers, "Where has this godlike man come from? He looks intently at my horses, surely he is experienced in horse-lore. Let him enter my presence quickly, for he is a warrior who shines like a god."

The enemy-destroyer came up to the king and said: "May you have victory, lord of the earth, and may blessings be upon you. I am experienced with horses and have always been highly thought of, king, so I will make an adroit master of your horses."

VIRÁTA said:

I will give you chariots, money and living quarters, for 12.5
you deserve to be the master of my horses. But tell me where you are from, who you are and how you have come here, and also what skill you have learned.

NÁKULA said:

Long ago I was the horse-master of Yudhi·shthira, the eldest brother of the five Pándavas, harasser of your enemies. I understand horses' nature and I am completely conversant with their training. I also know how to deal with difficult horses and have knowledge of all curative expertise. No horse of mine is ever agitated at all, much less are my mares vicious. People called me Gránthika—Yudhi·shthira, son of Pandu, included.

VIRÁTA said:

As of today, let all the horses and chariots I own be in your charge. Let my grooms and charioteers be subordinate

ye c' âpi ke cin mama vāji|yojakās
tvad|āśrayāḥ sārathayaś ca santu me.
12.10 idaṃ tav' êṣṭaṃ yadi vai, sur'|ôpama,
bravīhi yat te prasamīkṣitaṃ vasu.
na te 'nurūpaṃ haya|karma vidyate,
prabhāsi rāj" êva hi, saṃmato mama.
Yudhiṣṭhirasy' êva hi darśanena me
samaṃ tav' êdaṃ priyam atra darśanam.
kathaṃ tu bhṛtyaiḥ sa vinā|kṛto vane
vasaty a|nindyo, ramate ca Pāṇḍavaḥ?

VAIŚAMPĀYANA uvāca:

tathā sa gandharva|var'|ôpamo yuvā
Virāṭa|rājñā muditena pūjitaḥ.
na c' âinam anye 'pi viduḥ kathañ cana
priy'|âbhirāmaṃ vicarantam antarā.
evaṃ hi Matsye nyavasanta Pāṇḍavā
yath" â|pratijñābhir a|mogha|darśanāḥ.
a|jñāta|caryāṃ vyacaran samāhitāḥ
samudra|nemī|patayo 'tiduḥkhitāḥ.

JANAMEJAYA uvāca:

13.1 EVAṂ TE MATSYA|nagare pracchannāḥ kuru|nandanāḥ,
ata ūrdhvaṃ mahā|vīryāḥ kim akurvata vai, dvija?

VAIŚAMPĀYANA uvāca:

evaṃ Matsyasya nagare pracchannāḥ Kuru|nandanāḥ
ārādhayanto rājānaṃ yad akurvanta, tac chṛṇu.

to you, and if this is indeed what you want, godlike man, 12.10
then tell me what you regard good pay.

But this occupation with horses does not seem to befit you, since you shine like a king and I hold you in high regard. The sight of you here is as pleasing to me as if it were the sight of Yudhi·shthira himself. How does that virtuous son of Pandu live and amuse himself in the forest, deprived of his servants?

VAISHAMPÁYANA said:

So that youth, comparable to the best of the *gandhárvas*, was honored by delighted King Viráta. No one else recognized him in the meantime, as he behaved charmingly and pleasingly.

Thus the Pándavas, the sight of whom was not fruitless, dwelled in Matsya in accordance with their promises. Those lords of the earth encompassed by the sea carried out their duties unrecognized as promised, although they were extremely unhappy.

JANAM·ÉJAYA said:

WHAT DID THE highly heroic descendants of Kuru do 13.1
from that time onward while hiding in Viráta's city, twice-born brahmin?

VAISHAMPÁYANA said:

Hear what the descendants of Kuru did while hidden in Viráta's city striving to obtain the favor of the king.

Tṛṇabindu|prasādāc ca, Dharmasya ca mah"|ātmanaḥ
a|jñāta|vāsam evaṃ tu Virāṭa|nagare 'vasan.
Yudhiṣṭhiraḥ sabhā|stāro Matsyānām abhavat priyaḥ,
tath" âiva ca Virāṭasya sa|putrasya, viśām pate.
13.5 sa hy akṣa|hṛdaya|jñas tān krīḍayām āsa Pāṇḍavaḥ
akṣavatyāṃ yathā|kāmaṃ sūtra|baddhān iva dvijān.
a|jñātaṃ ca Virāṭasya, vijitya vasu dharma|rāṭ
bhrātṛbhyaḥ puruṣa|vyāghro yath"|ârhaṃ samprayacchati.
Bhimaseno 'pi māṃsāni, bhakṣyāṇi vividhāni ca
atisṛṣṭāni Matsyena vikrīṇīte Yudhiṣṭhire.
vāsāṃsi parijīrṇāni labdhāny antaḥ|pure 'rjunaḥ
vikrīṇānaś ca sarvebhyaḥ Pāṇḍavebhyaḥ prayacchati.
Sahadevo 'pi gopānāṃ veṣam āsthāya Pāṇḍavaḥ
dadhi, kṣīraṃ, ghṛtaṃ c' âiva Pāṇḍavebhyaḥ prayacchati.
13.10 Nakulo 'pi dhanaṃ labdhvā kṛte karmaṇi vājinām
tuṣṭe tasmin nara|patau Pāṇḍavebhyaḥ prayacchati.
Kṛṣṇā tu sarvān bhartṝṃs tān nirīkṣantī tapasvinī,
yathā punar a|vijñātā, tathā carati bhāminī.
evaṃ sampādayantas te tad" ânyonyaṃ mahā|rathāḥ
Virāṭa|nagare ceruḥ punar garbha|dhṛtā iva.
s'|āśaṅkā Dhārtarāṣṭrasya bhayāt Pāṇḍu|sutās tadā
prekṣamāṇās tadā Kṛṣṇām ūṣuś channā, nar'|âdhipa.
atha māse caturthe tu Brahmaṇaḥ su|mah"|ôtsavaḥ
āsīt samṛddho Matsyeṣu, puruṣāṇāṃ su|saṃmataḥ.
13.15 tatra mallāḥ samāpetur digbhyo, rājan, sahasraśaḥ,
samāje Brahmaṇo, rājan, yathā Paśu|pater iva.
mahā|kāyā, mahā|vīryāḥ, Kālakhañjā iv' âsurāḥ,
vīry'|ônmattā, bal'|ôdagrā, rājñā samabhipūjitāḥ.

Through the favor of Trina·bindu and high-souled Dharma, they lived in Viráta's city unrecognized. Yudhi·shthira the courtier became dear to the Matsyas and equally so to
Viráta and his son, lord of earth. The son of Pandu, perfectly 13.5
skilled at gambling, made them play dice games just as he wished, like birds bound on a string. But, unknown to Viráta, when the king of righteousness won, the tiger-like man gave his brothers as much as they were entitled to.

Bhima·sena sold meat and various foods that were distributed by the King of Matsya to Yudhi·shthira. Árjuna gave the traded, worn-out clothes that he obtained in the inner apartments to all the Pándavas. Saha·deva, the son of Pandu, who had adopted the guise of a cowherd, gave
yogurt, milk and clarified butter to the Pándavas. Nákula 13.10
gave the Pándavas the money he earned for his work with horses from the satisfied king. Austere Krishná looked to all her husbands, though the passionate lady behaved in such a way that she remained unrecognized. So these great warriors helped each other to prosper and lived in Viráta's city as if they were once again being carried in the womb. Even though the sons of Pandu were apprehensive from fear of Dhrita·rashtra's son, those lords of men lived concealed and watched over Krishná.

Then, in the fourth month, the magnificent festival of Brahma took place, held in particular esteem by the people
in Matsya. Wrestlers came to the kingdom by the thousand 13.15
from every direction, my king, like the celestials gathering to the dwelling of Brahma or Shiva, the lord of animals, my king. Huge in stature, with enormous courage like the demon Kala·khanjas, they had high opinions of their prowess

siṃha|skandha|kaṭi|grīvāḥ, sv|avadātā, manasvinaḥ,
a|sakṛl|labdha|lakṣās te raṅge pārthiva|sannidhau.

teṣām eko mahān āsīt, sarva|mallān ath' āhvayat.
āvalgamānaṃ taṃ raṅge n' ôpatiṣṭhati kaś cana.
yadā sarve vi|manasas te mallā hata|cetasaḥ,
atha sūdena taṃ mallaṃ yodhayām āsa Matsya|rāṭ.
13.20 nodyamānas tadā Bhīmo duḥkhen' âiv' âkaron matim,
na hi śaknoti vivṛte pratyākhyātuṃ nar'|âdhipam.
tataḥ sa puruṣa|vyāghraḥ śārdūla|śithilaś caran
praviveśa mahā|raṅge Virāṭam abhipūjayan.
babandha kakṣāṃ Kaunteyas tataḥ saṃharṣayan janam.
tatas tu Vṛtra|saṅkāśaṃ Bhīmo mallaṃ samāhvayat,
Jīmūtaṃ nāma taṃ tatra mallaṃ prakhyāta|vikramam.

tāv ubhau su|mah"|ôtsāhāv, ubhau bhīma|parākramāu,
mattāv iva mahā|kāyau vāraṇau ṣaṣṭi|hāyanau.
tatas tau nara|śārdūlau bāhu|yuddhaṃ samīyatuḥ
13.25 vīrau parama|saṃhṛṣṭāv, anyonya|jaya|kāṅkṣiṇau.
āsīt su|bhīmaḥ saṃpāto vajra|parvatayor iva.
ubhau parama|saṃhṛṣṭau balen', âti|balāv ubhau.
anyonyasy' ântaraṃ prepsū, paraspara|jay'|âiṣiṇau.

ubhau parama|saṃhṛṣṭau, mattāv iva mahā|gajau,
kṛta|pratikṛtaiś citrair, bāhubhiṣ ca su|saṅkaṭaiḥ,
sannipāt'|âvadhūtaiś ca, pramāth'|ônmathanais tathā,
kṣepaṇair, muṣṭibhiś c' âiva, varāh'|ôddhūta|niḥsvanaiḥ,
talair vajra|nipātaiś ca, prasṛṣṭābhis tath" âiva ca

and pride in their strength, and they were highly honored by the king. They had lion-like shoulders, hips and necks, and were spotless. They were in high spirits, for they had won prizes in the arena many times in the presence of kings.

One of them was enormous and challenged all the wrestlers, but no one would stand against him as he leaped around in the arena. When all the wrestlers were dishonored and depressed, the king of the Matsyas forced the wrestler to fight his cook. But Bhima made up his mind unhappily 13.20
when pushed forward, since he was not able to openly refuse the king. Tiger-like Kauntéya paid his respects to Viráta, entered the massive arena, moving like a relaxed tiger and girded his loins, delighting the crowd. Then Bhima challenged the Vritra-like wrestler called Jimúta, whose strength was notorious.

Both of them had enormous power, both had dread courage, like rutting sixty-year-old massive-bodied elephants. So that pair of tiger-like men took each other on in a wrestling match, incredibly cheerful heroes, each eager to 13.25
defeat the other. Their collision was terrible in the extreme, like a thunderbolt against a mountain. Both were supremely strong and clearly delighted with the other's strength. Eager to defeat each other, they tried to find their partner's weakness.

Both were enjoying themselves greatly, like massive, rutting elephants, with excellently varied difficult attacks and counterattacks, and they collided and shook each other off, harassed each other and threw each other down. They let fly at each other with clenched fists and roared when thrown

śalākā|nakha|pātaiś ca, pād'|ôddhūtaiś ca dāruṇaiḥ,
jānubhiś c' âśma|nirghoṣaiḥ, śirobhiś c' âvaghaṭṭanaiḥ.

13.30 tad yuddham abhavad ghoram a|śastraṃ bāhu|tejasā,
bala|prāṇena śūrāṇāṃ samāj'|ôtsava|sannidhau.
arajyata janaḥ sarvaḥ s'|ôtkruṣṭa|ninad'|ôtthitaḥ
balinoḥ saṃyuge, rājan, Vṛtra|Vāsavayor iva.
prakarṣaṇ'|ākarṣaṇayor, abhyākarṣa|vikarṣaṇaiḥ
ākarṣatur ath' ânyonyaṃ, jānubhiś c' âpi jaghnatuḥ.
tataḥ śabdena mahatā bhartsayantau parasparam
vyūḍh'|ôraskau, dīrgha|bhujau, niyuddha|kuśalāv ubhau,
bāhubhiḥ samasajjetām āyasaiḥ parighair iva.

cakarṣa dorbhyām utpātya Bhīmo mallam amitra|hā
ninadantam abhikrośañ śārdūla iva vāraṇam,
13.35 samudyamya mahā|bāhur bhrāmayām āsa vīryavān.
tato mallāś ca Matsyāś ca vismayaṃ cakrire param.
bhrāmayitvā śata|guṇaṃ gata|sattvam a|cetanam
pratyapiṃṣan mahā|bāhur mallaṃ bhuvi Vṛkodaraḥ.

up like boars. They let fly at each other with slaps like thunderbolts with the palms of their hands, and attacked each other with their fingernails, pointed like sticks, and with pitiless stamping of the feet. The contact of their knees and heads was like the clash of stones.

So the terrible fight between those champions was fought 13.30
without weapons but through the power of their arms, and their strength of spirit; a source of jubilation for the spectators gathered in the vicinity. Cheers and cries sprang up as everyone was engrossed in the conflict of those two powerful men like Vritra and Vásava, o king. The wrestlers drew away and toward each other again, struck their breasts with the palms of their hands in defiance and dragged each other down. Then, drawing toward one another, they even struck out with their knees. Each threatened the other in a booming voice. Broad-chested, long-armed and both skilled in fighting, those two wrestled together with arms like iron clubs.

Then Bhima, the slaughterer of his enemies, sprang up shouting and took hold of the screaming wrestler by the
arms, just as a tiger seizes a wild elephant, and the heroic 13.35
and long-armed man lifted him up and sent him spinning, causing exceptional astonishment among the athletes and the Matsyan people. When he had spun him around a hundred times till he was unconscious and senseless, long-armed Vrikódara crushed the wrestler on the ground.

tasmin vinihate vīre Jīmūte loka|viśrute
Virāṭaḥ paramaṃ harṣam agacchad bāndhavaiḥ saha.
praharṣāt pradadau vittaṃ bahu rājā mahā|manāḥ
Ballavāya mahā|raṅge, yathā Vaiśravaṇas tathā.
evaṃ sa su|bahūn mallān, puruṣāṃś ca mahā|balān
vinighnan Matsya|rājasya prītim āharad uttamām.
13.40 yad" âsya tulyaḥ puruṣo na kaś cit tatra vidyate,
tato vyāghraiś ca, siṃhaiś ca, dvi|radaiś c' âpy ayodhayat.
punar antaḥpura|gataḥ strīṇāṃ madhye Vṛkodaraḥ
yodhyate sma Virāṭena siṃhair mattair mahā|balaiḥ.

Bībhatsur api gītena sva|nṛtyena ca Pāṇḍavaḥ
Virāṭaṃ toṣayām āsa, sarvāś c' ântaḥpura|striyaḥ.
aśvair vinītair javanais tatra tatra samāgataiḥ
toṣayām āsa rājānaṃ Nakulo nṛpa|sattamam.
tasmai pradeyaṃ prāyacchat prīto rājā dhanaṃ bahu.
vinītān vṛṣabhān dṛṣṭvā Sahadevasya c' âbhitaḥ
dhanaṃ dadau bahu|vidhaṃ Virāṭaḥ puruṣa'|rṣabhaḥ.
13.45 Draupadī prekṣya tān sarvān kliśyamānān mahā|rathān
n' âtiprīta|manā, rājan, niḥśvāsa|param" âbhavat.
evaṃ te nyavasaṃs tatra pracchannāḥ puruṣa'|rṣabhāḥ
karmāṇi tasya kurvāṇā Virāṭa|nṛpates tadā.

And when brave, world-famous Jimúta was killed, Viráta and his relatives were extremely pleased. In his delight, the high-minded king granted great wealth to Bállava there in the vast arena, just like Kubéra, lord of wealth. So, killing a great many wrestlers and men of enormous strength, he brought exceptional joy to the king of the Matsyas. When 13.40
no comparable match could be found, then he fought with tigers, lions and double-tusked elephants. And Viráta made Vrikódara fight again, this time with mighty and exultant lions in the middle of the women's apartments.

Bibhátsu, the son of Pandu, also delighted Viráta and all the women within their apartments with his singing and his dancing. Nákula, too, satisfied the most venerable sovereign king with the well-trained, swift horses that gathered wherever he was. The king was pleased and so granted him great wealth. When he saw the well-trained bulls around Saha·deva, Viráta, himself a bull among men, gave him riches of great variety. But Dráupadi, watching all those great war- 13.45
riors suffering, was not best pleased in her mind, my king, and she sighed excessively. So it was that those bull-like men lived there in disguise, working for King Viráta.

14–24
KÍCHAKA'S LUST AND DEATH

VAIŚAMPĀYANA uvāca:

14.1 Vasamāneṣu Pārtheṣu Matsyasya nagare tadā
mahā|ratheṣu cchanneṣu māsā daśa samatyayuḥ.
Yājñasenī Sudeṣṇāṃ tu śuśrūṣantī, viśām pate,
avasat paricār'|ârhā su|duḥkhaṃ, Janamejaya.
tathā carantī Pāñcālī Sudeṣṇāyā niveśane
tāṃ devīṃ toṣayām āsa, tathā c' ântaḥpura|striyaḥ.
tasmin varṣe gata|prāye Kīcakas tu mahā|balaḥ
senā|patir Virāṭasya dadarśa Drupad'|ātmajām.
14.5 tāṃ dṛṣṭvā deva|garbh'|ābhāṃ carantīṃ devatām iva,
Kīcakaḥ kāmayām āsa Kāma|bāṇa|prapīḍitaḥ.
sa tu Kām'|âgni|saṃtaptaḥ Sudeṣṇām abhigamya vai,
prahasann iva senā|nīr idaṃ vacanam abravīt:
«n' êyaṃ mayā jātu pur" êha dṛṣṭā
rājño Virāṭasya niveṣane śubhā.
rūpeṇa c' ônmādayat' îva māṃ bhṛśaṃ
gandhena jātā madir" êva bhāminī.
kā deva|rūpā hṛdayaṅ|gamā, śubhe?
hy ācakṣva me kasya kuto 'tra, śobhane.
cittaṃ hi nirmathya karoti māṃ vaśe.
na c' ânyad atr' āuṣadham asti me matam!
aho tav' êyaṃ paricārikā śubhā
praty|agra|rūpā pratibhāti mām iyam
a|yukta|rūpaṃ hi karoti karma te.
praśāstu māṃ yac ca mam' âsti kiñ cana!
14.10 prabhūta|nāg'|âśva|rathaṃ, mahā|janaṃ,
samṛddhi|yuktaṃ, bahu|pāna|bhojanam,
mano|haraṃ, kāñcana|citra|bhūṣaṇaṃ
gṛhaṃ mahac chobhayatām iyaṃ mama!»

VAISHAMPÁYANA said:

THOSE MIGHTY warriors, the disguised Parthas, lived in the city of Matsya, and ten months passed. But the daughter of Yajña·sena, lord of the earth, attended Sudéshna, although she deserved a servant herself, and spent her time very miserably, Janam·éjaya. So it was that the Pancháli princess lived in Sudéshna's apartment, satisfying that lady and the women of the inner quarters. 14.1

Then, when the year had almost passed, mighty Kíchaka, the general of Viráta's army, saw the daughter of Drúpada. When he gazed at that woman who resembled a child of 14.5 the celestials, moving like a goddess, Kíchaka fell in love, tortured by Kama's arrow. So, scorched by Kama's fire, the general of the army came up to Sudéshna, and said these words with a hint of a smirk:

"Never before have I seen this beautiful woman in King Viráta's palace. The lady drives me violently mad with her beauty, just as new wine intoxicates with its fragrance. Who is this divinely gorgeous woman, who touches the heart, lovely lady? Tell me whose she is and where she comes from, splendid lady. She grinds my heart and makes me her slave. I believe there is no other medicine than her! Oh, this exquisite servant girl of yours seems young to me, and the work she does for you is unsuitable. Let her rule over me and whatever belongs to me! Let her illuminate my 14.10 charming home adorned with various golden ornaments, furnished with plenty of food and drink, endowed with prosperity and full of many people, as well as numerous chariots, horses and elephants!"

tataḥ Sudeṣṇām anumantrya Kīcakas
tataḥ samabhyetya nar'|âdhip'|ātmajām
uvāca Kṛṣṇām abhisāntvayaṃs tadā
mṛg'|êndra|kanyām iva jambuko vane:
«kā tvaṃ, kasy' âsi, kalyāṇi? kuto vā tvaṃ, var'|ānane,
prāptā Virāṭa|nagaraṃ? tattvam ācakṣva, śobhane.
rūpam agryaṃ, tathā kāntiḥ, saukumāryam an|uttamam,
kāntyā vibhāti vaktraṃ te, śaś'|âṅka iva nirmalam.
netre su|vipule, su|bhru, padma|patra|nibhe śubhe,
vākyaṃ te, cāru|sarv'|âṅgi, para|puṣṭa|rut'|ôpamam.
14.15 evaṃ|rūpā mayā nārī kā cid anyā mahī|tale
na dṛṣṭa|pūrvā, su|śroṇi, yādṛśī tvam, a|nindite.
Lakṣmīḥ padm'|ālayā kā tvam,
atha Bhūtiḥ, su|madhyame?
Hrīḥ, Śrīḥ, Kīrtir, atho Kāntir—
āsāṃ kā tvaṃ, var'|ānane?
at'|îva rūpiṇī kiṃ tvam Anaṅg'|âṅga|vihāriṇī?
atīva bhrājase, su|bhru, prabh" êv' êndor an|uttamā.
api c' êkṣaṇa|pakṣmāṇāṃ smita|jyotsn"|ôpamaṃ śubham,
divy'|âṃśu|raśmibhir vṛttaṃ divya|kānti|manoramam
nirīkṣya vaktra|candraṃ te lakṣmy" ânupamayā yutam,
kṛtsne jagati ko n' êha kāmasya vaśa|go bhavet?
14.20 hār'|âlaṅkāra|yogyau tu stanau c' ôbhau su|śobhanau,
su|jātau, sahitau lakṣmyā, pīnau, vṛttau, nirantarau,
kuḍmal'|âmburuh'|ākārau tava, su|bhru, payo|dharau,
kāma|pratodāv iva māṃ tudataś, cāru|hāsini.
valī|vibhaṅga|caturaṃ, stana|bhāra|vināmitam,

Then, once he had consulted with Sudéshna, Kíchaka went up to Princess Krishná and spoke these ingratiating words, like a jackal in the forest to a lioness, daughter of the king of beasts: "Who are you, and whom do you belong to, beautiful lady? Where have you come from to Viráta's city, my pretty-faced girl? Tell me truthfully, gorgeous lady.

Your beauty, loveliness and delicacy are exceptional, and your face shines with its allure like the dazzling moon. Fair-browed girl, you have large, beautiful eyes like lotus petals, and your speech is like the cry of the cuckoo, entirely beautiful-limbed lady. Never before have I seen any 14.15
other woman in this world as beautiful as you, irreproachable, shapely-hipped girl.

Are you Lakshmi who dwells in lotuses, also called Bhuti, slender-waisted lady? Or are you Hri, Shri, Kirti or Kanti, my lovely-faced girl? Or are you she who delights in the limbs of Kama, in astoundingly beautiful corporeal form? You shine so very brightly, lovely-browed lady, like the dazzling splendor of the moon. Who in the whole world would not become a slave to desire when they see your moon-like countenance, possessed of matchless charm, divinely bewitching and graceful, round with beams of celestial splendor, with its smile luminous like moonlight and even the aspect of your eyelashes?

Your breasts are both gorgeous and deserve pearl neck- 14.20
lace ornaments. They are excellently formed, graceful, full and round and sit tightly together. With the appearance of budding day lotuses, lovely-browed and sweet-smiling lady, your breasts are the goads of the fulfillment of desire driving me on. Now that I have seen your charming waist,

kar'|âgra|saṃmitaṃ madhyaṃ tav' êdaṃ, tanu|madhyame,
dṛṣṭv" âiva cāru jaghanaṃ sarit|pulina|saṃnibham,
kāma|vyādhir a|sādhyo mām apy ākrāmati, bhāmini.
jajvāla c' âgni|madano, dāv'|âgnir iva nirdayaḥ,
tvat|saṅgam'|âbhisaṅkalpa|vivṛddho māṃ dahaty ayam.
14.25 ātma|pradāna|varṣeṇa saṃgam'|âmbho|dhareṇa ca
śamayasva, var'|ārohe, jvalantaṃ manmath'|ânalam.
mac|citt'|ônmādana|karā manmathasya śar'|ôtkarāḥ
tvat|saṃgam'|āśā|niśitās tīvrāḥ, śaśi|nibh'|ānane,
mahyaṃ vidārya hṛdayam idaṃ nirdaya|vegitāḥ.
praviṣṭā hy, a|sit'|âpāṅgi, pracaṇḍāś, caṇḍa|dāruṇāḥ,
atyunmāda|samārambhāḥ prīty|unmāda|karā mama,
ātma|pradāna|sambhogair mām uddhartum ih' ârhasi.
citra|māly'|âmbara|dharā, sarv'|ābharaṇa|bhūṣitā,
kāmaṃ prakāmaṃ seva tvaṃ mayā saha, vilāsini.
n' ârhas' îh' â|sukhaṃ vastuṃ
sukh'|ârhā, sukha|varjitā.
prāpnuhy an|uttamaṃ saukhyaṃ
mattas tvaṃ, matta|gamini.
14.30 svādūny amṛta|kalpāni peyāni vividhāni ca
pibamānā mano|jñāni, ramamāṇā yathā sukham,
bhog'|ôpacārān vividhān, saubhāgyaṃ c' âpy an|uttamam,
pānaṃ piba, mahā|bhāge, bhogaiś c' ân|uttamaiḥ śubaiḥ.
idaṃ hi rūpaṃ prathamaṃ tav', ân|aghe,
nirarthakaṃ kevalam adya, bhāmini;
a|dhāryamāṇā srag iv' ôttamā śubhā;
na śobhase, sundari, śobhanā satī.

measuring only the width of a fingertip and slightly caved in due to the weight of your breasts, slender-waisted lady, and now that I have seen your pretty hips, like riverbanks, the incurable disease of desire seizes me, my spirited girl.

The fire of love blazes like a pitiless forest fire, and, fueled
by my hope of being with you, it scorches me. Extinguish 14.25
the burning fire of love, shapely-hipped lady, with your rain by giving yourself to me, with the cloud of our coming together. The love god's multitude of arrows are swift, intense and sharpened by my hope of union with you, my lunar-countenanced lady, and they have split my heart and torn my core.

O black-eyed girl, these violent, fierce and passionate arrows have pierced me, acting too wildly, creating mad desire, so you ought to strengthen me with the joys of embrace and by giving yourself to me. Decked in brightly colored garments and garlands, embellished with every ornament, enjoy love with me willingly, radiant girl.

You should not live here in misery, deprived of the happiness that you deserve, but may you rather obtain matchless joy from me, elephant-gaited girl. Drinking various 14.30
sweet and tasty nectar liquors, enjoying yourself as you wish, charming girl, and engaging in various pleasures and matchless prosperity, drink your wine with unrivaled joyful luxuries, you lucky lady. Your exquisite beauty, faultless, passionate lady, is indeed completely useless at the moment. It is like an exquisitely beautiful garland that is unworn. My gorgeous girl, you do not shine though you are indeed dazzling.

tyajāmi dārān mama ye purātanā!
bhavantu dāsyas tava, cāru|hāsini.
ahaṃ ca te, sundari, dāsavat sthitaḥ
sadā bhaviṣye vaśa|go, var'|ānane.»

DRAUPADY uvāca:

a|prārthanīyām iha māṃ, sūta|putr', âbhimanyase
nihīna|varṇāṃ sairandhrīṃ, bībhatsāṃ keśa|kāriṇīm.
14.35 para|dār" âsmi, bhadraṃ te, na yuktaṃ tava sāmpratam.
dayitāḥ prāṇināṃ dārā, dharmaṃ samanucintaya.
para|dāre na te buddhir jātu kāryā katham cana.
vivarjanaṃ hy a|kāryāṇām, etat su|puruṣa|vratam.
mithy"|âbhigṛdhno hi naraḥ pāp'|ātmā, moham āsthitaḥ
a|yaśaḥ prāpnuyād ghoraṃ, mahad vā prāpnuyād bhayam.

VAIŚAMPĀYANA said:

evam uktas tu sairandhryā Kīcakaḥ kāma|mohitaḥ,
jānann api su|durbuddhiḥ para|dār'|âbhimarśane,
doṣān bahūn prāṇa|harān, sarva|loka|vigarhitān,
provāc' êdaṃ su|durbuddhir Draupadīm a|jit'|êndriyaḥ:
14.40 «n' ârhasy evaṃ, var'|ārohe, pratyākhyātum, var'|ānane,
māṃ manmatha|samāviṣṭaṃ tvat|kṛte, cāru|hāsini.
pratyākhyāya ca māṃ, bhīru, vaśa|gaṃ priya|vādinam
nūnaṃ tvam, asit'|âpāṅgi, paścāt|tāpaṃ kariṣyasi.
ahaṃ hi, su|bhru, rājyasya kṛtsnasy' âsya, su|madhyame,
prabhur, vāsayitā c' âiva, vīrye c' â|pratimaḥ kṣitau.

I will abandon my previous wives! Let them become your slaves, sweet-smiling girl. I, too, stand before you as a slave and I will always be obedient, bewitching, lovely-faced lady."

DRÁUPADI said:

Son of a *suta*,* you long for me, but I should not be desired, for I am a low-caste servant, a loathsome hairdresser.
Besides, I am the wife of others, so good luck to you but 14.35
your advances are neither suitable nor proper. Remember the law that wives should be pitied while living. Your mind should certainly never be set on adultery at all. The good man's vow is to avoid forbidden acts. A wicked-hearted man who is unjustly covetous and undertakes folly obtains either a terrible reputation or great danger.

VAISHAMPÁYANA said:

Thus addressed by the *sairándhri*, Kíchaka, deluded by lust and incredibly foolish, although aware of the many sins involved in touching another man's wife, sins forbidden by the whole world and even destructive to life, the incredibly wicked-minded man full of uncontrolled passions, replied to Dráupadi:

"Shapely-hipped lady, you ought not to reject me, since 14.40
I am filled with desire for you, most beautiful-faced, sweet-smiling girl. By rejecting me when I am in your power and speaking kindly to you, you will surely regret it later, timid, black-eyed girl. For it is in fact I who am the mighty ruler of this whole kingdom. The people who live here rely on me, and I am incomparable in power on this earth, lovely-browed and slender-waisted girl.

pṛthivyāṃ mat|samo n' âsti kaś cid anyaḥ pumān iha
rūpa|yauvana|saubhāgyair bhogaiś c' ânuttamaiḥ śubhaiḥ.
sarva|kāma|samṛddheṣu bhogeṣv an|upameṣv iha,
bhoktavyeṣu ca, kalyāṇi, kasmād dāsye ratā hy asi?
14.45 mayā dattam idaṃ rājyaṃ, svāminy asi, śubh'|ānane.
bhajasva māṃ, var'|ārohe, bhuṅkṣva bhogān an|uttamān.»
evam uktā tu sā sādhvī Kīcaken' â|śubhaṃ vacaḥ
Kīcakaṃ pratyuvāc' êdaṃ garhayanty asya tad vacaḥ:

SAIRANDHRY uvāca:

mā, sūta|putra, muhyasva, m" âdya tyakṣyasva jīvitam!
jānīhi pañcabhir ghorair nityaṃ māṃ abhirakṣitām.
na c' âpy ahaṃ tvayā labhyā, gandharvāḥ patayo mama.
te tvāṃ nihanyuḥ kupitāḥ sādhv, alaṃ, mā vyanīnaśaḥ!
a|śakya|rūpaṃ puruṣair adhvānaṃ gantum icchasi.
yathā niś|cetano bālaḥ kūla|sthaḥ kūlam uttaram
tartum icchati, mand'|ātmā, tathā tvaṃ kartum icchasi.
14.50 antar mahīṃ vā yadi v" ōrdhvam utpateḥ,
samudra|pāraṃ yadi vā pradhāvasi,
tath" âpi teṣāṃ na vimokṣam arhasi;
pramāthino deva|sutā hi khe|carāḥ.
tvaṃ kāla|rātrīm iva kaś cid āturaḥ
kiṃ māṃ dṛḍhaṃ prārthayase 'dya, Kicaka?
kiṃ mātur aṅke śayito yathā śiśuś
candraṃ jighṛkṣur iva manyase hi mām?
teṣāṃ priyāṃ prārthayato na te bhuvi

There is no other man on earth who is my equal in appearance, youth, prosperity or even in matchlessly delightful pleasures. Why, then, instead of all excellent indulgences and the best amusements to be enjoyed do you take delight in slavery, lovely lady? You are mistress of this kingdom 14.45
which I give you, beautiful-faced girl. Choose me, shapely-hipped lady, and enjoy the greatest luxuries."

Thus addressed by Kíchaka in these menacing words, the pure girl replied to Kíchaka, reproaching him with this speech:

THE SAIRANDHRI said:

Son of a *suta*, do not be foolish and do not abandon your life! Know that I am always protected by my five frightening husbands, so you can't have me or my *gandhárva* husbands will become incensed and destroy you! Do not meet with your own end! You want to go down an impossible road for men. You are like an unthinking child standing on the shore, wishing to cross to the further side, foolish-souled man—this is how you wish to behave.

If you should fly inside the earth or into the sky or if 14.50
you rush to the other side of the sea, even then you will not deserve release from those flying *gandhárva* destroyers, the sons of the gods. Why do you proposition me today so perseveringly, Kíchaka, like a sick man longs for the night that is his last? Why do you set your heart on me as though you were a child sleeping on his mother's lap wishing to seize the moon? There will be no refuge for the man who propositions their dear wife, regardless of whether he has gone to the earth or sky. Kíchaka, will you not turn your

gatvā divaṃ vā śaraṇaṃ bhaviṣyati.
na vartate, Kicaka, te dṛśā śubhaṃ
yā tena saṃjīvanam arthayeta, sā?

VAIŚAṂPĀYANA uvāca:

15.1 PRATYĀKHYĀTO rāja|putryā Sudeṣṇāṃ Kīcako 'bravīt
a|maryādena kāmena ghoreṇ' âbhipariplutaḥ,
«yathā, Kaikeyi, sairandhrī sameyāt, tad vidhīyatām.
yen' ôpāyena sairandhrī bhajen māṃ gaja|gāminī,
taṃ, Sudeṣṇe, parīpsasva, prāṇān mohāt prahāsiṣam.»
tasya sā bahuśaḥ śrutvā vācaṃ vilapatas tadā
Virāṭa|mahiṣī devī kṛpāṃ cakre manasvinī.
sva|mantram abhisandhāya, tasy' ârtham anucintya ca,
udyogaṃ c' âiva Kṛṣṇāyāḥ, Sudeṣṇā sūtam abravīt:
15.5 «parvaṇi tvaṃ samuddiśya surām annaṃ ca kāraya,
tatr' âināṃ preṣayiṣyāmi sur"|āhārīṃ tav' ântikam.
tatra saṃpreṣitām enām vijane niravagrahe,
sāntvayethā yathā kāmaṃ, sāntvyamānā ramed yadi.»
ity uktaḥ sa viniṣkramya bhaginyā vacanāt tadā
surām āhārayām āsa rāj'|ârhāṃ, su|pariṣkṛtām,
bhakṣāṃś ca vividh'|ākārān, bahūṃś c', ôccāvacāṃs tadā
kārayām āsa kuśalair annaṃ, pānaṃ su|śobhanam.
tasmin kṛte tadā devī Kīcaken' ôpamantritā
Sudeṣṇā preṣayām āsa sairandhrīṃ Kīcak'|ālayam.

SUDEṢṆ" ôvāca:

15.10 uttiṣṭha, gaccha, sairandhri, Kīcakasya niveśanam.
pānam ānaya, kalyāṇi, pipāsā māṃ prabādhate.

sights upon what is good for you, so that you may save your life?

VAISHAMPÁYANA said:

REJECTED BY THE princess, Kíchaka was afflicted by terrible desire that transgressed all normal bounds, and he said to Sudéshna: "Kaikéyi, let it be arranged for the *sairándhri* to come to me. Sudéshna, preserve my life, so keen to slip away because of this distraction, by whichever means the elephant-gaited girl will love me." 15.1

Having repeatedly listened to his moaning, Viráta's powerful and intelligent queen felt compassion for Kíchaka. Reconciling her own deliberations with what she considered his motive to be and Krishná's effort, Sudéshna spoke
to the *suta*'s son: "At festival time have some food and wine 15.5
brought to you, and I will arrange for this woman to enter your presence to bring the wine, and there in the freedom of solitude you should coax her as you please, so that when cajoled she may enjoy herself."

Thus addressed, he left his sister's apartments. He procured well-prepared wine, fit for a king, and he had splendid food, drink and numerous different and variously made dishes cooked by experts. When this was done, Queen Sudéshna, as advised by Kíchaka, sent her *sairándhri* to Kíchaka's dwelling.

SUDÉSHNA said:

Get up, *sairándhri*, and go to Kíchaka's apartment to 15.10
fetch wine, beautiful lady, since thirst is tormenting me.

SAIRANDHRY uvāca:

na gaccheyam ahaṃ tasya, rāja|putri, niveśanam.
tvam eva, rājñi, jānāsi yathā sa nirapatrapaḥ.
na c' âham, an|avady'|âṅgi, tava veśmani, bhāmini,
kāma|vṛttā bhaviṣyāmi patīnāṃ vyabhicāriṇī.
tvaṃ c' âiva, devi, jānāsi yathā sa samayaḥ kṛtaḥ
praviśantyā mayā pūrvaṃ tava veśmani, bhāmini.
Kīcakas tu, su|keś'|ânte, mūḍho, madan|darpitaḥ.
so 'vamaṃsyati māṃ dṛṣṭvā. na yāsye tatra, śobhane.
15.15 santi bahvyas tava preṣyā, rāja|putri, vaś'|ânugāḥ.
anyāṃ preṣaya, bhadraṃ te, sa hi mām avamaṃsyate!

SUDEṢṆ" ôvāca:

«n' âiva tvāṃ jātu hiṃsyāt sa itaḥ saṃpreṣitā mayā.»
ity uktvā pradadau pātraṃ sa|pidhānaṃ hiraṇ|mayam.
sā śaṅkamānā rudatī daivaṃ śaraṇam īyuṣī
prātiṣṭhata sur"|āhārī Kīcakasya niveśanam.

SAIRANDHRY uvāca:

yath" âham anyaṃ bhartṛbhyo n' âbhijānāmi kaṃ cana,
tena satyena māṃ prāptāṃ mā kuryāt Kīcako vaśe.

VAIŚAMPĀYANA uvāca:

upātiṣṭhata sā Sūryaṃ muhūrtam a|balā tataḥ.
sa tasyās tanu|madhyāyāḥ sarvaṃ Sūryo 'vabuddhavān
15.20 antar|hitaṃ tatas tasyā rakṣo rakṣ'|ârtham ādiśat,
tac c' âināṃ n' âjahāt tatra sarv'|âvasthāsv a|ninditām.
tāṃ mṛgīm iva santrastāṃ dṛṣṭvā Kṛṣṇāṃ samīpa|gām

THE SAIRÁNDHRI said:

I should not go to his apartment, princess. You yourself, my queen, know how impudent he is. I will not become a woman who lives wantonly, nor will I be faithless to my husbands in your home, beautiful lady of faultless limbs. You also know, queen, the agreement we made before I entered your house, beautiful lady.

Kíchaka is dazed and made arrogant by love, lady with beautiful curly-tipped hair, and will treat me contemptuously when he sees me, so I will not go there, lovely lady.
You have many servants obedient to your will, princess, so 15.15
send another, bless you, for he will abuse me!

SUDÉSHNA said:

"He would certainly never harm you, for you have been sent from this place by me." When she had said this she gave her a gold cup with a cover. So, afraid and crying, she prayed to the gods for protection and set out for Kíchaka's dwelling to fetch the wine.

THE SAIRÁNDHRI said:

By the very fact that I know no one but my husbands, don't let Kíchaka make me subject to his will when I reach him.

VAISHAMPÁYANA said:

The powerless lady worshipped Surya for a moment. Then Surya, perceiving everything the slender-waisted girl
said, directed a guard there for her invisible protection. It did 15.20
not leave but remained with that blameless lady throughout everything that followed. Then, observing Krishná trembling like a doe as she stood nearby, the *suta* stood up, as

udatiṣṭhan mudā Sūto, nāvaṃ labdhv" êva pāra|gaḥ.

KĪCAKA uvāca:

16.1 SVĀGATAṂ TE, su|keś'|ânte! su|vyuṣṭā rajanī mama.
svāminī tvam anuprāptā, prakuruṣva mama priyam.
suvarṇa|mālāḥ, kambūś ca, kuṇḍale parihāṭake
nānā|pattana|je śubhre, maṇi|ratnaṃ ca śobhanam,
āharantu ca vastrāṇi kauśikāny, ajināni ca.
asti me śayanaṃ divyaṃ tvad|artham upakalpitam.
ehi tatra mayā sārdhaṃ, pibasva madhu|mādhavīm.

DRAUPADY uvāca:

apraiṣid rāja|putrī māṃ sur"|āhārīṃ tav' ântikam.
pānam āhara me kṣipram, ‹pipāsā me 'ti› c' âbravīt.

KĪCAKA uvāca:

16.5 «anyā, bhadre, nayiṣyanti rāja|putryāḥ pratiśrutam.»
ity evaṃ dakṣiṇe pāṇau Sūta|putraḥ parāmṛśat.

DRAUPADY uvāca:

yath" âiv' âhaṃ n' âbhicare kadā cit
patīn madād vai manas" âpi jātu,
ten' âiva satyena vaśī|kṛtaṃ tvāṃ
draṣṭ" âsmi pāpaṃ parikṛṣyamāṇam.

VAIŚAṂPĀYANA uvāca:

sa tām abhiprekṣya viśāla|netrāṃ
jighṛkṣamāṇaḥ paribhartsayantīm,
jagrāha tām uttara|vastra|deśe
sa Kīcakas tāṃ sahas" ākṣipantīm.

happy as a man who has found a boat to get to the other shore.

KÍCHAKA said:

LADY WITH CHARMING curly-tipped locks, welcome! The night has dawned beautifully for me, for I have won you as the mistress of my home, so do me a favor. Let golden garlands, conch shells, beautiful golden earrings fashioned in varied cities, a splendid jewel, silk clothes and antelope skins be brought for you. My divine bed has also been made ready for you. Come there with me and drink the honey-flower wine. 16.1

DRÁUPADI said:

The princess sent me to you to fetch wine. She told me to bring it to her quickly for she is thirsty.

KÍCHAKA said:

"Others will bring the princess what was promised to her, my dear." Saying this, the son of the *suta* seized her by her right hand. 16.5

DRÁUPADI said:

I have never been unfaithful to my husbands, not even in my mind, and by that truth I will see you subdued and dragged around, wicked as you are.

VAISHAMPÁYANA said:

Seeing that large-eyed lady threatening him, Kíchaka wanted to grab her, so he seized her by the tip of her upper garment as she ran away at speed. But when seized, the slender princess, breathing hard, threw him off very quickly, and the wicked man fell down like a tree cut from its roots.

pragṛhyamāṇā tu mahā|javena
muhur viniḥśvasya ca rāja|putrī
tayā samākṣipta|tanuḥ sa pāpaḥ
papāta śākh" îva nikṛtta|mūlaḥ.
sā gṛhītā vidhunvānā bhūmāv ākṣipya Kīcakam,
sabhāṃ śaraṇam āgacchad yatra rājā Yudhiṣṭhiraḥ.
16.10 tām Kīcakaḥ pradhāvantīṃ keśa|pāśe parāmṛśat,
ath' âināṃ paśyato rājñaḥ pātayitvā pad" âvadhīt.
tasya yo 'sau tad" ârkeṇa rākṣasaḥ saṃniyojitaḥ,
sa Kīcakam apovāha vāta|vegena, Bhārata.
sa papāta tadā bhūmau rakṣo|bala|samāhataḥ,
vighūrṇamāno, niśceṣṭaś, chinna|mūla iva drumaḥ.
tāṃ c' āsīnau dadṛśatur Bhimasena|Yudhiṣṭhirau
a|mṛṣyamāṇau Kṛṣṇāyāḥ Kīcakena parābhavam.
tasya Bhīmo vadhaṃ prepsuḥ Kīcakasya dur|ātmanaḥ
dantair dantāṃś tadā roṣān niṣpipeṣa mahā|manāḥ.
16.15 dhūma|cchāyā hy abhajatāṃ netre c' ôcchrita|pakṣmaṇī,
sa|svedā bhṛkuṭī c' ôgrā lalāṭe samavartata.
hastena mamṛde c' âiva lalāṭaṃ para|vīra|hā,
bhūyaś ca tvaritaḥ kruddhaḥ sahas" ôtthātum aicchata.
ath' âvamṛdnād aṅguṣṭham aṅguṣṭhena Yudhiṣṭhiraḥ
prabodhana|bhayād rājā Bhīmaṃ taṃ pratyaṣedhayat.
taṃ mattam iva mātaṅgaṃ vīkṣamāṇaṃ vanas|patim
sa tam āvarayām āsa Bhīmasenaṃ Yudhiṣṭhiraḥ,
«ālokayasi kiṃ vṛkṣaṃ, sūda, dāru|kṛtena vai!
yadi te dārubhiḥ kṛtyaṃ, bahir vṛkṣān nigṛhyatām.»

She threw Kíchaka to the floor when he took hold of her and then, trembling, she went to the court for protection,
where King Yudhi·shthira was. But Kíchaka grabbed her by 16.10
the knot of her hair as she ran, tripped her up and kicked her with his foot while the king looked on. Then the *rák-shasa* that had been assigned to her by the sun god pushed Kíchaka with the force of the wind, Bhárata. Then he fell to the ground, struck down by the force of the *rákshasa*, unconscious and powerless like a tree whose roots have been cut.

Bhima·sena and Yudhi·shthira saw her as they sat there and were incensed by the injury done to Krishná by Kíchaka. Bhima longed for the destruction of the black-hearted Kíchaka. The high-spirited man gnashed his teeth in rage. His 16.15
eyes were diffused with smoky shadows, and his eyelashes stood on end. Sweat ran across his forehead and his brows were formidably furrowed. The destroyer of enemy heroes wiped his forehead with his hand, and, hastened still more by his anger, he longed to get up at once.

But then King Yudhi·shthira, from fear of being discovered, squeezed his thumbs and held Bhima back. So Yudhi·shthira caused Bhima·sena, who was like an elephant in rut sizing up a mighty tree, the lord of the forest, to hold back and said, "Look for a tree for fuel, cook! If something has to be made with fuel, then cut down trees outside."

16.20 sā sabhā|dvāram āsādya rudatī Matsyam abravīt,
avekṣamāṇā su|śroṇī patīṃs tān dīna|cetasaḥ,
ākāram abhirakṣantī, pratijñā|dharma|saṃhitāṃ,
dahyamān" ēva raudreṇa cakṣuṣā Drupad'|ātmajā:

DRAUPADY uvāca:

yeṣāṃ vairī na svapiti ṣaṣṭhe 'pi viṣaye vasan,
teṣāṃ māṃ māninīṃ bhāryāṃ sūta|putraḥ pad" âvadhīt!
ye dadyur, na ca yāceyur brahmaṇyāḥ satya|vādinaḥ,
teṣāṃ māṃ māninīṃ bhāryāṃ sūta|putraḥ pad" âvadhīt!
yeṣāṃ dundubhi|nirghoṣo jyā|ghoṣaḥ śrūyate 'niśam,
teṣāṃ māṃ māninīṃ bhāryāṃ sūta|putraḥ pad" âvadhīt!
16.25 ye ca tejasvino, dāntā, balavanto, 'timāninaḥ,
teṣāṃ māṃ māninīṃ bhāryāṃ sūta|putraḥ pad" âvadhīt!
sarva|lokam imaṃ hanyur dharma|pāśa|sitās tu ye,
teṣāṃ māṃ māninīṃ bhāryāṃ sūta|putraḥ pad" âvadhīt!
śaraṇaṃ ye prapannānāṃ bhavanti śaraṇ'|ârthinām
caranti loke pracchannāḥ, kva nu te 'dya mahā|rathāḥ?
kathaṃ te sūta|putreṇa vadhyamānāṃ priyāṃ satīm
marṣayanti yathā klībā, balavanto 'mit'|âujasaḥ?
kva nu teṣāṃ a|marṣaś ca, vīryaṃ, tejaś ca vartate,
na parīpsanti ye bhāryāṃ vadhyamānāṃ dur|ātmanā?

Dráupadi approached the door of the assembly crying, and there the shapely-hipped lady saw her depressed husbands, but abiding by the duty of the pact she protected her disguise, and, eyes burning with fury, the daughter of Drúpada said to the King of Matsya: 16.20

DRÁUPADI said:

The son of the *suta* kicked me with his foot though I am the highly honored wife of those whose enemy cannot sleep even with six realms between them! The son of the *suta* kicked me with his foot though I am the highly honored wife of those who give to brahmins without asking for anything in return and who speak the truth! The son of the *suta* kicked me with his foot though I am the highly honored wife of those whose kettledrum beats and bowstring twangs
are heard incessantly! The son of the *suta* kicked me with 16.25
his foot though I am the highly honored wife of those who are exceedingly proud, possessed of great strength, generous and powerful. The son of the *suta* kicked me with his foot though I am the highly honored wife of those who could destroy this whole world were they not constrained by duty!

Where are those mighty warriors now, who wander the earth in disguise and provide protection for their suppliants who need shelter? How do they endure their dear, faithful wife being struck by the son of a *suta*, as though they are emasculated, despite the fact that they possess infinite energy? Where is their passion, courage and splendor, for they do not prevent their wife being struck by a wicked man?

16.30 may" âtra śakyaṃ kiṃ kartuṃ Virāṭe dharma|dūṣake,
yaḥ paśyan māṃ marṣayati vadhyamānām an|āgasam?
na rājā rājavat kiñ cit samācarati Kīcake.
dasyūnām iva dharmas te, na hi saṃsadi śobhate.
n' âham etena yuktaṃ vai hantuṃ, Matsya, tav' ântike!
sabhā|sado 'tra paśyantu Kīcakasya vyatikramam!
Kīcako na ca dharma|jño, na ca Matsyaḥ kathaṃ cana!
sabhā|sado 'py a|dharma|jñā, ya enaṃ paryupāsate.

VAIŚAMPĀYANA uvāca:

evaṃ|vidhair vacobhiḥ sā tadā Kṛṣṇ" âśru|locanā
upālabhata rājānaṃ Matsyānāṃ vara|varṇinī.

VIRĀṬA uvāca:

16.35 parokṣaṃ n' âbhijānāmi vigrahaṃ yuvayor aham.
artha|tattvam a|vijñāya kiṃ nu syāt kauśalaṃ mama?

VAIŚAMPĀYANA uvāca:

tatas tu sabhyā vijñāya Kṛṣṇāṃ bhūyo 'bhyapūjayan,
«sādhu sādhv! iti» c' âpy āhuḥ, Kīcakaṃ ca vyagarhayan.

SABHYĀ ūcuḥ:

yasy' êyaṃ cāru|sarv'|âṅgī bhāryā syād āyat'|ēkṣaṇā,
paro lābhas tu tasya syān na, ca śocet kathaṃ cana.
na h' īdṛśī manuṣyeṣu su|labhā vara|varṇinī
nārī sarv'|ânavady'|âṅgī. devīṃ manyāmahe vayam.

What can I do when Viráta transgresses rightful law by watching me being struck though I am blameless? The king does not behave toward Kíchaka in a way befitting royalty. Your law resembles that of demons and it does not shine in court. It is not right that I should be harmed in your presence, King of Matsya! Let all the courtiers observe Kíchaka's violation! Kíchaka does not know his moral duty, nor, it seems, does the King of Matsya know anything about it! And courtiers who serve such a man are also devoid of morality. 16.30

VAISHAMPÁYANA said:

So the flawless-complexioned and teary-eyed Krishná reproached the king of the Matsyan people with her righteous words.

VIRÁTA said:

I am not aware of what your quarrel was, while it was out of my sight. Without knowledge of the true cause, what experience could I have? 16.35

VAISHAMPÁYANA said:

When the courtiers found out what had happened, they honored Krishná greatly, saying, "Bravo, bravo!," but condemned Kíchaka.

THE COURTIERS said:

Whoever has that large-eyed, entirely lovely-limbed lady for his wife has the ultimate prize and would never grieve at all. Surely this flawless-complexioned lady's equal would be rare among mortals. To our mind this lady, of entirely faultless limbs, is a goddess.

VAIŚAMPĀYANA uvāca:

evaṃ sampūjayantas te Kṛṣṇāṃ prekṣya sabhā|sadaḥ.
Yudhiṣṭhirasya kopāt tu lalāṭe sveda āgamat.

16.40 ath' âbravīd rāja|putrīṃ Kauravyo mahiṣīṃ priyām:
«gaccha, sairandhri, m" âtra sthāḥ, Sudeṣṇāyā niveśanam.
bhartāram anurundhantyaḥ kliśyante vīra|patnayaḥ.
śuśrūṣayā kliśyamānāḥ pati|lokaṃ jayanty uta.
manye na kālaṃ krodhasya paśyanti patayas tava,
tena tvāṃ n' âbhidhāvanti gandharvāḥ sūrya|varcasaḥ.

a|kāla|jñ" âsi, sairandhri, śailūṣ" îva virodiṣi.
vighnaṃ karoṣi Matsyānāṃ dīvyatām rāja|saṃsadi.
gaccha, sairandhri. gandharvāḥ kariṣyanti tava priyam.
vyapaneṣyanti te duḥkhaṃ yena te vi|priyaṃ kṛtam.»

SAIRANDHRY uvāca:

16.45 atīva teṣāṃ ghṛṇinām arthe 'haṃ dharma|cāriṇī.
tasya tasy' âiva te vadhyā, yeṣāṃ jyeṣṭho 'kṣa|devitā.

VAIŚAMPĀYANA uvāca:

ity uktvā prādravat Kṛṣṇā Sudeṣṇāyā niveśanam
keśān muktvā ca su|śroṇī saṃrambhāl lohit'|ēkṣaṇā.
śuśubhe vadanaṃ tasyā rudatyāḥ su|ciraṃ tadā,
megha|lekhā|vinirmuktaṃ div' îva śaśi|maṇḍalam.

VAISHAMPÁYANA said:

So the courtiers honored Krishná when they saw her. But sweat had appeared on Yudhi·shthira's forehead from fury. The descendant of Kuru addressed the princess, his 16.40
dear wife: "Go to Sudéshna's apartments, *sairándhri*. Don't stay here. Heroes' wives are tormented when they oblige their husbands and suffer with obedience, but they win the husband's world. I imagine that your *gandhárva* husbands, luminous as the sun, do not consider this an appropriate time for anger, since they did not rush down to you.

You are unaware of the right occasion for things, *sairándhri*, as you cry like an actress and you interrupted gambling in the royal court of the king of the Matsyas. So go, *sairándhri*. The *gandhárvas* will do what you want. The misery you feel because of the violation you suffered will be wiped out."

THE SAIRÁNDHRI said:

I believe that I am a virtuous wife to compassionate hus- 16.45
bands, but the eldest of them is addicted to dice and so they are humbled by one and all.

VAISHAMPÁYANA said:

Having said this, Krishná ran to Sudéshna's apartments, with her hair fallen loose, crying, and her eyes red with anger. But her face was dazzling after her lengthy crying, like the disk of the moon in the heavens released from a line of clouds.

SUDEṢṆ" ôvāca:

kas tv" âvadhīd, var'|ārohe? kasmād rodiṣi, śobhane?
kasy' âdya na sukhaṃ, bhadre? kena te vi|priyaṃ kṛtam?

DRAUPADY uvāca:

Kīcako m" âvadhīt tatra sur"|āhārīṃ gatām tava,
sabhāyāṃ paśyato rājño yath" âiva vi|jane vane.

SUDEṢṆ" ôvāca:

16.50 ghātayāmi, su|keś'|ânte, Kīcakaṃ, yadi manyase,
yo 'sau tvāṃ kāma|saṃmatto dur|labhām avamanyate.

SAIRANDHRY uvāca:

anye c' âinaṃ vadhiṣyanti, yeṣām āgaḥ karoti saḥ!
manye c' âiv' âdya su|vyaktaṃ Yama|lokaṃ gamiṣyati!

VAIŚAṂPĀYANA uvāca:

17.1 SĀ HATĀ SŪTA|putreṇa rāja|patnī yaśasvinī
vadhaṃ Kṛṣṇā parīpsantī senā|vāhasya bhāminī.
jagām' āvāsam ev' âtha sā tadā Drupad'|ātmajā
kṛtvā śaucam yathā|nyāyaṃ kṛṣṇā sā tanu|madhyamā.
gātrāṇi, vāsasī c' âiva prakṣālya salilena sā
cintayām āsa rudatī tasya duḥkhasya nirṇayam.
«kiṃ karomi? kva gacchāmi?
kathaṃ kāryaṃ bhaven mama?»

SUDÉSHNA said:

Who has insulted you, shapely-hipped lady? Why are you crying, beautiful girl? Why are you unhappy now, my dear? Who has done you wrong?

DRÁUPADI said:

Kíchaka hit me when I went to fetch your wine in the court within the sight of the king, as if we were in a deserted wood.

SUDÉSHNA said:

I will have Kíchaka killed if you set your mind on it, lady 16.50
with lovely curly-tipped locks, for that man, maddened by his lust, treated you with contempt even though you are unavailable.

THE SAIRÁNDHRI said:

Others will kill him—those against whom he committed his violation! I think it is very clear that he will go to the realm of Yama even today!

VAISHAMPÁYANA said:

THE BEAUTIFUL AND illustrious Queen Krishná, thus 17.1
harmed by the *suta*'s son, desired first and foremost the murder of the army's general. Then the daughter of Drúpada went to her apartment and the dark-skinned, slender-waisted girl washed herself. When she had washed her body and clothes with running water, she cried and contemplated the dissolution of her misery. "What should I do? Where can I go? How can I accomplish my plan?"

ity evaṃ cintayitvā sā
Bhīmaṃ vai manas" âgamat.
17.5 «n' ânyaḥ kartā ṛte Bhīmān mam' âdya manasaḥ priyam.»
tata utthāya rātrau sā vihāya śayanaṃ svakam,
prādravan nātham icchantī Kṛṣṇā nāthavatī satī,
bhavanaṃ Bhīmasenasya kṣipram āyata|locanā,
duḥkhena mahatā yuktā mānasena manasvinī.

SAIRANDHRY uvāca:

tasmin jīvati pāpiṣṭhe senā|vāhe mama dviṣi
tat karma kṛtavān adya kathaṃ nidrāṃ niṣevase?

VAIŚAMPĀYANA uvāca:

evam uktv" âtha tāṃ śālāṃ praviveśa manasvinī
yasyāṃ Bhīmas tathā śete, mṛga|rāja iva śvasan
tasyā rūpeṇa sā śālā, Bhīmasya ca mah"|ātmanaḥ
17.10 saṃmūrchit" êva, Kauravya, prajajvāla ca tejasā.
sā vai mahānasaṃ prāpya Bhīmasenaṃ śuci|smitā
sarva|śvet" êva māheyī vane jātā tri|hāyaṇī
upātiṣṭhata Pāñcālī vāsit" êva vara'|ṛṣabham.
sā lat" êva mahā|śālaṃ phullaṃ Gomati|tīra|jam
pariṣvajata Pāñcālī madhyamaṃ Pāṇḍu|nandanam,
bāhubhyāṃ parirabhy' âinaṃ prābodhayad a|ninditā,
siṃhaṃ suptaṃ vane durge mṛga|rāja|vadhūr iva.
Bhīmasenam upāśliṣyadd hastin" îva mahā|gajam,
vīṇ" êva madhur|ālāpā Gāndhāraṃ sādhu mūrchatī,
abhyabhāṣata Pāñcālī Bhīmasenam a|ninditā:
17.15 «uttiṣṭh' ôttiṣṭha! kiṃ śeṣe, Bhīmasena, yathā mṛtaḥ?
n' â|mṛtasya hi pāpīyān bhāryām ālabhya jīvati.»

Pondering this, she hit upon the idea of Bhima, "There is no one but Bhima who can do what I want." So, getting up in the night and leaving her bed, large-eyed and protected Krishná ran quickly to the quarters of Bhima·sena, wanting her husband, for the spirited lady was afflicted with great grief in her mind. 17.5

THE SAIRÁNDHRI said:

How can you sleep while the man who committed that outrage today, my enemy, the most vile army general, is still alive?

VAISHAMPÁYANA said:

Saying this, the intelligent lady entered the apartment in which Bhima slept, breathing heavily like a lion, and the chamber, filled with her beauty and that of high-souled Bhima, seemed to intensify, Kaurávya, and blazed with splen- 17.10
dor. Once the sweet-smiling princess of Panchála had found Bhima·sena in the kitchen, she approached him like a three-year-old pure-white cow, born in the forest, approaches a bull when in season.

The princess of Panchála embraced the second son of Pandu like a creeper encircling a huge flowery *shala* tree near the shore of the Gómati, and, circling her arms around him, the virtuous lady woke him, as a lioness wakes a sleeping lion in an impassable forest. Clinging to Bhima·sena like a female elephant to a mighty bull elephant, the faultless princess of Panchála addressed Bhima·sena with sweet speech, like a
lute emitting the pure Gandhára note: "Get up, get up! 17.15
Why do you sleep, Bhima·sena, as if you were dead? Surely

sa saṃprahāya śayanaṃ rāja|putryā prabodhitaḥ
upātiṣṭhata megh'|âbhaḥ paryaṅke s'|ôpasaṃgrahe.
ath' âbravīd rāja|putrīṃ Kauravyo mahiṣīṃ priyām:
«ken' âsy arthena saṃprāptā tvarit' êva mam' ântikam?
na te prakṛtimān varṇaḥ, kṛśā pāṇḍuś ca lakṣyase.
ācakṣva pariśeṣeṇa, sarvaṃ vidyām ahaṃ yathā,
sukhaṃ vā yadi vā duḥkhaṃ, dveṣyaṃ vā yadi vā priyam.
yathāvat sarvam ācakṣva śrutvā jñāsyāmi yat kṣamam.
17.20 aham eva hi te, Kṛṣṇe, viśvāsyaḥ sarva|karmasu,
aham āpatsu c' âpi tvāṃ mokṣayāmi punaḥ punaḥ.
śīghram uktvā yathā|kāmaṃ yat te kāryaṃ vivakṣitam,
gaccha vai śayanāy' âiva, purā n' ânyena budhyate.»

DRAUPADY UVĀCA:

18.1 A|ŚOCYATVAṂ KUTAS tasyā yasyā bhartā Yudhiṣṭhiraḥ?
jānan sarvāṇi duḥkhāni kiṃ māṃ tvaṃ paripṛcchasi?
yan māṃ dāsī|pravādena prātikāmī tad" ânayat
sabhā|pariṣado madhye, tan māṃ dahati, Bhārata.
pārthivasya sutā nāma kā nu jīvati mādṛśī,
anubhūy' ēdṛśaṃ duḥkham anyatra Draupadīṃ, prabho?
vana|vāsa|gatāyāś ca Saindhavena dur|ātmanā,
parāmarśo dvitīyo vai soḍhum utsahate tu kā?
18.5 Matsya|rājñaḥ samakṣaṃ tu tasya dhūrtasya paśyataḥ
Kīcakena parāmṛṣṭā kā nu jīvati mādṛśī?
evaṃ bahu|vidhaiḥ kleśaiḥ kliśyamānāṃ ca, Bhārata,
na māṃ jānāsi, Kaunteya, kiṃ phalaṃ jīvitena me?

if a man is not dead then the wicked creature who molested his wife should not live."

Woken by the princess, he left his bed, resembling a cloud, and rose up onto his cushioned sofa. The descendant of Kuru spoke to the princess, his beloved wife: "Why have you come to me like this in a rush? You seem to have lost your usual color and seem thin and pale. Tell me all the facts in detail, regardless of whether they are pleasant or unpleasant, hateful or congenial. So tell me everything, and when I have heard it I will know what is appropriate.

I alone, Krishná, am entitled to your confidence in all 17.20
matters, since I am the one who rescues you time and again from misfortunes. Quickly tell me what you want and what needs doing, then go to your bed before others wake up."

DRÁUPADI said:

HOW IS THERE NO pity for the woman whose husband 18.1
is Yudhi·shthira? Why do you even ask me when you know all my miseries? A servant led me into the middle of an assembly of courtiers, calling me a slave—and that burns me, Bhárata.*

Which princess lives like me and has experienced misery of this kind other than Dráupadi, my lord? Who could endure a second violation such as I suffered at the hands of the wicked-souled Sáindhava when I lived in the forest?
Who lives like me, being kicked by Kíchaka in clear view of 18.5
the wicked King of Matsya? What is the point of me even living, if you, son of Kuntí, do not know that I am thus afflicted by many varied troubles, Bhárata?

yo 'yaṃ rājño Virāṭasya Kīcako nāma, Bhārata,
senā|nīḥ, puruṣa|vyāghra, śyālaḥ parama|durmatiḥ,
sa māṃ sairandhri|veṣeṇa vasantīṃ rāja|veśmani
nityam ev' āha duṣṭ'|ātmā, «bhāryā mama bhav' êti» vai.
ten' ôpamantryamāṇāyā vadh'|ârheṇa, sa|patna|han,
kālen' êva phalaṃ pakvaṃ hṛdayaṃ me vidīryate.
18.10 bhrātaraṃ ca vigarhasva jyeṣṭhaṃ dur|dyūta|devinam,
yasy" âsmi karmaṇā prāptā duḥkham etad an|antakam!
ko hi rājyaṃ parityajya, sarva|svaṃ c' ātmanā saha
pravrajyāy' âiva dīvyeta vinā dur|dyūta|devinam?
yadi niṣka|sahasreṇa, yac c' ânyat sāravad dhanam,
sāyaṃ|prātar adeviṣyad api saṃvatsarān bahūn,
rukmaṃ, hiraṇyaṃ, vāsāṃsi, yānaṃ, yugyam, aj'|âvikam,
aśv'|âśvatara|saṅghāṃś ca, na jātu kṣayam āvahet.
so 'yaṃ dyūta|pravādena śriyaḥ pratyavaropitaḥ
tūṣṇīm āste yathā mūḍhaḥ, svāni karmāṇi cintayan.
18.15 daśa nāga|sahasrāṇi hayānāṃ hema|mālinām
yaṃ yāntam anuyānt" îha so 'yaṃ dyūtena jīvati!
rathāḥ śata|sahasrāṇi nṛpāṇām a|mit'|âujasām
upāsanta mahā|rājam Indraprasthe Yudhiṣṭhiram.
śataṃ dāsī|sahasrāṇāṃ yasya nityaṃ mahānase
pātrī|hastaṃ divā|rātram atithīn bhojayaty uta,
eṣa niṣka|sahasrāṇi pradāya dadatāṃ varaḥ
dyūta|jena hy an|arthena mahatā samupāśritaḥ!
enaṃ hi svara|sampannā bahavaḥ sūta|māgadhāḥ
sāyaṃ|prātar upātiṣṭhan su|mṛṣṭa|maṇi|kuṇḍalāḥ.

Tiger-like Bhárata, the army's commander and King Viráta's utterly wicked-minded brother-in-law, Kíchaka by name, evil-souled man that he is, always says to me, as I live in the palace in the disguise of a *sairándhri*: "Become my wife." Being propositioned by this man who deserves death, slayer of your foes, my heart is tearing like fruit, ripened by the season.

Blame your older brother the despicable gambler, for it 18.10
is because of what he did that I have obtained this endless misery! Who but a despicable gambler would lay a bet, forsaking his kingdom and everything he owns, including me, for wandering in exile? Even if he had gambled from morning to evening for many years, betting golden coins by the thousand and other precious wealth, his gold, silver, robes, chariots, yoked teams, goats, sheep, and his multitudes of mules and horses would certainly not have suffered any depletion.

But now, deprived of his prosperity, which is scattered due to challenges at gambling, he sits silently like a fool and
ponders his own actions. The man who had ten thousand 18.15
horses decked in golden garlands when he journeyed away and back now supports himself through gambling with dice! Hundreds of thousands of chariots belonging to kings of unbounded energy waited on great King Yudhi·shthira at Indra·prastha. In his kitchen were a hundred thousand slave girls, plate in hand, constantly feeding guests day and night. The best of benefactors, who gave a thousand nishkas a day, is now dependent on the great evil of gambling! Numerous sweet-voiced encomiasts and panegyrists, wearing earrings of brightly polished gems, served this man dawn and dusk.

18.20 sahasram ṛṣayo yasya nityam āsan sabhā|sadaḥ,
tapaḥ|śrut'|ôpasaṃpannāḥ, sarva|kāmair upasthitāḥ,
aṣṭ'|âśīti|sahasrāṇi snātakā gṛha|medhinaḥ,
triṃśad dāsīka ek' âiko, yān bibharti Yudhiṣṭhiraḥ,
a|pratigrāhiṇāṃ c' âiva yatīnām ūrdhva|retasām
daśa c' âpi sahasrāṇi, so 'yam āste nar'|ēśvaraḥ!
a|nṛśaṃsyam, anukrośaṃ, saṃvibhāgas tath" âiva ca—
yasminn etāni sarvāṇi, so 'yam āste nar'|ēśvaraḥ!
andhān, vṛddhāṃs, tath" â|nāthān bālān rāṣṭreṣu durgatān
bibharti vividhān rājā dhṛtimān, satya|vikramaḥ,
saṃvibhāgamanā nityam ānṛśaṃsyād Yudhiṣṭhiraḥ,
18.25 sa eṣa nirayaṃ prāpto Matsyasya paricārakaḥ,
sabhāyāṃ devitā rājñaḥ Kaṅko brūte Yudhiṣṭhiraḥ!
Indraprasthe nivasataḥ samaye yasya pārthivāḥ
āsan bali|bhṛtaḥ sarve, so 'dy' ânyair bhṛtim icchati.
pārthivāḥ pṛthivī|pālā yasy' āsan vaśa|vartinaḥ,
sa vaśe vivaśo rājā pareṣām adya vartate.
pratāpya pṛthivīṃ sarvām raśmimān iva tejasā,
so 'yaṃ rājño Virāṭasya sabhā|stāro Yudhiṣṭhiraḥ.
yam upāsanta rājānaḥ sabhāyām ṛṣibhiḥ saha,
tam upāsīnam ady' ânyaṃ paśya, Pāṇḍava, Pāṇḍavam.
18.30 sadasyaṃ samupāsīnaṃ, parasya priya|vādinam
dṛṣṭvā Yudhiṣṭhiraṃ kopo vardhate mām a|saṃśayam.
a|tad|arhaṃ, mahā|prājñaṃ,
jīvit'|ârthe 'bhisaṃsthitam
dṛṣṭvā kasya na duḥkhaṃ syād
dharm'|ātmānaṃ Yudhiṣṭhiram?

A thousand sages endowed with austerity and learning 18.20
always sat in his court with every desire catered for. Yudhi·shthira once supported eighty-eight thousand *snátaka* householders with thirty slave girls for each, as well as ten thousand *yati* ascetics who had renounced the world and who accepted nothing, having raised their offspring—and now that king of men lives like this! The merciful, compassionate and sharing lord of men who possessed all these things now lives like this! King Yudhi·shthira, truly valiant and sharing, always supported various unfortunates from compassion: the blind, old, helpless and children in his
kingdoms. Now he has reached hell as the servant of Mat- 18.25
sya. Yudhi·shthira is a dice player called Kanka in the king's court!

When he was living at Indra·prastha, all the kings of earth bore him tribute under the terms of his treaty, but nowadays he wants support from others. The kings and princes of earth were subject to his will, but now that king, deprived of his own power, is subject to the will of others. Having illuminated the whole world with his splendor like the sun, that same Yudhi·shthira is now King Viráta's courtier. Pándava, see how another son of Pandu, whom kings and sages served in his court, now attends another man.

Seeing Yudhi·shthira attending and speaking obsequi- 18.30
ously to someone else, it is no wonder that my anger grows. Seeing the clever and virtuous-souled Yudhi·shthira attending someone else, which he does not deserve, just to support himself, who would not be miserable? Hero Bhárata, see how the another descendant of Bharata, who was once waited upon in court by the whole earth, now waits upon

upāste sma sabhāyāṃ yaṃ kṛtsnā, vīra, vasun|dharā
tam upāsīnam apy anyaṃ paśya, Bhārata, Bhāratam.
evaṃ bahu|vidhair duḥkhaiḥ pīḍyamānām a|nāthavat,
śoka|sāgara|madhya|sthāṃ kiṃ māṃ, Bhīma, na paśyasi?

DRAUPADY uvāca:

19.1 IDAṂ TU TE mahad duḥkhaṃ yat pravakṣyāmi, Bhārata,
na me 'bhyasūyā kartavyā, duḥkhād etad bravīmy aham.
sūda|karmaṇi hīne tvam a|same, Bharata'|rṣabha,
bruvan Ballava|jātīyaḥ, kasya śokaṃ na vardhayeḥ?
sūpa|kāraṃ Virāṭasya Ballavaṃ tvāṃ vidur janāḥ
preṣyatvaṃ samanuprāptaṃ, tato duḥkhataraṃ nu kim?
yadā mahānase siddhe Virāṭam upatiṣṭhasi
bruvāṇo Ballavaḥ sūdas, tadā sīdati me manaḥ.
19.5 yadā prahṛṣṭaḥ samrāṭ tvāṃ saṃyodhayati kuñjaraiḥ,
hasanty antaḥ|pure nāryo, mama t' ûdvijate manaḥ.
śārdūlair, mahiṣaiḥ, siṃhair āgāre yodhyase yadā
Kaikeyyāḥ prekṣamāṇāyās, tadā me kaśmalaṃ bhavet.
tata utthāya Kaikeyī sarvās tāḥ pratyabhāṣata
preṣyāḥ samutthitāś c' âpi Kaikeyīṃ tāḥ striyo 'bruvan,
prekṣya mām an|avady'|âṅgīṃ kaśmal'|ôpahatām iva,
«snehāt saṃvāsa|jād dharmāt sūdam eṣā śuci|smitā
yoddhyamānaṃ mahā|vīryam iyaṃ samanuśocati.
kalyāṇa|rūpā sairandhrī, Ballavaś c' âpi sundaraḥ.
19.10 strīṇāṃ cittaṃ ca dur|jñeyaṃ, yukta|rūpau ca me matau.
sairandhrī priya|saṃvāsān nityaṃ karuṇa|vādinī.
asmin rāja|kule c' êmau tulya|kāla|nivāsinau.»
iti bruvāṇā vākyāni sā māṃ nityam atarjayat.

someone else. Why, then, Bhima, do you not see that I am unfortunate, thus pained by many and various miseries, standing in the midst of a sea of troubles?

DRÁUPADI said:

I WILL EXPLAIN my great misery, Bhárata, but you should 19.1
not reproach me, for I am speaking out of pain. Bull of the Bharata race, whose anger would not grow when you perform chef's work, unworthy of you, calling yourself a member of Bállava jati? What is more sad than that people know you as Bállava, Viráta's chef, who has fallen into servitude? When the kitchen work is successfully done, you wait upon Viráta calling youself Bállava the cook, and so your mind sinks into depression.

When the supreme ruler is in a good mood, he makes 19.5
you fight with elephants and the women laugh inside their apartment, but my heart grieves. When you fight with tigers, buffaloes and lions in the inner quarters, and the Princess Kaikéyi watches, I faint. When Princess Kaikéyi rises and all the servant girls get up, too, and tell the princess that they find nothing wrong with my body when they examine it; that it seems I fell from fainting, she replies, "It is out of love and the duty derived from their intimate relationship that the sweet-smiling lady grieves for this cook who fights very heroically. The *sairándhri* is beautiful-looking and Bállava, too, is handsome. It is hard to know women's hearts, 19.10
but to my mind they are well suited. The *sairándhri* always laments because of the bond with her lover. Furthermore, they both started living in this royal family at the same time." She always derides me by saying such things.

krudhyantīṃ māṃ ca saṃprekṣya
samaśaṅkata māṃ tvayi.
tasyāṃ tathā bruvatyāṃ tu
duḥkhaṃ māṃ mahad āviśat.
tvayy evaṃ nirayaṃ prāpte Bhīme bhīma|parākrame,
śoke Yudhiṣṭhire magnā n' âhaṃ jīvitum utsahe.

yaḥ sa|devān manuṣyāṃś ca sarvāṃś c' âika|ratho 'jayat,
so 'yaṃ rājño Virāṭasya kanyānāṃ nartako yuvā.
19.15 yo 'tarpayad a|mey'|ātmā Khāṇḍave Jātavedasam,
so 'ntaḥpura|gataḥ Pārthaḥ kūpe 'gnir iva saṃvṛtaḥ.
yasmād bhayam amitrāṇāṃ sad" âiva puruṣa'|ṛṣabhāt,
sa loka|paribhūtena veṣeṇ' āste Dhanañjayaḥ.
yasya jyā|kṣepa|kaṭhinau bāhū parigha|sannibhau,
sa śaṅkha|paripūrṇābhyāṃ śocann āste Dhanañjayaḥ.
yasya jyā|tala|nirghoṣāt samakampanta śatravaḥ,
striyo gīta|svanaṃ tasya muditāḥ paryupāsate.
kirīṭaṃ sūrya|saṅkāśaṃ yasya mūrdhany aśobhata,
veṇī|vikṛta|keś'|ântaḥ so 'yam adya Dhanañjayaḥ!

19.20 taṃ veṇīkṛta|keś'|ântaṃ bhīma|dhanvānam Arjunam
kanyā|parivṛtaṃ dṛṣṭvā, Bhīma, sīdati me manaḥ.
yasminn astrāṇi divyāni samastāni mah"|ātmani,
ādhāraḥ sarva|vidyānāṃ sa dhārayati kuṇḍale!
spraṣṭuṃ rāja|sahasrāṇi tejas" âpratibhāni vai
samare n' âbhyavartanta, velām iva mah"|ârṇavaḥ,
so 'yaṃ rājño Virāṭasya kanyānāṃ narta|ko yuvā
āste veśa|praticchannah kanyānāṃ paricārakaḥ.

When she sees that I get angry, she suspects me when it comes to you. When she talks that way, great grief overwhelms me. Immersed in grief for Yudhi·shthira and for you now that you have reached this hell, Bhima of great prowess, I do not dare to live.

The youth who defeated all celestials and men in a single chariot now teaches Viráta's daughters to dance. Partha 19.15
of immeasurable soul who satisfied all-knowing Agni in Khándava has gone into the apartments of the palace like a fire hidden in a cave. Dhanan·jaya has gone from being a bull among men, the constant fear of his enemies, to living in a disguise that is despised by the world. Dhanan·jaya whose arms, like iron bars, are harsh, struck by the bowstring, now lives grieving with his arms covered with conch bracelets. His enemies trembled at the sound of the slap of his bowstring, but now joyful women worship the sound of his songs. Dhanan·jaya, whose head was adorned with a sun-like crown, now has braids with unnatural curls at the end!

My heart sinks when I see Árjuna, the terrifying bow- 19.20
man, with his hair in braids and curls at the end, living among women, Bhima. That high-minded master of all divine weapons and the vessel of all knowledge now wears earrings! The youth whom thousands of kings matchless in splendor could not touch when they attacked him in battle, just as the sea cannot defeat the shore, teaches King Viráta's daughters to dance, and lives concealed in a disguise, as the princesses' servant.

yasya sma ratha|ghoṣeṇa samakampata medinī
sa|parvata|vanā, Bhīma, saha|sthāvara|jaṅgamā,
19.25 yasmin jāte mahā|bhāge Kuntyāḥ śoko vyanaśyata,
sa śocayati mām adya, Bhīmasena, tav' ânujaḥ.
bhūṣitaṃ tam alaṅ|kāraiḥ, kuṇḍalaiḥ parihāṭakaiḥ,
kambu|pāṇinam āyāntaṃ dṛṣṭvā sīdati me manaḥ.
yasya n' âsti samo vīryaṃ kaś cid urvyāṃ dhanur|dharaḥ
so 'dya kanyā|parivṛto gāyann āste Dhanañjayaḥ.
dharme śaurye ca satye ca jīva|lokasya saṃmatam
strī|veṣa|vikṛtaṃ Pārthaṃ dṛṣṭvā sīdati me manaḥ.

yadā hy enaṃ parivṛtaṃ kanyābhir deva|rūpiṇam,
prabhinnam iva mātaṅgaṃ parikīrṇaṃ kareṇubhiḥ,
19.30 Matsyam artha|patiṃ Pārthaṃ Virāṭaṃ samupasthitam
paśyāmi turya|madhya|sthaṃ, diśo naśyanti me tadā.
nūnam āryā na jānāti kṛcchraṃ prāptaṃ Dhanañjayam,
Ajātaśatruṃ Kauravyaṃ magnaṃ dur|dyūta|devinam.

tathā dṛṣṭvā yavīyāṃsaṃ Sahadevaṃ gavāṃ patim
goṣu go|veṣam āyāntaṃ pāṇḍu|bhūt" âsmi, Bhārata.
Sahadevasya vṛttāni cintayantī punaḥ punaḥ
na nidrām abhigacchāmi, Bhīmasena, kuto ratim?
na vindāmi, mahā|bāho, Sahadevasya duṣ|kṛtam
yasminn evaṃ|vidhaṃ duḥkhaṃ prāpnuyāt satya|vikramaḥ.
19.35 dūyāmi, Bhārata|śreṣṭha, dṛṣṭvā te bhrātaraṃ priyam
goṣu go|vṛṣa|saṅkāśaṃ Matsyen' âbhiniveśitam,
saṃrabdhaṃ rakta|nepathyaṃ go|pālānāṃ puro|gamam
Virāṭam abhinandantam atha me bhavati jvaraḥ.

O Bhima, the earth together with her mountains and forests, as well as inanimate and animate objects, trembled at the sound of his chariot, and when the nobleman 19.25
was born Kuntí's sorrow vanished, but now, Bhima·sena, your brother Árjuna makes me grieve. Seeing him coming toward me adorned with accessories, golden earrings and conch bracelets on his wrists, my heart despairs. Dhanan·jaya, whom no archer on earth can match for heroism, now lives in the company of women, singing. My heart sinks when I see Partha, once the most highly esteemed man in the world in virtue, heroism and truth, now disguised as a woman.

When I see godlike Partha standing in the middle of the music hall, surrounded by women like an elephant in rut crowded with female elephants, as he attends Viráta, King 19.30
of Matsya, I don't know which way to turn. Surely my noble mother-in-law doesn't know that Dhanan·jaya has attained such hardship, and that Ajáta·shatru, of the Kuru race, is addicted to gambling and sunk in misfortune.

When I see the youngest, Saha·deva, coming toward me disguised as a cowherd, managing the cattle, I grow pale, Bhárata. I can't get to sleep as I reflect again and again on Saha·deva's circumstances. Where can I find peace, Bhima·sena? I cannot conceive what Saha·deva's sin was, long-armed hero, for which that truly valiant man should attain such
misery. O best of the race of Bharata, when I see your beloved 19.35
brother employed by the King of Matsya, in the disguise of a cowherd, I become depressed, and seeing him frustrated at the head of the cowherds, in a dyed red costume, pleasing Viráta, I grow feverish.

Sahadevaṃ hi me vīraṃ nityam āryā praśaṃsati,
mah"|âbhijana|saṃpannaḥ, śīlavān, vṛttavān iti.
«hrī|niṣevo, madhura|vāg, dhārmikaś ca, priyaś ca me,
sa te 'raṇyeṣu voḍhavyo, Yājñaseni, kṣapāsv api.
su|kumāraś ca, śūraś ca, rājānaṃ c' âpy anuvrataḥ
jyeṣṭh'|âpacāyinaṃ vīraṃ svayaṃ, Pāñcāli, bhojayeḥ.»
19.40 ity uvāca hi māṃ Kuntī rudatī, putra|gṛddhinī
pravrajantaṃ mah"|âraṇyaṃ taṃ pariṣvajya tiṣṭhatī.
taṃ dṛṣṭvā vyāpṛtaṃ goṣu, vatsa|carma|kṣap"|āśayam,
Sahadevaṃ yudhāṃ śreṣṭhaṃ kiṃ nu jīvāmi, Pāṇḍava?

yas tribhir nitya|saṃpanno rūpeṇ' âstreṇa medhayā,
so 'śva|bandho Virāṭasya. paśya kālasya paryayam!
abhyakīryanta vṛndāni Dāmagranthim udīkṣya tam
vinayantaṃ javen' âśvān mahā|rājasya paśyataḥ.
apaśyam enaṃ śrīmantaṃ Matsyaṃ bhrājiṣṇum uttamam
Virāṭam upatiṣṭhantaṃ, darśayantaṃ ca vājinaḥ.
19.45 kiṃ nu māṃ manyase, Pārtha, sukhin" îti, paran|tapa,
evaṃ duḥkha|śat'|āviṣṭā Yudhiṣṭhira|nimittatah?
ataḥ prativiśiṣṭāni duḥkhāny anyāni, Bhārata
vartante mayi, Kaunteya. vakṣyāmi, śṛṇu tāny api.
yuṣmāsu dhriyamāṇeṣu duḥkhāni vividhāṇy uta
śoṣayanti śarīraṃ me. kiṃ nu duḥkham ataḥ param?

My mother-in-law always taught me that brave Saha·deva possessed a noble mind, a good character and good behavior. "He is modest, sweet-speeched, virtuous and dear to me. You should take care of him even during the nights in the forests, Yajñaséni. He is a very tender and brave man, devoted to the king and respectful to his older brother, so
you should feed him yourself, Pancháli." So Kuntí spoke 19.40
to me, crying and longing for her son as she stood there embracing Saha·deva when he set out for the great forest. How can I live, Pándava, watching Saha·deva, that excellent warrior, working among cattle and sleeping on calfskins at night?

The man who is eternally funished with the three attributes of beauty, weapons and intelligence is now in charge of Viráta's horses. See how the times have changed! Hordes turn out to watch Dama·granthi now that he trains horses in speed while the great king looks on. I was watching him serving the venerable and most resplendent King Viráta of Matsya, showing him the horses.

So why do you think I am happy, son of Pritha, scorcher 19.45
of your enemies, when I am burdened by these hundred troubles on account of Yudhi·shthira? But then there are worse miseries, so listen to me, Bhárata, son of Kuntí, and I will tell you these as well. What could be worse than this utter misery: that these various troubles desiccate my body while you are all alive?

DRAUPADY uvāca:

20.1 «AHAṂ SAIRANDHRI|veṣeṇa carantī rāja|veśmani
śaucad" âsmi Sudeṣṇāyā akṣa|dhūrtasya kāraṇāt.
vikriyāṃ paśya me tīvrāṃ rāja|putryāḥ, paran|tapa!
ātma|kālam udīkṣantī sarvaṃ duḥkhaṃ kil' ântavat.
a|nityā kila martyānāṃ artha|siddhir, jay'|âjayau—
iti kṛtvā pratīkṣāmi bhartṝṇām udayaṃ punaḥ.
cakravat parivartante hy arthāś ca, vyasanāni ca—
iti kṛtvā pratīkṣāmi bhartṝṇām udayaṃ punaḥ.
20.5 parājaye ca hetuś ca sa, iti pratipālaye.
kiṃ māṃ na pratijānīṣe, Bhīmasena, mṛtām iva?
dattvā yācanti puruṣā, hatvā vadhyanti c' âpare,
pātayitvā ca pātyante parair, iti ca me śrutam.
na daivasy' âtibhāro 'sti, na c' âiv' âsy' âtivartanam.
iti c' âpy āgamaṃ bhūyo daivasya pratipālaye.
sthitaṃ pūrvaṃ jalaṃ yatra, punas tatr' âiva gacchati,
iti paryāyam icchantī pratīkṣe udayaṃ punaḥ.
daivena kila yasy' ârthaḥ su|nīto 'pi vipadyate
daivasya c' āgame yatnas tena kāryo vijānatā.
20.10 yat tu me vacanasy' âsya kathitasya prayojanam,
pṛccha māṃ duḥkhitāṃ tat tvaṃ, pṛṣṭā c' âtra bravīmi te.
mahiṣī Pāṇḍu|putrāṇāṃ, duhitā Drupadasya ca,
imām avasthāṃ saṃprāptā mad anyā kā jijīviṣet?
Kurūn paribhavet sarvān, Pāñcālān api, Bhārata,
Pāṇḍaveyāṃś ca saṃprāpto mama kleśo hy, arin|dama.
bhrātṛbhiḥ, śvaśuraiḥ, putrair bahubhiḥ parivāritā
evaṃ samuditā nārī kā tv anyā duḥkhitā bhavet?

DRÁUPADI said:

"I LIVE IN THE palace in the guise of a *sairándhri*, Sudéshna's cleaner, because of that gambler. See my horrible transformation, scorcher of the enemy, and I a princess! I spend my time looking forward to the end of all this misery. Indeed, having reflected on the impermanent nature of the aim, success, victory and failure of mortals, I expect prosperity for my husbands once more. 20.1

Prosperity and misfortune revolve like a wheel. It is with this in mind that I expect prosperity for my husbands once more. The same cause that brings victory to one man may 20.5
bring defeat to another, so I am hopeful. Bhima·sena, why do you not admit that I am like a dead person? I've heard that benefactors beg, even killers are subsequently killed, and revolutionaries are overthrown by others. Nothing is too difficult for fate, and no one is beyond its scope. So I expect the return of good fortune once more. Just as water comes back to where it once stood, so hoping for a transformation, I look to the return of prosperity. Truly, when one's best-laid plan is thwarted by destiny, the wise man should make an effort for the return of good fortune.

Ask me the point of what I'm saying, truly miserable 20.10
as I am, and asked I will tell you. Who else but me, the queen of the Pándavas and daughter of Drúpada, would wish to live being reduced to this situation? Foe-destroying Bhárata, the sorrow that has taken me over may disgrace all the Kurus, the Panchálas and the Pándavas. Which woman besides me, surrounded by brothers, my father-in-law and sons, wanting for nothing, would become this miserable?

nūnaṃ hi bālayā dhātur mayā vai vi|priyaṃ kṛtam,
yasya prasādād dur|nītaṃ prāpt" âsmi, Bharata'|ṛṣabha.
20.15 varṇ'|âvikāśam api me paśya, Pāṇḍava, yādṛśam,
tādṛśo me na tatr' āsīd duḥkhe paramake tadā.
tvam eva, Bhīma, jānīṣe yan me, Pārtha, sukhaṃ purā,
s" âhaṃ dāsītvam āpannā na śāntim a|vaśā labhe.

n' â|daivikam ahaṃ manye yatra Pārtho Dhanañjayaḥ
bhīma|dhanvā mahā|bāhur āste channa iv' ânalaḥ.
a|śakyā vedituṃ, Pārtha, prāṇināṃ vai gatir naraiḥ
vinipātam imaṃ manye yuṣmākaṃ hy a|vicintitam.

yasyā mama mukha|prekṣā yūyam Indra|samāḥ sadā
sā prekṣe mukham anyāsām avarāṇāṃ varā satī.
20.20 paśya, Pāṇḍava, me 'vasthāṃ, yathā n' ârhāmi vai, tathā.
yuṣmāsu dhriyamāṇeṣu paśya kālasya paryayam!
yasyāḥ sāgara|paryantā pṛthivī vaśa|vartinī
āsīt, s" âdya Sudeṣṇāyā bhīt" âhaṃ vaśa|vartinī.
yasyāḥ puraḥ|sarā āsan, pṛṣṭhataś c' ânugāminaḥ,
s" âham adya Sudeṣṇāyāḥ puraḥ, paścāc ca gāminī.

idaṃ tu duḥkhaṃ, Kaunteya,
mam' â|sahyaṃ, nibodha tat.
yā na jātu svayaṃ piṃṣe
gātr'|ôdvartanam ātmanaḥ
anyatra Kuntyā, bhadraṃ te,

Surely I must have committed some transgression in my childhood which offended the creator, through whose intervention I have attained such bad luck, o bull-like Bharata. Son of Pandu, look at my visible pallor, the like of which 20.15
I never had even during the worst troubles. You yourself know, Bhima, son of Pritha, what happiness I enjoyed in the past, but now I am afflicted with servitude, and without independence I cannot find any peace.

The fact that Dhanan·jaya, son of Pritha, the long-armed and terrifying bowman lives like a hidden fire suggests to me that it is the work of destiny. Partha, it is not possible for men to understand the course of living creatures' destiny, so I believe that your great fall could not have been avoided by prior planning.

Despite being an illustrious and virtuous wife, I who had all of you, like Indra, watching my face to ascertain my wishes must now watch the faces of others, my inferiors in social hierarchy. Look at my circumstances, son of Pandu. I 20.20
most assuredly do not deserve this. Despite all of you being alive, see how the times have changed! The earth as far as the ocean shores was under my control, but now I am under Sudéshna's control, and terrified of her. I had attendants in front and followers behind, but now I follow Sudéshna, going in front and behind.

Listen to this misery I've encountered, son of Kuntí. I had never even ground unguents for the body by myself, for anyone other than Kuntí, but now, bless you, I grind sandalwood. Look at my hands, son of Kuntí. They were certainly not like this before!" And, saying this, she showed him both her calloused hands. "I, who never feared either 20.25

sā pinasmy adya candanam.
paśya, Kaunteya, pāṇī me n' âiv' âbhūtāṃ hi yau purā.»
ity asya darśayāṃ āsa kiṇavantau karāv ubhau.
20.25 «bibhemi Kuntyā yā n' âhaṃ, yuṣmākaṃ vā kadā cana,
s" âdy' âgrato Virāṭasya bhītā tiṣṭhāmi kiṅkarī.,
kiṃ nu vakṣyati samrāṇ māṃ, varṇakaḥ su|kṛto, na vā.
n' ânya|piṣṭaṃ hi Matsyasya candanaṃ kila rocate.»

VAIŚAMPĀYANA uvāca:

sā kīrtayantī duḥkhāni Bhīmasenasya bhāminī
ruroda śanakaiḥ Kṛṣṇā Bhīmasenam udīkṣatī.
sā bāṣpa|kalayā vācā niḥśvasantī punaḥ punaḥ
hṛdayaṃ Bhīmasenasya ghaṭṭayant" îdam abravīt,
«n' âlpaṃ kṛtaṃ mayā, Bhīma, devānāṃ kilbiṣaṃ purā,
abhāgyā yatra jīvāmi martavye sati, Pāṇḍava.»
20.30 tatas tasyāḥ karau sūkṣmau, kiṇa|baddhau Vṛkodaraḥ
mukham ānīya vai patnyā ruroda para|vīra|hā.
tau gṛhītvā ca Kaunteyo bāṣpam utsṛjya vīryavān
tataḥ parama|duḥkh'|ārta idaṃ vacanam abravīt.

BHĪMASENA uvāca:

21.1 DHIG ASTU ME bāhu|balaṃ, Gāṇḍīvaṃ Phālgunasya ca,
yat te raktau purā bhūtvā pāṇī kṛta|kiṇāv imau!
sabhāyāṃ tu Virāṭasya karomi kadanaṃ mahat
tatra me kāraṇam bhāti Kaunteyo yat pratīkṣate.
atha vā Kīcakasy' âhaṃ pothayāmi padā śiraḥ
aiśvarya|mada|mattasya, krīḍann iva mahā|dvipaḥ.
apaśyaṃ tvāṃ yadā, Kṛṣṇe, Kīcakena padā hatām
tad" âiv' âhaṃ cikīrṣāmi Matsyānāṃ kadanaṃ mahat.
21.5 tatra māṃ dharma|rājas tu kaṭākṣeṇa nyavārayat.

Kuntí or you and your family, now stand in front of Viráta as a slave, terrified of what that great king will say to me about whether or not the unguent is well prepared, for the King of Matsya is not pleased if someone else grinds the sandalwood."

VAISHAMPÁYANA said:

Listing her miseries to Bhima·sena in this way, the passionate Krishná wept softly, fixing her gaze on Bhima·sena. Then, sighing again and again, in speech inarticulate through her tears, she spoke, stirring Bhima·sena's heart. "The offense I committed against the gods in the past must have been great, Bhima, son of Pandu, for, unfortunate though I am, I am alive, when I should be dead."

Then the slayer of enemy heroes, Vrikódara, bringing his 20.30
wife's delicate but calloused hands to his face, began to cry. Having grasped those hands, the heroic son of Kuntí shed tears, and then, suffering extreme pain, he spoke.

BHIMA·SENA said:

SHAME ON THE strength of my arms and on Phálgu- 21.1
na's Gandíva! Your hands were once red but now they have become calloused! I would have carried out a great slaughter in Viráta's court were it not for the fact that the son of Kuntí glanced at me, revealing his motive. Otherwise, like a frolicking elephant, I would have struck Kíchaka's head with my foot, intoxicated with pride in his power as he is. When I saw you, Krishná, kicked by Kíchaka's foot, I longed to carry out a mass slaughter of the Matsyas at that
very moment. But then the king of righteousness held me 21.5

tad ahaṃ tasya vijñāya sthita ev' âsmi, bhāmini.

yac ca rāṣṭrāt pracyavanaṃ, Kurūṇām a|vadhaś ca yaḥ,
Suyodhanasya, Karṇasya, Śakuneḥ Saubalasya ca,
Duḥśāsanasya pāpasya yan mayā n' āhṛtaṃ śiraḥ,
tan me dahati gātrāṇi, hṛdi śalyam iv' ârpitam.

mā dharmaṃ jahi, su|śroṇi, krodhaṃ jahi, mahā|mate.
idaṃ tu samupālambhaṃ tvatto rājā Yudhiṣṭhiraḥ
śṛṇuyād v" âpi, kalyāṇi, kṛtsnaṃ jahyāt sa jīvitam,
Dhanañjayo vā, su|śroṇi, yamau vā, tanu|madhyame.
lok'|ântara|gateṣv eṣu n' âhaṃ śakṣyāmi jīvitum.

21.10 purā Sukanyā bhāryā ca Bhārgavaṃ Cyavanaṃ vane
valmīka|bhūtaṃ śāmyantam anvapadyata bhāminī.
Nārāyaṇī c' Êndrasenā rūpeṇa yadi te śrutā,
patim anvacarad vṛddhaṃ purā varṣa|sahasriṇam.
duhitā Janakasy' âpi Vaidehī yadi te śrutā,
patim anvacarat Sītā mah"|âraṇya|nivāsinam.
rakṣasā nigrahaṃ prāpya Rāmasya mahiṣī priyā
kliśyamān" âpi, su|śroṇi, Rāmam ev' ânvapadyata.
Lopāmudrā tathā, bhīru, vayo|rūpa|samanvitā,
Agastim anvayādd hitvā kāmān sarvān a|mānuṣān.
21.15 Dyumatsena|sutaṃ vīraṃ Satyavantam a|ninditā
Sāvitry anucacār' âikā Yama|lokaṃ manasvinī.

back with a glance, and, understanding his point, I stayed quiet, passionate lady.

The fact that we left our kingdom, that there has been no murder of the Kurus and that I have failed to take the heads of Suyódhana, Karna, Súbala's son Shákuni and the wicked Duhshásana burns me to my limbs and sticks in my heart as though it were pierced by a javelin.

Don't abandon virtue, beautiful-hipped lady, and repress your anger, great-hearted woman. If King Yudhi·shthira should hear this reproach from you, he would end his whole life, lovely lady. If Dhanan·jaya and the twins should go to the next world, shapely-hipped and slender-waisted lady, I will not be able to live.

Long ago, the beautiful wife Sukánya followed Chyávana 21.10
of Bhrigu's race into the forest, and as he was in peaceful meditation he became part of an anthill. Perhaps you heard that Indra·sena, like Naráyani herself in beauty, long ago followed her husband, who was a thousand years old. Or perhaps you have heard of the Vidéhan princess, Jánaka's daughter, Sita, who followed her husband when he was living in the great forest. Rama's beloved wife was kidnapped by a *rákshasa*, and although she suffered, shapely-hipped lady, she still followed Rama. Lopa·mudra, timid lady, who was possessed of beauty and youth, followed Agásti, and
renounced all non-human pleasures, and intelligent and 21.15
virtuous Sávitri followed the brave Sátyavat, the son of Dyumat·sena, into the realm of Yama on her own.

yath" âitāḥ kīrtitā nāryo rūpavatyaḥ, pati|vratāḥ,
tathā tvam api, kalyāṇi, sarvaiḥ samuditā guṇaiḥ.
mā dīrghaṃ kṣama kālaṃ tvaṃ,
māsam ardhaṃ ca saṃmitam.
pūrṇe trayo|daśe varṣe
rājñāṃ rājñī bhaviṣyasi.

DRAUPADY uvāca:

ārtay" âitan mayā, Bhīma, kṛtaṃ bāṣpa|pramocanam,
a|pārayantyā duḥkhāni; na rājānam upālabhe.
kim uktena vyatītena, Bhīmasena mahā|bala?
pratyupasthita|kālasya kāryasy' ân|antaro bhava.
21.20 mam' êha, Bhīma, Kaikeyī rūp'|âbhibhava|śaṅkayā
nityam udvijate, rājā kathaṃ neyād imām iti.
tasyā viditvā taṃ bhāvaṃ, svayaṃ c' ân|ṛta|darśanaḥ
Kicako 'yaṃ su|duṣṭ'|ātmā sadā prārthayate hi mām.
tam ahaṃ kupitā, Bhīma, punaḥ kopaṃ niyamya ca
abruvaṃ kāma|sammūḍham: «ātmānaṃ rakṣa Kīcaka!
gandharvāṇām ahaṃ bhāryā pañcānāṃ mahiṣī priyā.
te tvāṃ nihanyuḥ kupitāḥ śūrāḥ sāhasa|kāriṇaḥ.»
evam uktaḥ su|duṣṭ'|ātmā Kīcakaḥ pratyuvāca ha:
«n' âhaṃ bibhemi, sairandhri, gandharvāṇāṃ, śuci|smite.
21.25 śataṃ śata|saharāṇi gandharvāṇām ahaṃ raṇe
samāgataṃ haniṣyāmi. tvaṃ, bhīru, kuru me kṣaṇam.»
ity ukte c' âbruvaṃ mattaṃ kām'|āturam ahaṃ punaḥ:
«na tvaṃ pratibalaś c' âiṣāṃ gandharvāṇāṃ yaśas|vinām.
dharme sthit" âsmi satataṃ, kula|śīla|samanvitā.
n' êcchāmi kañ cid vadhyantaṃ, tena jīvasi, Kīcaka.»

So like these beautiful women, devoted to their husbands, whom I have listed, you, too, beautiful girl, are possessed of every virtue. Be patient for a short while more, for there is only another fortnight to go, and then, when the thirteenth year is complete, you will become a queen of kings.

DRÁUPADI said:

I've only been crying, Bhima, because of the pain of being unable to bear my troubles, and I do not reproach the king. What is the point of dwelling on the past, mighty Bhima·sena? Be immediately ready for the work of the hour at hand.

O Bhima, Kaikéyi, overpoweringly jealous of my beauty, 21.20
is always scared that the king would have me brought to him. Aware of this, thoroughly wicked-souled Kíchaka, who has shown himself to be of false character, always propositions me. Though I am offended, Bhima, I once again restrain my anger and say to that man made foolish by lust, "Protect yourself, Kíchaka, for I am the wife and beloved queen of five *gandhárvas*, and they will kill you since they are brave and incensed at you acting rashly."

But, spoken to this way, the wicked-souled Kíchaka replied to me: "I am not afraid of *gandhárvas*, sweet-smiling
sairándhri. I will kill a hundred—hundreds of thousands 21.25
of *gandhárvas* gathered in battle, so, then, timid girl, give in this instant." When he spoke to me that way, I spoke to the lovesick and lust-ridden man again, saying: "You are no match for those splendid *gandhárvas*. I always abide by virtue and have a respectable family and good character. I do

evam uktaḥ sa duṣṭ'|ātmā prāhasat svanavat tadā.

atha māṃ tatra Kaikeyī preṣayat praṇayena tu
ten' âiva dośitā pūrvaṃ bhrātṛ|priya|cikīrṣayā,
«surām ānaya, kalyāṇi, Kīcakasya niveśanāt.»
21.30 sūta|putras tu māṃ dṛṣṭvā mahat sāntvam avartayat.
sāntve pratihate kruddhaḥ parāmarśa|man" âbhavat.

viditvā tasya saṅkalpaṃ Kīcakasya dur|ātmanaḥ
tath" âhaṃ rāja|śaraṇaṃ javen' âiva pradhāvitā.
sandarśane tu māṃ rājñaḥ sūta|putraḥ parāmṛśat.
pātayitvā tu duṣṭ'|ātmā pad" âhaṃ tena tāḍitā.
prekṣate sma Virāṭas tu, Kaṅkas tu, bahavo janāḥ:
rathinaḥ, pīṭha|mardāś ca, hasty|ārohāś ca, nai|gamāḥ.
upālabdho mayā rājā, Kaṅkaś c' âpi punaḥ punaḥ,
tato na vārito rājñā, na tasy' â|vinayaḥ kṛtaḥ.
21.35 yo 'yaṃ rājño Virāṭasya Kīcako nāma sārathiḥ
tyakta|dharmā, nṛśaṃsaś ca nara|strī|sammataḥ priyaḥ.

śūro, 'bhimānī, pāp'|ātmā, sarv'|ârtheṣu ca mugdhavān,
dār'|āmarśī, mahā|bhāga, labhate 'rthān bahūn api.
āhared api vittāni pareṣāṃ krośatām api.
na tiṣṭhate sma san|mārge, na ca dharmaṃ bubhūṣati.
pāp'|ātmā, pāpa|bhāvaś ca, kāma|bāṇa|vaś'|ânugaḥ,
a|vinītaś ca duṣṭ'|ātmā pratyākhyātaḥ punaḥ punaḥ.
darśane darśane hanyād yadi, jahyāṃ ca jīvitam!

not wish for anyone's death, and that is why you live, Kíchaka." When he heard this, the wicked-souled man laughed loudly.

Then Kaikéyi sent me, previously compromised by affection for her brother, and, wishing to do him a favor, saying, "Girl, bring wine from Kíchaka's apartment." And the *su-* 21.30
ta's son, upon seeing me, began with very gentle speech, but when his cajoling words were disregarded he became angry and violent.

Understanding wicked-hearted Kíchaka's motive, I rushed quickly to where the king was and then, in the sight of the king, the *suta*'s son attacked me. Once he had tripped me up, that wicked soul kicked me with his foot, in sight of Viráta and Kanka and many people: charioteers, companions, elephant-riders and citizens. I reproached the king and Kanka over and over again, but the king did not restrain him, nor was anything done about his rude behavior. Kí- 21.35
chaka is, after all, King Viráta's chief general, so, cruel and devoid of virtue though he may bc, he is neverthelss held dear by man and wife.

Strong, proud, sinful at heart, adulterous and lost in every object of pleasure, illustrious man, he also obtains great wealth. He takes the wealth of others for himself, even if they cry out. He never stands on the path of what is right, and is never intent on virtue. Wicked-souled, wicked in character, submissive to the arrows of lust, ill-mannered and evil-hearted, he has been rejected repeatedly, but as soon as he sees me he will rape me, and then I will definintely end my life!

tad dharme yatamānānāṃ mahān dharmo naśiṣyati.
21.40 samayaṃ rakṣyamāṇāyāṃ bhāryā vo na bhaviṣyati.
bhāryāyāṃ rakṣyamāṇāyāṃ prajā bhavati rakṣitā,
prajāyāṃ rakṣyamāṇāyām ātmā bhavati rakṣitaḥ.
ātmā hi jāyate tasyāṃ, tena Jāyāṃ vidur budhāḥ,
bhartā tu bhāryayā rakṣyaḥ, «kathaṃ jāyān mam' ôdare?»
vadatāṃ varṇa|dharmāṃś ca brāhmaṇānām iti śrutaḥ:
kṣatriyasya sadā dharmo n' ânyaḥ śatru|nibarhaṇāt.
paśayato dharma|rājasya Kīcako māṃ pad" âvadhīt,
tava c' âiva samakṣe vai, Bhīmasena mahā|bala!
tvayā hy ahaṃ paritrātā tasmād ghorāj Jaṭāsurāt.
21.45 Jayadrathaṃ tath" aiva tvam ajaiṣīr bhrātṛbhiḥ saha.
jah' îmam api pāpiṣṭhaṃ yo 'yaṃ mām avamanyate.
Kīcako rāja|vāllabhyāc
chokakṛn mama, Bhārata.
tam evaṃ kāma|saṃmattaṃ
bhinddhi, kumbham iv' âśmani.
yo nimittam an|arthānāṃ bahūnāṃ mama, Bhārata,
taṃ cej jīvantam ādityaḥ prātar abhyudayiṣyati,
viṣam ālodya pāsyāmi, mā Kīcaka|vaśam gamam.
śreyo hi maraṇaṃ mahyaṃ, Bhīmasena, tav' âgrataḥ.

VAIŚAMPĀYANA uvāca:

ity uktvā prārudat Kṛṣṇā Bhīmasy'|ôraḥ samāśritā.
Bhīmaś ca tāṃ pariṣvajya, mahat sāntvam prayujya ca,
21.50 āśvāsayitvā bahuśo bhṛśam ārtāṃ su|madhyamām,
hetu|tattv'|ârtha|saṃyuktair vacobhir Drupad'|ātmajām,

Your great virtue will be lost, as you persevere for merit
after this. You will have no wife as you protect your agree- 21.40
ment. When one's wife is protected, one's progeny is in turn protected, and, when one's progeny is protected, one's own self is in turn protected. It is because one reproduces oneself in one's wife that the wise know her as Jaya, and the husband should be protected by the wife, thinking, "How else will he be born in my womb?"

I have heard it said by the brahmins discussing the duties of the castes that the duty of the kshatriya is nothing other than always destroying foes. Kíchaka kicked me in the presence of the king of righteousness, and even in your presence, Bhima·sena of great strength! I was rescued from
that frightful Jatásura by you, and it was also you, along 21.45
with your brothers, who conquered Jayad·ratha. Now kill this most evil of men who insulted me as well. Kíchaka, due to his position as the king's favorite, makes grief for me, Bhárata. So break this man besotted with lust like a jar on a stone.

If the sun rises on him at daybreak and this man who is the cause of my many misfortunes, Bhárata, is still living, then I will mix poison and drink it to avoid becoming subject to Kíchaka's will. It is better that my death should be before yours, Bhima·sena.

VAISHAMPÁYANA said:

Having spoken in this way, Krishná wept, leaning on Bhima's chest. Bhima, embracing her, began to console her
a great deal. He comforted the violently unhappy slender- 21.50
waisted daughter of Drúpada with words filled with truth

pramṛjya vadanaṃ tasyāḥ pāṇin" âśru|samākulam,
Kīcakaṃ manas" âgacchat sṛkkiṇī parisaṃlihan.
uvāca c' âināṃ duḥkh'|ārtāṃ Bhīmaḥ krodha|samanvitaḥ:

BHĪMASENA uvāca:

22.1 TATHĀ, BHADRE, kariṣyāmi yathā tvaṃ, bhīru, bhāṣase.
adya taṃ sūdayiṣyāmi Kīcakaṃ saha|bāndhavam.
asyāḥ pradoṣe śarvaryāḥ kuruṣv' ânena saṅgatam
duḥkhaṃ śokaṃ ca nirdhūya, Yājñaseni śuci|smite.
y" âiṣā nartana|śāl" êha Matsya|rājena kāritā
div" âtra kanyā nṛtyanti, rātrau yānti yathā|gṛham.
tatr' âsti śayanaṃ divyaṃ, dṛḍh'|âṅgaṃ, su|pratiṣṭhitam.
tatr' âsya darśayiṣyāmi pūrva|pretān pitā|mahān.
22.5 yathā ca tvāṃ na paśyeyuḥ kurvāṇāṃ tena saṃvidam,
kuryās tathā tvaṃ, kalyāṇi, yathā sannihito bhavet.

VAIŚAṂPĀYANA uvāca:

tathā tau kathayitvā nu, bāṣpam utsṛjya duḥkhitau
rātri|śeṣaṃ tam atyugraṃ dhārayām āsatur hṛdi.
tasyāṃ rātryāṃ vyatītāyāṃ prātar utthāya Kīcakaḥ
gatvā rāja|kulāy' âiva Draupadīm idam abravīt:
«sabhāyāṃ paśyato rājñaḥ pātayitvā pad" âhanam,
na c' âiv' ālabhase trāṇam abhipannā balīyasā.
pravāden' êha Matsyānāṃ rājā nāmn" âyam ucyate.
aham eva hi Matsyānāṃ rājā vai vāhinī|patiḥ.
22.10 māṃ sukhaṃ pratipadyasva dāso, bhīru, bhavāmi te.
ahnāya tava, su|śroṇi, śataṃ niṣkān dadāmy aham,

and reason. When he had wiped her tearful face with his hand, he licked the corners of his mouth and pondered over Kíchaka in his mind. Full of anger, Bhima then said to the lady afflicted with pain:

BHIMA·SENA said:

I WILL DO WHAT you ask, my lovely, timid lady. I will kill 22.1
Kíchaka and his clan soon.

Sweet-smiling Yajñaséni, renounce misery and grief, and arrange a meeting with him tomorrow evening. The girls dance in the dancing hall built by the King of Matsya during the day, but at night they go home. Inside stands a celestial, sure-footed and sturdy bed, and there I will show him his
deceased ancestors. But, beautiful girl, you must arrange the 22.5
rendezvous so that there is no one nearby who will witness what happens.

VAISHAMPÁYANA said:

So they both spoke and shed their tears in their misery, enduring the last part of the night very impatiently in their hearts.

When the night had passed, Kíchaka got up in the morning, went to the palace and said this to Dráupadi: "I tripped you up and kicked you in full sight of the king, but when attacked by too strong a person you found no protection. Rumor has it that he is the king of the Matsyas in name alone. In fact, I am the king of the Matsyas, since I'm commander of the forces. So, my timid lady, treat me nicely and 22.10
I will become your slave. Beautiful-hipped girl, I will give you one hundred *nishkas* at once, and later one hundred

dāsī|śataṃ ca te dadyāṃ, dāsānāṃ api c' âparam,
rathaṃ c' âśvatarī|yuktam. astu nau, bhīru, saṅgamaḥ.»

DRAUPADY uvāca:

evaṃ me samayaṃ tv adya pratipadyasva, Kīcaka:
na tvāṃ sakhā vā, bhrātā vā jānīyāt saṅgataṃ mayā.
anupravādād bhīt" âsmi gandharvāṇāṃ yaśasvinām.
evaṃ me pratijānīhi, tato 'haṃ vaśa|gā tava.

KĪCAKA uvāca:

evam etat kariṣyāmi yathā, su|śroṇi, bhāṣase.
eko, bhadre, gamiṣyāmi śūnyam āvasathaṃ tava
22.15 samāgam'|ârthaṃ, rambh'|ôru, tvayā madana|mohitaḥ,
yathā tvāṃ n' âiva paśyeyur gandharvāḥ sūrya|varcasaḥ

DRAUPADY uvāca:

yad etan nartan'|āgāraṃ Matsya|rājena kāritam,
div" âtra kanyā nṛtyanti, rātrau yānti yathā|gṛham
tamisre tatra gacchethā, gandharvās tan na jānate.
tatra doṣaḥ parihṛto bhaviṣyati na saṃśayaḥ.

VAIŚAMPĀYANA uvāca:

tam artham api jalpantyāḥ Kṛṣṇāyāḥ Kīcakena ha
divas'|ârdhaṃ samabhavan māsen' âiva samaṃ, nṛpa.
Kīcako 'tha gṛhaṃ gatvā bhṛśaṃ harṣa|pariplutaḥ
sairandhrī|rūpiṇaṃ mūḍho mṛtyuṃ taṃ n' âvabuddhavān.
22.20 gandh'|ābharaṇa|mālyeṣu vyāsaktaḥ sa viśeṣataḥ
alañ|cakre tad" ātmānaṃ sa|tvaraḥ kāma|mohitaḥ.
tasya tat kurvataḥ karma kālo dīrgha iv' âbhavat,

slave girls and one hundred slaves will be given to you, as well as a chariot yoked with mules, so let's unite, timid lady."

DRÁUPADI said:

Kíchaka, these are my terms for doing this with you: neither your friends nor your brothers should know about your relationship with me. I am afraid of a rumor reaching those splendid *gandhárvas*. Promise me this, and then I will obey your will.

KÍCHAKA said:

I will do just as you say, shapely-hipped lady, and I will go alone, my dear, without companions to your apartment
for our rendezvous, plaintain-thighed girl, infatuated with 22.15
love for you, so that those *gandhárvas*, resplendent as the sun, do not see you.

DRÁUPADI said:

When it's dark, go to the town's dance hall, which was built by the King of Matsya, where the girls dance in the day, but leave at night to go home, since the *gandhárvas* do not know it. There doubtless we will avoid blame.

VAISHAMPÁYANA said:

The afternoon seemed as long as a month to Krishná, as she reflected on the subject of her conversation with Kícha-ka, my king. But Kíchaka, a fool unaware that death bore the guise of a *sairándhri*, went home, overwhelmed with
excessively violent lust. Made foolish with desire, he was 22.20
intently engaged in hurriedly attaching garlands, ornaments and fragrances to himself, and while he was doing this he was thinking of the large-eyed lady, and the time seemed to

anucintayataś c' âpi tām ev' āyata|locanām.
āsīd abhyadhikā c' âpi śrīḥ śriyaṃ pramumukṣataḥ,
nirvāṇa|kāle dīpasya vartīm iva didhakṣataḥ.
kṛta|saṃpratyayas tasyāḥ Kīcakaḥ kāma|mohitaḥ
n' âjānād divasaṃ yāntaṃ cintayānaḥ samāgamam.
tatas tu Draupadī gatvā tadā Bhīmaṃ mahānase
upātiṣṭhata kalyāṇī Kauravyaṃ patim antikam.
22.25 tam uvāca su|keśāntā: «Kīcakasya mayā kṛtaḥ
saṅgamo nartan'|āgāre, yath" âvocaḥ, paran|tapa.
śūnyaṃ sa nartan'|āgāram āgamiṣyati Kīcakaḥ
eko niśi, mahā|bāho. Kīcakaṃ taṃ niṣūdaya.
taṃ sūta|putraṃ, Kaunteya, Kīcakaṃ mada|darpitam
gatvā tvaṃ nartan'|āgāraṃ nirjīvaṃ kuru, Pāṇḍava.
darpāc ca sūta|putro 'sau gandharvān avamanyate.
taṃ tvaṃ, praharatāṃ śreṣṭha, hradān nāgam iv' ôddhara.
aśru duḥkh'|âbhibhūtāyā mama mārjasva, Bhārata,
ātmanaś c' âiva, bhadraṃ te, kuru mānaṃ kulasya ca.»

BHĪMASENA uvāca:

22.30 svāgataṃ te, var'|ārohe! yan māṃ vedayase priyam,
na hy anyaṃ kañ cid icchāmi sahāyaṃ, vara|varṇini.
yā me prītis tvay" ākhyātā Kīcakasya samāgame
hatvā Hiḍimbaṃ sā prītir mam' āsid, vara|varṇini.
satyaṃ, bhrātṝś ca, dharmaṃ ca puras|kṛtya bravīmi te,
Kīcakaṃ nihaniṣyāmi, Vṛtraṃ deva|patir yathā.
taṃ gahvare, prakāśe vā pothayiṣyāmi Kīcakam.

drag. His beauty, though about to be extinguished like the wick of an eagerly burning lamp, was extraordinary. Kíchaka had complete faith in Dráupadi, for he was made foolish by lust, and he did not notice that the day had passed as he dwelled on the meeting.

But beautiful Dráupadi entered her Kuru husband's presence in the kitchen, and stood before him. The lady with 22.25
lovely curly-tipped hair said to him: "Just as you told me, the meeting with Kíchaka has been arranged for the dancing hall, scorcher of your enemy. Kíchaka will arrive alone at the empty dancing hall at night, long-armed man, so kill Kíchaka! Son of Kuntí, go to the dancing hall and make sure that Kíchaka, the son of the *suta*, who is haughty with arrogance, dies, Pándava.

For it is because of his arrogance that the *suta*'s son disrespects the *gandhárva*s. Greatest of aggressors, raise him up just as Krishna raised the *naga* from the water. Bhárata, wash away my tears, since I am afflicted with grief, and defend both your own honor and that of the Kuru race, bless you."

BHIMA·SENA said:

Welcome, shapely-hipped lady! I wish for no other as- 22.30
sistance than the good news you give me, flawlessly complexioned lady. The joy I feel as you tell me of my meeting with Kíchaka is that same exhilaration I felt when I killed Hidímba, flawless-complexioned lady. I swear to you truthfully, by my brothers and the law first and foremost, that I will kill Kíchaka just as the lord of the gods killed Vritra. Regardless of whether it be in secret or in the open, I will

atha ced api yotsyanti, hiṃse Matsyān api dhruvam!
tato Duryodhanaṃ hatvā pratipatsye vasun|dharām.
kāmaṃ Matsyam upāstāṃ hi Kuntī|putro Yudhiṣṭhiraḥ!

DRAUPADY uvāca:

22.35 yathā na santyajethās tvaṃ satyaṃ vai mat|kṛte, vibho,
nigūḍhas tvaṃ tathā, Pārtha, Kīcakaṃ taṃ niṣūdaya.

BHĪMASENA uvāca:

evam etat kariṣyāmi, yathā tvaṃ, bhīru, bhāṣase.
adya taṃ sūdayiṣyāmi Kīcakaṃ saha bāndhavaiḥ
a|dṛśyamānas tasy' âtha tamasvinyām, a|nindite,
nāgo bilvam iv' ākramya pothayiṣyāmy ahaṃ śiraḥ
a|labhyām icchatas tasya Kīcakasya dur|ātmanaḥ.

VAIŚAMPĀYANA said:

Bhīmo 'tha prathamaṃ gatvā rātrau channa upāviśat,
mṛgaṃ harir iv' â|dṛśyaḥ pratyākāṅkṣata Kīcakam.
Kīcakaś c' âpy alaṅ|kṛtya yathā|kāmam upāgamat
taṃ velaṃ nartan'|āgāraṃ Pāñcālī|saṅgam'|āśayā.
22.40 manyamānaḥ sa saṅketam āgāraṃ prāviśac ca tat.
pravíśya ca sa tad veśma tamasā saṃvṛtaṃ mahat,
pūrv'|āgataṃ tatas tatra Bhīmam a|pratim'|âujasam
ek'|ânt'|âvasthitaṃ ca tam āsasāda sa dur|matiḥ.
śayānaṃ śayane tatra sūta|putraḥ parāmṛṣat
jājvalyamānaṃ kopena Kṛṣṇā|dharṣaṇa|jena ha.
upasaṅgamya c' âiv' âinaṃ Kīcakaḥ kāma|mohitaḥ
harṣ'|ônmathita|citt'|ātmā smayamāno 'bhyabhāṣata:

destroy Kíchaka, and if the Matsyas should fight for him then I will certainly kill them, too! Then, when I have killed Duryódhana, I will recover the earth. Let Yudhi·shthira, the son of Kuntí, serve the King of Matsya's whim!

DRÁUPADI said:

My lord, kill Kíchaka in secret so that you should not 22.35
need to renounce that which you have truly sworn to me, son of Pritha.

BHIMA·SENA said:

I will do it as you instruct, timid lady, and I will kill Kíchaka and his relatives today, unseen in the darkness of night, faultless lady. Just as an elephant crushes the woodapple tree, so I will crush the head of wicked-souled Kíchaka, who lusts after what is not his to take.

VAISHAMPÁYANA said:

First thing that night, Bhima sat down in disguise, expecting Kíchaka, like a lion lying hidden expecting a deer. Then, when Kíchaka had decorated himself to his liking, he came to the dancing hall at the arranged time in the hope
of meeting Pancháli, and reflecting on their rendezvous, he 22.40
entered the building.

Once he had entered the apartment cloaked in thick darkness, that wicked-minded man approached Bhima of unequaled power, who had come earlier and was settled in his place. The *suta*'s son touched him as he lay in the bed, burning with rage owing to the offense to Krishná. Foolish from lust, Kíchaka even came close, his heart and soul whirling with joy, and, smiling, he said:

«prāpitaṃ te mayā vittaṃ bahu|rūpam an|antakam,
yat kṛtaṃ dhana|ratn'|āḍhyaṃ dāsī|śata|paricchadam,
22.45 rūpa|lāvaṇya|yuktābhir yuvatībhir alaṅ|kṛtam
gṛhaṃ c' ântaḥ|puraṃ, su|bhru, krīḍā|rati|virājitam.
tat sarvaṃ tvāṃ samuddiśya sahas" âham upāgataḥ.
a|kasmān māṃ praśaṃsanti sadā gṛha|gatāḥ striyaḥ,
‹su|vāsā, darśanīyaś ca n' ânyo 'sti tvādṛśaḥ pumān!›»

BHĪMSENA uvāca:

diṣṭyā tvaṃ darśanīyo 'si, diṣṭy" ātmānaṃ praśaṃsasi!
īdṛśas tu tvayā sparśaḥ spṛṣṭa|pūrvo na karhi cit.
sparśaṃ vetsi vidagdhas tvaṃ kāma|dharma|vicakṣaṇaḥ!
strīṇāṃ prīti|karo n' ânyas tvat|samaḥ puruṣas tv iha!

VAIŚAṂPĀYANA uvāca:

ity uktvā taṃ mahā|bāhur Bhīmo bhīma|parākramaḥ
sahas" ôtpatya Kaunteyaḥ prahasy' êdam uvāca ha,
22.50 «adya tvāṃ bhaginī pāpaṃ kṛṣyamāṇaṃ mayā bhuvi
drakṣyate 'dri|pratīkāśaṃ, siṃhen' êva maha|gajam.
nirābādhā tvayi hate sairandhrī vicariṣyati,
sukham eva cariṣyanti sairandhryāḥ patayaḥ sadā.»
tato jagrāha keśeṣu mālyavatsu mahā|balaḥ.
sa keśeṣu parāmṛṣṭo balena balināṃ varaḥ,
ākṣipya keśān vegena bāhvor jagrāha Pāṇḍavam.
bāhu|yuddhaṃ tayor āsīt kruddhayor nara|siṃhayoḥ,
vasante vāsitā|hetor balavad gajayor iva,
Kīcakānāṃ tu mukhyasya, narāṇām uttamasya ca,

"I have given you the infinite and varied possessions I earned: wealth abounding in jewels, a retinue of a hundred slave girls, a house furnished with young beautiful and ele- 22.45
gant women to do the work, and interior apartments with glorious pleasures and pastimes, beautiful-browed girl. I came here quickly after I designated all this for you and inexplicably women came from the house and kept incessantly praising me, saying, 'There is no man to match you in good looks and dress sense!'"

BHIMA·SENA said:

I congratulate you on your handsomeness and I congratulate you on your self-adulation! Your touch was never quite like this in the past. You have mastered caresses, you are an expert and you are experienced in the art of love! You give women pleasure and there is no man like you!

VAISHAMPÁYANA said:

Having said this, long-armed Kauntéya, Bhima of terrifying prowess, got up quickly and, laughing, said, "Today your 22.50
sister will see me drag you to the ground, wretch that you are, like a mighty elephant being brought down by a lion. When you are dead, the *sairándhri* will live unmolested, and the *sairándhri*'s husbands will always live happily."

Then the hugely powerful man seized Kíchaka by his garlanded hair, but when that foremost of mighty men was violently grabbed by the hair, he freed his hair forcibly and seized the son of Pandu's arms. So a bare fistfight broke out between those two furious lion-like men; the head of the Kíchaka clan and that most excellent man, like a pair of
mighty elephants for a female elephant in spring, or like 22.55

22.55 Vāli|Sugrīvayor bhrātroḥ pur" êva kapi|siṃhayoḥ.
anyonyam api saṃrabdhau, paraspara|jay'|âiṣiṇau
tataḥ samudyamya bhujau,
pañca|śīrṣāv iv' ôragau,
nakha|daṃṣṭrābhir anyonyaṃ
ghnantaḥ krodha|viṣ'|ôddhatau.
vegen' âbhihato Bhīmaḥ Kīcakena balīyasā
sthira|pratijñaḥ sa raṇe padān na calitaḥ padam.
tāv anyonyaṃ samāśliṣya prakarṣantau paras|param
ubhāv api prakāśete pravṛddhau vṛṣabhāv iva.
tayor hy āsīt su|tumulaḥ saṃprahāraḥ su|dāruṇaḥ
nakha|dant'|āyudhavator vyāghrayor iva dṛptayoḥ.
22.60 abhipaty' âtha bāhubhyāṃ pratyagṛhṇād a|marṣitaḥ,
mātaṅga iva mātaṅgaṃ prabhinna|karaṭā|mukham.
sa c' âpy enaṃ tadā Bhīmaḥ pratijagrāha vīryavān
tam ākṣipat Kīcako 'tha balena balināṃ varaḥ.
tayor bhuja|viniṣpeṣād ubhayor balinos tadā
śabdaḥ samabhavad ghoro veṇu|sphoṭa|samo yudhi.
ath' âinam ākṣipya balād gṛha|madhye Vṛkodaraḥ
dhūtayām āsa vegena, vāyuś caṇḍa iva drumam.
Bhīmena ca parāmṛṣṭo dur|balo balinā raṇe
prāspandata yathā|prāṇaṃ,vicakarṣa ca Pāṇḍavam
22.65 īṣad|ākalitaṃ c' âpi krodhād druta|padaṃ sthitam.
Kīcako balavān Bhīmaṃ jānubhyām ākṣipad bhuvi.
pātito bhuvi Bhīmas tu Kīcakena balīyasā
utpapāt' âtha vegena, daṇḍa|pāṇir iv' Ântakaḥ.

the fight long ago, between the brothers Valin and Sugríva, lions among monkeys.

Both were furiously angry, each eager for victory over the other. Both raised their arms like five-headed serpents, then both men attacked each other with their nails and teeth in unbridled anger. When forcibly attacked by the mighty Kíchaka with force, the faithful Bhima did not move his feet one step in the onslaught. As they were locked together and dragging each other along, both shone like fully grown boars.

The battle between the two of them was extremely fierce and cruel, since they fought with teeth and nails like wild
tigers. Then they threw each other over, impatient with 22.60
grappling arms like a pair of elephants facing each other with split temples. The heroic Bhima seized Kíchaka but Kíchaka, himself marvelously strong, then violently threw him down.

During the fight between those two powerful men, a terrifying noise like splitting bamboo resounded from the collision of their arms. Vrikódara threw Kíchaka forcefully inside the room and shook him savagely, just as a hurricane-force wind shakes a tree. Attacked by mighty Bhima in the fight, he became weak and trembled, though he hit out at
the son of Pandu as much as his breath would allow, and, a 22.65
little shaken, the son of Pandu even took a quick step back in anger when seized. So mighty Kíchaka felled Bhima to his knees on the floor, but Bhima, tripped to the ground by the mighty Kíchaka, quickly rose up again like Yama, mace in hand.

sparghayā ca bal'|ônmattau tāv ubhau Sūta|Pāṇḍavau
niśīthe paryakarṣetāṃ balinau nirjane sthale.
tatas tad bhavanaṃ śreṣṭhaṃ prākampata muhur|muhuḥ,
balavac c' âpi saṃkruddhāv anyonyaṃ prati garjataḥ.
talābhyām sa tu Bhīmena vakṣasy abhihato balī
Kīcako roṣa|saṃtaptaḥ padān na calitaḥ padam.
22.70 muhūrtaṃ tu sa taṃ vegaṃ sahitvā bhuvi duḥ|saham
balād ahīyata tadā sūto Bhīma|bal'|ârditaḥ.

tam hīyamānaṃ vijñāya Bhīmaseno mahā|balaḥ
vakṣasy ānīya vegena mamard' âinaṃ vicetasam.
krodh'|āviṣṭo viniḥśvasya punaś c' âinaṃ Vṛkodaraḥ
jagrāha jayatāṃ śreṣṭhaḥ keśeṣv eva tadā bhṛśam.
gṛhītvā Kīcakaṃ Bhīmo virarāja mahā|balaḥ,
śardūlaḥ piśit'|ākāṅkṣī gṛhītv' êva mahā|mṛgam.
tata enam pariśrāntam upalabhya Vṛkodaraḥ
yojayām āsa bāhubhyāṃ, paśuṃ raśanayā yathā.
22.75 nadantaṃ ca mahā|nādaṃ bhinna|bherī|sama|svanam
bhrāmayām āsa su|ciraṃ visphurantam a|cetasam.
pragṛhya tarasā dorbhyāṃ kaṇṭhaṃ tasya Vṛkodaraḥ
apīḍayata Kṛṣṇāyās tadā kop'|ôpaśāntaye.

atha taṃ bhagna|sarv'|āṅgaṃ, vyāviddha|nayan'|âmbaram
ākramya ca kaṭī|deśe jānunā Kīcak'|âdhamam
apīḍayata bāhubhyāṃ paśu|māram amārayat.
taṃ viṣīdantam ājñāya Kīcakaṃ Pāṇḍu|nandanaḥ
bhūtale bhrāmayām āsa, vākyaṃ c' êdam uvāca ha,
«ady' âham an|ṛṇo bhūtvā bhrātur bhāry"|âpahāriṇam
śāntiṃ labdho 'smi paramāṃ hatvā sairandhri|kaṇṭakam.»

Intoxicated with their own strength, both the mighty *suta* and the son of Pandu harassed the other in that lonely spot in the middle of the night. As they roared at each other in their fury, the excellent, sturdy building kept trembling incessantly. When Bhima struck him on the chest with the flat of his hands, mighty Kíchaka blazed with rage, but did not budge an inch. Having endured that unbearable 22.70
earthly force, the *suta* became weakened, afflicted by Bhima's strength.

Noticing that he was weakening, enormously powerful Bhima·sena violently pulled him to his chest and pounded him into near-unconsciousness. Vrikódara, the best of victors, absorbed in his anger, kept breathing hard and seized Kíchaka violently by the hair. The glistening and enormously powerful Bhima took hold of Kíchaka and roared like a tiger greedy for meat, which has just caught a huge deer. Vrikódara then took hold of him, when he was totally exhausted, and bound him with his arms, like a beast with rope. Then for a long while he spun the quivering and in- 22.75
sensible Kíchaka, who kept roaring loudly and bellowing like a broken trumpet. Vrikódara quickly grasped his neck in his arms and squeezed in order to soothe Krishná's anger.

Then, with his knees, he attacked the waist of that vilest of the Kíchakas, all of whose various limbs were broken and whose eyes were closed, and he squeezed him with his arms and killed him as one slaughters beasts. When the Pándava realized that Kíchaka was motionless, he rolled him on the floor, and said these words, "Now that I have killed the thorn in the *sairándhri*'s side, the man who wanted to

22.80 ity evam uktvā puruṣa|pravīras
tam Kīcakaṃ krodha|sarāga|netraḥ
āsrasta|vastr'|ābharaṇaṃ sphurantam
udbhrānta|netraṃ vyasum utsasarja.
niṣpiṣya pāṇinā pāṇiṃ saṃdaṣṭ'|âuṣṭha|puṭaṃ balī,
samākramya ca saṃkruddho balena balināṃ varaḥ,
tasya pādau ca, pāṇī ca, śiro, grīvāṃ ca sarvaśaḥ
kāye praveśayām āsa, paśor iva Pināka|dhṛk.
tam sammathita|sarv'|âṅgaṃ,
māṃsa|piṇḍ'|ôpamaṃ kṛtam
Kṛṣṇāyā darśayām āsa
Bhīmaseno mahā|balaḥ.
uvāca ca mahā|tejā Draupadīṃ yoṣitāṃ varām:
«paśy' âinam, ehi, Pāñcāli, kāmuko 'yaṃ yathā kṛtaḥ!»
22.85 evam uktvā mahā|rājo Bhīmo bhīma|parākramaḥ
pādena pīḍayām āsa tasya kāyaṃ dur|ātmanaḥ.
tato 'gniṃ tatra prajvālya, darśayitvā tu Kīcakam,
Pāñcālīṃ sa tadā vīra idaṃ vacanam abravīt:
«prārthayanti, su|keś'|ânte, ye tvāṃ śīla|guṇ'|ânvitām,
evaṃ te, bhīru, vadhyante, Kīcakaḥ śobhate yathā.»
tat kṛtvā duṣ|karaṃ karma Kṛṣṇāyāḥ priyam uttamam,
tathā sa Kīcakam hatvā, gatvā roṣasya vai śamam,
āmantrya Draupadīṃ Kṛṣṇāṃ kṣipram āyān mahānasam.
Kīcakaṃ ghātayitvā tu Draupadī yoṣitāṃ varā
prahṛṣṭā, gata|saṃtāpā sabhā|pālān uvāca ha:
22.90 «Kīcako 'yaṃ hataḥ śete gandharvaiḥ patibhir mama,
para|strī|kāma|saṃmattas. tatr' āgacchata, paśyata.»

violate our wife, I am released from my debt to my brothers and I have found supreme peace."

Then that foremost of men, eyes red from anger, let go of 22.80
the still trembling Kíchaka, whose clothes and ornaments had fallen loose, and whose eyes were rolling. Rubbing his hands together and biting his lips, that furious, mighty and extremely powerful man pummeled him again, forcing all his legs, arms, head and neck inside the trunk of his body, like the trident-bearer did to the beast.*

When he had crushed all his limbs and turned him into a lump of flesh, the mighty Bhima·sena showed him to Krishná. The man of great splendor said to Dráupadi, the foremost of women: "Look, Pancháli, at what has happened
to this lustful man!" Once he had said this, Bhima, the 22.85
great king of terrifying prowess, pressed that wicked-souled man's body down with his foot. Then he lit a torch and showed Kíchaka to Pancháli, and the hero said these words: "Those who proposition you, lady with lovely curly-tipped hair, though you have a good character and virtues, will be slaughtered, timid one, just as Kíchaka has been killed." Now that he had completed this difficult task, but one most dear to Krishná, he became calm after his wrath, and once he had said goodbye to Dráupadi Krishná he quickly returned to the kitchen.

Now that Dráupadi, the most excellent of women, had brought about Kíchaka's death, she was delighted, for her grief was gone, and she said to the keepers of the assembly:
"Come and see how Kíchaka, who was intoxicated with lust 22.90
for other people's wives, lies dead, killed by my *gandhárva* husbands."

tac chrutvā bhāṣitaṃ tasyā nartan'|āgāra|rakṣiṇaḥ
sahas" âiva samājagmur ādāy'|ôlkāḥ sahasraśaḥ.
tato gatv" âtha tad veśma Kīcakaṃ vinipātitam
gat'|âsuṃ dadṛśur bhūmau rudhireṇa samukṣitam.
pāṇi|pāda|vihīnaṃ tu dṛṣṭvā ca vyathit" âbhavan,
nirīkṣanti tataḥ sarve paraṃ vismayam āgatāḥ.
a|mānuṣaṃ kṛtaṃ karma taṃ dṛṣṭvā vinipātitam,
«kv' âsya grīvā? kva caraṇau? kva pāṇī? kva siras tathā?»
iti sma taṃ parīkṣante gandharveṇa hataṃ tadā.

VAIŚAMPĀYANA uvāca:

23.1 TASMIN KĀLE samāgamya sarve tatr' âsya bāndhavāḥ
ruruduḥ Kīcakaṃ dṛṣṭvā, parivārya samantataḥ.
sarve saṃhṛṣṭa|romāṇaḥ, saṃtrastāḥ prekṣya Kīcakam,
tathā saṃbhinna|sarv'|âṅgaṃ, kūrmaṃ sthala iv' ôddhṛtam,
pothitaṃ Bhīmasenena tam, Indreṇ' êva dānavam.
saṃskārayitum icchanto bahir netuṃ pracakramuḥ.
dadṛśus te tataḥ Kṛṣṇāṃ sūta|putrāḥ samāgatāḥ
a|dūrāc c' ân|avady'|âṅgīṃ stambham āliṅgya tiṣṭhatīm.
23.5 samaveteṣu sarveṣu tām ūcur upakīcakāḥ,
«hanyatāṃ śīghram asatī, yat|kṛte Kīcako hataḥ!
atha vā n' âiva hantavyā, dahyatāṃ kāminā saha.
mṛtasy' âpi priyaṃ kāryaṃ sūta|putrasya sarvathā.»

Hearing her words, the dancing-hall guards came quickly in their thousands, holding torches. Once they had gone into the room, they saw Kíchaka thrown down to the ground, dead, and spattered with red blood. Seeing him without his arms and legs, they were horrified, and as they all gazed at him they were astounded. Having witnessed the inhuman assault that had been perpetrated, they said, "Where is his neck? Where are his legs? Where are his arms, and where is his head?" Seeing him this way they concluded that he was killed by a *gandhárva*.

VAISHAMPÁYANA said:

AT THAT TIME, all his relatives arrived, and, surrounding 23.1
Kíchaka on all sides, they cried when they saw him. They were all terrified and their hair stood on end upon seeing him with all his limbs shattered, like a tortoise dragged out to dry land, crushed by Bhima·sena as if he were a *dánava* crushed by Indra.

They took him outside, for they wished to perform the last rites. The *suta* clansmen gathered together and caught sight of faultless-limbed Krishná nearby, as she stood clinging to a pillar. When they were all gathered together, the 23.5
Kíchakas shouted, "Let that unfaithful wife be put to death, for Kíchaka was slaughtered for her sin! Or if she should not be killed in this way then let her be cremated with the man who lusted for her! We should act in complete accordance with what the dead *suta*'s son would have wanted."

tato Virāṭam ucus te: «Kīcako 'syāḥ kṛte hataḥ.
sah' ânen' âdya dahyema. tad anujñātum arhasi.»
parākramaṃ tu sūtānāṃ matvā rāj" ânvamodata
sairandhryāḥ Sūta|putreṇa saha dāhaṃ viśām patiḥ.
tāṃ samāsādya vitrastāṃ Kṛṣṇāṃ kamala|locanām
momuhyamānāṃ te tatra jagṛhuḥ Kīcakā bhṛśam.
23.10 tatas tu tāṃ samāropya, nibadhya ca su|madhyamām
jagmur udyamya te sarve śmaśān' âbhimukhās tadā.
hriyamāṇā tu sā, rājan, sūta|putrair a|ninditā
prākrośan nātham icchantī Kṛṣṇā nāthavatī satī.

DRAUPADY uvāca:

Jayo, Jayanto, Vijayo, Jayatseno, Jayadbalaḥ,
te me vācaṃ vijānantu! Sūta|putrā nayanti mām!
yeṣāṃ jyā|tala|nirghoṣo visphūrjitam iv' âśaneḥ
vyaśrūyata mahā|yuddhe bhīma|ghoṣas tarasvinām,
ratha|ghoṣaś ca balavān gandharvāṇāṃ tarasvinām,
te me vācaṃ vijānantu: sūta|putrā nayanti mām!

VAIŚAMPĀYANA uvāca:

23.15 tasyās tāḥ kṛpaṇā vācaḥ Kṛṣṇāyāḥ paridevitam
śrutv" âiv' âbhyāpatad Bhīmaḥ śayanād a|vicārayan.

BHĪMASENA uvāca:

ahaṃ śṛṇomi te vācaṃ tvayā, sairandhri, bhāṣitām.
tasmāt te Sūta|putrebhyo bhayaṃ, bhīru, na vidyate!

Then they said to Viráta: "Kíchaka has been killed for her misconduct, so now we will cremate him with another. You ought to give your permission." Aware of the *sutas'* great prowess, the king, the lord of earth, gave his permission for the *sairándhri* to be burned with the *suta's* son. So the Kíchakas came up to the terrified and bewildered, lotus-
eyed Krishná and seized her violently. Having placed the 23.10
slender-waisted girl on the bier and tied her up, they all picked her up and went toward the cemetery. Carried off by the *suta's* sons, my king, the blameless and chaste Krishná, who had her husbands for protection, longed for the appearance of her guardian hero.

DRÁUPADI said:

Jaya, Jayánta, Víjaya, Jayat·sena and Jayad·bala hear my words! The *suta's* sons are leading me away! May the swift, energetic *gandhárvas*, whose terrifying roars are heard in battle, whose bowstring produces a deafening twang like the roar of thunder and the sound of whose chariot is deafening, perceive my words: the sons of the *suta* are leading me away!

VAISHAMPÁYANA said:

Hearing miserable Krishná's plaintive words, Bhima got 23.15
up from his bed without hesitating.

BHIMA·SENA said:

I have heard what you said, *sairándhri*, and so, timid lady, you should not be afraid of the *suta* clan!

VAIŚAMPĀYANA uvāca:

ity uktvā sa mahā|bāhur vijajṛmbhe jighāṃsayā.
tataḥ sa vyāyataṃ kṛtvā veṣaṃ, viparivartya ca,
a|dvāreṇ' âbhyavaskandya nirjagāma bahis tadā.
sa Bhīmasenaḥ prākārād āruhya tarasā drumam
śmaśān' âbhimukhaḥ prāyād, yatra te Kīcakā gatāḥ.
sa laṅghayitvā prākāraṃ, niḥsṛtya ca pur'|ôttamāt,
javena patito Bhīmaḥ sūtānām agratas tadā.
23.20 citā|samīpe gatvā sa tatr' âpaśyad vanas|patim
tāla|mātraṃ, mahā|skandhaṃ, mūrdha|śuṣkaṃ, viśām pate.
taṃ nāgavad upakramya, bāhubhyāṃ parirabhya ca
skandham āropayām āsa daśa|vyāmaṃ paran|tapaḥ.
sa taṃ vṛkṣaṃ daśa|vyāmaṃ sa|skandha|viṭapaṃ balī
pragṛhy' âbhyadravat sūtān, daṇḍa|pāṇir iv' Ântakaḥ.

ūru|vegena tasy' âtha nyagrodh'|âśvattha|kiṃśukāḥ
bhūmau nipatitā vṛkṣāḥ saṅghaśas tatra śerate.
taṃ siṃham iva saṃkruddhaṃ dṛṣṭvā gandharvam āgatam
vitresuḥ sarvaśaḥ sūtā viṣāda|bhaya|kampitāḥ.
23.25 «gandharvo balavān eti kruddha, udyamya pādapam!
sairandhrī mucyatāṃ śīghraṃ, yato no bhayam āgatam!»
te tu dṛṣṭvā tam āviddhaṃ Bhīmasenena pādapam
vimucya Draupadīṃ tatra prādravan nagaraṃ prati.

dravatas tāṃs tu saṃprekṣya sa vajrī dānavān iva
śataṃ pañc'|âdhikaṃ Bhīmaḥ prāhiṇod Yama|sādanam
vṛkṣeṇ' aitena, rāj'|êndra, prabhañjana|suto balī.
tata āśvāsayat Kṛṣṇāṃ sa vimucya, viśāṃ|pate.

VAISHAMPÁYANA said:

Having said this, the long-armed man stretched, keen to kill, and completely changed his outfit. Then Bhima·sena leaped through a forbidden door and rushed outside. He quickly climbed up a tree and over a wall and then made his way toward the cemetery where the Kíchakas had gone. Once he had leaped across the wall and left the most excellent city, Bhima quickly flew to where the *suta*s were.

As he approached the funeral pyre he saw a massive forest 23.20
tree, as big as a palm tree, with a huge trunk but a shriveled top, lord of earth. The scorcher of foes took hold of the tree, measuring ten *vyama*s, with his arms, uprooted it like an elephant, and then put it on his shoulder. Next, the mighty man, holding the tree, which spanned ten *vyama*s in branches and trunk, rushed to where the *suta*s were like Yama, mace in hand.

The banyans, fig trees and *kínshuka* trees fell to the ground at the force of his thighs and lay there in clumps. Seeing the *gandhárva* approaching them like a furious lion, the *suta*s were completely terrified and trembled with de-
spondency and fear. "The mighty *gandhárva* is furious and 23.25
has uprooted a tree! Quickly release the *sairándhri*, for she is the reason we are in this danger!" Eyeing the tree that Bhima·sena had uprooted, they released Dráupadi and ran back to the city.

Watching them running away, Bhima, the mighty son of the wind god, like the wielder of the thunderbolt killing the *dánava*s, dismissed at least one hundred and five to the house of Yama with that tree, lord of kings. Then, once he untied her, he comforted Krishná, lord of earth. The

uvāca ca mahā|bāhuḥ Pāñcālīṃ tatra Draupadīm
aśru|pūrṇa|mukhīṃ dīnāṃ dur|dharṣaḥ sa Vṛkodaraḥ:
23.30 «evaṃ te, bhīru, vadhyante ye tvāṃ kliśyanty an|āgasam.
praihi tvaṃ nagaraṃ, Kṛṣṇe, na bhayaṃ vidyate tava.
anyen' âhaṃ gamiṣyāmi Virāṭasya mahānasam.»

pañc'|âdhikaṃ śataṃ tac ca nihataṃ tena, Bhārata,
mahā|vanam iva cchinnaṃ śiśye vigalita|drumam.
evaṃ te nihatā, rājan, śataṃ pañca ca Kīcakāḥ,
sa ca senā|patiḥ pūrvam, ity etat Sūta|ṣaṭ|śatam.
tad dṛṣṭvā mahad āścaryaṃ narā nāryaś ca saṅgatāḥ
vismayaṃ paramaṃ gatvā n' ôcuḥ kiñ cana, Bhārata.

VAIŚAṂPĀYANA uvāca:

24.1 TE DṚṢṬVĀ NIHATĀN Sūtān rājñe gatvā nyavedayan,
«gandharvair nihatā, rājan, sūta|putrā mahā|balāḥ.
yatha vajreṇa vai dīrṇaṃ parvatasya mahac chiraḥ,
vyatikīrṇāḥ pradṛśyante tathā sūtā mahī|tale.
sairandhrī ca vimukt" âsau punar āyāti te gṛham.
sarvaṃ saṃśayitaṃ, rājan, nagaraṃ te bhaviṣyati.
yathā|rūpā ca sairandhrī, gandharvāś ca mahā|balāḥ,
puṃsām iṣṭaś ca viṣayo maithunāya na saṃśayaḥ.
24.5 yathā sairandhri|doṣeṇa na te, rājann, idaṃ puram
vināśam eti vai kṣipraṃ, tathā nītir vidhīyatām.»

long-armed and indomitable Vrikódara said to the miserable Princess of Pancháli, Dráupadi, whose face was full of tears: "So, timid lady, this is how those who torment you, 23.30
though you are sinless, are killed. Go back to the city, Krishná, you no longer have anything to fear. I will go to Viráta's kitchen another way."

So, Bhárata, he destroyed at least one hundred and five, and they lay there as if they were a great forest of chopped, felled trees. So it was that one hundred and five Kíchakas were killed, my king. Counting the commander of the army, who was killed first, it was one hundred and six *suta*s in the end. When men and women gathered together and saw this extraordinarily astounding incident, they were overcome with the greatest astonishment and no one could speak, Bhárata.

VAISHAMPÁYANA said:

WHEN THEY SAW the dead *suta*s, they went to the king and 24.1
related it: "King, the *suta*'s mighty sons were killed by the *gandhárva*s. The *suta*s can be seen scattered on the surface of the ground like massive mountain peaks dislodged by the force of the wind. The *sairándhri* has been released and has returned to the palace. The whole city will be in turmoil, my king. The *sairándhri* is beautiful and the *gandhárva*s exceedingly powerful, and without doubt men's primary
concern is sex. Therefore, king, quickly arrange matters to 24.5
prevent our city's being annihilated because of the wrongs done to the *sairándhri*."

teṣāṃ tad vacanaṃ śrutvā Virāṭo vāhinī|patiḥ
abravīt, «kriyatām eṣāṃ Sūtānāṃ parama|kriyā.
ekasminn eva te sarve su|samiddhe hut'|âśane
dahyantāṃ Kīcakāḥ śīghraṃ, ratnair gandhaiś ca sarvaśaḥ.»
Sudeṣṇām abravīd rājā mahiṣīṃ jāta|sādhvasaḥ:
«sairandhrīm āgatāṃ brūyā mam' âiva vacanād idam:
‹gaccha, sairandhri, bhadraṃ te, yathā|kāmaṃ, var'|ānane.
bibheti rājā, su|śroṇi, gandharvebhyaḥ parābhavāt.›
24.10 na hi tām utsahe vaktuṃ svayaṃ gandharva|rakṣitām.
striyas tv a|doṣās tāṃ vaktum atas tvāṃ prabravīmy aham.»
atha muktā bhayāt Kṛṣṇā, Sūta|putrān nirasya ca,
mokṣitā Bhīmasenena jagāma nagaraṃ prati,
trāsit' êva mṛgī bālā śārdūlena manasvinī,
gātrāṇi, vāsasī c' âiva prakṣālya salilena sā.
tāṃ dṛṣṭvā puruṣā, rājan, prādravanta diśo daśa,
gandharvāṇāṃ bhaya|trastāḥ, ke cid dṛṣṭvā nyamīlayan.
tato mahānasa|dvāri Bhīmasenam avasthitaṃ
dadarśa, rājan, Pāñcālī yathā mattaṃ mahā|dvipam.
24.15 taṃ vismayantī śanakaiḥ saṃjñābhir idam abravīt:
«gandharva|rājāya namo yen' âsmi parimocitā.»

BHĪMASENA uvāca:

ye yasyāḥ vicarant" îha puruṣā vaśa|vartinaḥ,
tasyās te vacanaṃ śrutvā hy an|ṛṇā viharantv ataḥ.

Having listened to their advice, Viráta, the commander in chief of the army, said, "Let the *sutas*' last rites be performed. Let all the Kíchakas be burned together quickly on one well-fueled fire with jewels and perfumes all around." Becoming panic-stricken, he said to Sudéshna, his queen: "Give the *sairándhri* this message from me when she arrives: 'Go where you please, *sairándhri*, bless you, most beautiful-faced lady. The king is afraid, shapely-hipped lady, because of the destruction wrought by the *gandhárvas*.' Since she is 24.10
protected by the *gandhárvas*, I do not dare to tell her this myself, but women are blameless, so I am telling this to you."

So, liberated from her fear of the now crushed *suta*'s sons, and freed by Bhima·sena, the intelligent Krishná, like a young doe frightened by a tiger, returned to the city and washed her limbs and clothes with water. But when they saw her the citizens ran away in all directions, my king, trembling from fear of the *gandhárvas*, and some shut their eyes when they saw her.

Then, at the door to the kitchen, the Princess of Panchála saw Bhima·sena standing there, my king, like a huge elephant in rut. Amazed by him, she quietly said this, which 24.15
they both understood: "I pay homage to the king of the *gandhárvas* who freed me."

BHIMA·SENA said:

The men who lived here, subject to the will of a woman, will wander free from their debt, now that they have heard her words.

VAIŚAMPĀYANA uvāca:

tataḥ sā nartan'|āgāre Dhanañjayam apaśyata
rājñaḥ kanyā Virāṭasya nartayānaṃ mahā|bhujam.
tatas tā nartan'|āgārād viniṣkramya sah'|Ârjunāḥ
kanyā dadṛśur āyāntīṃ kliṣṭāṃ Kṛṣṇām an|āgasam.

KANYĀ ūcuḥ:

diṣṭyā, sairandhri, mukt" âsi! diṣṭy" âsi punar āgatā!
diṣṭyā vinihatāḥ Sūtā ye tvāṃ kliśyanty an|āgasam!

BṚHANNAL" ôvāca:

24.20 kathaṃ, sairandhri, mukt" âsi? kathaṃ pāpāś ca te hatāḥ?
icchāmi vai tava śrotuṃ sarvam eva yathā|tatham.

SAIRANDHRY uvāca:

Bṛhannale, kiṃ nu tava sairandhryā kāryam adya vai,
yā tvaṃ vasasi, kalyāṇi, sadā kanyā|pure sukham?
na hi duḥkhaṃ samāpnoṣi, sairandhrī yad upāśnute!
tena māṃ duḥkhitām evaṃ pṛcchase prahasann iva!

BṚHANNAL" ôvāca:

Bṛhannal" âpi, kalyāṇi, duḥkham āpnoty an|uttamam
tiryag|yoni|gatā, bāle, na c' âinam avabudhyase.
tvayā sah' ôṣitā c' âsmi, tvaṃ ca sarvaiḥ sah' ôṣitā.
kliśyantyāṃ tvayi, su|śroṇi, ko nu duḥkhaṃ na cintayet?
24.25 na tu kena cid atyantaṃ kasya cidd hṛdayaṃ kva cit

VAISHAMPÁYANA said:

Then she saw long-armed Dhanan·jaya in the dancing hall teaching King Viráta's daughters to dance. As they were leaving the dancing hall along with Árjuna, the girls caught sight of the tormented though blameless Krishná, approaching.

THE GIRLS said:

Sairándhri, thank heaven you have been saved! Thank heaven you have made it back again! You are lucky that the *suta*s who were tormenting you, though you are blameless, have been killed!

BRIHAN·NALA said:

How have you been saved, *sairándhri*? How were those 24.20
wicked men killed? I want to hear the whole story from you, just as it happened.

THE SAIRÁNDHRI said:

Fortunate Brihan·nala, what concern of yours is the *sairándhri*'s business now, when you always live happily in the women's quarters? You do not bear the pain that the *sairándhri* has to bear! That is why you question me, aggrieved as I am, as though you are mocking me!

BRIHAN·NALA said:

Noble lady, Brihan·nala, too, feels the utmost pain. She has become a beast, and you, young lady, have no comprehension of this. I have lived with you, and you too have lived with all of us. Shapely-hipped lady, when you are tormented, who does not feel your pain? No one's heart can 24.25

veditum śakyate nūnam, tena mām n' âvabudhyase.

VAIŚAMPĀYANA uvāca:

tataḥ sah' âiva kanyābhir Draupadī rāja|veśma tat
praviveśa Sudeṣṇāyāḥ samīpam upagāminī.
tām abravīd rāja|putrī Virāṭa|vacanād idam:
«sairandhri, gamyatāṃ śīghraṃ yatra kāmayase gatim.
rājā bibheti te, bhadre, gandharvebhyaḥ parābhavāt.
tvaṃ c' âpi taruṇī, su|bhru, rūpeṇ' â|pratimā bhuvi,
puṃsām iṣṭaś ca viṣayo, gandharvāś c' âti|kopanāḥ.»

SAIRANDHRY uvāca:

trayo|daś'|âha|mātraṃ me rājā kṣamyatu, bhāmini.
kṛta|kṛtyā bhaviṣyanti gandharvās te, na saṃśayaḥ.
24.30 tato mām upaneṣyanti, kariṣyanti ca te priyam.
dhruvaṃ ca śreyasā rājā yokṣyate saha bāndhavaiḥ.

be perfectly understood by another, so by that logic you do not understand me.

VAISHAMPÁYANA said:

Dráupadi and the girls entered the royal apartment, going into Sudéshna's presence. The princess spoke these words to her at Viráta's request: "*Sairándhri*, please go wherever you wish, but quickly. The king is afraid of you, my dear, due to the destruction wrought by the *gandhárva*s. You are young, beautiful-eyebrowed girl, and are unmatched on earth in beauty. You are an object of desire for men and the *gandhárva*s are exceedingly angry."

THE SAIRÁNDHRI said:

Beautiful lady, let the king suffer me to remain here for thirteen days more. The *gandhárva*s will doubtless have
achieved their aims. Then they will take me away and do 24.30
you favors. The king and his kin will certainly experience the benefit.

25–30
THE KÁURAVAS' SCHEME

VAIŚAMPĀYANA uvāca:

25.1 KĪCAKASYA TU ghātena s'|ânujasya, viśām pate,
atyahitaṃ cintayitvā vyasmayanta pṛthag|janāḥ.
tasmin pure, jana|pade sañjalpo 'bhūc ca saṅghaśaḥ,
śauryādd hi vallabho rājño mahā|sattvaḥ sa Kīcakaḥ
āsīt prahartā sainyānāṃ, dār'|āmarṣī ca dur|matiḥ.
sa hataḥ khalu pāp'|ātmā gandharvair duṣṭa|pūruṣaḥ.
ity ajalpan, mahā|rāja, par'|ânīka|vināśanam
deśe deśe manuṣyāś ca Kīcakaṃ duṣ|pradharṣaṇam.
25.5 atha vai Dhārtarāṣṭreṇa prayuktā ye bahiś|carāḥ
mṛgayitvā bahūn grāmān, rāṣṭrāṇi, nagarāṇi ca,
saṃvidhāya yath"|ādiṣṭaṃ, yathā|deśa|pradarśanam,
kṛta|kṛtyā nyavartanta te carā nagaraṃ prati.
tatra dṛṣṭvā tu rājānaṃ Kauravyaṃ Dhṛtarāṣṭra|jam
Droṇa|Karṇa|Kṛpaiḥ sārdhaṃ, Bhīṣmeṇa ca mah"|ātmanā,
saṅgataṃ bhrātṛbhiś c' âpi, Trigartaiś ca mahā|rathaiḥ,
Duryodhanaṃ sabhā|madhye āsīnam idam abruvan.

CARĀ ūcuḥ:

kṛto 'smābhiḥ paro yatnas teṣām anveṣaṇe sadā
Pāṇḍavānāṃ, manuṣy'|êndra, tasmin mahati kānane
25.10 nirjane, mṛga|saṅkīrṇe, nānā|druma|lat"|ākule,
latā|pratāna|bahule, nānā|gulma|samāvṛte.
na ca vidmo gatā yena Pārthāḥ su|dṛḍha|vikramāḥ.

VAISHAMPÁYANA said:

EACH AND EVERY person was amazed by the slaughter of Kíchaka and his clan, lord of men, reflecting on that excessive violence. In the city and the country districts, the general gossip was that the great Kíchaka was dear to the king on account of his valor, but that he was wicked-minded, an abuser of warriors and an adulterer. Furthermore, it was said that the wicked man of sinful soul was definitely killed by the *gandhárvas*. So the people gossiped from place to place in this way, great king, about unbeatable Kíchaka, the annihilator of enemy armies. 25.1

When the spies employed by Dhrita·rashtra's son who had examined many villages, kingdoms and cities had completed their examination according to what was prescribed in the places assigned to them, and they were satisfied with what they achieved, they turned back, going to their city. When they saw the king of the Kurus, Dhrita·rashtra's son, together with Drona, Karna and Kripa, as well as high-souled Bhishma, his brothers and the great chariot-warrior Tri·gartas, they spoke to him as he sat in the midst of court. 25.5

THE SPIES said:

We have constantly made the utmost effort, lord of men,
searching for those Pándavas in the great forest, but it is 25.10
uninhabited and full of deer, overgrown with a mass of various trees and creepers, abundant in creepers and tendrils, and dense with various thickets. However, the path that the Parthas of resolutely firm prowess took could not be found.

mārgamāṇāḥ pada|nyāsaṃ teṣu teṣu tathā tathā:
giri|kūṭeṣu tuṅgeṣu, nānā|jana|padeṣu ca,
jan'|ākīrṇeṣu deśeṣu, kharvaṭeṣu pureṣu ca,
nar'|êndra, bahuśo 'nviṣṭā, n' âiva vidmaś ca Pāṇḍavān.
atyantaṃ vā vinaṣṭās te, bhadraṃ tubhyaṃ, nara'|rṣabha.
vartmāny anveṣyamāṇā vai rathināṃ, rathi|sattama,
na hi vidmo gatiṃ teṣāṃ, vāsaṃ hi, nara|sattama.
25.15 kiṃ cit kālaṃ, manuṣy'|êndra, sūtānām anugā vayam
mṛgayitvā yathā|nyāyaṃ vedit'|ârthāḥ sma tattvataḥ.
prāptā Dvāravatīṃ sūtā vinā Pārthaiḥ, paran|tapa.
na tatra Kṛṣṇā, rāj'|êndra, Pāṇḍavāś ca mahā|vratāḥ.
sarvathā vipranaṣṭās te. namas te, Bharata'|rṣabha.
na hi vidmo gatiṃ teṣāṃ, vāsaṃ v" âpi mah"|ātmanām.
Pāṇḍavānāṃ pravṛttiṃ ca vidmaḥ, karm' âpi vā kṛtam.
sa naḥ śādhi, manuṣy'|êndra, ata ūrdhvaṃ, viśām pate,
anveṣaṇe Pāṇḍavānāṃ bhūyaḥ kiṃ karavāmahe.
imāṃ ca naḥ priyāṃ, vīra, vācaṃ bhadravatīṃ śṛṇu.
25.20 yena Trigartā nihatā balena mahatā, nṛpa,
sūtena rājño Matsyasya Kīcakena balīyasā,
sa hataḥ patitaḥ śete gandharvair niśi, Bhārata,
a|dṛśyamānair duṣṭ'|ātmā, bhrātṛbhiḥ saha sodaraiḥ!
priyam etad upaśrutya śatrūṇāṃ ca parābhavam,
kṛta|kṛtyaś ca, Kauravya, vidhatsva yad an|antaram.

We have searched for their footprints in these places and beyond: on the lofty summits of mountains and among various communities. We have searched in places full of people and mountain villages, lord of men, going in many directions, but there is no information about the Pándavas. Bull-like man, bless you, they may have been completely destroyed. Although we searched for the tracks of their chariot wheels, greatest of charioteers, there is no evidence of their path or their current abode, best of men.

For some time, lord of men, we followed their charioteers, 25.15
and, having investigated thoroughly, we discovered what we wished to know. The charioteers reached Dváravati without the Parthas, scorcher of your enemies. Krishná wasn't there, lord of kings, nor were the Pándavas who practice religious observance. They have completely disappeared. Salutations to you, bull-like Bharata. There was no evidence of the path or the current abode of the high-souled Pándavas. We know about their conduct and the deeds they have done. Instruct us later, lord of men and earth, as to what we should do next in the search for the sons of Pandu.

But now, hero, listen to our pleasing and auspicious report. The Matsyan king's mighty warrior, my lord, who was 25.20
responsible for the Tri·gartans' extremely violent destruction, the evil-souled Kíchaka, lies fallen, killed by unseen *gandhárvas* at night, Bhárata, along with his clan! So now that you have heard this welcome news of the destruction of your enemies and have thus achieved one of your aims, descendant of Kuru, instruct us as to what should be done next.

VAIŚAMPĀYANA uvāca:

26.1 TATO DURYODHANO rājā jñātvā teṣāṃ vacas tadā
ciram antar|manā bhūtvā pratyuvāca sabhā|sadaḥ:
«su|duḥkhā khalu kāryāṇāṃ gatir vijñātum antataḥ.
tasmāt sarve nirīkṣadhvaṃ kva nu te Pāṇḍavā gatāḥ
alp'|âvaśiṣṭaṃ kālasya gata|bhūyiṣṭham antataḥ
teṣām a|jñāta|caryāyām asmin varṣe trayo|daśe.
asya varṣasya śeṣaṃ ced vyatīyur iha Pāṇḍavāḥ,
nivṛtta|samayās te hi satya|vrata|parāyaṇāḥ.
26.5 kṣaranta iva nāg'|êndrāḥ, sarve hy āśīviṣ'|ôpamāḥ
duḥkhā bhaveyuḥ saṃrabdhāḥ Kauravān prati te dhruvam.
sarve kālasya vettāraḥ, kṛcchra|rūpa|dharāḥ sthitāḥ.
praviśeyur jita|krodhās tāvad eva punar vanam,
tasmāt kṣipraṃ bubhūṣadhvaṃ
yathā te 'tyantam a|vyayam
rājyaṃ nir|dvandvam, a|vyagraṃ,
niḥ|sapatnaṃ ciraṃ bhavet.»
ath' âbravīt tataḥ Karṇaḥ, «kṣipraṃ gacchantu, Bhārata,
anye dhūrtā narā, dakṣā, nibhṛtāḥ, sādhu|kāriṇaḥ.
carantu deśān saṃvītāḥ, sphītāñ janapad'|ākulān,
tatra goṣṭhīṣu ramyāsu, siddha|pravrajiteṣu ca,
26.10 paricāreṣu, tīrtheṣu, vividheṣv ākareṣu ca.
vijñātavyā manuṣyais tais tarkayā su|vinītayā,
vividhais tat|paraiḥ samyak, taj|jñair, nipuṇa|saṃvṛtaiḥ,
anveṣṭavyāḥ su|nipuṇaiḥ Pāṇḍavāś channa|vāsinaḥ
nadī|kuñjeṣu, tīrtheṣu, grāmeṣu, nagareṣu ca,

VAISHAMPÁYANA said:

KING DURYÓDHANA understood their report, but was 26.1
perplexed for a long while, and then addressed his courtiers: "It is very difficult to finally ascertain the course of events with certainty. Therefore, everyone speculate as to where the Pándavas have gone, for little time remains in this thirteenth year of the last part of their unrecognized exile.

If the Pándavas see through the remainder of this year, they will have completed their end of the bargain, wholly devoted to their vow of truth. Then they will be like streaming 26.5
lords of elephants, or the most virulently poisonous snakes, pained and eternally furious toward the Kurus. They are all men who understand the meaning of time, and they are spending their time wearing painful disguises. Therefore, quickly make every effort to ensure that they subdue their anger and return to the forest again, and to ensure that the kingdom may remain absolutely and unchangingly undisputed, undisturbed and unclaimed by another for a long time."

Karna then said, "Send out different spies quickly; ones who are intelligent, cunning and skilled, Bhárata. Let them wander in disguise, to flourishing areas and populous communities, and from there into pleasant assemblies and successful colonies. Let them go into places of worship, pilgrim- 26.10
ages, into mines and various places. They must be hunted by such men using well-trained logic. The sons of Pandu who are living in disguise must be sought by various, completely devoted men, themselves in disguise, all skilled and knowledgeable in their task, as well as very experienced. The

āśrameṣu ca ramyeṣu, parvateṣu, guhāsu ca.»

ath' âgraj'|ânantara|jaḥ pāpa|bhāv'|ânurāgavān
jyeṣṭhaṃ Duḥśāsanas tatra bhrātā bhrātaram abravīt:
«yeṣu naḥ pratyayo, rājaṃś, cāreṣu, manuj'|âdhipa,
te yāntu datta|deyā vai bhūyas tān parimārgitum.
26.15 etac ca Karṇo yat prāha, sarvam īhāmahe tathā.
yath''|ôddiṣṭaṃ carāḥ sarve mṛgayantu yatas tataḥ.
ete c' ânye ca bhūyāṃso deśād deśaṃ yathā|vidhi.

na tu teṣāṃ gatir, vāsaḥ, pravṛttiś c' ôpalabhyate.
atyantaṃ vā nigūḍhās te, pāraṃ v' ôrmim ato gatāḥ.
vyālair v' âpi mah''|âraṇye bhakṣitāḥ śūra|māninaḥ!
atha vā viṣamaṃ prāpya vinaṣṭāḥ śāśvatīḥ samāḥ.
tasmān mānasam a|vyagraṃ kṛtvā tvaṃ, Kuru|nandana,
kuru kāryaṃ mah''|ôtsāhaṃ, manyase yan, nar'|âdhipa.»

VAIŚAMPĀYANA uvāca:

27.1 ATH' ÂBRAVĪN mahā|vīryo Droṇas tattv'|ârtha|darśivān,
«na tādṛśā vinaśyanti, na prayānti parābhavam.
śūrāś ca, kṛta|vidyāś ca, buddhimanto, jit'|êndriyāḥ,
dharma|jñāś ca, kṛta|jñāś ca, dharma|rājam anuvratāḥ
nīti|dharm'|ârtha|tattva|jñaṃ, pitṛvac ca samāhitam,
dharme sthitaṃ, satya|dhṛtiṃ, jyeṣṭhaṃ jyeṣṭh'|ânuyāyinaḥ,
anuvratā mah''|ātmānaṃ bhrātaro bhrātaraṃ, nṛpa,
Ajātaśatruṃ śrīmantaṃ sarva|bhrātṝn anuvratam.
27.5 teṣāṃ tathā vidheyānāṃ nibhṛtānāṃ mah''|ātmanām
kim arthaṃ nītimān Pārthaḥ śreyo n' âiṣāṃ kariṣyati?

Pándavas must be pursued at riverbanks, holy areas, villages and cities, ashrams and pleasant mountains and caves."

Then Duhshásana, the second-born son, a man who took pleasure in being wicked, said to his older brother: "Lord of men, my king, only allow trusted spies, paid their rewards in advance to go and search a second time. We fully approve 26.15
of this idea and that which Karna mentioned. Let all the spies search as has been suggested. Let these men and others search from place to place, in the proper manner.

But their path, abode and occupation will not be ascertained. Either they are very secretly hidden or have crossed the ocean. Or maybe, arrogant as they are, they have even been eaten by beasts in the great forest! Or then again maybe they have come across something dangerous and are totally gone for good. Therefore, descendant of the Kuru race, be calm and collected in your mind, and do what must be done energetically, lord of men, as you see fit."

VAISHAMPÁYANA said:

THEN THE MIGHTY Drona, who saw the truth of the 27.1
matter, said, "Men such as they do not get annihilated nor do they come to their ruin. They are brave, learned and wise and have control over their senses. They are learned in moral law, correct in their conduct, and both devoted to and dependent on their eldest brother, the king of righteousness, who is truly skilled in politics, virtue and profit and who is devoted to them in return like a father, strictly truthful and adhering to virtue. They are brothers who are devoted to their high-souled and glorious sibling, Ajáta·shatru, my
king, who is attached to his brothers in turn. So why should 27.5

tasmād yatnāt pratīkṣante kālasy' ôdayam āgatam.
na hi te nāśam ṛccheyur, iti paśyāmy ahaṃ dhiyā.
sāmprataṃ c' âiva yat kāryaṃ, tac ca kṣipram a|kālikam
kriyatāṃ sādhu sañcintya. vāsaś c' âiṣāṃ pracintyatām
yathāvat Pāṇḍu|putrāṇāṃ sarv'|ârtheṣu dhṛt'|ātmanām.
dur|jñeyāḥ khalu śūrās te, dur|āpās, tapasā vṛtāḥ.
śuddh'|ātmā, guṇavān Pārthaḥ, satyavān, nītimān, śuciḥ.
tejo|rāśir a|saṅkhyeyo gṛhṇīyād api cakṣuṣā.
27.10 vijñāya, kriyatāṃ. tasmād bhūyaś ca mṛgayāmahe
brāhmaṇaiś, cārakaiḥ, siddhair, ye c' ânye tad|vido janāḥ.»

VAIŚAMPĀYANA uvāca:

28.1 TATAḤ ŚĀNTANAVO Bhīṣmo Bharatānāṃ pitā|mahaḥ
śrutavān, deśa|kāla|jñas, tattva|jñaḥ, sarva|dharma|vit,
ācārya|vāky'|ôparame tad vākyam abhisandadhat.
hit'|ârthaṃ samuvāc' âināṃ bhāratīṃ Bhāratān prati,
Yudhiṣṭhire samāsaktāṃ dharma|jñe, dharma|saṃvṛtām,
a|satsu dur|labhāṃ nityaṃ, satāṃ c' âbhimatāṃ sadā.

Partha, who is conversant in political science, not bring about prosperity for his high-souled, faithful and obedient brothers?

Therefore, they diligently look forward to the return of their good fortune. These men do not perish in ruin. This is what I see through wise reflection. So now do what must quickly be done at once, after proper consideration. Contemplate the whereabouts of the sons of Pandu, firm-minded in every matter.

They are certainly hard to discover, inaccessible and hidden through their asceticism. The son of Pritha is pure-souled, virtuous, holy, politically astute and truthful. That incalcuable mass of splendor can overpower his enemies with a mere glance. Knowing this, do what is right. There- 27.10
fore let us search again with brahmins, spies, holy experts and whoever else could know something of them."

VAISHAMPÁYANA said:

THEN THE BHARATAS' grandfather, Bhishma, the son of 28.1
Shántanu, who was learned in the Vedas, understood time and space, and was aware of the truth and familiar with all law, applauded the speech, once the teacher had finished speaking. He addressed the Bharatas for their own good, in words that showed his affection for Yudhi·shthira, a man acquainted with divine law, and which conformed to virtue, always hard for the wicked to grasp but eternally agreeable to the good.

Bhīṣmaḥ samavadat tatra giraṃ sādhubhir arcitām,
«yaś c' âiṣa brāhmaṇaḥ prāha Droṇaḥ sarv'|ârtha|tattva|vit,
28.5 sarva|lakṣaṇa|sampannāḥ, sādhu|vrata|samanvitāḥ,
śruta|vrat'|ôpapannāś ca, nānā|śruti|samanvitāḥ,
vṛddh'|ânuśāsane yuktāḥ, satya|vrata|parāyaṇāḥ,
samayaṃ samaya|jñās te pālayantaḥ, śuci|vratāḥ,
kṣatra|dharma|ratā nityaṃ, Keśav'|ânugatāḥ sadā,
pravīra|puruṣās te vai, mah"|ātmāno mahā|balāḥ.

n' âvasīditum arhanti udvahantaḥ satāṃ dhuram.
dharmataś c' âiva guptās te su|vīryeṇa ca Pāṇḍavāḥ
na nāśam adhigaccheyur, iti me dhīyate matiḥ.
tatra buddhiṃ pravakṣyāmi Pāṇḍavān prati, Bhārata,
na tu nītiḥ su|nītasya śakyate 'nvoṣituṃ paraiḥ.
28.10 yat tu śakyam ih' âsmābhis tān vai sañcintya Pāṇḍavān,
buddhyā prayuktaṃ, na drohāt pravakṣyāmi, nibodha tat.
na tv iyaṃ mādṛśair nītis tasya vācyā kathañ cana.
sā tv iyaṃ sādhu vaktavyā, na tv a|nītiḥ kathañ cana.

vṛddh'|ânuśāsane, tāta, tiṣṭhatā, satya|śīlinā,
avaśyaṃ tv iha dhīreṇa, satāṃ madhye vivakṣatā
yath"|ârham iha vaktavyaṃ, sarvathā dharma|lipsayā.
tatra n' âhaṃ tathā manye, yath" âyam itaro janaḥ,
nivāsaṃ dharma|rājasya varṣe 'smin vai trayo|daśe.

The address that Bhishma gave was worshipped by the wise, and went as follows: "The brahmin Drona, who is familiar with the truth of all matters, has already said this. They are endowed with every auspicious marking, observe 28.5
religious vows. They are furnished with Vedic vows and familiar with various sciences. They follow the advice of their elders, rely on vows of truth, are well aware of the conditions of their agreement and those virtuous men keep them. They always delight in the requirements of their kshatriya caste, are constant followers of Késhava, men of enormous heroism, high-souled and enormously strong.

They bear the burden of good men and so ought not to have been ruined. The Pándavas are protected, in accordance with virtue and by means of their great valor, and they will not reach their destruction. This is my opinion, as I see it. I shall present my advice as regards the Pándavas, Bhárata, though the policy of a wise tactician cannot be comprehended by others. It is possible for us to consider 28.10
and discuss the Pándavas wisely, but understand that I will not speak from treachery. For advice of that kind should never be given by people like me. Wise advice of this sort should indeed be uttered, but never bad policy.

My son, the man who stands obedient to the old and dedicated to the truth, and most certainly the man who speaks with composure in the midst of the wise, should always speak in this manner if he wishes to obtain virtue. So I do not agree with the others here as regards the abode of Yudhi·shthira, the king of righteousness, in this thirteenth year.

tatra, tāta, na teṣāṃ hi rājñāṃ bhāvyam a|sāmpratam,
28.15 pure, jana|pade c' âpi, yatra rājā Yudhiṣṭhiraḥ.
dāna|śīlo, vadānyaś ca, nibhṛto, hrī|niṣevakaḥ
jano jana|pade bhāvyo, yatra rājā Yudhiṣṭhiraḥ.
priya|vādī, sadā dānto bhavyaḥ, satya|paro janaḥ,
hṛṣṭaḥ, puṣṭaḥ, śucir, dakṣo, yatra rājā Yudhiṣṭhiraḥ.
n' âsūyako, na c' âp' īrṣur, n' âbhimānī, na matsarī
bhaviṣyati janas tatra, svayaṃ dharmam anuvrataḥ.
brahma|ghoṣāś ca bhūyāṃsaḥ, pūrṇ'|āhutyas tath" âiva ca,
kratavaś ca bhaviṣyanti bhūyāṃso bhūri|dakṣiṇāḥ.

sadā ca tatra parjanyaḥ samyag|varṣī, na saṃśayaḥ,
sampanna|sasyā ca mahī, nir|ātaṅkā bhaviṣyati.
28.20 guṇavanti ca dhānyāni, rasavanti phalāni ca,
gandhavanti ca mālyāni, śubha|śabdā ca bhāratī.
vāyuś ca sukha|saṃsparśo, niṣpratīpaṃ ca darśanam,
na bhayaṃ tv āviśet tatra, yatra rājā Yudhiṣṭhiraḥ.

gāvaś ca bahulās tatra, na kṛśā na ca dur|balāḥ,
payāṃsi, dadhi|sarpīṃṣi rasavanti, hitāni ca,
guṇavanti ca peyāni, bhojyāni rasavanti ca
tatra deśe bhaviṣyanti, yatra rājā Yudhiṣṭhiraḥ.
rasāḥ, sparśāś ca, gandhāś ca, śabdāś c' âpi guṇ'|ânvitāḥ,
dṛśyāni ca prasannāni, yatra rājā Yudhiṣṭhiraḥ.

My son, the king of the city or community in which 28.15
King Yudhi·shthira is staying will certainly not have any misfortune. The people in the community where King Yudhi·shthira resides must be generous, munificent, gentle and modest. The people where King Yudhi·shthira lives will always be pleasant in their speech, restrained, observant of the truth, happy, healthy, honest and industrious. They would not be discontented, nor even envious, conceited or selfish; rather, the population there would be devoted to their respective duties. The sounds of hymns will be constant, sacrifices will be performed with full oblations and there will always be plentiful gifts for brahmins.

In that land the clouds will assuredly produce just the right amount of rain, and the land will be well supplied with
crops and free from fear. The grain there will be good quality, 28.20
the fruit will be juicy, the garlands will be sweetly fragranced, and speech will be full of pleasant words. The wind will be pleasant to the touch, judgments will be unopposed and nothing would bring about fear, wherever King Yudhi·shthira may be.

The cows will be numerous there and none would be emaciated or weak. The mild and sour milk and butter would be tasty and wholesome. There in the land where King Yudhi·shthira lives, the drink is of good quality and the food is appetizing. Where King Yudhi·shthira lives, the objects of the senses such as taste, touch, smell and speech are endowed with excellent qualities.

28.25 dharmāś ca tatra sarvais tu sevitāś ca dvi|jātibhiḥ,
svaiḥ svair guṇaiś ca saṃyuktā asmin varṣe trayo|daśe
deśe tasmin bhaviṣyanti, tāta, Pāṇḍava|saṃyute.
saṃprītimāñ janas tatra, santuṣṭaḥ, śucir, a|vyayaḥ,
devat'|âtithi|pūjāsu sarva|bhāv'|ânurāgavān,
iṣṭa|dāno, mah"|ôtsāhaḥ, sva|sva|dharma|parāyaṇaḥ.

a|śubhādd hi śubha|prepsur, iṣṭa|yajñaḥ, śubha|vrataḥ
bhaviṣyati janas tatra, yatra rājā Yudhiṣṭhiraḥ.
tyakta|vāky'|ânṛtas, tāta, śubha|kalyāṇa|maṅgalaḥ,
śubh'|ârth'|ēpsuḥ, śubha|matir, yatra rājā Yudhiṣṭhiraḥ,
28.30 bhaviṣyati janas tatra nityaṃ c' êṣṭa|priya|vrataḥ.

dharm'|ātmā śakyate jñātuṃ n' âpi, tāta, dvi|jātibhiḥ,
kiṃ punaḥ prākṛtais, tāta, Pārtho vijñāyate kva cit,
yasmin satyaṃ, dhṛtir, dānaṃ, parā śāntir, dhruvā kṣamā,
hṛīḥ, śrīḥ, kīrtiḥ, paraṃ teja, ānṛśaṃsyam, ath' ārjavam?
tasmāt tatra nivāsaṃ tu channaṃ yatnena dhīmataḥ,
gatiṃ ca paramāṃ tatra n' ôtsahe vaktum anyathā.
evam etat tu sañcintya yat|kṛte, manyase hitam,
tat kṣipraṃ kuru, Kauravya, yady evaṃ śraddadhāsi me.»

VAIŚAMPĀYANA UVĀCA:

29.1 TATAḤ ŚĀRADVATO vākyam ity uvāca Kṛpas tadā,
«yuktaṃ, prāptaṃ ca vṛddhena Pāṇḍavān prati bhāṣitam,
dharm'|ârtha|sahitaṃ, ślakṣṇaṃ, tattvataś ca sa|hetukam,
tatr'|ânurūpaṃ Bhīṣmeṇa. mam' âpy atra giraṃ śṛṇu:

Laws of duty will be respected by all twice-born men, 28.25
according to their own qualities. In this, the thirteenth year, the people in that place where the Pándavas are united will be unchangingly pleasant, contented and full of delight. They will love with their whole being, worshipping guests and the gods, and love generosity. They will have great energy, and be intent on their own virtue.

Where King Yudhi·shthira lives, the people will strive to obtain what is pure rather than impure, be keen sacrificers and pure-vowed. Where King Yudhi·shthira lives they will have abandoned useless deceitful speech, my son, and be happy in virtuous felicity, eager to achieve honest goals,
and pure-minded. The people there will always be dearly 28.30
devoted to agreeable vows.

My boy, the virtuous-souled man cannot be found by brahmins, so how, then, my son, could the son of Pritha, in whom there is truth, satisfaction, generosity, supreme peace and sure forgiveness, modesty, success, fame, great splendor, kindness and sincerity, be found again anywhere by normal people? Therefore, since this wise man has diligently hidden his abode I do not dare speculate any further on his last course. So give it some thought, and, once you've finished, quickly do whatever you think appropriate, Kaurávya, if you do trust me."

VAISHAMPÁYANA said:

THEN KRIPA, THE SON of Sharádvata, said this: "What 29.1
the venerable Bhishma said concerning the Pándavas is appropriate and proper, in conjunction with duty and profit, sincere, truthful, well founded and suitable. But listen to my

teṣāṃ c' âiva gatis tīrthair, vāsaś c' âiṣāṃ pracintyatām,
nītir vidhīyatāṃ c' âpi, sāmprataṃ yā hitā bhavet.
n' âvajñeyo ripus, tāta, prākṛto 'pi bubhūṣatā,
kiṃ punaḥ Pāṇḍavās, tāta, sarv'|âstra|kuśalā raṇe?
29.5 tasmāt satraṃ praviṣṭeṣu Pāṇḍaveṣu mah"|ātmasu,
gūḍha|bhāveṣu, channeṣu, kāle c' ôdayam āgate,
sva|rāṣṭre, para|rāṣṭre ca jñātavyaṃ balam ātmanaḥ.
udayaḥ Pāṇḍavānāṃ ca prāpte kāle na saṃśayaḥ.
nivṛtta|samayāḥ Pārthā mah"|ātmāno, mahā|balāḥ,
mah"|ôtsāhā bhaviṣyanti Pāṇḍavā hy a|mit'|âujasaḥ.
tasmād balaṃ ca, kośaś ca, nītiś c' âpi vidhīyatām,
yathā|kāl'|ôdaye prāpte samyak taiḥ sandadhāmahe.
tāta, buddhy" âpi tat sarvaṃ budhyasva balam ātmanaḥ,
niyataṃ sarva|mitreṣu: balavatsv a|baleṣu ca.
29.10 ucc'|âvacaṃ balaṃ jñātvā, madhya|sthaṃ c' âpi, Bhārata,
prahṛṣṭam, a|prahṛṣṭaṃ ca sandadhāma tathā paraiḥ.
sāmnā, dānena, bhedena, daṇḍena, bali|karmaṇā,
nyāyen' ākramya ca parān, balāc c' ānamya dur|balān,
sāntvayitvā tu mitrāṇi, balaṃ c' ābhāṣyatāṃ sukham.
su|kośa|bala|saṃvṛddhaḥ samyak siddhim avāpsyasi.
yotsyase c' âpi balibhir aribhiḥ pratyupasthitaiḥ
anyais tvaṃ, Pāṇḍavair v" âpi, hīnaiḥ sva|bala|vāhanaiḥ.

opinion, too, for a moment. Their course and abode should be contemplated by suitable agents, and an advantageous and appropriate policy should be formulated as well.

Young man, even an ordinary enemy should not be disregarded by the man who strives to survive, my son, so how much more so is this true when it comes to the Pándavas,
who are skilled in all weapons in battle? Therefore, by the 29.5
time that the high-souled Pándavas who entered the forest and are now hidden and disguised reappear, you should ascertain your strength in your own kingdom and indeed your strength in others' kingdoms.

Doubtless the time has arrived for the Pándavas' reappearance. The high-souled, mighty, greatly energetic and splendid sons of Pritha will appear once the stipulations of the agreement have lapsed. Therefore, your strength, treasury and policy, too, must be prepared so that when the time of their resurgence has arrived you may be reconciled with them. Once you have attended to these things, my son, also consider how your own strength is limited by all your enemies, both strong and weak. Once you know your forces, 29.10
the variance and the indifference, Bhárata, as well as which are content and which discontent, then form alliances with enemies.

By conciliation, bribery, betrayal, violence and tribute, and by the established rules of foreign policy, attack your enemies and subdue the weak through force, then conciliate your friends and army by telling them what they want to hear. When you have augmented your substantial treasury and strengthened your army, you will obtain complete success. Quite apart from the Pándavas, who lack forces and

evaṃ sarvaṃ viniścitya vyavasāyaṃ sva|dharmataḥ
yathā|kālaṃ, manuṣy'|êndra, ciraṃ sukham avāpsyasi.»

VAIŚAMPĀYANA uvāca:

30.1 ATHA RĀJĀ Trigartānāṃ Suśarmā ratha|yūthapaḥ
prāpta|kālam idaṃ vākyam uvāca tvarito balī,
a|sakṛn nikṛtaḥ pūrvaṃ Matsya|Śālveyakaiḥ, prabho,
Sūten' âiva ca Matsyasya Kīcakena punaḥ punaḥ,
bādhito bandhubhiḥ sārdhaṃ balād balavatāṃ, vibho,
sa Karṇam abhyudīkṣy' âtha Duryodhanam abhāṣata.
«a|sakṛn Matsya|rājñā me rāṣṭraṃ bādhitam ojasā.
praṇetā Kīcakas tasya balavān abhavat purā.
30.5 krūro, 'marṣī sa duṣṭ'|ātmā, bhuvi prakhyāta|vikramaḥ.
nihataḥ sa tu gandharvaiḥ pāpa|karmā nṛśaṃsavān.
tasmin vinihate rājā hata|darpo, nirāśrayaḥ
bhaviṣyati, nirutsāho Virāṭa, iti me matiḥ.
tatra yātrā mama matā, yadi te rocate, 'n|agha,
Kauravāṇāṃ ca sarveṣāṃ, Karṇasya ca mah"|ātmanaḥ.
etat prāptam ahaṃ manye kāryam ātyayikaṃ hi naḥ.
rāṣṭraṃ tasy' âbhiyāsyāmo bahu|dhānya|samākulam!
ādadāmo 'sya ratnāni, vividhāni vasūni ca,
grāmān, rāṣṭrāṇi vā tasya hariṣyāmo vibhāgaśaḥ.
30.10 atha vā go|sahasrāṇi śubhāni ca, bahūni ca,

chariots of their own, you will also fight with other mighty enemies who present themselves. Having resolved all your strategies in this manner, according to your own duty, lord of men, you will obtain lasting happiness."

VAISHAMPÁYANA said:

THEN THE MIGHTY king of the Tri·gartas, Sushárman, a 30.1
warrior and leader of hosts of chariots, who had been repeatedly humiliated in the past by the Matsyas and the Shalvéyakans, my lord, as well as repeatedly humiliated by Kíchaka, the King of Matsya's general, quickly made a speech when his moment had come. Since he and his relatives had been oppressed through the force of those mighty men, king, he glanced at Karna and addressed Duryódhana.

"My kingdom has been oppressed repeatedly by the mighty King of Matsya. The powerful Kíchaka was once his
general. Cruel, intolerant and wicked-souled, his prowess 30.5
was famous in rumors throughout the world. That malicious miscreant has been killed by the *gandhárvas*. Now that this man is dead, King Viráta's pride has been destroyed and he has no refuge. He will, in my opinion, become despondent. O sinless man, I believe we should invade, if it pleases you, as well as all the Káuravas and high-souled Karna. I reckon that we should act swiftly upon the opportunity we have gained.

Let us invade his kingdom, which abounds in masses of corn! We will take his jewels and various wealth and seize
his villages and kingdoms proportionately to our status. Or 30.10
let us seize thousands of his splendid cattle of various kinds, once we have attacked his city by force. Let us ally the

vividhāni hariṣyāmaḥ pratipīḍya puraṃ balāt.
Kauravaiḥ saha saṅgatya Trigartaiś ca, viśām pate,
gās tasy' âpaharāmo 'dya, sarvaiś c' âiva su|saṃhatāḥ.
saṃvibhāgena kṛtvā tu nibadhnīmo 'sya pauruṣam,
hatvā c' âsya camūṃ kṛtsnāṃ vaśam ev' ānayāmahe.
taṃ vaśe nyāyataḥ kṛtvā sukhaṃ vatsyāmahe vayam,
bhavatāṃ bala|vṛddhiś ca bhaviṣyati na saṃśayaḥ.»

tac chrutvā vacanaṃ tasya Karṇo rājānam abravīt:
«s'|ûktaṃ Suśarmaṇā vākyaṃ. prāpta|kālaṃ hitaṃ ca naḥ.
30.15 tasmāt kṣipraṃ viniryāmo yojayitvā varūthinīm,
vibhajya c' âpy anīkāni, yathā vā manyase, 'n|agha.
prājño vā Kuru|vṛddho 'yaṃ sarveṣāṃ naḥ pitā|mahaḥ,
ācāryaś ca yathā Droṇaḥ, Kṛpaḥ Śāradvatas tathā.
saṃmantrya c' āśu gacchāmaḥ sādhan'|ârthaṃ, mahī|pateḥ.
kiṃ ca naḥ Pāṇḍavaiḥ kāryaṃ hīn'|ârtha|bala|pauruṣaiḥ?
aty|antaṃ vā pranaṣṭās te, prāptā v" âpi Yama|kṣayam.
yāmo, rājan, nirudvignā Virāṭa|nagaraṃ vayam,
ādāsyāmo hi gās tasya, vividhāni vasūni ca.»

tato Duryodhano rājā vākyam ādāya tasya tat
Vaikartanasya Karṇasya, kṣipram ājñāpayat svayam
30.20 śāsane nitya|saṃyuktaṃ Duḥśāsanam an|antaram:
«saha vṛddhais tu saṃmantrya kṣipram yojaya vāhinīm!
yath'|ôddeśaṃ ca gacchāmaḥ sahitās tatra Kauravaiḥ.
Suśarmā ca yath'|ôddiṣṭaṃ deśaṃ yātu mahā|rathaḥ,
Trigartaiḥ sahito rājā, samagra|bala|vāhanaḥ.
prāg eva hi su|saṃvīto Matsyasya viṣayaṃ prati

Káuravas with the Tri·gartas, lord of earth, and take away his cattle today in all their herds. Uniting in cooperation, we will either obstruct his force or bring him under our control by killing his entire army. When we have brought him under our command we will live happily, and doubtless your power will be augmented."

When he had listened to what he had to say, Karna said to the king: "Sushárman has delivered a good speech. This opportunity that has fallen into our lap is to our advantage.
Therefore, sinless man, if you agree, draw up your army 30.15
and arrange it into divisions, and let us set out quickly. Alternatively, let the invasion be organized according to how the wise and aged Kuru grandfather of us all, the teacher Drona, and Kripa, the son of Sharádvat, see fit. Consulting together, let us quickly set out to procure our aim, lord of earth. What do we need to do about the Pándavas when they are destitute of wealth, force and men? They are either entirely lost or have reached the realm of Yama. My king, let's go confidently to Viráta's city, and plunder his cattle and various wealth."

When King Duryódhana had accepted the advice of Karna, the son of the sun, he quickly commanded his brother
Duhshásana, who was born immediately after him, and who 30.20
was always obedient to his orders: "Consult with the elders and quickly organize the army! We will go to the assigned place with the Káuravas. Let the great warrior King Sushárman go to the designated place with his Tri·gartas and all his army and chariots and horses. He should go to the kingdom of Matsya in the lead without giving away the plan, and we will set out behind him one day later to the

jaghanyato vayaṃ tatra yāsyāmo divas'|ântare
viṣayaṃ Matsya|rājasya su|samṛddhaṃ su|saṃhatāḥ.
te yāntu sahitās tatra Virāṭa|nagaraṃ prati,
kṣipraṃ gopān samāsādya gṛhṇantu vipulaṃ dhanam.
gavāṃ śata|sahasrāṇi śrīmanti, guṇavanti ca
vayam apy anugṛhṇīmo, dvi|dhā kṛtvā varūthinīm.»

30.25 te sma gatvā yath"|ôddiṣṭāṃ diśaṃ vahner, mahī|pate,
sannaddhā rathinaḥ sarve sa|padātā, bal'|ôtkaṭāḥ,
prativairaṃ cikīrṣanto, goṣu gṛddhā, mahā|balāḥ.
ādātuṃ gāḥ Suśarm" âtha kṛṣṇa|pakṣasya saptamīm,
apare divase sarve, rājan, saṃbhūya Kauravāḥ
aṣṭamyāṃ te nyagṛhṇanta go|kulāni sahasraśaḥ.

prosperous kingdom of the King of Matsya, in close units. Let them go together to Viráta's city and quickly approach the cowherds and seize the abundant wealth. We, too, will form our army into two divisions and seize hundreds of thousands of excellent, auspiciously marked cattle."

Then all those armed Tri·gartan chariot-warriors went 30.25
to the prescribed place, lord of earth, with their incredibly powerful infantry, great powerful men, eager to wage hostilities and dearly longing for the cattle. Sushárman then went on the seventh day of the black fortnight to seize the cattle, and on the next, eighth day, all the Káuravas and their troops, king, seized the cattle in their thousands.

31–39

TWO CATTLE RAIDS

VAIŚAMPĀYANA UVĀCA:

31.1 TATAS TEṢĀṂ, mahā|rāja,
tatr' âiv' â|mita|tejasām
chadma|liṅga|praviṣṭānāṃ
Pāṇḍavānāṃ mah"|ātmanām
vyatītaḥ samayaḥ samyag vasatāṃ vai pur'|ôttame,
kurvatāṃ asya karmāṇi Virāṭasya, mahī|pateḥ.
Kīcake tu hate rājā Virāṭaḥ para|vīra|hā
parāṃ saṃbhāvanāṃ cakre Kuntī|putre Yudhiṣṭhire.
tatas trayo|daśasy' ânte tasya varṣasya, Bhārata,
Suśarmaṇā gṛhītaṃ tad go|dhanaṃ tarasā bahu.
31.5 tato javena mahatā gopaḥ puram ath' āvrajat.
sa dṛṣṭvā Matsya|rājaṃ ca rathāt praskandya kuṇḍalī
śūraiḥ parivṛtaṃ yodhaiḥ
kuṇḍal'|âṅgada|dhāribhiḥ,
saṃvṛtaṃ mantribhiḥ, sārdhaṃ
Pāṇḍavaiś ca mah"|ātmabhiḥ,
taṃ sabhāyāṃ mahā|rājam āsīnaṃ rāṣṭra|vardhanam,
so 'bravīd upasaṃgamya Virāṭaṃ praṇatas tadā:
«asmān yudhi vinirjitya, paribhūya sa|bāndhavān,
gavāṃ śata|sahasrāṇi Trigartāḥ kālayanti te.
tān parīpsasva, rāj'|êndra, mā neśuḥ paśavas tava!»
tac chrutvā nṛpatiḥ senāṃ Matsyānāṃ samayojayat
31.10 ratha|nāg'|âśva|kalilāṃ, patti|dhvaja|samākulām.
rājāno, rāja|putrāś ca tanutrāṇy atha bhejire
bhānamanti, vicitrāṇi, śūra|sevyāni bhāgaśaḥ.
sa|vajr'|āyasa|garbhaṃ tu kavacaṃ tatra kāñcanam
Virāṭasya priyo bhrātā Śatānīko 'bhyahārayat.
sarva|pārasavaṃ varma kalyāṇa|paṭalaṃ, dṛḍham,
Śatānīkād avara|jo Madirākṣo 'bhyahārayat.

VAISHAMPÁYANA said:

THEN, GREAT KING, the entire period of the agreement to live in the excellent city came to an end for the high-souled and immeasurably energetic Pándavas, who had entered into the service of Viráta, lord of earth, hidden in disguises. When Kíchaka was killed, King Viráta, the slayer of enemy heroes, put the greatest faith in Yudhi·shthira, the son of Kuntí. And at the end of the thirteenth year, Bhárata, Sushárman swiftly seized Viráta's great wealth of cattle. 31.1

An earringed herdsman very hurriedly came to the city 31.5
and jumped down from his chariot when he saw the King of Matsya surrounded by brave fighters wearing earrings and bracelets, and encircled by counselors and the high-souled sons of Pandu. He went up to the great king, the augmenter of his kingdom, who was sitting in his court, and bowing to Viráta he addressed him: "The Tri·gartas along with our allied friends are defeating and disgracing us in battle and carrying off our cattle by the hundreds of thousands. O lord of kings, quickly make an effort to rescue your cattle so they don't become lost!"

Hearing this, the king organized the Matsyan army into
formation, full of horses, elephants and chariots and 31.10
abounding in infantry and standards. The kings and princes, each in their turn, put on their gleaming, beautifully decorated armor, fit for heroes. Viráta's dear brother, Shataníka, put on a suit of golden armor that had an impenetrable iron lining. Madiráksha, younger than Shataníka, put on solid, strong steel armor with a beautiful exterior. The king of the Matsyas put on seemingly unbreakable armor, decorated with a hundred suns, a hundred circles, a hundred dots and

śata|sūryaṃ, śat'|āvartaṃ, śata|bindu, śat'|âkṣimat,
a|bhedya|kalpaṃ Matsyānāṃ rājā kavacam āharat.
utsedhe yasya padmāni śataṃ saugandhikāni ca,
31.15 suvarṇa|pṛṣṭhaṃ, sūry'|ābhaṃ, Sūryadatto 'bhyahārayat.
dṛḍham āyasa|garbhaṃ ca śvetaṃ varma śat'|âkṣimat
Virāṭasya suto jyeṣṭho vīraḥ Śaṅkho 'bhyahārayat.
śataśaś ca tanutrāṇi yathā|svaṃ te mahā|rathāḥ
yotsyamānā anahyanta deva|rūpāḥ prahāriṇaḥ.
s'|ûpaskareṣu, śubhreṣu, mahatsu ca mahā|rathāḥ
pṛthak kāñcana|sannāhān ratheṣv aśvān ayojayan.
sūrya|candra|pratīkāśe rathe divye hiraṇ|maye
mah"|ânubhāvo Matsyasya dhvaja ucchiśriye tadā.
ath' ânyān vividh'|ākārān dhvajān hema|pariṣkṛtān
31.20 yathā|svaṃ kṣatriyāḥ śūrā ratheṣu samayojayan.
atha Matsyo 'bravīd rājā Śatānīkaṃ jaghanya|jam:
«Kaṅka|Ballava|Gopālā, Dāmagranthiś ca vīryavān
yudhyeyur, iti me buddhir vartate, n' âtra saṃśayaḥ.
eteṣām api dīyantāṃ rathā dhvaja|patākinaḥ,
kavacāni ca citrāṇi, dṛḍhāni ca, mṛdūni ca
pratimuñcantu gātreṣu, dīyantām āyudhāni ca.
vīr'|âṅga|rūpāḥ puruṣā nāga|rāja|kar'|ôpamāḥ,
n' ême jātu na yudhyerann, iti me dhīyate matiḥ.»
etac chrutvā tu nṛpater vākyaṃ tvarita|mānasaḥ
Śatānīkas tu Pārthebhyo rathān, rājan, samādiśat,
31.25 Sahadevāya, rājñe ca, Bhīmāya, Nakulāya ca.
tān prahṛṣṭāṃs tataḥ sūtā rāja|bhakti|puraskṛtāḥ
nirdiṣṭā nara|devena rathāñ śīghram ayojayan.
kavacāni vicitrāṇi, mṛdūni ca, dṛḍhāni ca
Virāṭaḥ prādiśad yāni teṣām akliṣṭa|karmaṇām,
tāny āmucya śarīreṣu daṃśitās te paran|tapāḥ.

a hundred eyes. Surya·datta wore armor that was as large as 31.15
a hundred sweet-smelling lotuses in size, overlaid with gold, and as glorious in appearance as the sun. Viráta's eldest son, the hero Shankha, dressed in armor with a solid-steel lining, decorated with a hundred white eyes.

And so those hundreds of godlike mighty warriors, girded with weapons, and about to fight, each dressed in his armor. Next, the mighty warriors each yoked their golden-armored horses to their great, well-equipped, glittering white chariots in turn. The King of Matsya's mighty banner was raised on his celestial golden chariot, luminous as the sun and
the moon. Then each of the kshatriya heroes fastened other 31.20
golden-embellished banners of various designs to their chariots.

The King of Matsya said to Shataníka, his younger brother: "My decision is that Kanka, Bállava, Go·pala, and Dama·granthi, who possess great heroism, will also fight; no doubt about it. Give them chariots furnished with banners and beautifully painted, solid but comfortable armor. Equip their bodies and give them weapons. Endowed with heroic physique, with arms like elephant trunks, I cannot imagine that those men are not fighters."

Having heard the king's speech, quick-witted Shataníka ordered chariots, my king, for the sons of Pritha— for 31.25
Saha·deva, King Yudhi·shthira, Bhima and Nákula. The charioteers, cheerful and occupied with serving the king, quickly yoked the chariots when ordered by that god among men. The scorchers of the foe, unwearied in battle, strapped the variously decorated, comfortable yet solid armor, which Viráta had ordered for them, onto their bodies.

rathān hayaiḥ su|saṃpannān āsthāya ca nar'|ôttamāḥ
niryayur muditāḥ Pārthāḥ śatru|saṅgh'|âvamardinaḥ.
tarasvinaś, channa|rūpāḥ, sarve yuddha|viśāradāḥ
rathān hema|paricchannān āsthāya ca mahā|rathāḥ
31.30 Virāṭam anvayuḥ Pārthāḥ sahitāḥ Kuru|puṅgavāḥ
catvāro bhrātaraḥ śūrāḥ Pāṇḍavāḥ satya|vikramāḥ.

bhīmāś ca matta|mātaṅgā prabhinna|karaṭā|mukhāḥ,
kṣarantaś c' âiva nāg'|êndrāḥ su|dantāḥ, ṣaṣṭi|hāyanāḥ,
sv|ārūḍhā yuddha|kuśalaiḥ, śikṣitā hasti|sādibhiḥ
rājānam anvayuḥ paścāc, calanta iva parvatāḥ.
viśāradānāṃ, mukhyānāṃ, hṛṣṭānāṃ, cāru|jīvinām
aṣṭau ratha|sahasrāṇi, daśa nāga|śatāni ca,
ṣaṣṭiś c' âśva|sahasrāṇi Matsyānām abhiniryayuḥ.
tad anīkaṃ Virāṭasya śuśubhe, Bharata'|rṣabha,
31.35 saṃprayātaṃ tadā, rājan, nirīkṣantaṃ gavāṃ padam.
tad bal'|âgryaṃ Virāṭasya saṃprasthitam aśobhata
dṛḍh'|āyudha|jan'|ākīrṇaṃ gaj'|âśva|ratha|saṅkulam.

VAIŚAMPĀYANA uvāca:

32.1 NIRYĀYA NAGARĀC chūrā vyūḍh'|ânīkāḥ prahāriṇaḥ
Trigartān aspṛśan Matsyāḥ sūrye pariṇate sati.
te Trigartāś ca Matsyāś ca saṃrabdhā, yuddha|durmadāḥ,
anyonyam abhigarjanto, goṣu gṛddhā, mahā|balāḥ.
bhīmāś ca matta|mātaṅgās tomar'|âṅkuśa|noditāḥ,
Grāmaṇīyaiḥ samārūḍhāḥ kuśalair hasti|sādibhiḥ.

Then those greatest of men, the sons of Pritha, oppressors of multitudes of enemies, stood on their chariots, which were well furnished with horses, and set out delighted. So all those energetic, battle-experienced, mighty warriors, whose true identities were hidden, stationed on gold-plated chariots, the four brave Partha brothers, the sons of Pandu, whose 31.30
strength was their truth, the bull-like Kurus, followed Viráta together.

Terrible and intoxicated elephants, bearing rent temples and faces, streaming, sixty-year-old elephant lords with fine tusks, trained and well ridden by elephant-riders skilled in battle, followed behind the king like moving mountains. The foremost experienced Matsyan warriors who cheerfully followed had eight thousand chariots, one thousand elephants and sixty thousand horses. Bull of the Bharata race, Viráta's army shone beautifully as it advanced inspecting the 31.35
footprints of the cattle, my king. Viráta's mighty force shone as it set out, crowded with men bearing strong weapons and teeming with chariots, horses and elephants.

VAISHAMPÁYANA said:

As THE SUN RIPENED, the brave champion Matsyan army, 32.1
which had set out from the city, divided into battle formation, came upon the Tri·gartas. Both the Tri·gartas and the Matsyas were enraged and furious for battle, and the mighty groups each roared at one another, both longing for the cattle. The fearful rutting elephants, ridden by skilled Gramaníyan elephant-riders, were driven on with hooks and lances.

teṣāṃ samāgamo ghoras, tumulo, loma|harṣaṇaḥ,
ghnatāṃ paras|paraṃ, rājan, Yama|rāṣṭra|vivardhanaḥ,
32.5 dev'|Âsura|samo, rājann, āsīt sūrye 'valambati
padāti|ratha|nāg'|êndra|hay'|āroha|bal'|âughavān.
anyonyam abhyāpatatāṃ, nighnatāṃ c' êtar'|êtaram
uditaṣṭhad rajo bhaumaṃ, na prājñāyata kiñ cina.

pakṣiṇaś c' âpatan bhūmau sainyena rajas" āvṛtāḥ.
iṣubhir vyatisarpadbhir ādityo 'ntaradhīyata
khadyotair iva saṃyuktam antarikṣaṃ vyarājata.
rukma|pṛṣṭhāni cāpāni vyatiṣiktāni dhanvinām,
patatāṃ loka|vīrāṇāṃ savya|dakṣiṇam asyatām.
rathā rathaiḥ samājagmuḥ, pādātaiś ca padātayaḥ,
32.10 sādinaḥ sādibhiś c' âiva, gajaiś c' âpi mahā|gajāḥ.
asibhiḥ, paṭṭiśaiḥ, prāsaiḥ, śaktibhis, tomarair api
saṃrabdhāḥ samare, rājan, nijaghnur itar'|êtaram.
nighnantaḥ samare 'nyonyaṃ śūrāḥ parigha|bāhavaḥ
na śekur abhisaṃrabdhāḥ śurān kartum parāṅ|mukhān.

kṛtt'|ôttar'|ôṣṭhaṃ, su|nasaṃ, kṛtta|keśam, alaṅ|kṛtam
a|dṛśyata śiraś chinnaṃ, rajo|dhvastaṃ, sa|kuṇḍalam.
adṛśyaṃs tatra gātrāṇi śaraiś chinnāni bhāgaśaḥ,
śāla|skandha|nikāśāni kṣatriyāṇāṃ mahā|mṛdhe.
nāga|bhoga|nikāśaiś ca bāhubhiś candan'|ôkṣitaiḥ
32.15 āstīrṇā vasudhā bhāti, śirobhiś ca sa|kuṇḍalaiḥ.
rathināṃ rathibhiś c' âtra saṃprahāro 'bhyavartata,
sādibhiḥ sādināṃ c' âpi, padātīnāṃ padātibhiḥ,
upāśāmyad rajo bhaumaṃ rudhireṇa prasarpatā.

There was a frightful, hair-raising tumult of murders on
both sides, expanding Yama's kingdom, my king. As the sun 32.5
slid down, the clash between their multitudes of infantry
and cavalry, chariots and elephants, o king, was like that
between the gods and the *ásura*s. As both sides flew at each
other, mutually hacking at one another, the dust that flew up
from the ground ensured that nothing could be discerned.

Birds fell to the ground covered with dust from the army.
Even the sun disappeared as the arrows flew, and the sky
glittered as though it were brimming over with fireflies.
The archers' gilt bows got all tangled as the heroes of this
world, shooting right and left, fell. Chariots clashed against
chariots and infantry collided with infantry, while riders 32.10
encountered riders and elephants fought with elephants.
With swords, spears, barbed missiles, javelins and lances
they furiously overpowered each other in the conflict, my
king. The brave men, whose arms were like iron bars, killed
each other in the battle, but despite their fury neither side
was able to make the brave rival side flee.

Decapitated heads were seen rolling in the dust: wearing
earrings, with their upper lips cut, handsomely nosed, or ornamented on their trimmed hair. The limbs of the warriors
could be seen ripped to shreds by arrows in the great battle,
resembling the trunks of *shala* trees. The ground glistened,
strewn as it was with sandal-smeared arms, resembling the
coils of snakes, and with heads still wearing earrings. As 32.15
chariots attacked and rushed at chariots, riders at riders,
and infantry at infantry, the dust that settled ran over the
ground with blood.

kaśmalaṃ c' âviśad ghoraṃ, nirmaryādam avartata.
upāviśan garutmantaḥ śarair gāḍhaṃ pravejitāḥ,
antarikṣe gatir yeṣāṃ, darśanaṃ c' âpy arudhyata.
te ghnantaḥ samare 'nyonyaṃ śūrāḥ parigha|bāhavaḥ
na śekur abhisaṃrabdhāḥ śūrān kartuṃ parāṅ|mukhān.

Śatānīkaḥ śataṃ hatvā, Viśālākṣaś catuḥ|śatam,
praviṣṭau mahatīṃ senāṃ Trigartānāṃ mahā|rathau.
32.20 tau praviṣṭau mahā|senāṃ balavantau manasvinau
ārcchetāṃ bāhu|saṃrabdhau keśā|keśi rathā|rathi.
lakṣayitvā Trigartānāṃ tau praviṣṭau ratha|vrajam.
agrataḥ Sūryadattaś ca, Madirākṣaś ca pṛṣṭhataḥ,
Virāṭas tatra saṃgrāme hatvā pañca|śatān rathān,
hayānāṃ ca śatāny aṣṭau hatvā pañca mahā|rathān,
caran sa vividhān mārgān rathena ratha|sattamaḥ.

Trigartānāṃ Suśarmāṇam ārcchad rukma|rathaṃ raṇe.
tau vyavāharatāṃ tatra mah"|ātmānau mahā|balau,
anyonyam abhigarjantau, go|ṣṭheṣu vṛṣabhāv iva.
32.25 tato rājā Trigartānāṃ Suśarmā yuddha|durmadaḥ
Matsyaṃ samīyād rājānaṃ dvairathena nara'|rṣabhaḥ.

Some men sank into terrible faintheartedness and exceeded all boundaries of decency. Vultures and scavengers landed on the ground since their path and sight were obstructed by the tightly packed arrows flying through the sky. Though the brave, raging warriors, with arms like iron bars, attacked each other, they were not able to make their brave opponents flee.

Shataníka killed a hundred men, Vishaláksha four hundred, and by so doing that pair of mighty warriors infiltrated
the massive Tri·gartan army. When those two powerful and 32.20
intelligent men had penetrated the great army, they fought by grappling arm to arm, head to head and chariot to chariot. When they spotted the densest formation of Tri·gartan chariots, they made their way inward toward it. With Surya·datta in front of him and Madiráksha behind him, Viráta, that most excellent charioteer, annihilated five hundred chariots as well as obliterating eight hundred cavalrymen and five mighty warriors in the battle, performing various maneuvers on his chariot.

Then Tri·gartan Sushárman took to his golden chariot in battle, and the pair of them, Sushárman and Viráta, both high-souled and massively powerful, met one another as enemies and roared ferociously at each other, like bulls in
a cattle pen. King Sushárman of Tri·garta, the battle-crazed 32.25
bull-like man, challenged the Matsyan king to single chariot combat.

tato rathābhyāṃ rathinau vyatīyatur a|marṣaṇau
śarān vyasṛjatāṃ śīghraṃ, toya|dhārā ghanā iva.
anyonyaṃ c' âpi saṃrabdhau viceratur a|marṣaṇau,
kṛt'|âstrau niśitair bāṇair, asi|śakti|gadā|bhṛtau.
tato rājā Suśarmāṇaṃ vivyādha daśabhiḥ saraiḥ,
pañcabhiḥ pañcabhiś c' âsya vivyādha caturo hayān.
tath" âiva Matsya|rājānaṃ Suśarmā yuddha|durmadaḥ
pañcāśadbhiḥ śitair bāṇair vivyādha param'|âstra|vit.
32.30 tataḥ sainyaṃ, mahā|rāja, Matsya|rāja|Suśarmaṇoḥ
n' abhyajānat tad" ânyonyaṃ sainyena rajas" āvṛtam.

VAIŚAMPĀYANA uvāca:

33.1 TAMAS" ÂBHIPLUTE loke, rajasā c' âiva, Bhārata,
atiṣṭhan vai muhūrtaṃ tu vyūḍh'|ânīkāḥ prahāriṇaḥ.
tato 'ndha|kāraṃ praṇudann udatiṣṭhata candramāḥ,
kurvāṇo vimalāṃ rātriṃ, nandayan kṣatriyān yudhi.
tataḥ prakāśam āsādya punar yuddham avartata
ghora|rūpaṃ, tatas te sma n' âvaikṣanta paras|param.

tataḥ Suśarmā Traigartaḥ saha bhrātrā yavīyasā
abhyadravan Matsya|rājaṃ ratha|vrātena sarvaśaḥ.
33.5 tato rathābhyāṃ praskandya bhrātarau kṣatriya'|rṣabhau
gadā|pāṇī, su|saṃrabdhau samabhyadravatāṃ rathān.
tath" âiva teṣāṃ tu balāni tāni
kruddhāny ath' ânyonyam abhidravanti
gad"|âsi|khaḍgaiś ca, paraśvadhaiś ca,
prāsaiś ca tīkṣṇ'|âgra|supīta|dhāraiḥ.

Next, like dense clouds streaming rain, those impatient charioteers swiftly fired their arrows as they attacked on their cars. Incensed with each other, the pair of truculent men, trained in weaponry, attacked one another with sharpened arrows, both equipped with a mace, spear and sword. Then King Viráta pierced Sushárman with ten arrows and struck his four horses with five arrows each. But battle-crazed Sushárman was also acquainted with the highest weaponry, and he pierced the Matsyan king with fifty sharpened shafts.
Until finally, mighty king, the troops belonging to the Mat- 32.30
syan king and Sushárman could not distinguish each other, for the entire array was veiled with dust.

VAISHAMPÁYANA said:

THEN, WHEN THE world was overwhelmed with the dark- 33.1
ness and dust, Bhárata, the soldiers rested for a while, although still divided into their army companies and divisions. Later the moon rose, chasing away the blinding dark. Making the night luminous, the moon gladdened the kshatriyas for battle. Then, once it was bright, the conflict started up again. But it took on such a dreadful form that the soldiers could not recognize each other.

Sushárman the Tri·gartan, along with his younger brother and chariots on all sides, rushed all together at the King
of Matsya, but then those furious brothers, the bull-like 33.5
warriors, leaped down from their vehicles, mace in hand, and charged at the chariots. The enraged troops rushed at each other with maces, swords and scimitars, as well as hatchets, barbed missiles and sharp-pointed copper-bladed arrows.

balaṃ tu Matsyasya balena rājā
sarvaṃ Trigart'|âdhipatiḥ Suśarmā
pramathya, jitvā ca prasahya Matsyaṃ,
Virāṭam ojasvinam abhyadhāvat.
tau nihatya pṛthag dhuryāv ubhau tau pārṣṇi|sārathī
vi|rathaṃ Matsya|rājānaṃ jīva|grāham agṛhṇatām.
tam unmathya Suśarm" âtha, yuvatīm iva kāmukaḥ,
syandanaṃ svaṃ samāropya prayayau śīghra|vāhanaḥ.
33.10 tasmin gṛhīte vi|rathe Virāṭe balavattare
prādravanta bhayān Matsyās, Trigartair arditā bhṛśam.
teṣu santrasyamāneṣu Kuntī|putro Yudhiṣṭhiraḥ
pratyabhāṣan mahā|bāhuṃ Bhīmasenam arin|damam:
«Matsya|rājaḥ parāmṛṣṭas Trigartena Suśarmaṇā!
taṃ mocaya, mahā|bāho, na gacched dviṣatāṃ vaśam!
uṣitāḥ sma sukhaṃ sarve, sarva|kāmaiḥ su|pūjitāḥ.
Bhīmasena, tvayā kāryā tasya vāsasya niṣkṛtiḥ.»

BHĪMASENA uvāca:

aham enaṃ paritrāsye śāsanāt tava, pārthiva.
paśya me su|mahat karma yudhyataḥ saha śatrubhiḥ
33.15 sva|bāhu|balam āśritya tiṣṭha tvaṃ bhrātṛbhiḥ saha.
ek'|ântam āśrito, rājan, paśya me 'dya parākramam.
su|skandho 'yaṃ mahā|vṛkṣo gadā|rūpa iva sthitaḥ
aham enam apārujya drāvayiṣyāmi śātravān.

And once King Sushárman, lord of the Tri·gartas, had assaulted, defeated and conquered the whole Matsyan force with his own troops, he rushed toward Viráta, the King of Matsya, who was, however, pretty powerful himself. When the two brothers had separately killed both Viráta's horses and outer drivers, they took the King of Matsya, who had lost his chariot, alive as a prisoner. Sushárman treated him roughly, like a lustful man treats a young woman, and made him climb aboard his own chariot. Then the two of them quickly drove away.

When the very powerful Viráta, without his chariot, was 33.10
captured, the Matsyas ran away in panic; overly tormented by the chariots and weapons. But when they were terrified, Yudhi·shthira, the son of Kuntí, said to the massive armed Bhima·sena, the conqueror of his enemies: "The king of the Matsyas has been seized by Sushárman the Tri·gartan! Long-armed man, free him to prevent his becoming subject to the control of his enemies! We all lived happily, well honored, with all our desires catered to, so, Bhima·sena, you should repay him for his hospitality."

BHIMA·SENA said:

I will rescue him at your command, king. You stand with our brothers and watch my enormously mighty achievement in fighting with the enemies, relying purely on the 33.15
strength of my own arms. King, behold my prowess now, as I rely purely on this one talent. I will uproot that enormous tree with the huge trunk, just standing there like a mace, and I will rout the enemy.

VAIŚAMPĀYANA uvāca:

taṃ mattam iva mātaṅgaṃ vīkṣamāṇaṃ vanas|patim
abravīd bhrātaraṃ vīraṃ Dharma|rājo Yudhiṣṭhiraḥ:
«mā, Bhīma, sāhasaṃ kārṣīs, tiṣṭhatv eṣa vanas|patiḥ.
mā tvaṃ vṛkṣeṇa karmāṇi kurvāṇam ati|mānuṣam
janāḥ samavabudhyeran, ‹Bhīmo 'yam! iti,› Bhārata.
anyad ev' āyudhaṃ kiñ cit pratipadyasva mānuṣam,
33.20 cāpaṃ vā yadi vā śaktiṃ, nistriṃśaṃ vā paraśvadham.
yad eva mānuṣaṃ, Bhīma, bhaved anyair a|lakṣitam,
tad ev' āyudham ādāya mokṣay' āśu mahī|patim.
yamau ca cakra|rakṣau te bhavitārau mahā|balau.
sahitāḥ samare tatra Matsya|rājaṃ parīpsata.»

evam uktas tu vegena Bhimaseno mahā|balaḥ
gṛhītvā tu dhanuḥ śreṣṭhaṃ javena su|mahā|javaḥ
vyamuñcac chara|varṣāṇi, sa|toya iva toyadaḥ.
taṃ Bhīmo bhīma|karmāṇaṃ Suśarmāṇam ath' âdravat,
Virāṭaṃ samavekṣy' âinaṃ, «tiṣṭha tiṣṭh'! êti» c' âvadat.
33.25 Suśarmā cintayām āsa kāl'|ântaka|Yam'|ôpamam,
«tiṣṭha tiṣṭh'! êti» bhāṣantaṃ pṛṣṭhato ratha|puṅgavaḥ,
«dṛṣyatām su|mahat karma! mahad yuddham upasthitam!»
parāvṛtto dhanur gṛhya Suśarmā bhrātṛbhiḥ saha.

nimeṣ'|ântara|mātreṇa Bhīmasenena te rathāḥ,
rathānāṃ ca, gajānāṃ ca, vājināṃ ca sa|sādinām
sahasra|śata|saṅghātāḥ śūrāṇām ugra|dhanvinām
pātitā Bhīmasenena Virāṭasya samīpataḥ.
pattayo nihatās teṣāṃ gadāṃ gṛhya mah"|ātmanā.

VAISHAMPÁYANA said:

Yudhi·shthira, the king of righteousness, said to his mighty brother, who was like an elephant in rut as he eyed the forest lord: "Bhima, don't act rashly, but let the forest lord remain where it is. Don't perform superhuman acts with that tree. People will recognize you and say, 'This is Bhima!,' Bhárata. So take some human weapon such as a bow 33.20
or spear or sword or axe. So taking some human weapon, Bhima, which won't be such a giveaway to others, quickly rescue the great king. The powerful twins will defend your wheels, and together strive to win back the King of Matsya."

Thus addressed, the mighty Bhima·sena quickly took his best bow and almost instantaneously shot a downpour of arrows, like a shower from a rain cloud. Then Bhima ran toward Sushárman; himself a man of terrifying deeds, and catching sight of Viráta, he shouted, "Stay there, stay there!"
But Sushárman, the bull-like chariot-warrior, appraised the 33.25
situation and noticed Bhima bchind him likc all-dcstroying Time in the form of Yama, shouting, "Stay there, stay there! Watch this extraordinary feat! The great battle is at hand!" So, turning back with his brothers, Sushárman took up his bow.

But in the twinkling of an eye Bhima·sena brought down those chariots and then hundreds of thousands of chariot, elephant and horse units with their charioteers. Fierce archer heroes were toppled by high-souled Bhima·sena in full sight of Viráta. Then, taking up his mace, he massacred their infantry.

tad dṛṣṭvā tādṛśaṃ yuddhaṃ Suśarmā yuddha|dur|madaḥ
cintayām āsa manasā, «kiṃ śeṣaṃ hi balasya me?
aparo dṛśyate sainye purā magno mahā|bale.»
33.30 ākarṇa|pūrṇena tadā dhanuṣā pratyadṛśyata
Suśarmā, sāyakāṃs tīkṣṇān kṣipate ca punaḥ punaḥ.
tataḥ samastās te sarve turagān abhyacodayan,
divyam astraṃ vikurvāṇās, Trigartān praty amarṣaṇāḥ.
tān nivṛtta|rathān dṛṣṭvā Pāṇḍavān sā mahā|camūḥ.
Vairāṭiḥ parama|kruddho yuyudhe param' âdbhutam.
sahasram avadhīt tatra Kuntī|putro Yudhiṣṭhiraḥ,
Bhīmaḥ sapta sahasrāṇi Yama|lokam adarśayat.
Nakulaś c' âpi sapt' âiva śatāni prāhiṇoc charaiḥ,
śatāni trīṇi śūrāṇāṃ Sahadevaḥ pratāpavān
33.35 Yudhiṣṭhira|samādiṣṭo nijaghne puruṣa'|rṣabhaḥ.
tato 'bhyapatad atyugraḥ Suśarmāṇam udāyudhaḥ
hatvā tāṃ mahatīṃ senāṃ Trigartānāṃ mahā|rathaḥ.
tato Yudhiṣṭhiro rājā tvaramāṇo mahā|rathaḥ
abhipatya Suśarmāṇaṃ śarair abhyāhanad bhṛśam,
Suśarm" âpi su|saṃrabdhas tvaramāṇo Yudhiṣṭhiram
avidhyan navabhir bāṇaiś, caturbhiś caturo hayān.
tato, rājann, āśu|kārī Kuntī|putro Vṛkodaraḥ
samāsādya Suśarmāṇam aśvān asya vyapothayat.
pṛṣṭha|gopāṃś ca tasy' âtha hatvā parama|sāyakaiḥ
33.40 ath' âsya sārathiṃ kruddho rath'|ôpasthād apātayat.
cakra|rakṣaś ca śūro vai Madirākṣo 'tiviśrutaḥ
samāyād vi|rathaṃ dṛṣṭvā Trigartaṃ, prāharat tadā.

Watching such combat, battle-crazed Sushárman contemplated the situation in his mind, thinking, "What is left of my forces? My younger brother seems to have drowned in this mighty army some time ago." So, with his bow fully 33.30 extended as far as his ear, Sushárman looked for his target and kept firing sharp arrows again and again. But the whole force of Viráta's mighty army drove their horses on and assaulted the Tri·gartas, producing celestial weapons, when they noticed the Pándavas turning their chariots back for an attack. Utterly enraged, Viráta's son also fought fantastically.

Yudhi·shthira, the son of Kuntí, killed a thousand men, while Bhima compelled seven thousand to look upon the realm of Yama. Nákula, too, sent down seven hundred with his arrows, while the majestic Saha·deva, a bull among men, killed three hundred brave soldiers under direction from Yu- 33.35 dhi·shthira. Then the hugely formidable and mighty warrior flew at Sushárman with his weapons raised, once he had killed a huge force of the Tri·gartas. King Yudhi·shthira, the great chariot-warrior, hastily flew at Sushárman and violently struck him with arrows, but Sushárman, utterly furious, rushed at Yudhi·shthira and hit him with nine shafts and each of his four horses with four arrows.

Then, my king, Vrikódara, the son of Kuntí, a man of swift action, came up to Sushárman and crushed his horses. Once he had killed the guards at his back with excellent arrows, enraged, he sent the charioteer tumbling from the 33.40 middle of the chariot. When the brave wheel guard, the famous Madiráksha, noticed that the Tri·gartan king had lost his chariot, he advanced and attacked. Then the mighty Viráta leaped down from Sushárman's chariot, seized his

tato Virāṭaḥ praskandya rathād atha Suśarmaṇaḥ
gadāṃ tasya parāmṛśya tam ev' âbhyadravad balī.
sa cacāra gadā|pāṇir vṛddho 'pi taruṇo yathā.
palāyamānaṃ Traigartaṃ dṛṣṭvā Bhīmo 'bhyabhāṣata:
«rāja|putra, nivartasva! na te yuktaṃ palāyanam!
anena vīryeṇa kathaṃ gās tvaṃ prārthayase balāt?
kathaṃ c' ânucarāṃs tyaktvā śatru|madhye viṣīdasi?»
33.45 ity uktaḥ sa tu Pārthena Suśarmā ratha|yūthapaḥ
«tiṣṭha tiṣṭh'! êti!» Bhīmaṃ sa sahas" âbhyadravad balī.
Bhīmas tu bhīma|saṃkāśo rathāt praskandya Pāṇḍavaḥ
prādravat tūrṇam a|vyagro jīvit'|epsuḥ Suśarmaṇaḥ.
taṃ Bhīmaseno dhāvantam abhyadhāvata vīryavān
Trigarta|rājam ādātuṃ, siṃhaḥ kṣudra|mṛgaṃ yathā.
abhidrutya Suśarmāṇaṃ keśa|pakṣe parāmṛśat,
samudyamya tu roṣāt taṃ niṣpipeṣa mahī|tale.
padā mūrdhni mahā|bāhuḥ prāharad vilapiṣyataḥ,
tasya jānuṃ dadau Bhīmo, jaghne c' âinam aratninā.
sa moham agamad rājā prahāra|vara|pīḍitaḥ.
33.50 tasmin gṛhīte, virathe Trigartānāṃ mahā|rathe
abhajyata balaṃ sarvaṃ Traigartaṃ tad bhay'|āturam.
nivartya gās tataḥ sarvāḥ Pāṇḍu|putrā mahā|rathāḥ,
avajitya Suśarmāṇaṃ, dhanaṃ c' ādāya sarvaśaḥ,
sva|bāhu|bala|sampannā, hrī|niṣevā yata|vratāḥ,
Virāṭasya mah"|ātmānaḥ parikleśa|vināśanāḥ
sthitāḥ samakṣaṃ te sarve tv. atha Bhīmo 'bhyabhāṣata,

mace and ran after him. Though an old man, he moved, mace in his hand, as though he were still young.

And, seeing the Tri·gartan king running away, Bhima said to him: "Prince, turn back! Your escape is not seemly! With this level of valor, how could you wish to forcibly steal the cattle? And how can you forsake your follower and sink so low in the midst of your enemies?"

Spoken to in this way by Pritha's son, Sushárman, the lord 33.45
of a multitude of chariots, said, "Stay there! Stay there!," and the mighty man charged swiftly at Bhima. But Bhima, the terrifying-looking son of Pandu, leaped down from his chariot and ran at full pelt, entirely focused and longing for the life of Sushárman. Powerful Bhima·sena chased the escaping Tri·gartan king in order to seize him, just like a lion chasing a little deer.

Once he had caught up with Sushárman, he seized him by the knot of his hair and lifted him up out of rage. Then he pounded him into the ground. Long-armed Bhima kicked him in the head as he wailed, and clamping his knee on his chest he beat him with his fists. The king was totally overwhelmed by the beating and became senseless.

When this mighty Tri·gartan warrior was deprived of his 33.50
chariot and captured, the whole Tri·gartan army, sick from fear, divided and fled. But the powerful Pándava warriors, who had turned back the cattle, defeated Sushárman and won wealth in general. Endowed with strength of arms, practitioners of modesty and observers of vows, they all stood in Viráta's presence as the men who had destroyed the high-souled king's problems. Bhima then spoke, saying,

«n' âyaṃ pāpa|samācāro matto jīvitum arhati;
kiṃ tu śakyaṃ mayā kartuṃ yad rājā satataṃ ghṛṇī?»
gale gṛhītvā rājānam ānīya vi|vaśaṃ vaśam
tata enaṃ viceṣṭantaṃ baddhvā Pārtho Vṛkodaraḥ
33.55 ratham āropayām āsa vi|saṃjñaṃ pāṃsu|guṇṭhitaṃ.
abhyetya raṇa|madhya|stham abhyagacchad Yudhiṣṭhiram
darśayām āsa Bhīmas tu Suśarmāṇaṃ nar'|âdhipam.
provāca puruṣa|vyāghro Bhīmam āhava|śobhinam
taṃ rājā prāhasat dṛṣṭvā «mucyatāṃ vai nar'|âdhamaḥ.»
evam ukto 'bravīd Bhīmaḥ Suśarmāṇaṃ mahā|balam:

BHĪMA uvāca:

«jīvituṃ c' êcchase, mūḍha, hetuṃ me gadataḥ śṛṇu.
‹dāso 'sm' îti› tvayā vācyaṃ saṃsatsu ca sabhāsu ca.
evaṃ te jīvitaṃ dadyām. eṣa yuddha|jito vidhiḥ.»
tam uvāca tato jyeṣṭho bhrātā sa|praṇayaṃ vacaḥ.

YUDHIṢṬHIRA uvāca:

33.60 muñca, muñc' âdham'|ācāraṃ, pramāṇaṃ yadi te vayam.
dāsa|bhāvaṃ gato hy eṣa Virāṭasya mahī|pateḥ.
a|dāso gaccha, mukto 'si, m" âivaṃ kārṣīḥ kadā cana!

VAIŚAṂPĀYANA uvāca:

34.1 EVAM UKTE TU sa|vrīḍaḥ Suśarm" āsīd adho|mukhaḥ.
sa mukto 'bhyetya rājānam abhivādya pratasthivān.
visṛjya tu Suśarmāṇaṃ Pāṇḍavās te hata|dviṣaḥ
sva|bāhu|bala|saṃpannā, hrī|niṣevā, yata|vratāḥ
saṃgrāma|śiraso madhye tāṃ rātriṃ sukhino 'vasan.

"This crazed miscreant does not deserve to live, but what can I do when the king is so compassionate?" And, having seized the helpless king by the throat, Vrikódara, the son of Pritha, subdued him. And binding the struggling man
he lifted him, now unconcious and caked in dirt, into the 33.55
chariot. Then Bhima made his way up to Yudhi·shthira, the lord of men, who was standing in the center of the battlefield, and showed King Sushárman to him. The tiger-like king said to Bhima, the ornament of war, when he had seen Sushárman and laughed: "Release this vilest of men." Thus addressed, Bhima said to the mighty Sushárman:

BHIMA said:

"If, fool, you want to live, then listen to the crux of what I'm saying. You must say 'I am a slave' in assemblies and courts. This is the condition on which I allow you to live. This is the winning combatant's customary right." Then his elder brother addressed him affectionately in these words:

YUDHI·SHTHIRA said:

Let him go. Release this man who is guilty of the vilest 33.60
conduct if you accept me as an authority. This man has become great King Viráta's slave. Go a free man, you are released, but don't ever do such things again!

VAISHAMPÁYANA said:

WHEN HE WAS spoken to in this manner, Sushárman was 34.1
ashamed and hung his head, looking down at the floor. Now that he had been released, he went up to the king, saluted him and left. Endowed with strength in their arms, the modest and vow-observing Pándavas, who had let Sushárman go and killed their enemies, spent the night happily in the

tato Virāṭaḥ Kaunteyān ati|mānuṣa|vikramān
arcayām āsa vittena mānena ca mahā|rathān.

VIRĀṬA uvāca:

yath" âiva mama ratnāni, yuṣmākaṃ tāni vai tathā.
kāryaṃ kuruta vai sarve yathā|kāmaṃ, yathā|sukham.
34.5 dadāmy alaṅ|kṛtāḥ kanyā, vasūni vividhāni ca,
manasaś c' âpy abhipretaṃ, yuddhe śatru|nibarhaṇāḥ!
yuṣmākaṃ vikramād adya mukto 'haṃ svastimān iha!
tasmād bhavanto Matsyānām īśvarāḥ sarva eva hi!

VAIŚAMPĀYANA uvāca:

tath" âbhivādinaṃ Matsyaṃ Kauraveyāḥ pṛthak pṛthak
ūcuḥ prāñjalayaḥ sarve Yudhiṣṭhira|purogamāḥ:
«pratinandāma te vākyaṃ sarvaṃ c' âiva, viśām pate,
eten' âiva pratītāḥ sma yat tvaṃ mukto 'dya śatrubhiḥ.»
tato 'bravīt prītamanā Matsya|rājo Yudhiṣṭhiram
punar eva mahā|bāhur Virāṭo rāja|sattamaḥ:
34.10 «ehi, tvām abhiṣekṣyāmi, Matsya|rājas tu no bhavān!
manasaś c' âpy abhipretaṃ yath"|êṣṭaṃ, bhuvi dur|labham,
tat te 'haṃ sampradāsyāmi. sarvam arhati no bhavān:
ratnāni, gāḥ, su|varṇaṃ ca, maṇi|muktam ath' âpi ca.
Vaiyāghrapadya, vipr'|êndra, sarvath' âiva namo 'stu te.
tvat|kṛte hy adya paśyāmi rājyaṃ, santānam eva ca!
yataś ca jāta|saṃrambho na ca śatru|vaśaṃ gataḥ!»

middle of the army's vanguard. Viráta then honored those superhumanly strong warrior sons of Kuntí with wealth and respect.

VIRÁTA said:

My jewels are yours as much as mine. All of you, do what you want: whatever takes your fancy. I will give you 34.5
ornamented women, every kind of wealth and whatever your heart desires, crushers of the enemy in battle! Today your valor has saved me and so I am blessed in this world! Therefore, all of you are lords of the Matsyas!

VAISHAMPÁYANA said:

The descendants of the Kurus, led by Yudhi·shthira, joined their hands together and each replied to the King of Matsya, who had spoken in this manner, addressing him in this way: "Lord of earth, we are all delighted with your words, but are already happy that today you have been freed from your enemies." The Matsyan king, Viráta, the long-armed greatest of sovereigns, was gladdened and again said
to Yudhi·shthira: "Come, I will consecrate you as King of 34.10
Matsya! Next, I will bestow upon you whatever the heart desires, whatever is longed for in this world, irrespective of how difficult it may be to acquire. For as our lord you deserve everything: jewels, cattle, gold, gems and pearls. Lord of brahmins of the Vyaghra·pad line, may every manner of homage be paid to you. For it is because of what you did that today I look upon my kingdom and my family! When violent fury surrounded me, I did not fall under the power of my enemies!"

tato Yudhiṣṭhiro Matsyaṃ punar ev' âbhyabhāṣata:
«pratinandāmi te vākyaṃ. mano|jñaṃ, Matsya, bhāṣase!
34.15 ānṛśaṃsya|paro nityaṃ, su|sukhī satataṃ bhava.
gacchantu dūtās tvaritaṃ nagaraṃ tava, pārthiva,
suhṛdāṃ priyam ākhyātuṃ, ghoṣayantu ca te jayam!»
tatas tad|vacanān Matsyo dūtān rājā samādiśat:
«ācakṣadhvaṃ puraṃ gatvā saṃgrāma|vijayaṃ mama!
kumāryaḥ samalaṃkṛtya paryāgacchantu me purāt,
vāditrāṇi ca sarvāṇi, gaṇikāś ca sv|alaṃkṛtāḥ.»
etāṃ c' ājñāṃ tataḥ śrutvā rājñā Matsyena noditāḥ
tām ājñāṃ śirasā kṛtvā prasthitā hṛṣṭa|mānasāḥ.
te gatvā tatra tāṃ rātrim atha sūry'|ôdayaṃ prati
Virāṭasya pur'|âbhyāśe dūtā jayam aghoṣayan.

VAIŚAMPĀYANA uvāca:

35.1 YĀTE TRIGARTĀN Matsye tu, paśūṃs tān vai parīpsati,
Duryodhanaḥ sah'|âmātyo Virāṭam upayād atha.
Bhīṣmo, Droṇaś ca, Karṇaś ca, Kṛpaś ca param'|âstra|vit,
Drauṇiś ca, Saubalaś c' âiva, tathā Duḥśāsanaḥ, prabho,
Viviṃśatir, Vikarṇaś ca, Citrasenaś ca viryavān
Durmukho, Duḥśalaś c' âiva, ye c' âiv' ânye mahā|rathāḥ—
ete Matsyān upāgamya Virāṭasya mahī|pateḥ
ghoṣān vidrāvya tarasā go|dhanaṃ jahrur ojasā.
35.5 ṣaṣṭiṃ gavāṃ sahasrāṇi Kuravaḥ kālayanti ca,
mahatā ratha|vaṃśena parivārya samantataḥ.

Then Yudhi·shthira again addressed the King of Matsya: "I am delighted with the gratifying speech you gave, King of Matsya! Always be kind to others, and eternally fortu- 34.15
nate. Now let messengers quickly go to your city, king, to announce the good news to our friends. Let them shout of your victory!" So the Matsyan king ordered messengers in accordance with his advice, saying, "Go to the city and declare my victory in battle! Let the noble ladies and courtesans come out from the city, decked in ornaments with all their musical instruments." Having heard the command, and being driven on by the King of Matsya, they took the order upon themselves and left with joy in their hearts. When they got there that night, the messengers shouted about Viráta's victory at the city gates at dawn.

VAISHAMPÁYANA said:

Now, WHEN THE King of Matsya had gone after the 35.1
King of Tri·garta, eager to retrieve his cattle, Duryódhana and his counselors invaded Viráta's kingdom. Bhishma, Drona, Karna and Kripa acquainted with the best weapons, Ashvatthâman, the son of Drona, Súbala's son, and Duhshásana, o lord, Vivínshati, Vikárna and the valiant Chitra·sena, Dúrmukha and Dúhshala—these and other great warriors came upon the Matsyas, quickly drove off King Viráta's herdsmen and stole his wealth of cattle by force. The Kurus, having surrounded them on all sides with their 35.5
huge force of chariots, rustled sixty thousand cattle.

go|pālānāṃ tu ghoṣasya hanyatāṃ tair mahā|rathaiḥ
ārāvaḥ su|mahān āsīt saṃprahāre bhayaṅ|kare.
gop'|âdhyakṣo bhaya|trasto ratham āsthāya sa|tvaraḥ
jagāma nagarāy' âiva parikrośaṃs tad" ârtavat.
sa praviśya puraṃ rājño nṛpa|veśm' âbhyayāt tataḥ.
avatīrya rathāt tūrṇam ākhyātuṃ praviveśa ha.

dṛṣṭvā Bhūmiñjayaṃ nāma putraṃ Matsyasya māninam
tasmai tat sarvam ācaṣṭa rāṣṭrasya paśu|karṣaṇam:
35.10 «ṣaṣṭiṃ gavāṃ sahasrāṇi Kuravaḥ kālayanti te.
tad vijetuṃ samuttiṣṭha go|dhanaṃ, rāṣṭra|vardhana.
rāja|putra, hita|prepsuḥ kṣipraṃ niryāhi ca svayam!
tvāṃ hi Matsyo mahī|pālaḥ śūnya|pālam ih' âkarot.
tvayā pariṣado madhye ślāghate sa nar'|âdhipaḥ,
‹putro mam' ânurūpaś ca, śūraś c' êti, kul'|ôdvahaḥ,
iṣv|astre nipuṇo yodhaḥ, sadā vīraś ca me sutaḥ.›

tasya tat satyam ev' âstu manuṣy'|êndrasya bhāṣitam!
āvartaya Kurūn jitvā pasūn, paśumatāṃ vara;
nirdah' âiṣām anīkāni bhīmena śara|tejasā.
35.15 dhanuś|cyutai rukma|puṅkhaiḥ śaraiḥ sannata|parvabhiḥ
dviṣatāṃ bhindhy anīkāni, gajānām iva yūtha|paḥ.
pāś'|ôpadhānāṃ, jyā|tantrīṃ, cāpa|daṇḍāṃ, mahā|svanām,
śara|varṇāṃ dhanur|vīṇāṃ śatru|madhye pravādaya.

An incredibly loud cry of horror erupted from the cowherds as they were killed by those great warriors in the fear-inducing battle. The superintendent of the cowherds, trembling with fear, quickly got on a chariot and went to the city, howling out loud in his suffering. Upon entering the city, he went to the king's royal palace, then, once he had quickly alighted from his chariot, he went in to tell his story.

And, seeing the proud son of the King of Matsya, a man named Bhumin·jaya, he told him everything about the kin-
dom's cattle rustling, saying: "The Kurus stole sixty thou- 35.10
sand cattle, so get up, augmenter of the kingdom, to have victory over the wealth of cattle. Prince, if you wish to benefit your country, quickly go out yourself! The King of Matsya made you substitute in his vacant role. That lord of men boasts about you in the middle of the assembly, saying, 'My son is brave in my image, a chip off the old block, and a skilled archer. My son is always a hero.'

May the lord of men's words be proved to be true! Bring back your cattle, best of cattle barons, once you've defeated the Kurus, and scorch their armies with the terrible energy of
your arrows. Like the leader of a herd of elephants, break the 35.15
armies of your enemies with well-prepared golden-winged arrows shot from your bow. Make your bow resonate in the midst of the enemy like *vina*: for its edges are the cushioned rests, the string is the chord, the staff is the crossbar for the strings, and its arrows are its loud musical notes.

śvetā rajata|saṅkāśā rathe yujyantu te hayāḥ,
dhvajaṃ ca siṃhaṃ sauvarṇam ucchrayantu tava, prabho.
rukma|puṅkhāḥ, prasann'|âgrā, muktā hastavatā tvayā
chādayantu śarāḥ sūryaṃ rājñāṃ mārga|nirodhakāḥ!
raṇe jitvā Kurūn sarvān, vajra|pāṇir iv' âsurān,
yaśo mahad avāpya tvaṃ praviś' êdaṃ puraṃ punaḥ!
35.20 tvaṃ hi rāṣṭrasya paramā gatir, Matsya|pateḥ sutaḥ,
yathā hi Pāṇḍu|putrāṇām Arjuno jayatāṃ varaḥ.
evam eva gatir nūnaṃ bhavān viṣaya|vāsinām.
gatimanto vayaṃ tv adya sarve viṣaya|vāsinaḥ.»

strī|madhya uktas ten' âsau tad vākyam abhayaṃ|karam
antaḥ|pure ślāghamāna idaṃ vacanam abravīt:

UTTARA uvāca:

36.1 ADY' ÂHAM anugaccheyaṃ dṛḍha|dhanvā gavāṃ padam,
yadi me sārathiḥ kaś cid bhaved aśveṣu kovidaḥ!
taṃ tv ahaṃ n' âvagacchāmi, yo me yantā bhaven naraḥ.
paśyadhvaṃ sārathiṃ kṣipraṃ mama yuktaṃ prayāsyataḥ.
aṣṭāviṃśati|rātraṃ vā, māsaṃ vā nūnam antataḥ,
yat tad" āsīn mahad yuddhaṃ, tatra me sārathir hataḥ.

sa labheyaṃ yadā tv anyaṃ haya|yāna|vidaṃ naram,
tvarāvān adya yātv" âhaṃ, samucchrita|mahā|dhvajam
36.5 vigāhya tat par'|ânīkaṃ gaja|vāji|rath'|ākulam,
śastra|pratāpa|nirvīryān Kurūn jitv" ānaye paśūn.
Duryodhanaṃ, Śāntanavaṃ,

Yoke your silvery-gleaming white horses to your chariot and raise your golden lion standard, my lord. Let your golden-winged and sharp-pointed arrows, released by your dextrous arms, provide shade from the sun and block the path of those kings! Once you have defeated the Kurus in battle, just as the wielder of the thunderbolt defeated the *ásuras*, and obtained great fame, then return again to the city! You, as Prince of Matsya, are the kingdom's last resort, 35.20
just as Árjuna, that best of victors, is the Pándavas' last resort. Surely, in this manner, you are the sanctuary for those who live in this territory. Today we who live in this realm all take our refuge in you."

Addressed by that man in those confidence-building words, the prince, who was among the women in their apartments, boasted in these words:

ÚTTARA said:

I WOULD GO OUT now with my sturdy bow, following the 36.1
tracks of the cattle, if there were any man experienced with horses to be my charioteer! But I cannot find any man who would be my driver. Quickly look for a charioteer to join me. since I'm rearing to go. My own charioteer was killed during the great battle, which lasted at least twenty-eight days if not a month.

I will raise my standard without delay and set out the moment I find another man who is experienced with horses. I will penetrate the enemy army full of elephants, horses 36.5
and chariots, defeat the Kurus, who are weak in power and weapons, and lead back the cattle. I will make Duryódhana, Bhishma, the son of Shántanu, Karna, Kripa, Drona and

Karṇaṃ Vaikartanaṃ, Kṛpam,
Droṇaṃ ca saha putreṇa,
mah"|êṣv|āsān samāgatān
vitrāsayitvā saṅgrāme, dānavān iva vajra|bhṛt,
anen' âiva muhūrtena punaḥ pratyānaye paśūn.
śūnyam āsādya Kuravaḥ prayānty ādāya go|dhanam.
kiṃ tu śakyaṃ mayā kartuṃ, yad ahaṃ tatra n' âbhavam?
paśyeyur adya me vīryaṃ Kuravas te samāgatāḥ:
‹kiṃ nu Pārtho 'rjunaḥ sākṣād ayam asmān prabādhate?›

VAIŚAMPĀYANA uvāca:

36.10 śrutvā tad Arjuno vākyaṃ rājñaḥ putrasya bhāṣataḥ
atīta|samaye kāle, priyāṃ bhāryām a|ninditām,
Drupadasya sutāṃ, tanvīṃ, Pāñcālīṃ, pāvak'|ātmajām,
saty'|ārjava|guṇ'|ôpetāṃ, bhartuḥ priya|hite ratām
uvāca rahasi prītaḥ Kṛṣṇāṃ sarv'|ârtha|kovidaḥ:
«Uttaraṃ brūhi, kalyāṇi, kṣipraṃ mad|vacanād idam:
‹ayaṃ vai Pāṇḍavasy' āsīt sārathiḥ saṃmato, dṛḍhaḥ,
mahā|yuddheṣu saṃsiddhaḥ. sa te yantā bhaviṣyati.›»

tasya tad vacanaṃ strīṣu bhāṣataś ca punaḥ punaḥ,
na s" âmarṣata Pāñcālī Bibhatsoḥ parikīrtanam.
36.15 ath' âinam upasaṃgamya strī|madhyāt sā tapasvinī,
vrīḍamān" êva śanakair idaṃ vacanam abravīt:
«yo 'sau bṛhad vāraṇ'|ābho yuvā, su|priya|darśanaḥ,
‹Bṛhannal" êti› vikhyātaḥ, Pārthasy' āsīt sa sārathiḥ.
dhanuṣy an|avaraś c' āsīt tasya śiṣyo mah"|ātmanaḥ.
dṛṣṭa|pūrvo mayā, vīra, carantyā Pāṇḍavān prati.
yadā tat Pāvako dāvam adahat Khāṇḍavaṃ mahat,

his son, Ashvattháman, and the other assembled great lords tremble, just as the wielder of the thunderbolt made the *dánava*s tremble, and in another instant I will lead the cattle back again. The Kurus have found an empty battlefield and so they are leaving, taking the wealth of cattle. But what can I do when I am not there? The assembled Kurus will behold my valor this very day, saying: "Could this man really be Árjuna himself, the son of Pritha, who is driving us away?"

VAISHAMPÁYANA said:

Having listened to what the prince had to say, after 36.10
the meeting and a little time had passed, Árjuna spoke to his dear faultless wife, the daughter of Drúpada, the slim Princess of Pancháli, who was born from pure fire, who possessed the virtues of truth and honesty, and was devoted to what was pleasing and beneficial to her husbands. Árjuna, skilled in all matters, spoke affectionately to Krishná in private: "My beautiful girl, tell Úttara my message without delay: 'This man was Pándava's reliable and esteemed charioteer, successful in great battles. He will be your driver.'"

Hearing the prince's words repeated time and again among the women, the Princess of Pancháli could not endure Úttara's boasting about Bibhátsu. So, stepping out 36.15
from the midst of the women, the poor, bashful lady said gently, "The exceptionally handsome youth called Brihan·nala, who resembles a mighty elephant, was Partha's charioteer. He was the best with a bow and a pupil of that high-souled man. I have seen this hero before, while I was working for the Pándavas. When Agni scorched the great Khándava forest, it was this man who kept Árjuna's excellent

Arjunasya tad" ânena saṃgṛhītā hay'|ôttamāḥ.
tena sārathinā Pārthaḥ sarva|bhūtāni sarvaśaḥ
ajayat Khāṇḍava|prasthe. na hi yant" âsti tādṛśaḥ.»

UTTARA uvāca:

36.20 sairandhri, jānāsi tathā yuvānaṃ,
na|puṃsako n' âiva bhaved yath" âsau.
ahaṃ na śaknomi Bṛhannalāṃ, śubhe,
vaktuṃ svayaṃ, ‹yaccha hayān mam'!› êti vai.

DRAUPADY uvāca:

«y" êyaṃ kumārī su|śroṇī bhaginī te yavīyasī,
asyāḥ sā, vīra, vacanaṃ kariṣyati na saṃśayaḥ.
yadi vai sārathiḥ sa syāt, Kurūn sarvān, na saṃśayaḥ,
jitvā, gāś ca samādāya dhruvam āgamanaṃ bhavet.»
evam uktaḥ sa sairandhryā bhaginīṃ pratyabhāṣata:
«gaccha tvam, an|avady'|âṅgi, tām ānaya Bṛhannalām.»
sā bhrātrā preṣitā śīghram agacchan nartanā|gṛham,
yatr' āste sa mahā|bāhuś channaḥ satreṇa Pāṇḍavaḥ.

VAIŚAMPĀYANA uvāca:

37.1 SĀ PRĀDRAVAT kāñcana|mālya|dhāriṇī,
jyeṣṭhena bhrātrā prahitā, yaśasvinī
Sudakṣiṇā vedi|vilagna|madhyā,
sā padma|patr'|ābha|nibhā, śikhaṇḍinī,
tanvī, śubh'|âṅgī, maṇi|citra|mekhalā,
Matsyasya rājño duhitā, śriyā vṛtā,
tan narta|nāgāram arāla|pakṣmā
śata|hradā megham iv' ânvapadyata.
sā hasti|hast'|ôpama|saṃhit'|ôrūḥ,
sv|aninditā, cāru|datī, su|madhyamā
āsādya taṃ vai vara|mālya|dhāriṇī

horses in check, and it was with this man as his charioteer that Árjuna, the son of Pritha, completely defeated all living creatures in Khándava·prastha. There is no driver like him."

ÚTTARA said:

Sairándhri, you know this youth and what this eunuch may or may not be. But I cannot say "Take charge of my horses!" to Brihan·nala myself, fair lady. 36.20

DRÁUPADI said:

"The hero will doubtless carry out the command of the passionate, shapely-hipped princess; your younger sister. If he were your charioteer, there is no doubt that you would certainly return having defeated all the Kurus and taken back the cattle." Thus addressed by the *sairándhri*, he spoke to his sister: "Go, faultless-limbed lady, and bring back Brihan·nala." And sent by her brother she went quickly to the dancing hall, where that long-armed son of Pandu was hidden in disguise.

VAISHAMPÁYANA said:

So IN THIS MANNER the illustrious Sudákshina was sent by her older brother. The slender, wasp-waisted girl wore a garland and a golden necklace. She resembled Lakshmi, dressed in peacock feathers, slim-figured, with flawless limbs, and wearing a belt of various gems. The Princess of Matsya, endowed with grace and curled eyelashes, flew to the dance hall just as the thousand-flashing thunderbolt shoots to a cloud. The beautiful girl, each of whose close-fitting thighs were like an elephant's trunk, the faultless girl with straight teeth and slim waist, adorned with an excellent garland, approached Partha as a female elephant approaches a male. 37.1

Pārthaṃ śubhā, nāga|vadhūr iva dvipam.
sā ratna|bhūtā, manasaḥ priy", ârcitā
sutā Virāṭasya, yath" Êndra|lakṣmīḥ,
su|darśanīyā, pramukhe yaśasvinī
prīty" âbravīd Arjunam āyat'|ēkṣaṇā.
37.5 su|saṃhat'|ôruṃ, kanak'|ôjjvalat|tvacaṃ
Pārthaḥ kumārīṃ sa tad" âbhyabhāṣata:
«kim āgamaḥ kāñcana|mālya|dhāriṇī,
mṛg'|âkṣi? kiṃ tvaṃ tvarit' êva, bhāmini?
kiṃ te mukhaṃ, sundari, na prasannam?
ācakṣva tattvaṃ mama śīghram, aṅgane!»

sa tāṃ dṛṣṭvā viśāl'|âkṣīṃ rāja|putrīṃ sakhīṃ tathā prahasann abravīd, rājan, «kim āgamanam?» ity uta. tam abravīd rāja|putrī samupetya nara'|rṣabham, praṇayaṃ bhāvayantī sā sakhī|madhya idaṃ vacaḥ, «gāvo rāṣṭrasya Kurubhiḥ kālyante no, Bṛhannale. tā vijetuṃ mama bhrātā prayāsyati dhanur|dharaḥ. nā|ciraṃ nihatas tasya saṃgrāme ratha|sārathiḥ. tena n' āsti samaḥ sūto yo 'sya sārathyam ācaret.

37.10 tasmai prayatamānāya sārathy|arthaṃ, Bṛhannale, ācacakṣe haya|jñāne sairandhrī kauśalaṃ tava. Arjunasya kil' āsīs tvaṃ sārathir dayitaḥ purā; tvay" âjayat sahāyena pṛthivīṃ Pāṇḍava'|rṣabhaḥ. sā sārathyaṃ mama bhrātuḥ kuru sādhu, Bṛhannale. purā dūrataraṃ gāvo hriyante Kurubhir hi naḥ. ath' âitad vacanaṃ me 'dya niyuktā na kariṣyasi praṇayād ucyamānā tvaṃ, parityakṣyāmi jīvitam!»

And that precious jewel of a girl, Viráta's daughter, who was dear to everyone's heart and honored like the personification of Indra's good fortune, very large-eyed, beautiful and renowned for her charm, greeted Árjuna. Partha then said to 37.5
the shapely and snug-thighed princess with skin of golden radiance: "Why have you come, doe-eyed girl, dressed in your golden garland? And what is your hurry, lovely lady? Why is your face not looking pleased, beautiful girl? Tell me quickly and truthfully, lady of well-rounded limbs!"

Seeing the princess, his wide-eyed friend, my king, he smilingly asked why she had come. The princess came up to that bull-like man, and in the midst of her friends she spoke affectionately, saying, "Our kingdom's cattle has been stolen by the Kurus, Lady Brihan·nala. My brother will go out to defeat them, bow in hand, but not long ago his charioteer was killed in battle. He has no equal who can act as my brother's charioteer.

Lady Brihan·nala, when he was trying to find a charioteer, 37.10
the *sairándhri* told him of your skill in horse-lore. You were, in fact, once Árjuna's favorite charioteer, and it was with you that the bull-like Pándava conquered the world. So, Brihan·nala, become my brother's excellent charioteer. The Kurus will certainly have led our cattle farther away by now than before. If you do not act in accordance with my request, even when I have commanded you, asking out of affection, then I will forsake my life!"

evam uktas tu su|śroṇyā tayā sakhyā param|tapaḥ
jagāma rāja|putrasya sakāśam a|mit'|âujasaḥ.
37.15 tam āvrajantaṃ tvaritaṃ, prabhinnam iva kuñjaram,
anvagacchad viśāl'|âkṣī, śiśuṃ gaja|vadhūr iva.
dūrād eva tu tāṃ prekṣya rāja|putro 'bhyabhāṣata:
«tvayā sārathinā Pārthaḥ Khāṇḍave 'gnim atarpayat,
pṛthivīm ajayat kṛtsnāṃ Kuntī|putro Dhanañjayaḥ!
sairandhrī tvāṃ samācaṣṭe, sā hi jānāti Pāṇḍavān.
saṃyaccha māmakān aśvāṃs tath" âiva tvaṃ, Bṛhannale,
Kurubhir yotsyamānasya go|dhanāni parīpsataḥ.
Arjunasya kil' āsīs tvaṃ sārathir dayitaḥ purā
tvay" âjayat sahāyena pṛthivīṃ Pāṇḍava'|rṣabhaḥ!»
37.20 evam uktā pratyuvāca rāja|putraṃ Bṛhannalā:
«kā śaktir mama sārathyaṃ kartuṃ saṅgrāma|mūrdhani?
gītaṃ vā, yadi vā nṛtyaṃ, vāditraṃ vā pṛthag|vidham—
tat kariṣyāmi, bhadraṃ te, sārathyaṃ tu kuto mama?»

UTTARA uvāca:

Bṛhannale, gāyano vā nartano vā punar bhava;
kṣipraṃ me ratham āsthāya nigṛhṇīṣva hay'|ôttamān!

VAIŚAMPĀYANA uvāca:

sa tatra narma|saṃyuktam akarot Pāṇḍavo bahu
Uttarāyāḥ pramukhataḥ sarvaṃ jānann arin|damaḥ.
ūrdhvam utkṣipya kavacaṃ śarīre pratyamuñcata;

Thus addressed by his shapely-hipped friend, that infinitely energetic enemy-scorcher entered the prince's presence, and, like a female elephant after her calf, the large-eyed 37.15
girl followed him as he strode quickly, like a bull elephant with split temples. Catching sight of him while he was still quite far in the distance, the prince addressed him:

"With you as his charioteer, Dhanan·jaya Partha, son of Kuntí, satisfied Agni at Khándava and conquered the whole world! The *sairándhri* has told me about you, and she knows the Pándavas. So take charge of my horses in the same manner as you once did, Brihan·nala, when I do battle with the Kurus, for I am eager to retrieve my wealth of cattle. You were, in fact, once Árjuna's favorite charioteer, and it was with you as his companion that the bull of the Pándava race conquered the world!"

Thus addressed, Brihan·nala replied to the prince: "What 37.20
ability do I have to be a charioteer at the forefront of battle? If it's song, dance, musical instruments or various things of this kind that you want, then, bless you, I will perform, but from where will I find charioteering skills?"

ÚTTARA said:

Brihan·nala, be a singer or dancer again later, but, for now, quickly get on my chariot and take control of my excellent horses!

VAISHAMPÁYANA said:

Then the son of Pandu, the destroyer of his enemies, although well aware of everything he needed to do, made a great game of it in front of Úttara. When he lifted his armor high in the air, trying to put it on his body, the large-eyed

kumāryas tatra taṃ dṛṣṭvā prāhasan pṛthu|locanāḥ.

37.25 sa tu dṛṣṭvā vimuhyantaṃ svayam ev' Ôttaras tataḥ
kavacena mah"|ârheṇa samanahyad Bṛhannalām.
sa bibhrat kavacaṃ c' âgryaṃ
svayam apy aṃśumat|prabham,
dhvajaṃ ca siṃham ucchritya
sārathye samakalpayat.
dhanūṃṣi ca mah"|ârhāṇi, bāṇāṃś ca rucirān bahūn
ādāya prayayau vīraḥ sa Bṛhannala|sārathiḥ.

ath' Ôttarā ca kanyāś ca sakhyas tām abruvaṃs tadā:
«Bṛhannale, ānayethā vāsāṃsi rucirāṇi ca
pāñcālik'|ârthaṃ citrāṇi, sūkṣmāṇi ca, mṛdūni ca,
vijitya saṃgrāma|gatān Bhīṣma|Droṇa|mukhān Kurūn!»
37.30 evaṃ tā bruvatīḥ kanyāḥ sahitāḥ Pāṇḍu|nandanaḥ
pratyuvāca hasan Pārtho megha|dundubhi|niḥsvanaḥ.

BṚHANNAL" ôvāca:

yady Uttaro 'yaṃ saṃgrāme vijeṣyati mahā|rathān,
ath' āhariṣye vāsāṃsi divyāni rucirāṇi ca!

VAIŚAṂPĀYANA uvāca:

evam uktvā tu Bībhatsus tataḥ prācodayadd hayān
Kurūn abhimukhaḥ śūro nānā|dhvaja|patākinaḥ.
tam Uttaraṃ vīkṣya rath'|ôttame sthitaṃ,
Bṛhannalāyāḥ sahitaṃ, mahā|bhujam,
striyaś ca, kanyāś ca, dvijāś ca su|vratāḥ
pradakṣiṇaṃ cakrur, ath' ūcur aṅganāḥ,
«yad Arjunasya' ṛṣabha|tulya|gāminaḥ
pur" âbhavat Khāṇḍava|dāha|maṅgalam,
Kurūn samāsādya raṇe, Bṛhannale,
sah' Ôttareṇ' âdya tad astu maṅgalam.»

royal ladies laughed as they watched. Seeing him so bewildered, Úttara dressed Brihan·nala in the highly valuable armor, and wearing excellent armor himself, which was as bright as the sun, he hoisted his banner bearing a lion, and made Brihan·nala his charioteer. Once he had taken many expensive bows and beautiful arrows, the hero set out with Brihan·nala as his charioteer. 37.25

His friend Uttará and the girls said to him: "Brihan·nala, bring back radiant clothes of pretty, delicate and soft cloth for our dolls, once you have defeated the assembled Kurus, led by Bhishma and Drona!" So the girls spoke together in 37.30
this way and Partha, the descendant of the Pándava race, smiled and replied in a voice that sounded like the thunder of clouds.

BRIHAN·NALA said:

If Úttara here defeats those warriors in battle, then I will bring back some heavenly and gorgeous cloth!

VAISHAMPÁYANA said:

After he had said this, the hero Bibhátsu drove the horses on toward the Kurus, who were flying various standards and banners. When the women, girls and vow-observing brahmins caught sight of long-armed Úttara standing on his most excellent chariot with Brihan·nala, they performed the rite of circling the chariot, and the women said, "May the same good outcome be yours today, Brihan·nala, when you encounter the Kurus in battle with Úttara, which Árjuna of bull-like strides was blessed with long ago when he burned the forest of Khándava."

VAIŚAMPĀYANA uvāca:

38.1 SA RĀJA|DHĀNYĀ niryāya Vairāṭir a|kuto|bhayaḥ
«prayāh', îty» abravīt sūtaṃ «yatra te Kuravo gatāḥ.
samavetān Kurūn sarvān jigīṣūn avajitya vai
gās teṣāṃ kṣipram ādāya punar eṣyāmy ahaṃ puram.»
tatas tāṃś codayām āsa sad|aśvān Pāṇḍu|nandanaḥ.
te hayā nara|siṃhena noditā vāta|raṃhasaḥ
ālikhanta iv' ākāśam ūhuḥ kāñcana|mālinaḥ.
n' âti|dūram atho gatvā Matsya|putra|Dhanañjayau
avekṣetām amitra|ghnau Kurūṇāṃ balināṃ balam.
38.5 śmaśānam abhito gatvā āsasāda Kurūn atha,
tāṃ Śamīm anvavekṣetāṃ, vyūḍh'|ânīkāṃś ca sarvaśaḥ.
tad anīkaṃ mahat teṣāṃ vibabhau sāgar'|ôpamam,
sarpamāṇam iv' ākāśe vanaṃ bahula|pādapam.
dadṛśe pārthivo reṇur janitas tena sarpatā,
dṛṣṭi|praṇāśo bhūtānāṃ diva|spṛk, Kuru|sattama.
tad anīkaṃ mahad dṛṣṭvā gaj'|âśva|ratha|saṅkulam,
Karṇa|Duryodhana|Kṛpair guptaṃ, Śāntanavena ca,
Droṇena ca sa|putreṇa mah"|êṣv|āsena dhīmatā,
hṛṣṭa|romā bhay'|ôdvignaḥ Pārthaṃ Vairāṭir abravīt:

UTTARA uvāca:

38.10 n' ôtsahe Kurubhir yoddhuṃ! roma|harṣaṃ hi paśya me!
bahu|pravīram, atyugraṃ, devair api dur|āsadam
pratiyoddhuṃ na śakṣyāmi Kuru|sainyam an|antakam!
n' āśaṃse Bhāratīṃ senāṃ praveṣṭuṃ bhīma|kārmukām,
ratha|nāg'|âśva|kalilāṃ, patti|dhvaja|samākulām.

VAISHAMPÁYANA said:

ONCE THEY HAD left the royal enclosure, Viráta's fearless son said to his charioteer: "Go to where the Kurus have gone. Once I have defeated all the assembled Kurus, who wish for victory themselves, and have quickly retrieved my cattle, I will return to the city." So the descendant of the Pándava race urged on the excellent horses. Driven by that lion-like man, the golden-harnessed steeds were swift as the wind and galloped as though they were grazing the ether. 38.1

They had not gone too far when the Matsyan prince and Dhanan·jaya, destroyers of their enemies, saw the force of the mighty Kurus. Approaching the Kurus, going near 38.5
the cemetery, they both inspected the *shami* tree and the army completely arrayed in its divisions. Their enormous army sounded like the mighty ocean and resembled a dense forest of trees crawling through the sky. O best of the Kurus, the dust that that creeping army kicked up from the ground was clearly visible. It blinded all living creatures and touched the heavens. Viráta's son shuddered with fear and his hair stood on end as he stared at that mighty army furnished with elephants, horses and chariots, and guarded by Karna, Duryódhana, Bhishma, Drona, the learned man and great archer, along with Ashvattháman, his son. He said to Partha:

ÚTTARA said:

I do not dare to fight with the Kurus! Look how my hair 38.10
is standing on end! I cannot fight this infinite Kuru army, filled with numerous extremely vicious heroes! It would prove a difficult army to attack even for the gods! I do not hope to penetrate that Bháratan army of terrifying bowmen,

dṛṣṭv" âiva hi parān ājau manaḥ pravyathat' îva me.
yatra Droṇaś ca, Bhīṣmaś ca, Kṛpaḥ, Karṇo, Viviṃśatiḥ,
Aśvatthāmā, Vikarṇaś ca, Somadattaś ca Bāhlikaḥ,
Duryodhanas tathā vīro rājā ca rathināṃ varaḥ,
dyutimanto mah"|êṣv|āsāḥ sarve yuddha|viśāradāḥ.
38.15 dṛṣṭv" âiva hi Kurūn etān vyūḍh'|ânīkān prahāriṇaḥ,
hṛṣitāni ca romāṇi, kaśmalaṃ c' āgataṃ mama.

VAIŚAMPĀYANA uvāca:

a|vijāto vijātasya maukhyāt dhūrtasya paśyataḥ
paridevayate mandaḥ sakāśe Savyasācinaḥ.
«Trigartān me pitā yātaḥ śūnye saṃpraṇidhāya mām!
sarvāṃ senām upādāya na me sant' îha sainikāḥ!
so 'ham eko bahūn bālaḥ kṛt'|âstrān a|kṛta|śramaḥ
pratiyoddhuṃ na śakṣyāmi! nivartasva, Bṛhannale.»

BṚHANNAL" ôvāca:

bhayena dīna|rūpo 'si dviṣatāṃ harṣa|vardhanaḥ!
na ca tāvat kṛtaṃ karma paraiḥ kiñ cid raṇ'|âjire.
38.20 svayam eva ca mām āttha, «vaha māṃ Kauravān prati!»
so 'ham tvāṃ tatra neṣyāmi yatr' âite bahulā dhvajāḥ.
madhyam āmiṣa|gṛdhrāṇāṃ Kurūṇām ātatāyinām
neṣyāmi tvāṃ, mahā|bāho, pṛthivyām api yudhyatām.

brimming with chariots, elephants and horses, and full of infantry and flags. My mind trembles just looking at the enemy on the battlefield.

There's Drona, and Bhishma, and there's Kripa, Karna, Vivínshati, Ashvattháman, Vikárna, Soma·datta and Báhlika, and then Duryódhana the hero king and the best of charioteers, and the majestic great bowmen, all skilled in warcraft. Looking at that warrior Kuru army arrayed 38.15
in battle formation, my hair is standing on end and I'm growing faint.

VAISHAMPÁYANA said:

And Úttara, the foolish man who was born low-minded, wailed from stupidity in front of Árjuna, while the ambidextrous and cunning man, who was born high-minded, was watching him. Úttara said, "My father has gone to confront the Tri·gartas, leaving me behind in an empty city! He took the entire army with him, so there are no soldiers left for me! I cannot fight against so many skilled warriors all on my own! I am only an inexperienced boy! Turn back, Brihan·nala."

BRIHAN·NALA said:

Your fear makes you look wretched and it increases the joy of your enemies! So far the enemy hasn't even done anything on the battlefield. It was you yourself who told 38.20
me to take you to the Kurus! So I will take you where those dense banners are. I will take you, long-armed man, into the midst of those Kurus, whose bows are drawn to kill, like vultures eager for prey, and so I would even if they were fighting inside the earth itself.

tathā strīṣu pratiśrutya pauruṣaṃ, puruṣeṣu ca
katthamāno 'bhiniryāya kim arthaṃ na yuyutsase?
na ced vijitya gās tās tvaṃ gṛhān vai pratiyāsyasi,
prahasiṣyanti vīrās tvāṃ, narā nāryaś ca saṃgatāḥ,
aham apy atra sairandhryā khyātā sārathya|karmaṇi;
na ca śakṣyāmy a|nirjitya gāḥ prayātuṃ puraṃ prati.
38.25 stotreṇa c' âiva sairandhryās, tava vākyena tena ca,
kathaṃ na yudhyeyam ahaṃ Kurūn sarvān? sthiro bhava!

UTTARA uvāca:

kāmaṃ harantu Matsyānāṃ
bhūyāṃsaṃ Kuravo dhanam.
prahasantu ca māṃ nāryo
narā v" âpi, Bṛhannale!
saṅgrāme na ca kāryaṃ me. gāvo gacchantu c' âpi me!
śūnyaṃ me nagaraṃ c' âpi! pituś c' âiva bibhemy aham!

VAIŚAṂPĀYANA uvāca:

ity uktvā prādravad bhīto rathāt praskandya kuṇḍalī,
tyaktvā mānaṃ ca darpaṃ ca, visṛjya sa|śaraṃ dhanuḥ.

BṚHANNAL" ôvāca:

n' âiṣa śūraiḥ smṛto dharmaḥ kṣatriyasya palāyanam!
śreyas tu maraṇaṃ yuddhe, na bhītasya palāyanam!

VAIŚAṂPĀYANA uvāca:

38.30 evam uktvā tu Kaunteyaḥ so 'vaplutya rath'|ôttamāt
tam anvadhāvad dhāvantaṃ rāja|putraṃ Dhanañjayaḥ.
dīrghāṃ veṇīṃ vidhunvānaḥ sādhu, rakte ca vāsasī.
vidhūya veṇīṃ dhāvantam a|jānanto 'rjunaṃ tadā

You assured us of your manliness, boasting among both men and women when we set out, so why won't you fight now? If you return without winning and retrieving the cattle, then brave men and women will congregate and laugh at you, and I cannot go back to the city without having retrieved the cattle, either, since the *sairándhri* waxed lyrical about my charioteering ability. It is because of the *sairán-* 38.25
dhri's praise and your speech that I am here, so how could I fail to fight all the Kurus? Be still!

ÚTTARA said:

Let the Kurus steal most of the Matsyan wealth if they want, or let men and women laugh at me, Brihan·nala! Let the cattle go! Let my city be empty! Even let me be afraid of my father, but battle isn't necessary!

VAISHAMPÁYANA said:

Once he'd said these things, the earringed and frightened prince leaped down from his chariot and ran away, abandoning his pride and self-respect as he threw away his bow and arrows.

BRIHAN·NALA said:

Running away is not the law prescribed by the brave for warriors! Death in battle is better than running away in terror!

VAISHAMPÁYANA said:

After he had said this, Dhanan·jaya, the son of Kuntí, 38.30
jumped down from the excellent chariot and chased the prince as he ran away. His single long braid and pure red garments blew around him. Then some soldiers, unaware

sainikāḥ prāhasan ke cit tathā|rūpam avekṣya tam.
taṃ śīghram abhidhāvantaṃ samprekṣya Kuravo 'bruvan,
«ka eṣa veṣa|saṃchanno bhasmany eva hut'|âśanaḥ?
kiṃ cid asya yathā puṃsaḥ, kiṃ cid asya yathā striyaḥ.
sārūpyam Arjunasy' êva, klība|rūpaṃ bibharti ca.
tad ev' âitac chiro|grīvaṃ, tau bāhū parigh'|ôpamau,
tadvad ev' âsya vikrāntaṃ. n' âyam anyo Dhanañjayāt!
38.35 amareṣv iva dev'|Êndro mānuṣeṣu Dhanañjayaḥ.
ekaḥ ko 'smān upāyāyād anyo loke Dhanañjayāt?
ekaḥ putro Virāṭasya śūnye sannihitaḥ pure.
sa eṣa kila niryāto bāla|bhāvān, na pauruṣāt!
satreṇa nūnaṃ channaṃ hi carantaṃ Pārtham Arjunam
Uttaraḥ sārathiṃ kṛtvā niryāto nagarād bahiḥ.
sa no manyāmahe dṛṣṭvā bhīta eṣa palāyate!
taṃ nūnam eṣa dhāvantaṃ jighṛkṣati Dhanañjayaḥ.»
iti sma Kuravaḥ sarve vimṛśantaḥ pṛthak pṛthak;
na ca vyavasituṃ kiṃ cid uttaraṃ śaknuvanti te
38.40 channaṃ tathā taṃ satreṇa Pāṇḍavaṃ prekṣya, Bhārata.
Uttaraṃ tu pradhāvantam abhidrutya Dhanañjayaḥ
gatvā pada|śataṃ tūrṇaṃ keśa|pakṣe parāmṛśat.
so 'rjunena parāmṛṣṭaḥ paryadevayad ārtavat,
bahulaṃ, kṛpaṇaṃ c' âiva Virāṭasya sutas tadā.

that it was Árjuna who was running with his hair shaking about, laughed at the figure they saw. As they watched him running away in haste the Kurus said,

"Who is this man, disguised like fire covered with ashes? There is something male and yet something female about him. Though he bears a eunuch's appearance, he resembles the form of Árjuna. He has the same head and neck, arms like maces, and the stride is his as well! He is none other
than Dhanan·jaya! Dhanan·jaya among men is like Indra 38.35
among the celestials. Who in the world would come out against us all alone other than Dhanan·jaya?

One of Viráta's sons was left in the empty city, and that man certainly came out due to immaturity rather than true manliness! Surely it is Úttara who has left the city and made Árjuna Partha his charioteer, who lived hidden in disguise. It seems that the former has seen us and is running away terrified! And surely Dhanan·jaya is desperate to catch him as he runs away."

All the Kurus reflected on these things, each in their turn,
but they were unable to decide anything for certain, upon 38.40
seeing the son of Pandu concealed in his disguise, Bhárata.

Dhanan·jaya caught up with Úttara as he was running away, having gone a mere one hundred strides at great speed, and seized him by the knot of his hair. Caught by Árjuna, Viráta's son began to cry very wretchedly, as if in pain.

UTTARA uvāca:

śṛṇuyās tvaṃ hi, kalyāṇi Bṛhannale su|madhyame,
nivartaya rathaṃ kṣipram; jīvan bhadrāni paśyati.
śata|kumbhasya śuddhasya śataṃ niṣkān dadāmi te,
maṇīn aṣṭau ca vaidūryān hema|baddhān, mahā|prabhān,
hema|daṇḍa|praticchannaṃ rathaṃ yuktaṃ ca su|vrataiḥ,
mattāṃś ca daśa mātaṅgān. muñca māṃ tvaṃ, Bṛhannale!

VAIŚAMPĀYANA uvāca:

38.45 evam|ādīni vākyāni vilapantam a|cetasam
prahasya puruṣa|vyāghro rathasy' ântikam ānayat.
ath' âinam abravīt Pārtho bhay'|ārtaṃ naṣṭa|cetasam:
«yadi n' ôtsahase yoddhuṃ śatrubhiḥ, śatru|karṣaṇa,
ehi, me tvaṃ hayān yaccha yudhyamānasya śatrubhiḥ!
prayāhy etad rath'|ânīkaṃ mad|bāhu|bala|rakṣitaḥ,
a|pradhṛṣyatamaṃ ghoraṃ, guptaṃ vīrair mahā|rathaiḥ.
mā bhais tvaṃ, rāja|putr'|âgrya, kṣatriyo 'si, paran|tapa.
kathaṃ, puruṣa|śārdūla, śatru|madhye viṣīdasi?
ahaṃ vai Kurubhir yotsye, vijeṣyāmi ca te paśūn,
praviśy' âitad rath'|ânīkam a|pradhṛṣyaṃ dur|āsadam.
38.50 yantā bhava, nara|śreṣṭha, yotsye 'haṃ Kurubhiḥ saha.»
evaṃ bruvāṇo Bībhatsur Vairāṭim a|parājitaḥ
samāśvāsya muhūrtaṃ tam Uttaraṃ, Bharata'|rṣabha.
tata enaṃ viceṣṭantam a|kāmaṃ bhaya|pīḍitam
ratham āropayām āsa Pārthaḥ praharatāṃ varaḥ.

ÚTTARA said:

Listen, noble and fair-waisted Brihan·nala, turn back the chariot quickly, for the man who lives sees good fortune. I will give you one hundred *nishka*s of pure gold, eight brilliant cat's-eye gems set in gold, a chariot furnished with a golden flagpole and yoked with excellent horses and even ten rutting elephants. Release me, Brihan·nala!

VAISHAMPÁYANA said:

The tiger among men laughed and dragged the senseless 38.45
man toward the chariot as he wailed moaning pleas. Partha said to the terrified man who had lost his mind: "If you do not dare to fight with the enemy, tormentor of your foes, then take charge of the horses for me as I fight the enemy! Protected by the strength of my arms, enter the terrifying and invincible army of chariots, guarded by great and heroic warriors.

Don't be afraid, scorcher of the enemy and foremost of princes, for you are a kshatriya. How can you sink so low in the midst of the enemy, tiger-like man? I will penetrate that dangerous and invincible army of chariots, fight with
the Kurus and win back the cattle. Be my charioteer, best 38.50
of men, and I will fight the Kurus." Speaking in this way to Viráta's son, Bibhátsu, o bull-like Bharata, undefeated by his enemies, comforted Úttara for a moment. Then Partha, the greatest of destroyers, lifted the senseless and reluctant man, struck by fear, onto the chariot.

VAIŚAMPĀYANA uvāca:

39.1 TAṂ DṚṢṬVĀ klība|veṣeṇa ratha|sthaṃ nara|puṃgavam,
śamīm abhimukhaṃ yāntaṃ, ratham āropya c' Ôttaram
Bhīṣma|Droṇa|mukhās tatra Kuravo rathi|sattamāḥ
vitrasta|manasaḥ sarve Dhanaṃjaya|kṛtād bhayāt.
tān avekṣya hat'|ôtsāhān, utpātān api c' âdbhutān,
guruḥ śastra|bhṛtāṃ śreṣṭho Bhāradvājo 'bhyabhāṣata,
«caṇḍāś ca vātāḥ saṃvānti rūkṣāḥ, śarkara|varṣiṇaḥ;
bhasma|varṇa|prakāśena tamasā saṃvṛtaṃ nabhaḥ.
39.5 rūkṣa|varṇāś ca jaladā dṛśyante 'dbhuta|darśanāḥ.
niḥsaranti ca kośebhyaḥ śastrāṇi vividhāni ca.
śivāś ca vinadanty etā dīptāyāṃ diśi dāruṇāḥ.
hayāś c' âśrūṇi muñcanti, dhvajāḥ kampanty a|kampitāḥ.
yādṛśāny atra rūpāṇi sandṛśyante bahūni ca,
yattā bhavantas tiṣṭhantu; sādhvasaṃ samupasathitam.
rakṣadhvam api c' ātmānaṃ, vyūhadhvaṃ vāhinīm api.
vaiśasaṃ ca pratīkṣadhvaṃ, rakṣadhvaṃ c' âpi go|dhanam!
eṣa vīro mah"|êṣv|āsaḥ sarva|śastra|bhṛtāṃ varaḥ
āgataḥ klība|veṣeṇa Pārtho. n' âsty atra saṃśayaḥ.
39.10 nadī|ja, Laṅkeśa|van'|âri|ketur
Nagāhvayo nāma Nagāri|sūnuḥ
eṣo 'ṅganā|veṣa|dharaḥ Kirīṭī
jitv" êva yo neṣyati c' âdya gāvaḥ!
sa eṣa Pārtho vikrāntaḥ Savyasācī paraṃ|tapaḥ!

VAISHAMPÁYANA said:

WATCHING THE bull-like man stand on the chariot in 39.1
eunuch's clothing, lifting Úttara onto his car, and driving toward the *shami* tree, the excellent Kuru warriors, with Bhishma and Drona at their head, all trembled in their hearts from fear and the suspicion that it was Dhanan·jaya. Noticing their vanishing resolve, and the astounding portents, the guru son of Bharad·vaja, the best of those who wield weapons, said,

"The winds blow fierce and dry, raining down gravel, and the sky is covered with darkness and an ashen luminescence.
The clouds have taken on a strange form, both water-laden 39.5
and yet dry in their appearance. Various weapons are slipping from their sheaths. Pitiless jackals howl on all sides of the blazing horizon. The horses are weeping and our banners tremble without any visible cause.

When such numerous omens appear, danger is at hand, so stand ready, protect yourself, and arrange your army. Expect butchery and protect the wealth of cattle! This great archer hero, the best of all who wield weapons, who has come in eunuch's clothing, is in fact Partha, no doubt about it.

Son of the Ganges, this is Kirítin wearing women's clothes; 39.10
he who has the enemy of the grove of Lankésha for his emblem,* Nagáhvaya* by name, son of Nagári,* and today once he has defeated us, he will lead the cattle away! This is valiant Partha, the ambidextrous scorcher of the enemy!

n' â|yuddhena nivarteta sarvair api sur'|Âsuraiḥ.
kleśitaś ca vane śūro, Vāsaven' âpi śikṣitaḥ,
a|marṣa|vaśam āpanno, Vāsava|pratimo yudhi.
n' êh' âsya pratiyoddhāram ahaṃ paśyāmi, Kauravāḥ.
Mahādevo 'pi Pārthena śrūyate yudhi toṣitaḥ
kirāta|veṣa|pracchanno girau Himavati prabhuḥ.»

KARṆA uvāca:

sadā bhavān Phālgunasya guṇair asmān vikatthase;
na c' Ârjunaḥ kalā|pūrṇo mama, Duryodhanasya ca!

DURYODHANA uvāca:

39.15 yady eṣa Pārtho, Rādheya, kṛtaṃ kāryaṃ bhaven mama;
jñātāḥ punaś cariṣyanti dvādaś' ābdān, viśāṃ pate!
ath' âiṣa kaś cid ev' ânyaḥ klība|veṣeṇa mānavaḥ,
śarair enaṃ su|niśitaiḥ pātayiṣyāmi bhū|tale!

VAIŚAṂPĀYANA uvāca:

tasmin bruvati tad vākyaṃ Dhārtarāṣṭre, paraṃ|tapa,
Bhīṣmo, Droṇaḥ, Kṛpo, Drauṇiḥ pauruṣaṃ tad apūjayan.

He would not turn away from battle even if it were against all the gods and *ásuras*. Vásava's brave pupil, who suffered in the forest, is like Indra in battle, and is coming in obedience to his rage. Therefore, Kurus, I do not see an opponent for him in battle. It is said that even Lord Maha·deva, disguised in the attire of a hunter, was satisfied in battle by Partha on Mount Himálaya."

KARNA said:

You always humble us, sir, with the virtues of Phálguna, but Árjuna is no match for even a fraction of me or Duryódhana!

DURYÓDHANA said:

If this is Partha, Radhéya,then my task has been accom- 39.15
plished, for if recognized then the Pándavas will wander again for another twelve years, lord of earth! And, if he is some other man in a eunuch's attire, then I will bring him down to the ground with my well-sharpened arrows!

VAISHAMPÁYANA said:

When Dhrita·rashtra's son had said these words, enemy-scorcher, Bhishma, Drona, Kripa and Ashvattháman, Drona's son, praised his manliness.

40–52
THE RECOGNITION OF ÁRJUNA

VAIŚAMPĀYANA uvāca:

40.1 TĀM ŚAMĪM upasaṃgamya Pārtho Vairāṭim abravīt
sukumāraṃ samājñāya, saṅgrāme n' âti|kovidam:
«samādiṣṭo mayā kṣipraṃ dhanūṃṣy avahar', Ôttara,
n' êmāni hi tvadīyāni soḍhuṃ śakṣyanti me balam,
bhāraṃ c' âpi guruṃ voḍhuṃ, kuñjaraṃ vā pramarditum,
mama vā bāhu|vikṣepaṃ śatrūn iha vijeṣyataḥ.
tasmād, Bhūmiṃjay', āroha śamīm etāṃ palāśinīm-
asyāṃ hi Pāṇḍu|putrāṇāṃ dhanūṃṣi nihitāny uta—
Yudhiṣṭhirasya, Bhīmasya, Bībhatsor, yamayos tathā—
40.5 dhvajāḥ śarāś ca śūrāṇāṃ, divyāni kavacāni ca.
atra c âitan mahā|vīryaṃ dhanuḥ Pārthasya Gāṇḍivam,
ekaṃ śata|sahasreṇa saṃmitaṃ, rāṣṭra|vardhanam,
vyāyāma|saham aty|arthaṃ, tṛṇa|rāja|samaṃ mahat,
sarv'|āyudha|mahā|mātraṃ, śatru|saṃbādha|kārakam,
su|varṇa|vikṛtaṃ, divyaṃ, ślakṣṇam, āyatam, a|vraṇam,
alaṃ bhāraṃ guruṃ voḍhuṃ, dāruṇaṃ, cāru|darśanam.
tādṛśāny eva sarvāṇi balavanti dṛḍhāni ca
Yudhiṣṭhirasya, Bhīmasya, Bībhatsor, yamayos tatha.»

UTTARA uvāca:

41.1 ASMIN VṚKṢE KIL' ôdbaddhaṃ śarīram, iti naḥ śrutam.
tad ahaṃ rāja|putraḥ san spṛśeyaṃ pāṇinā katham?
n' âivaṃ|vidhaṃ mayā yuktam ālabdhuṃ kṣatra|yoninā
mahatā rāja|putreṇa mantra|yajña|vidā satā.
spṛṣṭavantaṃ śarīraṃ māṃ śava|vāham iv' â|śucim

VAISHAMPÁYANA said:

ONCE THEY REACHED the *shami* tree, Partha realized 40.1
that the prince was not especially experienced in battle, and he said to Viráta's son: "Quickly take down the
bows as I direct you, Úttara, for yours are not able to take
my strength and heavy weight, when I destroy horses and
elephants, nor can they cope with the extension of my arms
as I strive to conquer our enemies. Therefore, Bhumin·jaya,
climb this leafy *shami* tree, for the bows of the Pándavas—
Yudhi·shthira, Bhima, Bibhátsu and the twins—are hidden
inside, as well as the banners, arrows and celestial armor of 40.5
those brave men.

The bow of great energy is there: the Gandíva of Árjuna, son of Pritha, which on its own is measured as equal to hundreds of thousands of other bows and is the augmenter of kingdoms. It is large like bamboo and can withstand excessive strain. That destroyer of the enemy is the largest of all weapons in size. It is adorned with gold, beautiful, smooth and long, without splinters or cuts, and equal to heavy weight, hard and handsome. All those belonging to Yudhi·shthira, Bhima, Bibhátsu and the twins are similarly powerful and sturdy."

ÚTTARA said:

WE HAVE HEARD that a corpse is tied up in this tree, or so 41.1
they say. So how can I, who am a prince, touch it with my
hand? Since I was born as a kshatriya, a great prince who is
conversant with mantras and sacrifices, it is not proper or
suitable for me to touch it. How can you, Brihan·nala, make

kathaṃ vā vyavahāryaṃ vai kurvīthās tvaṃ, Bṛhannale?

BṚHANNAL" ôvāca:

vyavahāryaś ca, rāj'|êndra, śuciś c' âiva bhaviṣyasi.
dhanūṃṣy etāni, mā bhais tvaṃ, śarīraṃ n' âtra vidyate!
41.5 dāyādaṃ Matsya|rājasya, kule jātaṃ manasvinām,
tvāṃ kathaṃ ninditaṃ karma kārayeyaṃ, nṛp'|ātmaja?

VAIŚAMPĀYANA uvāca:

evam uktaḥ sa Pārthena rathāt praskandya kuṇḍalī
āruhoha śamī|vṛkṣaṃ Vairāṭir a|vaśas tadā.
tam anvaśāsac chatru|ghno rathe tiṣṭhan Dhanañjayaḥ,
«avaropaya vṛkṣ'|âgrād dhanūṃṣy etāni mā|ciram,
so 'pahṛtya mah"|ârhāṇi dhanūṃṣi pṛthu|vakṣasām,
pariveṣṭana|patrāṇi vimucya samupānayat.
tathā saṃnahanāny eṣāṃ parimucya samantataḥ
apaśyad Gāṇḍivaṃ tatra caturbhir aparaiḥ saha.
41.10 teṣāṃ vimucyamānānāṃ dhanuṣām arka|varcasām
viniśceruḥ prabhā divyā, grahāṇām udayeṣv iva.
sa teṣāṃ rūpam ālokya, bhoginām iva jṛmbhatām,
hṛṣṭa|romā, bhay'|ôdvignaḥ, kṣaṇena samapadyata.
saṃspṛśya tāni cāpāni bhānumanti bṛhanti ca
Vairāṭir Arjunaṃ, rājann, idaṃ vacanam abravīt:

UTTARA uvāca:

42.1 BINDAVO JĀTA|rūpasya śataṃ yasmin nipātitāḥ
sahasra|koṭi|sauvarṇāḥ, kasy' âitad dhanur uttamam?
vāraṇā yatra sauvarṇāḥ pṛṣṭhe bhāsanti daṃśitāḥ,
su|pārśvaṃ su|grahaṃ c' âiva kasy' âitad dhanur uttamam?

me an unclean carrier of corpses by forcing me to touch a dead body?

BRIHAN·NALA said:

Lord of kings, you will remain clean as always, for there is
no corpse in there—just bows! So do not fear. Prince, how 41.5
could I force you, the heir to the King of Matsya, born into
a family of wise ancestors, to perform a forbidden act?

VAISHAMPÁYANA said:

Thus addressed by Partha, the earringed son of Viráta leaped down from the chariot and unwillingly climbed the *shami* tree. Dhanan·jaya, the murderer of his enemies, stood on the chariot and said "Quickly bring those bows down from the top of the tree."

So he took down the highly-costly bows belonging to
the broad-chested Pándavas, and releasing them from their
leafy covering, he brought them down. Cutting their ropes
on all sides, he saw the Gandíva there with four others. As 41.10
they were untied, the celestial glory of those bows, luminous
as the sun, shone forth in all directions like the rising of the
planets. When he saw their forms like yawning serpents, his
hair stood on end, and for a moment he was overcome with
terror. Touching those splendid, massive bows, the son of
Viráta said to Árjuna, my king:

ÚTTARA said:

WHOSE SUPERB bow is this, with a hundred golden dots 42.1
and a thousand golden points adorning it? Whose is this
excellent-sided, superb bow with invincible golden-tusked
elephants gleaming on the back, so easy to handle? Whose

tapanīyasya śuddhasya pṛṣṭhe yasy' êndra|gopakāḥ
pṛṣṭhe vibhaktāḥ śobhante, kasy' âitad dhanur uttamam?
sūryā yatra ca sauvarṇās trayo bhāsanti daṃśitāḥ
tejasā prajvalanto hi, kasy' âitad dhanur uttamam?
42.5 śalabhā yatra sauvarṇās tapanīya|vibhūṣitāḥ,
suvarṇa|maṇi|citraṃ ca kasy' âitad dhanur uttamam?

ime ca kasya nārācāḥ sahasrā loma|vāhinaḥ,
samantāt kala|dhaut'|âgrā, upāsaṅge hiraṇ|maye?
vipāṭhāḥ pṛthavaḥ kasya, gārdhra |patrāḥ, śilā|śitāḥ,
hāridra|varṇāḥ, su|mukhāḥ, pītāḥ, sarv'|āyasāḥ śarāḥ?
kasy' âyam a|sitaś cāpaḥ pañca|śārdūla|lakṣaṇaḥ,
varāha|karṇa|vyāmiśrāñ śarān dhārayate daśa?
kasy' ême pṛthavo, dīrghāś, candra|bimb'|ârdha|darśanāḥ
śatāni sapta tiṣṭhanti nārācā rudhir|āśanāḥ?
42.10 kasy' ême śuka|patr'|ābhaiḥ pūrvair ardhaiḥ, su|vāsasaḥ,
uttarair āyasaiḥ pītair, hema|puṅkhaiḥ śilā|śitaiḥ?

guru|bhāra|saho, divyaḥ, śātravāṇāṃ bhayaṃ|karaḥ
kasy' âyaṃ sāyako dīrghaḥ śilī|pṛṣṭhaḥ, śilī|mukhaḥ?
vaiyāghra|kośe nihito, hema|citra|tsarur, mahān,
su|phalaś, citra|kośaś ca kiṅkiṇī|sāyako mahān?
kasya hema|tsarur, divyaḥ khaḍgaḥ parama|nirmalaḥ,
kasy' âyaṃ vimalaḥ khaḍgo gavye kośe samarpitaḥ?

hema|tsarur, an|ādhṛṣyo, Naiṣadhyo, bhāra|sādhanaḥ,
kasya pāñcanakhe kośe sāyako hema|vigrahaḥ?
42.15 pramāṇa|rūpa|saṃpannaḥ, pīta, ākāśa|sannibhaḥ
kasya hema|maye kośe su|tapte pāvaka|prabhe

is this superb bow, made of pure fire-tested gold, with ornamental fireflies shining on the back of the staff? Whose is this superb bow, adorned with three glittering, golden suns,
which blazes with splendor? Whose is this superb bow of 42.5
gold, variously jeweled and decorated with insects of pure, fire-tested gold?

Who do these thousand, fully-feathered arrows with gold and silver tips in a golden quiver belong to? Whose are these numerous, large arrows made entirely of iron, which are decorated with vulture feathers, sharpened with stones, fine-pointed and yellow and greenish in color? Whose is this quiver emblazoned with five tigers, which carries ten various boar-eared arrows? And whose are these seven hundred, blood-drinking, long and wide arrows that are shaped like
half-moons? Whose are these well-feathered arrows with 42.10
greenish-golden shafts made from parrot plumage, with the upper iron parts sharpened on stones?

Whose is this excellent, long and heavy-weighted sword, bringing terror to the enemy, with a frog emblem on the back and pointed like a frog's mouth? Whose is this massive sword, decorated with jingling bells and a variegated golden hilt with a good blade kept inside a variegated, tiger-skin scabbard? Whose is this excellent, gold-hilted sword, a perfectly unsullied and spotless scimitar placed in a cow's-leather scabbard?

Whose is this golden-hilted, invincible, Níshadhan and deeply effective sword with a golden blade, kept in a goat
scabbard? Whose is this sword, endowed with great size 42.15
and beauty, similar to the gem-like color of the sky, kept in a beautifully blazing and bright shining, golden scabbard?

nistriṃśo 'yaṃ guruḥ, pītaḥ, sāyakaḥ para|nirvraṇaḥ?
kasy' âyaṃ a|sitaḥ khaḍgo, hema|bindubhir āvṛtaḥ,
āśīviṣa|sama|sparśaḥ, para|kāya|prabhedanaḥ,
guru|bhāra|saho, divyaḥ, sapatnānāṃ bhaya|pradaḥ?
nirdiśasva yathā|tattvaṃ mayā pṛṣṭā, Bṛhannale,
vismayo me paro jāto dṛṣṭvā sarvam idaṃ mahat.

BṚHANNAL" ôvāca:

43.1 YAN MĀṂ PŪRVAM ih' âpṛcchaḥ śatru|sen"|âpahāriṇam,
Gāṇḍīvam etat Pārthasya lokeṣu viditaṃ dhanuḥ
sarv'|āyudha|mahā|mātraṃ śātakumbha|pariṣkṛtam
etat tad Arjunasy' āsīd Gāṇḍīvaṃ param'|āyudham,
yat tac chata|sahasreṇa saṃmitaṃ rāṣṭra|vardhanam,
yena devān manuṣyāṃś ca Pārtho vijayate mṛdhe.
citram ucc'|âvacair varṇaiḥ, ślakṣṇam, āyatam, a|vraṇam,
deva|dānava|gandharvaiḥ pūjitaṃ śāśvatīḥ samāḥ.
43.5 etad varṣa|sahasraṃ tu Brahmā pūrvam adhārayat;
tato 'n|antaram ev' âtha Prajāpatir adhārayat
trīṇi pañca|śataṃ c' âiva; Śakro 'śīti ca pañca ca;
Somaḥ pañca|śataṃ rājā; tath" âiva Varuṇaḥ śatam;
Pārthaḥ pañca ca ṣaṣṭiṃ ca varṣāṇi śveta|vāhanaḥ.
mahā|vīryaṃ mahā|divyam etat tad dhanur uttamam.
etat Pārtham anuprāptaṃ Varuṇāc, cāru|darśanam,
pūjitaṃ sura|martyeṣu, bibharti paramaṃ vapuḥ.

Whose is this heavy, merciless sword, undamaged by the enemy, with a dark blade and decorated with golden dots, the touch of which is like that of a poisonous snake, and which can slice open the bodies of one's enemies; a long and heavy-weighted, excellent sword, bringing terror to the enemy?

Brihan·nala, give me a truthful answer to my question, for my amazement has grown great upon seeing all this tremendous equipment.

BRIHAN·NALA said:

THE ONE YOU asked about first is Gandíva, a bow known throughout worlds, which belongs to Árjuna, the son of Pritha, and is able to destroy enemy armies. It is the largest and greatest weapon that belongs to Árjuna and is decorated with gold. On its own it is equal to a hundred thousand weapons, and it is the augmenter of kingdoms. Partha has conquered the gods and mortals with this bow in battle. It is decorated with variegated colors. It is smooth, long and without blemish, and is constantly worshipped by gods, *dánavas* and *gandhárvas* alike. 43.1

Brahma wielded it first for a thousand years, and then Praja·pati immediately took it up for five hundred and three years. Next, Shakra for eighty-five years, then King Soma for five hundred years, and Váruna for one hundred. Then white-horsed Partha kept it for sixty-five years. This superb bow possesses mighty strength and is greatly divine. This handsome bow was obtained by Partha from Váruna. It is worshipped by gods and mortals and possesses the greatest beauty. 43.5

su|pārśvaṃ Bhīmasenasya jāta|rūpa|grahaṃ dhanuḥ,
yena Pārtho 'jayat kṛtsnāṃ diśaṃ prācīṃ paraṃ|tapaḥ.
indra|gopaka|citraṃ ca yad etac cāru|darśanam,
rājño Yudhiṣṭhirasy' âitad, Vairāṭe, dhanur uttamam.
43.10 sūryā yasmiṃs tu sauvarṇāḥ prakāśante prakāśinaḥ
tejasā prajvalanto vai, Nakulasy' âitad āyudham.
śalabhā yatra sauvarṇās tapanīya|vicitritāḥ,
etan Mādrī|sutasy' âpi Sahadevasya kārmukam.
ye tv ime kṣura|saṅkāśāḥ sahasrā loma|vāhinaḥ,
ete 'rjunasya, Vairāṭe, śarāḥ sarpa|viṣ'|ôpamāḥ.
ete jvalantaḥ saṅgrāme tejasā śīghra|gāminaḥ
bhavanti vīrasy' âkṣayyā, vyūhataḥ samare ripūn.
ye c' ême pṛthavo, dīrghāś, candra|bimb'|ârdha|darśanāḥ,
ete Bhīmasya niśitā ripu|kṣaya|karāḥ śarāḥ.
43.15 hāridra|varṇā ye tv ete hema|puṅkhāḥ śilā|śitāḥ,
Nakulasya kalāpo 'yaṃ pañca|śārdūla|lakṣaṇaḥ.
yen' âsau vyajayat kṛtsnāṃ pratīcīṃ diśam āhave
kalāpo hy eṣa tasy' āsīn Mādrī|putrasya dhīmataḥ.
ye tv ime bhāskar'|ākārāḥ sarva|pārasavāḥ śarāḥ,
ete citra|kriy'|ôpetāḥ Sahadevasya dhīmataḥ.
ye tv ime niśitāḥ, pītāḥ, pṛthavo, dīrgha|vāsasaḥ,
hema|puṅkhās, tri|parvāṇā, rājña ete mahā|śarāḥ.
yas tv ayaṃ sāyako dīrghaḥ śilī|pṛṣṭhaḥ, śilī|mukhaḥ,
Arjunasy' âiṣa saṅgrāme guru|bhāra|saho dṛḍhaḥ.
43.20 Vaiyāghra|kośaḥ su|mahān Bhīmasenasaya sāyakaḥ,
guru|bhāra|saho, divyaḥ, śātravāṇāṃ bhayaṃ|karaḥ.

The bow with the excellent sides and golden handle belongs to Bhima·sena, and it was with this weapon that the enemy-scorcher conquered the whole of the eastern region. That superb and handsome bow, decorated with pictures of fireflies, belongs to King Yudhi·shthira, o son of Viráta. This 43.10
one on which brilliant, golden suns are glittering and blazing with splendor is Nákula's weapon. This bow, adorned with insects of pure fire-tested gold, belongs to Saha·deva, the son of Madri.

And these thousand razor-sharp, feathered arrows, like poisonous snakes, belong to Árjuna, son of Viráta. When shot at the enemy in battle, they become inexhaustible in power and blaze with brilliance, flying swiftly in the conflict. These long, broad, sharp arrows which resemble a half-moon and bring destruction to the enemy belong to Bhima.

This quiver, emblazoned with five images of tigers, full 43.15
of yellow shafts, sharpened on stone, endowed with golden wings, belongs to Nákula. And this is the quiver with which the intelligent son of Madri conquered the whole western region in battle. These arrows, made entirely of iron, which resemble the rays of the sun and are covered with paintings, belong to the intelligent Saha·deva.

These numerous coppery, sharp, long and golden-feathered great arrows with three knots belong to King Yudhi·shthira. This long sword with a frog emblem on the back, pointed like a frog's mouth, is Árjuna's heavy-weighted solid weapon in battle. That massive heavy-weighted, ex- 43.20
cellent sword which brings fear to the enemy, encased in a tiger-skin scabbard, belongs to Bhima·sena.

su|phalaś, citra|kośaś ca, hema|tsarur, an|uttamaḥ
nistriṃśaḥ Kauravasy' âiṣa dharma|rājasya dhīmataḥ.
yas tu pāñca|nakhe kośe nihitaś citra|yodhane,
Nakulasy' âiṣa nistriṃśo guru|bhāra|saho, dṛḍhaḥ.
yas tv ayaṃ vipulaḥ khaḍgo gavye kośe samarpitaḥ,
Sahadevasya viddhy enaṃ sarva|bhāra|sahaṃ, dṛḍham.

UTTARA uvāca:

44.1 SUVARṆA|VIKṚTĀN' îmāny āyudhāni mah"|ātmanām
rucirāṇi prakāśante Pārthānām āśu|kāriṇām.
kva nu svid Arjunaḥ Pārthaḥ, Kauravyo vā Yudhiṣṭhiraḥ,
Nakulaḥ, Sahadevaś ca, Bhīmasenaś ca Pāṇḍavaḥ?
sarva eva mah"|ātmānaḥ, sarv'|âmitra|vināśanāḥ,
rājyam akṣaiḥ parākīrya na śrūyante kathaṃ cana.
Draupadī kva ca Pāñcālī, «strī|ratnam» iti viśrutā?
jitān akṣais tadā Kṛṣṇā tān ev' ânvagamad vanam?

ARJUNA uvāca:

44.5 aham asmy Arjunaḥ Pārthaḥ, sabhā|stāro Yudhiṣṭhiraḥ,
Ballavo Bhīmasenas tu pitus te rasa|pācakaḥ.
aśva|bandho 'tha Nakulaḥ, Sahadevas tu go|kule.
sairandhrīṃ Draupadīṃ viddhi, yat|kṛte Kīcakā hatāḥ.

The merciless sword with the excellent blade, multicolored scabbard and superb golden hilt belongs to the wise Káurava Yudhi·shthira, king of righteousness. This solid, heavy-weighted, cruel sword, designed for many types of battle and enclosed in a goat scabbard, belongs to Nákula. Lastly, this large scimitar which is massive and very powerful, encased in a cow's-leather scabbard, belongs to Saha·deva.

ÚTTARA said:

THESE GOLD-PLATED weapons, which belong to the high- 44.1
souled, swift-acting Parthas, look beautiful. But where is Árjuna, the son of Pritha, or Yudhi·shthira of the Kuru race, and Nákula and Saha·deva and Bhima·sena, the sons of Pandu? Since they lost their kingdom in a game of dice, all those high-souled men, the destroyers of all their enemies, have been neither seen nor heard of at all. Where is Dráupadi Krishná, the Pancháli princess, said to be the "jewel among women," who followed them to the forest after their defeat at gambling?

ÁRJUNA said:

I am Árjuna, the son of Pritha. Yudhi·shthira is your 44.5
father's courtier and Bhima·sena is Bállava, your father's chef. Nákula is the groom of the horses and Saha·deva is the cowherd. Know that Dráupadi is the *sairándhri* for whose sake the Kíchakas were killed.

UTTARA uvāca:

daśa Pārthasya nāmāni yāni pūrvaṃ śrutāni me.
prabrūyās tāni yadi me, śraddadhyām sarvam eva te.

ARJUNA uvāca:

hanta te 'haṃ samācakṣe daśa nāmāni yāni me,
Vairāṭe, śṛṇu tāni tvaṃ, yāni pūrvaṃ śrutāni te
ek' âgra mānaso bhūtvā śṛṇu sarvaṃ samāhitaḥ:
Arjunaḥ Phālguno Jiṣṇuḥ Kirīṭī Śvetavāhanaḥ
Bībhatsur Vijayaḥ Kṛṣṇaḥ Savyasācī Dhanaṃjayaḥ.

UTTARA uvāca:

44.10 ken' âsi Vijayo nāma, ken' âsi Śvetavāhanaḥ?
Kirīṭī nāma ken' âsi, Savyasācī kathaṃ bhavān?
Arjunaḥ, Phālguno, Jiṣṇuḥ, Kṛṣṇo, Bībhatsur eva ca,
Dhanaṃjayaś ca ken' âsi? brūhi tan mama tattvataḥ.
śrutā me tasya vīrasya kevalā nāma|hetavaḥ.
tat sarvaṃ yadi me brūyāḥ, śraddadhyāṃ sarvam eva te.

ARJUNA uvāca:

sarvāñ jana|padāñ jitvā, vittam ādāya kevalam,
madhye dhanasya tiṣṭhāmi ten' âhur māṃ Dhanaṃjayam.
abhiprayāmi saṅgrāme yad ahaṃ yuddha|dur|madān,
n' âjitvā vinivartāmi, tena māṃ Vijayaṃ viduḥ.
44.15 śvetāḥ kāñcana|sannāhā rathe yujyanti me hayāḥ
saṅgrāme yudhyamānasya, ten' âhaṃ Śveta|vāhanaḥ.
Uttarābhyāṃ Phalgunībhyāṃ nakṣatrābhyām ahaṃ divā
jāto Himavataḥ pṛṣṭhe, tena māṃ Phālgunaṃ viduḥ.
purā Śakreṇa me dattaṃ yudhyato dānava'|rṣabhaiḥ
kirīṭaṃ mūrdhni sūry'|ābhaṃ, ten' āhur māṃ Kirīṭīnam.

ÚTTARA said:

I will believe you if you can recite all ten names of Árjuna, the son of Pritha, which I have heard before.

ÁRJUNA said:

Well, then, I will recite my ten names, son of Viráta. Listen to the names you have heard before, and, focusing your mind on this one matter, listen intently to the whole list: Árjuna, Phálguna, Jishnu, Kirítin, Shveta·váhana, Bibhátsu, Víjaya, Krishna, Savya·sachin and Dhanan·jaya.

ÚTTARA said:

Why are you called Víjaya, and why are you called Sh- 44.10
veta·váhana? Why is your name Kirítin and how did you become Savya·sachin? Tell me truly why you are called Árjuna, Phálguna, Jishnu, Krishna, Bibhátsu and Dhanan·jaya. I have heard about all the names of that hero, and so if you can tell me about all of them, then I will trust you.

ÁRJUNA said:

They called me Dhanan·jaya because once I had conquered all peoples and taken away all their treasure I lived in the midst of wealth. They call me Víjaya because when I go out to war I do not return without having defeated
the battle-crazed. I am called Shveta·váhana because white 44.15
horses decorated with gold are yoked to my chariot when I fight in battle. They call me Phálguna because I was born on the far side of Mount Himálaya on a day during the appearance of the constellation Úttara Phálguna, and they call me Kirítin on account of the crown that was put on my head by Shakra long ago, when I fought the bull-like *dánava*s.

na kuryāṃ karma bībhatsaṃ
yudhyamānaḥ kathaṃ ca na,
tena deva|manuṣyeṣu
Bībhatsur iti viśrutaḥ.
ubhau me dakṣiṇau pāṇī Gāṇḍīvasya vikarṣaṇe,
tena deva|manuṣyeṣu Savyasāc" îti māṃ viduḥ.
44.20 pṛthivyāṃ catur|antāyāṃ varṇo me dur|labhaḥ samaḥ,
karomi karma śuklaṃ ca, tasmān mām Arjunaṃ viduḥ.
ahaṃ dur|āpo, dur|dharṣo, damanaḥ, Pāka|śāsaniḥ,
tena deva|manuṣyeṣu Jiṣṇur nām" âsmi viśrutaḥ.
Kṛṣṇa ity eva daśamaṃ nāma cakre pitā mama,
kṛṣṇ'|âvadātasya tataḥ priyatvād bālakasya vai.

VAIŚAMPĀYANA uvāca:

tataḥ sa Pārthaṃ Vairāṭir abhyavādayad antikāt:
«ahaṃ Bhūmiṃjayo nāma, nāmn" âham api c' Ôttaraḥ.
diṣṭyā tvāṃ, Pārtha, paśyāmi! svāgataṃ te, Dhanaṃjaya!
lohit'|âkṣa, maha|bāho, nāga|rāja|kar'|ôpama,
44.25 yad a|jñānād avocaṃ tvāṃ, kṣantum arhasi tan mama.
yatas tvayā kṛtaṃ pūrvaṃ citraṃ karma su|duṣ|karam,
ato bhayaṃ vyatītaṃ me, prītiś ca paramā tvayi.»

UTTARA uvāca:

45.1 ĀSTHĀYA RUCIRAṂ, vīra, rathaṃ sārathinā mayā,
katamaṃ yāsyase 'nīkam? ukto yāsyāmy ahaṃ tvayā.

I am known as Bibhátsu by the gods and mortals alike because I have never committed an abhorrent act while fighting. They call me Savya·sachin among both the heavenly immortals and men because both my hands can draw the Gandíva. My complexion is hard to match throughout 44.20
the four ends of the earth and I commit only pure acts, and therefore they call me Árjuna. I am known by the name of Jishnu among gods and men because I am unapproachable, inviolable, a tamer of enemies and the son of the punisher of Paka. My father created Krishna, my tenth name, from affection for his perfectly dazzling, black-skinned boy.

VAISHAMPÁYANA said:

Then the son of Viráta said to Partha: "I am called Bhumin·jaya as well as Úttara. Thank heaven I'm looking at you, Partha! Welcome, Dhanan·jaya! Red-eyed man with long arms like elephant trunks, you ought to forgive the 44.25
things I said to you in my ignorance. The various tasks you have achieved in the past were so incredibly difficult that now my fear has vanished and I feel the greatest affection toward you."

ÚTTARA said:

NOW THAT YOU have got into this beautiful chariot, hero, 45.1
with me as your charioteer, which part of the army will you go to? I will go where you direct me.

ARJUNA uvāca:

prīto 'smi, puruṣa|vyāghra. na bhayaṃ vidyate tava.
sarvān nudāmi te śatrūn raṇe, raṇa|viśārada.
sva|stho bhava, mahā|bāho, paśya māṃ śatrubhiḥ saha
yudhyamānaṃ vimarde 'smin, kurvāṇaṃ bhairavaṃ mahat.
etān sarvān upāsaṅgān kṣipraṃ badhnīhi me rathe,
ekaṃ c' āhara nistriṃśaṃ jāta|rūpa|pariṣkṛtam.

VAIŚAMPĀYANA uvāca:

45.5 Arjunasya vacaḥ śrutvā tvarāvān Uttaras tadā
Arjunasy' āyudhān gṛhya śīghreṇ' âvātarat tataḥ.

ARJUNA uvāca:

ahaṃ vai Kurubhir yotsyāmy, avajeṣyāmi te paśūn.
saṃkalpa|pakṣa|vikṣepaṃ, bāhu|prākāra|toraṇam,
tri|daṇḍa|tūṇa|saṃbādham, aneka|dhvaja|saṃkulam,
vyākṣepaṇaṃ krodha|kṛtaṃ, nemī|ninada|dundubhi
nagaraṃ te mayā guptaṃ rath'|ôpasthaṃ bhaviṣyati.
adhiṣṭhito mayā saṃkhye ratho Gāṇḍīva|dhanvanā
a|jeyaḥ śatru|sainyānāṃ, Vairāṭe, vyetu te bhayam.

UTTARA uvāca:

45.10 bibhemi n' âham etetṣāṃ, jānāmi tvāṃ sthiraṃ yudhi,
Keśaven' âpi saṅgrāme, sākṣād Indreṇa vā samam.
idaṃ tu cintayann evaṃ parimuhyāmi kevalam!
niścayaṃ c' âpi dur|medhā na gacchāmi kathaṃ cana.
evaṃ yukt'|âṅga|rūpasya, lakṣaṇaiḥ sūcitasya ca
kena karma|vipākena klībatvam idam āgatam?

ÁRJUNA said:

I am pleased with you, tiger-like man. There is no need for your fear, since I will drive away all your enemies in battle, skilled battle-warrior. Be confident, long-armed man, and watch me as I fight against your enemies in this battle, doing great and terrible things. Quickly attach all those quivers to my chariot and take a single sword adorned with gold.

VAISHAMPÁYANA said:

Once he'd listened to Árjuna's orders, Úttara hurriedly 45.5
took Árjuna's weapons, then climbed down quickly.

ÁRJUNA said:

I will fight with the Kurus and win back your cattle. The interior of this chariot will become a city under my protection: my determination shall form a winged assault, my arms will be ramparts and entrances. It will be thronged with the triple pole and quivers, and packed with many banners. My fury will be like a catapult and the clatter of my wheels will be like kettledrums! This chariot, directed by me, the Gandíva bowman, in battle, will be invincible among the enemy army, son of Viráta, so let your fear be gone.

ÚTTARA said:

I do not fear these men, for I know that your firmness in 45.10
battle makes you like Késhava in conflict, or like Indra in human form. But musing on this I am entirely bewildered! For, idiot that I am, I cannot come to any conclusion on this problem. What deed can cause such a delightful man, endowed with such beauty in his limbs and auspicious markings, to be in the predicament of being a eunuch? To my

manye tvāṃ klība|veṣeṇa carantaṃ śūlapāṇinam,
gandharva|rāja|pratimaṃ, devaṃ v" âpi śata|kratum.

ARJUNA uvāca:

bhrātur niyogāj jyeṣṭhasya saṃvatsaram idaṃ vratam
carāmi vrata|caryaṃ ca, satyam etad bravīmi te.
45.15 n' âsmi klībo, mahā|bāho, paravān dharma|saṃyutaḥ
samāpta|vratam uttīrṇaṃ viddhi māṃ tvaṃ, nṛp'|ātmaja.

UTTARA uvāca:

paramo 'nugraho me 'dya, yatas tarko na me vṛthā!
na h' īdṛśāḥ klība|rūpā bhavanti tu, nar'|ôttama.
sahāyavān asmi raṇe, yudhyeyam a|marair api.
sādhvasaṃ hi pranaṣṭaṃ me. kiṃ karomi? bravīhi me!
ahaṃ te saṃgrahīṣyāmi hayāñ śatru|rath'|ārujān,
śikṣito hy asmi sārathye tīrthataḥ, puruṣa'|rṣabha.
Dāruko Vāsudevasya yathā, Śakrasya Mātaliḥ,
tathā māṃ viddhi sārathye śikṣitaṃ, nara|puṃgava!
45.20 yasya yāte na paśyanti bhūmau kṣiptaṃ padaṃ padam,
dakṣiṇāṃ yo dhuraṃ yuktaḥ, Sugrīva|sadṛśo hayaḥ.
yo 'yaṃ dhuraṃ dhurya|varo vāmāṃ vahati śobhanaḥ,
taṃ manye Meghapuṣpasya javena sadṛśaṃ hayam.
yo 'yaṃ kāñcana|sannāhaḥ pārṣṇiṃ vahati śobhanaḥ,
samaṃ Śaibyasya taṃ manye, javena balavattaram.
yo 'yaṃ vahati me pārṣṇiṃ dakṣiṇām abhitaḥ sthitaḥ,

mind, you seem like Shiva, trident in hand, or the king of the *gandhárvas*, or the god Indra, who had performed the hundred sacrifices, merely living in the disguise of a eunuch.

ÁRJUNA said:

I tell you truthfully, I am living in accordance with a vow at the command of my older brother for this year only. I 45.15
am not really a eunuch, long-armed man, but rather know me, prince, as one who has acted as though I were, out of obedience to another and for the accumulation of religious merit.

ÚTTARA said:

Today you have done me the greatest kindness, since I find that my speculation was not idle! Someone like you is not really a eunuch, greatest of men. Now I have a companion in battle and I could fight against even the immortals! My fear has been destroyed. What shall I do? Tell me! I will take the reins of your horses, which can demolish enemy chariots, since I have been trained in driving by a worthy teacher, bull-like man. Know that I was trained in driving up to the standards of Vasudéva's Dáruka or Shakra's Mátali, bull-like hero!

The horse yoked to the right-hand pole is like Krishna's 45.20
Sugríva, for it travels so fast that its hoofprints are invisible! The fine-looking horse who bears the left-hand pole is the best and most excellent of yoked creatures, and to my mind is Megha·pushpa's equal in terms of speed. This glittering golden-armored horse bearing the rear left pole is, in my opinion, equal to Shaibya in speed, but stronger. This horse standing near the right, bearing the pole, is considered to

Balāhakād api mataḥ sa jave vīryavattaraḥ!
tvām ev' âyaṃ ratho voḍhuṃ saṅgrāme 'rhati dhanvinam.
tvaṃ c' êmaṃ ratham āsthāya yoddhum arho mato mama.

VAIŚAMPĀYANA uvāca:

45.25 tato vimucya bāhubhyāṃ valayāni sa vīryavān,
citre kāñcana|sannāhe pratyamuñcat tadā tale,
kṛṣṇān bhaṅgimataḥ keśāñ śveten' ôdgrathya vāsasā.
ath' âsau prāṅ|mukho bhūtvā śuciḥ, prayata|mānasaḥ,
abhidadhyau mahā|bāhuḥ sarv'|âstrāṇi rath'|ôttame.
ūcuś ca Pārthaṃ sarvāṇi prāñjalīni nṛp'|ātma|jam:
«ime sma, param'|ôdārāḥ kiṃ|karāḥ, Pāṇḍu|nandana.»
praṇipatya tataḥ Pārthaḥ, samālabhya ca pāṇinā:
«sarvāṇi mānasān' îha bhavat', êty» abhyabhāṣata.
pratigṛhya tato 'strāṇi prahṛṣṭa|vadano 'bhavat,
adhijyaṃ tarasā kṛtvā Gāṇḍīvaṃ vyākṣipad dhanuḥ.
45.30 tasya vikṣipyamāṇasya dhanuṣo 'bhūn mahā|dhvaniḥ
yathā śailasya mahataḥ śailen' âiv' âvajaghnataḥ.
sa|nirghāt" âbhavad bhūmir,
diksu vāyur vavau bhṛśam,
papāta mahatī c' ôlkā,
diśo na pracakāśire.
bhrānta|dhvajaṃ khaṃ tad" āsīt,
prakampita|mahā|drumam.
tam śabdaṃ Kuravo 'jānan, visphoṭam aśaner iva,
yad Arjuno dhanuḥ|śreṣṭhaṃ bāhubhyām ākṣipad rathe.

UTTARA uvāca:

«ekas tvaṃ, Pāṇḍava|śreṣṭha, bahūn etān mahā|rathān
kathaṃ jeṣyasi saṅgrāme sarva|śastr'|âstra|pāra|gān?
a|sahāyo 'si, Kaunteya, sa|sahāyāś ca Kauravāḥ.

be more powerful than Baláhaka in speed! This chariot is worthy of conveying a bowman such as yourself into battle, and you deserve to fight stationed on this chariot! Or at least that's what I think.

VAISHAMPÁYANA said:

Then, when he had taken the bracelets off his arms, the 45.25
powerful man put multicolored gloves, decorated with gold, onto his hands, and then tied up his curly black hair with a white piece of cloth. Having faced the east on his superb chariot, that long-armed hero became pure, concentrating his mind and meditating upon all his weapons. All performing the anjali gesture, they said to Partha: "We are here as your illustrious servants, son of Pandu." Once he had bowed to them, Partha took hold of them with his hand and said to them: "All of you be present in my mind."

Then, when he had taken his weapons, his face beamed with joy, and, having quickly strung his bow, Gandíva, he
plucked it. The great twang of the bow being plucked re- 45.30
verberated just like one mighty mountain crashing against another. A huge meteor fell and the world became dark. The banner was shaking and the mighty tree trembled. The Kurus recognized the sound like the crash of thunder, aware that it was Árjuna on a chariot drawing his best bow in his arms.

ÚTTARA said:

"You are alone, best of the Pándavas, but they are many great warriors. How will you defeat all those men in battle, who have mastered every kind of weapon? You, son of Kuata eṣa, mahā|bāho, bhītas tiṣṭhāmi te 'grataḥ.»

45.35 uvāca Pārtho, «mā bhaiṣīḥ,» prahasya svanavat tadā,
«yudhyamānasya me, vīra, gandharvaiḥ su|mahā|balaiḥ
sahāyo ghoṣa|yātrāyāṃ, kas tad" āsīt sakhā mama?
tathā pratibhaye tasmin deva|dānava|saṃkule
Khāṇḍave yudhyamānasya, kas tad" āsīt sakhā mama?
Nivātakavacaiḥ sārdhaṃ, Paulomaiś ca mahā|balaiḥ
yudhyato deva|rāj'|ârthe, kaḥ sahāyas tad" âbhavat?
svayaṃ|vare tu Pāñcālyā rājabhiḥ saha saṃyuge
yudhyato bahubhis, tāta, kaḥ sahāyas tad" âbhavat?

45.40 upajīvya guruṃ Droṇaṃ, Śakraṃ, Vaiśravaṇam, Yamam,
Varuṇaṃ, Pāvakaṃ c' âiva, Kṛpaṃ, Kṛṣṇaṃ ca Mādhavam,
Pināka|pāṇinaṃ c' âiva, katham etān na yodhaye?
rathaṃ vāhaya me śīghraṃ; vyetu te mānaso jvaraḥ.»

VAIŚAṂPĀYANA uvāca:

46.1 UTTARAṂ SĀRATHIṂ kṛtvā, śamīṃ kṛtvā pradakṣiṇam,
āyudhaṃ sarvam ādāya prayayau Pāṇḍava'|rṣabhaḥ.
dhvajaṃ siṃhaṃ rathāt tasmād apanīya mahā|rathaḥ,
praṇidhāya śamī|mūle, prāyād Uttara|sārathiḥ.

devīṃ māyāṃ rathe yuktāṃ vihitāṃ Viśvakarmaṇā,
kāñcanaṃ siṃha|lāṅgūlaṃ dhvajaṃ vānara|lakṣaṇam
manasā cintayām āsa, prasādaṃ Pāvakasya ca.
sa ca tac cintitaṃ jñātvā dhvaje bhūtāny adeśayat.

ntí, have no follower, but the Kurus have many. So this is why I stand beside you terrified, long-armed man."

Partha said, "Don't be afraid," and he laughed loudly, 45.35
"What friend did I have with me as a follower, hero, when I fought with the fantastically powerful *gandhárvas* during the herdsmen's procession? Who was my companion when I fought against the gods and the *dánavas* at Khándava in that formidable conflict? And when I fought for the sake of the king of the gods with the powerful Niváta·kávachas and Paulómas, who then was my companion? And when I fought with numerous kings in the conflict at the *svayam·vara* of the Princess of Pancháli, young man, who then was my ally?

I have made good use of Drona, Shakra, Váishravana, Ya- 45.40
ma, Váruna, Agni and Kripa, Krishna *Mádhava* and even the trident-bearer, Shiva, as my teachers, so why should I not fight them? Drive my chariot quickly and let the fever in your mind disappear."

VAISHAMPÁYANA said:

ONCE HE HAD made Úttara his chariot driver, and per- 46.1
formed the circumambulation of the *shami* tree, the bull of the Pándavas set out, taking his entire arsenal. The great warrior took down the lion banner from the chariot, deposited it at the root of the *shami* tree and set off with Úttara as his driver.

He meditated in his mind on his own banner being attached to his chariot, golden and bearing the image of a monkey with a lion's tail, which was a celestial illusion devised by Vishva·karman. When he had meditated in his

46.5 sa|patākaṃ, vicitr'|âṅgaṃ, s'|ôpāsaṅgaṃ, mahā|balam
khāt papāta rathe tūrṇaṃ divya|rūpaṃ mano|ramam.
rathaṃ tam āgatam dṛṣṭvā dakṣiṇaṃ prākarot tadā.

rathaṃ āsthāya Bībhatsuḥ Kaunteyaḥ Śvetavāhanaḥ
baddha|godh"|âṅgulitrāṇaḥ, pragṛhīta|śarāsanaḥ
tatah prāyād udīcīṃ ca kapi|pravara|ketanaḥ.
svanavantaṃ mahā|śaṅkhaṃ balavān ari|mardanaḥ
prādhamad balam āsthāya, dviṣatāṃ loma|harṣaṇam.
tatas te javanā dhuryā jānubhyām agaman mahīm,
Uttaraś c' âpi santrasto rath'|ôpastha upāviśat.
46.10 saṃsthāpya c' âśvān Kaunteyaḥ, samudyamya ca raśmibhiḥ,
Uttaraṃ ca pariṣvajya samāśvāsayad Arjunaḥ.

ARJUNA uvāca:

mā bhais tvaṃ, rāja|putr'|âgrya, kṣatriyo 'si, paraṃ|tapa.
kathaṃ tu, puruṣa|vyāghra, śatru|madhye viṣīdasi?
śrutās te śaṅkha|śabdāś ca, bherī|śabdāś ca puṣkalāḥ,
kuñjarāṇāṃ ca nadatāṃ vyūḍh'|ânīkeṣu tiṣṭhatām.
sa tvaṃ katham ih' ânena śaṅkha|śabdena bhīṣitaḥ,
vivarṇa|rūpo, vitrastaḥ, puruṣaḥ prākṛto yathā?

mind on the favor of Agni, then Pávaka himself understood his intention and assigned those creatures to his banner. The 46.5
mighty and beautiful flagstaff, of divine form, variously and charmingly decorated on its body, with a flag and quiver attached, quickly fell from the sky onto the chariot. Seeing it reach the chariot, he circumambulated it.

Then, standing on the chariot. Bibhátsu, the son of Kuntí, Shveta·váhana, who had the distinguished ensign of a monkey, bound his fingers into a leather guard strap, and took up his bow and arrows, setting out toward the north. That powerful crusher of the enemy, using his strength, blew his mighty loud-resounding conch shell, hair-raising to his enemies. The excellent swift horses dropped on their knees to the ground, and even Úttara trembled and collapsed inside the chariot. So the son of Kuntí made the horses get 46.10
up and restrained them with the reins. Árjuna also embraced Úttara, encouraging him.

ÁRJUNA said:

Don't be afraid, foremost of princes, for you are a kshatriya, enemy-scorcher. How, tiger-like man, have you sunk down in the midst of the enemy? You must have heard the sounds of conch shells and the powerful boom of kettledrums, and of bellowing elephants standing in the ordered divisions of armies. So how are you so scared of the sound of this conch, pale and trembling, as if you were a normal person?

UTTARA uvāca:

«śrutā me śaṅkha|śabdāś ca, bherī|śabdāś ca puṣkalāḥ,
kuñjarāṇāṃ ninadatāṃ vyūḍh'|ânīkeṣu tiṣṭhatām;
46.15 n' âivaṃ|vidhaḥ śaṅkha|śabdaḥ purā jātu mayā śrutaḥ!
dhvajasya c' âpi rūpaṃ me dṛṣṭa|pūrvaṃ na h' īdṛśam,
dhanuṣaś c' âiva nirghoṣaḥ śruta|pūrvo na me kva cit!
asya śaṅkhasya śabdena, dhanuṣo niḥsvanena ca,
a|mānuṣāṇāṃ śabdena bhūtānāṃ dhvaja|vāsinām,
rathasya ca ninādena mano muhyati me bhṛśam!
vyākulāś ca diśaḥ sarvā, hṛdayaṃ vyathat' îva me.
dhvajena pihitāḥ sarvā diśo na pratibhānti me,
Gāṇḍīvasya ca śabdena karṇau me badhirī|kṛtau!»
sa muhūrtaṃ prayātaṃ tu Pārtho Vairāṭim abravīt:

ARJUNA uvāca:

46.20 ek'|ântaṃ ratham āsthāya
padbhyāṃ tvam avapīḍayan,
dṛḍhaṃ ca raśmīn saṃyaccha.
śaṅkhaṃ dhmāsyāmy ahaṃpunaḥ.

VAIŚAṂPĀYANA uvāca:

tataḥ śaṅkham upādhmāsīd, dārayann iva parvatān,
guhā girīṇāṃ ca tadā, diśaḥ, śailāṃs tath" âiva ca.
Uttaraś c' âpi saṃlīno rath'|ôpastha upāviśat.
tasya śaṅkhasya śabdena, ratha|nemi|svanena ca,
Gāṇḍīvasya ca ghoṣeṇa pṛthivī samakampata.
taṃ samāśvāsayām āsa punar eva Dhanañjayaḥ.

ÚTTARA said:

"I have heard plenty of conch-shell sounds and kettle-drum booms and I have indeed heard the sounds of bellowing elephants lined up in the ordered divisions of armies, but I have never before heard such a piercing sound from a 46.15
conch! Nor have I ever seen a design of banner such as this before, and I have never heard such a twang from a bow anywhere! What with the sound of the conch, the twang of the bow, the shriek of these inhuman creatures living on your banner and the clatter of this chariot, my mind is totally bewildered! My entire sense of direction is muddled, too, and my heart is agitated. The whole sky is concealed by the banner, and hidden from my view! And my ears have been deafened by the sound of Gandíva!" Partha instantly said to Viráta's son as he was on the verge of passing out:

ÁRJUNA said:

Stand steady on the chariot, pressing down with your feet 46.20
and take firm control of the reins, for I will blow the conch shell again.

VAISHAMPÁYANA said:

Then there was a mountain-splitting blast from the conch shell, cleaving apart the hiding places in hills, mountain peaks and all directions. Úttara once again sat cowering inside the chariot, and the earth itself trembled at the blare of the conch, the clatter of the chariot and the reverberating twang of Gandíva. So Dhanan·jaya once again comforted him.

DROṆA uvāca:

yathā rathasya nirghoṣo, yathā megha udīryate,
kampate ca yathā bhūmir, n' âiṣo 'nyaḥ Savyasācinaḥ.

46.25 śastrāṇi na prakāśante, na prahṛṣyanti vājinaḥ.
agnayaś ca na bhāsante samiddhās. tan na śobhanam!
praty ādityaṃ ca naḥ sarve mṛgā ghora|pravādinaḥ,
dhvajeṣu ca nilīyante vāyasās. tan na śobhanam.

śakunāś c' âpasavyā no vedayanti mahad bhayam.
go|māyur eṣa senāyāṃ rudan madhyena dhāvati,
an|āhataś ca niṣkānto mahad vedayate bhayam.
bhavatāṃ roma|kūpāṇi prahṛṣṭāny upalakṣaye.
dhruvaṃ vināśo yuddhena kṣatriyāṇāṃ pradṛśyate.
46.30 jyotīṃṣi na prakāśante; dāruṇā mṛga|pakṣiṇaḥ;
utpātā vividhā ghorā dṛśyante kṣatra|nāśanāḥ.
viśeṣata ih' âsmākaṃ nimittāni vināśane.

ulkābhiś ca pradīptābhir bādhyate pṛtanā tava;
vāhanāny a|prahṛṣṭāni rudant' îva, viśām pate.
upāsate ca sainyāni gṛdhrās tava samantataḥ.
tapsyase vāhinīṃ dṛṣṭvā Pārtha|bāṇa|prapīḍitām.
parābhūtā ca vaḥ senā, na kaś cid yoddhum icchati.
vivarṇa|mukha|bhūyiṣṭhāḥ sarve yodhā vicetasaḥ.
gāḥ saṃprasthāpya tiṣṭhāmo vyūḍh'|ânīkāḥ, prahāriṇaḥ.

DRONA said:

From the clash of the chariot, from the way the clouds are stirring and from the way the earth itself is trembling, this can be none other than Savya·sachin. Our weapons no 46.25
longer gleam and our horses are unhappy. The fires do not blaze though they are kindled. This is not auspicious! All our animals are crying out terribly, staring at the sun, and the crows are alighting on our banners. This is not auspicious.

The vultures on our right signify great danger. This jackal running through the middle of our army is howling, and the ugly brute has not been killed, which portends great danger. I notice that the hairs on your bodies are bristling with goose bumps. This portends a fixed destruction of kshatriyas in battle. Bright things do not gleam and beasts 46.30
and birds seem violent. Various horrifying portents of the destruction of kshatriyas are appearing. These omens of destruction are for us in particular.

Your army is troubled by the blazing meteors and the horses appear to be miserable and crying, lord of earth. Vultures are flying all around the army. You will repent when you have seen your army afflicted by the son of Pritha's arrows. In fact, the army has yielded already, for there is no one who wants to fight. All our warriors have pale faces and are witless. Once we've forced the cattle to move forward, let us stay here with our army ordered in divisions, ready for the attack.

VAIŚAMPĀYANA uvāca:

47.1 ATHA DURYODHANO rājā samare Bhīṣmam abravīt,
Droṇaṃ ca ratha|śārdūlaṃ, Kṛpaṃ ca su|mahā|ratham:
«ukto 'yam artha ācāryo mayā Karṇena c' â|sakṛt.
punar eva pravakṣyāmi, na hi tṛpyāmi taṃ bruvan.

parābhūtair hi vastavyaṃ taiś ca dvādaśa vatsarān
vane jana|pade jñātair, eṣa eva paṇo hi naḥ.
teṣāṃ na tāvan nivṛttaṃ vartate tu trayodaśam;
ajñāta|vāso Bībhatsur ath' âsmābhiḥ samāgataḥ.
47.5 a|nivṛtte tu nirvāse yadi Bībhatsur āgataḥ,
punar dvā|daśa|varṣāṇi vane vatsyanti Pāṇḍavāḥ!
lobhād vā te na jānīyur, asmān vā moha āviśat;
hīn'|âtiriktam eteṣāṃ Bhīṣmo veditum arhati.

arthānāṃ ca punar dvaidhe nityaṃ bhavati saṃśayaḥ;
anyathā cintito hy arthaḥ, punar bhavati so 'nyathā.
uttaraṃ mārgamāṇānāṃ Matsyānāṃ ca yuyutsatām
yadi Bībhatsur āyātas, tadā kasy' âparādhnumaḥ.
Trigartānāṃ vayaṃ hetor Matsyān yoddhum ih' āgatāḥ.
Matsyānāṃ viprakārāṃs te bahūn asmān akīrtayan.
47.10 teṣāṃ bhay'|âbhibhūtānāṃ tad asmābhiḥ pratiśrutam,
prathamaṃ tair grahītavyaṃ Matsyānāṃ go|dhanaṃ mahat
saptamyām apar'|âhṇe vai tathā tais tu samāhitam.
aṣṭamyāṃ punar asmābhir ādityasy' ôdayaṃ prati
imā gāvo grahītavyā gate Matsye gavāṃ padam.
te vā gāś c' ānayiṣyanti, yadi vā syuḥ parājitāḥ,

VAISHAMPÁYANA said:

THEN KING Duryódhana, on the field of battle, said to Bhishma, Drona, that tiger among warriors and Kripa, the excellent charioteering warrior: "I have mentioned this matter many times before to the teacher, as has Karna, but I will say it again, for I am not satisfied with its discussion. 47.1

This was our wager: that if defeated they would have to live in the forest and kingdoms, still known to us, for twelve years, and in their thirteenth year, which is not yet over, but
still running, they would live unknown. Now Bibhátsu has 47.5
appeared before us. If Bibhátsu appears before the exile is finished then the Pándavas will live for twelve more years in the forest! Whether it is from their impatience to rule or whether some delusion has fooled us, Bhishma ought to know what amount of their exile remains or has passed.

There is always doubt and duality when it comes to the objects of desire, and a matter considered one way may actually turn out quite differently. If Bibhátsu has come, then what sin have we committed by coming out wanting to fight the Matsyas and rustle their cattle in the north? We have come here to fight against the Matsyas on behalf of the Tri·gartans. We heard from men, overcome by fear, of the numerous injuries perpetrated by the Matsyas.

We agreed between us that first they should seize the Mat- 47.10
syas' great wealth of cattle on the afternoon of the seventh lunar day, and on the eighth day at sunrise we should seize these cattle while the King of Matsya was gone on the trail of the other cattle. Either they are leading away the cattle or they may be defeated, and may be approaching us having formed an alliance with the Matsyan king. Or, alternatively,

asmān vā hy upasaṃdhāya kuryur Matsyena saṃgatam.
atha vā tān apāhāya Matsyo jana|padaiḥ saha
sarvayā senayā sārdhaṃ saṃvṛto bhīma|rūpayā
āyātaḥ kevalaṃ rātrim asmān yoddhum ih' āgataḥ.

teṣām eva mahā|vīryaḥ kaś cid eṣa puraḥ|saraḥ
asmān jetum ih' āyāto Matsyo v" âpi svayaṃ bhavet.
47.15 yady eṣa rājā Matsyānāṃ, yadi Bībhatsur āgataḥ,
sarvair yoddhavyam asmābhir, iti naḥ samayaḥ kṛtaḥ.
atha kasmāt sthitā hy ete ratheṣu ratha|sattamāḥ,
Bhīṣmo, Droṇaḥ, Kṛpaś c' âiva, Vikarṇo, Drauṇir eva ca,
saṃbhrānta|manasaḥ sarve, kāle hy asmin mahā|rathāḥ?

n' ânyatra yuddhāc chreyo 'sti, tath" ātmā praṇidhīyatām.
ācchinne go|dhane 'smākam api devena vajriṇā,
Yamena v" âpi saṅgrāme, ko Hāstinapuraṃ vrajet?
śarair ebhiḥ praṇunnānāṃ, bhagnānāṃ gahane vane,
ko hi jīvet padātīnāṃ, bhaved aśveṣu saṃśayaḥ?»

47.20 Duryodhana|vacaḥ śrutvā Rādheyas tv abravīd vacaḥ,
«ācāryaṃ pṛṣṭhataḥ kṛtvā tathā nītir vidhīyatām.
jānāti hi mataṃ teṣām, atas trāsayat' îha naḥ.
Arjune c' âsya samprītim adhikām upalakṣaye.
tathā hi dṛṣṭvā Bībhatsum upāyāntam praśaṃsati.
yathā senā na bhajyeta, tathā nītir vidhīyatām.
hreṣitaṃ hy upaśṛṇvāne Droṇe sarvaṃ vighaṭṭitaṃ.
a|deśikā mah"|âraṇye grīṣme śatru|vaśaṃ gatā
yathā na vibhramet senā, tathā nītir vidhīyatām.

the King of Matsya, along with his people, has driven them off and, surrounded by his whole fearsome-looking army, he is approaching and will come to fight us for the whole night.

Perhaps some mighty hero of theirs has come as a forerunner to conquer us, or perhaps it is the King of Matsya
himself. But, regardless of whether it is the king of the Mat- 47.15
syas or Bibhátsu who has come, we must all fight him. This is the agreement we made. So why are these most excellent chariot-warriors, Bhishma, Drona, Kripa and Vikárna and Ashvattháman, Drona's son, standing on their chariots all terrified in their minds now, though they are all mighty chariot-warriors?

There is nothing else better than fighting, so a decision must be made. If we had to fight with the divine thunderbolt-wielder or Yama for the cattle we rustled, who would go back to Hástina·pura? Which of the infantry will live when they are scared away to the impenetrable forest and broken by those arrows, when even the cavalry's escape is in doubt?"

Having heard Duryódhana's speech, Karna said these 47.20
words: "Prepare matters, but ignore the teacher and put our tactics into action. For he knows the way that others think and he makes us scared. I notice his exceeding affection for Árjuna. Seeing Bibhátsu approach, he praises him. But let us arrange our tactics so our army doesn't break. Everything is in disarray because Drona has heard the neighing of Árjuna's horses. Let us organize our tactics so that the army, strangers in a great forest in the hot season, should not become bewildered and fall under the enemy's control.

iṣṭā hi Pāṇḍavā nityam ācāryasya viśeṣataḥ.
āsayann a|par'|ârthaś ca, kathyate sma svayaṃ tathā.
47.25 aśvānām hreṣitaṃ śrutvā kaḥ praśaṃsā|paro bhavet?
sthāne v" âpi, vrajanto vā sadā hreṣanti vājinaḥ,
sadā ca vāyavo vānti, nityaṃ varṣati Vāsavaḥ!
stanayitnoś ca nirghoṣaḥ śrūyate bahuśas tathā.
kim atra kāryaṃ Pārthasya? kathaṃ vā sa praśasyate?
anyatra kāmād, dveṣād vāv roṣād asmāsu kevalāt.

ācāryā vai kāruṇikāḥ, prājñāś c', â|pāpa|darśinaḥ;
n' âite mahā|bhaye prāpte saṃpraṣṭavyāḥ kathañ cana.
prāsādeṣu vicitreṣu, goṣṭhīṣ', ûpavaneṣu ca
kathā vicitrāḥ kurvāṇāḥ paṇḍitāś tatra śobhanāḥ.
47.30 bahūny āścarya|rūpāṇi kurvāṇā jana|saṃsadi,
ijy' âstre c' ôpasandhāne paṇḍitās tatra śobhanāḥ.
pareṣāṃ vivara|jñāne, manuṣya|cariteṣu ca,
hasty|aśva|ratha|caryāsu, khar'|ôṣṭr'|âj'|âvi|karmaṇi,
go|dhaneṣu, pratolīṣu, vara|dvāra|mukheṣu ca,
anna|saṃskāra|doṣeṣu paṇḍitās tatra śobhanāḥ.

paṇḍitān pṛṣṭhataḥ kṛtvā pareṣāṃ guṇa|vādinaḥ,
vidhīyatāṃ tathā nītir, yathā vadhyo bhavet paraḥ.
gāvaś ca saṃpratiṣṭhāpya, senāṃ vyūhya samantataḥ,
ārakṣāś ca vidhīyantāṃ yatra yotsyāmahe parān.»

The Pándavas were always the teacher's special favorites. They are selfish and have made him stay, but he betrays himself. Who would praise someone having merely heard 47.25
the neigh of his horses? Horses always neigh regardless of whether they're standing still or moving, the wind always blows and Indra always brings rain! The crack of thunder is frequently heard. What does Partha have to do with it? Why is he praised for it? It is either entirely from affection for him or from complete enmity and anger toward us.

Teachers are compassionate, wise and without visible sin, but in times of great danger they should never be consulted. It is in beautiful palaces, assemblies and gardens that teachers shine, telling diverse stories. Doing many extraordinary 47.30
things in the assembly or with regard to the implement of sacrifices—these are the areas where teachers shine. In matters of knowing others' faults, in matters of men's characters, in knowing about elephants, horses and chariots, in matters of treating donkeys, camels, goats and sheep as well as wealth of cattle, in public road building and choosing gateways, and in the problems with food preparation: these are the areas in which teachers shine.

Ignoring teachers who tell us the merits of our enemies, let us organize our tactics so the enemy can be annihilated. Take control of the cattle and arrange the army into divisions on all sides and let guards be set up where we will fight our enemies."

KARNA uvāca:

48.1 SARVĀN ĀYUṢMATO bhītān, saṃtrastān iva lakṣaye,
a|yuddha|manasaś c' âiva, sarvāṃś c' âiv' ân|avasthitān.
yady eṣa rājā Matsyānāṃ, yadi Bībhatsur āgataḥ,
aham āvārayiṣyāmi, vel" êva makar'|ālayam.

mama cāpa|prayuktānāṃ śarāṇāṃ nata|parvaṇām
n' āvṛttir gacchatāṃ teṣāṃ, sarpāṇām iva sarpatām.
rukma|puṅkhāḥ, su|tīkṣṇ'|âgrā, muktā hastavatā mayā,
chādayantu śarāḥ Pārthaṃ, śalabhā iva pāda|pam.
48.5 śarāṇāṃ puṅkha|saktānāṃ maurvy" âbhihatayā dṛḍham
śrūyatāṃ talayoḥ śabdo, bheryor āhatayor iva.

samāhito hi Bībhatsur varṣāṇy aṣṭau ca pañca ca,
jāta|snehaś ca yuddhe 'smin mayi saṃprahariṣyati.
pātrī|bhūtaś ca Kaunteyo, brāhmaṇo guṇavān iva,
śar'|âughān pratigṛhṇātu mayā muktān sahasraśaḥ.
eṣa c' âiva mah"|êṣv|āsas triṣu lokeṣu viśrutaḥ;
ahaṃ c' âpi nara|śreṣṭhād Arjunān n' âvarah kva cit!

itaś c' êtaś ca nirmuktaiḥ kāñcanair gārdhra|vājitaiḥ
dṛśyatām adya vai vyoma, kha|dyotair iva, saṃvṛtam.
48.10 ady' âham ṛṇam akṣayyaṃ purā vācā pratiśrutam
Dhārtarāṣṭrāya dāsyāmi, nihatya samare 'rjunaṃ.
antarā chidyamānānāṃ puṅkhānāṃ vyatiśīryatām,
śalabhānām iv' ākāśe, pracāraḥ saṃpradṛśyatām.

KARNA said:

I SEE ALL THESE men in peak fitness are scared and trembling, in an unfit state of mind for battle, and all unsettled. If the man who is approaching turns out to be the king of the Matsyas or Bibhátsu, I will ward him off as the coast wards off the ocean, home of monsters. 48.1

Shot from my bow, these smooth arrows like gliding snakes will not miss their target. Released from my hands, these golden-winged and razor-sharp-pointed arrows will cover Partha like locusts on a tree. The sound of the winged 48.5
arrows shot firmly from my bowstring will resound on my palm and wrist guards as though they were a couple of kettle drums being struck.

Bibhátsu will certainly attack me in this conflict, but since he has spent thirteen years devout in meditation, it will only be benignly. The son of Kuntí, a brahmin of merit, has become a fitting recipient, so let him receive the thousands of arrows I will release upon him in downpours. This great archer is indeed renowned throughout all three worlds, but I am in no way inferior to Árjuna, the best of men!

Today may the sky, filled with the golden, vulture-feathered arrows released on all sides, look as though it were swarming with fireflies. Today, by killing Árjuna in battle, I 48.10
will repay that undecaying debt, promised in a speech long ago to the son of Dhrita·rashtra. Let my winged arrows, split in the middle, fly forward with the appearance of fireflies in the ether.

Indr'|âśani|sama|sparśaṃ, mah"|Êndra|sama|tejasam
ardayiṣyāmy ahaṃ Pārtham, ulkābhir iva kuñjaram.
rathād atirathaṃ śūraṃ, sarva|śastra|bhṛtāṃ varam,
vivaśaṃ Pārtham ādāsye, Garutmān iva panna|gam.
tam agnim iva dur|dharṣam asi|śakti|śar'|êndhanam,
Pāṇḍav'|âgnim ahaṃ dīptaṃ, pradahantam iv' â|hitam,
48.15 aśva|vega|puro|vāto, rath'|âugha|stanayitnumān,
śara|dhāro mahā|meghah, śamayiṣyāmi Pāṇḍavam!

mat|kārmuka|vinirmuktāḥ Pārtham āśīviṣ'|ôpamāḥ
śarāḥ samabhisarpantu, valmīkam iva panna|gāḥ.
su|tejanai, rukma|puṅkhaiḥ, su|dhautair, nata|parvabhiḥ
ācitaṃ paśya Kaunteyaṃ, karṇikārair iv' âcalam.
Jāmadagnyān mayā hy astraṃ yat prāptam ṛṣi|sattamāt,
tad upāśritya, vīryaṃ ca, yudhyeyam api Vāsavam!

dhvaj'|âgre vānaras tiṣṭhan bhallena nihato mayā
ady' âiva patatāṃ bhūmau vinadan bhairavān ravān.
48.20 śatror mayā vipannānāṃ bhūtānāṃ dhvaja|vāsinām
diśaḥ pratiṣṭhamānānām astu śabdo divaṃ|gamaḥ.
adya Duryodhanasy' âhaṃ śalyaṃ hṛdi cira|sthitam
sa|mūlam uddhariṣyāmi Bībhatsuṃ pātayan rathāt!
hat'|âśvaṃ vi|rathaṃ Pārthaṃ, pauruṣe paryavasthitam,
niḥśvasantaṃ yathā nāgam, adya paśyantu Kauravāḥ.
kāmaṃ gacchantu Kuravo dhanam ādāya kevalam,
ratheṣu v" âpi tiṣṭhanto yuddhaṃ paśyantu māmakam!

I will torment Partha, just as an elephant is tormented by firebrands, even though his touch is like Indra's thunderbolt and he is as energetic as great Indra himself. I will seize powerless Partha just like Gáruda seizing a snake, despite the fact that he is an excellent, brave chariot-warrior and the best of all who bear weapons. Though the son of Pandu is an unextinguishable fire, kindled with swords, spears and arrows, I will put out that blazing fire of the Pándavas
who consumes his enemies, by becoming a mighty cloud 48.15
raining down arrows. The speed of my horses will be the preceding wind and my multitude of chariots will constitute the thunder!

Released from my bow, let my arrows like poisonous snakes glide into Partha like serpents into an anthill! See the son of Kuntí heaped with my fantastically splendid, golden-winged, smooth-polished arrows like a hill covered with *karnikára* flowers. Relying on the strength of the weapon I received from that most excellent sage, the son of Jamad·agni, I would even fight Indra!

Today the monkey stationed on the top of his banner will fall to the ground, roaring horrible cries when struck
by my missile. May the shrieks of those creatures, who live 48.20
in the enemy's banner, reach heaven as I torment and scatter them in all directions. Today I will remove the spear stuck in Duryódhana's heart by its roots, as I topple Bibhátsu from his chariot! Let the Kurus see him today when his horses are killed and he has lost his chariot, intent on his heroism and hissing like a snake. Let the Kurus go if they want and take the whole wealth of cattle, or let them stay on their chariots and watch my battle!

KṚPA uvāca:

49.1 SAD" ÂIVA TAVA, Rādheya, yuddhe krūratarā matiḥ!
n' ârthānāṃ prakṛtiṃ vetsi, n' ânubandham avekṣase.
māyā hi bahavaḥ santi śāstram āśritya cintitāḥ.
teṣāṃ yuddhaṃ tu pāpiṣṭhaṃ vedayanti purā|vidaḥ.
deśa|kālena saṃyuktaṃ yuddhaṃ vijaya|daṃ bhavet.
hīna|kālaṃ tad ev' êha phalaṃ na labhate punaḥ.
deśe kāle ca vikrāntaṃ kalyāṇāya vidhīyate.
ānukūlyena kāryāṇām antaraṃ saṃvidhīyate.
bhāraṃ hi ratha|kārasya na vyavasyanti paṇḍitāḥ!
49.5 paricintya tu Pārthena saṃnipāto na naḥ kṣamaḥ.
ekaḥ Kurūn abhyagacchad, ekaś c' Âgnim atarpayat.
ekaś ca pañca varṣāṇi brahma|caryam adhārayat,
ekaḥ Subhadrām āropya dvairathe Kṛṣṇam āhvayat.
ekaḥ kirāta|rūpeṇa sthitaṃ Rudram ayodhayat.
asminn eva vane Pārtho hṛtāṃ Kṛṣṇām avājayat.
ekaś ca pañca varṣāṇi Śakrād astrāṇy aśikṣata,
ekaḥ so 'yam ariṃ jitvā Kurūṇām akarod yaśaḥ.
eko gandharva|rājānaṃ Citrasenam arin|damaḥ
vijigye tarasā saṅkhye, senāṃ prāpya su|durjayām.
49.10 tathā Nivātakavacāḥ Kālakhañjāś ca dānavāḥ
daivatair apy a|vadhyās te ekena yudhi pātitāḥ!

KRIPA said:

RADHÉYA, YOUR mind is always too savage and set on 49.1
battle! You do not understand the fundamental nature of matters, nor do you take the consequences into consideration. There are numerous tactics that can be taken from the shastras which deserve consideration. Of these, battle is regarded as the most sinful by those who understand history. Success is possible only when the time and place are suitable for battle. At this inopportune moment, no benefit will be gained. Mighty valor at the right time and place proves to be advantageous. But it is by its suitability that something is proved to be advantageous or otherwise. Teachers do not make decisions based on the work of a chariot-maker!

So, bearing all this in mind, conflict with Partha is not 49.5
to our benefit. He alone saved the Kurus, and all alone he satisfied Agni. Alone he bore the life of an ascetic brahmin for five years, and once he had picked Subhádra up onto his chariot he challenged Krishna alone to single-car combat. Alone he fought with Rudra as he stood before him in the disguise of a hunter. It was in this very forest that Partha won back Krishná when she had been kidnapped.

He alone has learned the science of the weapons from Indra for five years, and he alone created the fame of the Kurus by defeating his enemies. That conqueror of his enemies single-handedly defeated Chitra·sena, the king of the *gandhárvas*, and speedily finished off his near-unbeatable army
in battle. He single-handedly brought down in battle the 49.10
Niváta·kávachas, Kala·khanjas and *dánavas* whom even the gods could not destroy!

ekena hi tvayā, Karṇa, kiṃ nām' êha kṛtaṃ purā
ek' âikena yathā teṣāṃ bhūmi|pālā vaśe kṛtāḥ?
Indro 'pi hi na Pārthena saṃyuge yoddhum arhati.
yas ten' āśaṃsate yoddhuṃ, kartavyaṃ tasya bheṣajam!
āśīviṣasya kruddhasya pāṇim udyamya dakṣiṇam,
avamucya pradeśinyā daṃṣṭrām ādātum icchasi!
atha vā kuñjaraṃ mattam eka eva caran vane
an|aṅkuśaṃ samāruhya nagaraṃ gantum icchasi!
49.15 samiddhaṃ pāvakaṃ c' âiva ghṛta|medo|vasā|hutam
ghṛt'|âktaś, cīra|vāsās tvaṃ madhyen'|ôtsartum icchasi!
ātmānaṃ kaḥ samudbadhya,
kaṇṭhe baddhvā mahā|śilām,
samudraṃ tarate dorbhyāṃ?
tatra kiṃ nāma pauruṣam?
a|kṛt'|âstraḥ kṛt'|âstraṃ vai, balavantaṃ su|dur|balaḥ;
tādṛśaṃ, Karṇa, yaḥ Pārthaṃ yoddhum icchet sa dur|matiḥ.
asmābhir hy eṣa nikṛto varṣāṇ' îha trayo|daśa,
siṃhaḥ pāśa|vinirmukto na naḥ śeṣaṃ kariṣyati?
ek'|ânte Pārtham āsīnaṃ, kūpe 'gnim iva saṃvṛtam,
a|jñānād abhyavaskandya prāptāḥ smo bhayam uttamam.
49.20 saha yudhyāmahe Pārtham āgataṃ yuddha|durmadam.
sainyās tiṣṭhantu saṃnaddhā, vyūḍh'|ânīkāḥ, prahāriṇaḥ.
Droṇo, Duryodhano, Bhīṣmo,
bhavān, Drauṇis, tathā vayam
sarve yudhyāmahe Pārthaṃ,
Karṇa, mā sāhasaṃ kṛthāḥ.

But what exactly have you achieved single-handedly up to this point, Karna, to rival those Pándavas, who have each in their turn subjugated earth-lords? Even Indra is not worthy to fight with Partha in battle. So the man who actively wants to fight with him should have his head examined!*

You want to remove the fangs of an angry poisonous
snake by stretching out your right hand and reaching with
your forefinger! Or, alternatively, wandering alone in the
forest, you want to climb onto a furious elephant without
restraints and ride it to town! Or, dressed in silk and smeared 49.15
with clarified butter, you want to walk through the middle
of a bright, blazing fire full of grease, fat and butter!

Who would bind himself and tie a massive rock to his own neck, then swim across the ocean with his bare arms? What is there in this which merits the name of manliness? He is a stupid man, Karna, who wishes to fight Partha—like an extremely weak and unskilled man who wishes to fight against a mighty and practiced opponent.

We tricked him, and now that he is liberated from his
thirteen-year bond won't this lion finish us once and for
all? Now that we have encountered Partha concealed in his
secret hiding place like fire in a well, we have reached the
gravest danger. But we ought to fight against battle-crazed 49.20
Partha now that he has come here.

So let our armed soldiers stand in their ranks within the divisions of the army, ready to attack. Let us, Drona, Duryódhana, Bhishma, yourself and Ashvattháman all fight Partha, but don't act rashly, Karna. We six chariot-warriors will gather and stand and fight against resolute Partha, who is as savage as thunderbolt-wielding Indra. We, who are ourselves

vayaṃ vyavasitaṃ Pārthaṃ, Vajra|pāṇim iv' ôddhatam,
ṣaḍ rathāḥ pratiyudhyema, tiṣṭhema yadi saṃhatāḥ.
vyūḍh'|ânīkāni sainyāni, yattāḥ parama|dhanvinaḥ,
yudhyāmahe 'rjunaṃ saṅkhye, dānavā iva Vāsavam.

AŚVATTHĀM" ôvāca:

50.1 NA CA TĀVAJ jitā gāvo, na ca sīm'|ântaraṃ gatāḥ,
na Hāstinapuraṃ prāptās. tvaṃ ca, Karṇa, vikatthase?
saṅgrāmāṃś ca bahūñ jitvā, labdhvā ca vipulaṃ dhanam,
vijitya ca parāṃ senāṃ, n' āhuḥ kiṃ cana pauruṣam.
dahaty agnir a|vākyas tu, tūṣṇīṃ bhāti divākaraḥ.
tūṣṇīṃ dhārayate lokān vasu|dhā sa|car'|âcarān.

cāturvarṇyasya karmāṇi vihitāni svayaṃbhuvā,
dhanaṃ yair adhigantavyaṃ, yac ca kurvan na duṣyati.
50.5 adhītya brāhmaṇo devān yājayeta, yajeta vā.
kṣatriyo dhanur āśritya yajec c' âiva, na yājayet.
vaiśyo 'dhigamya vittāni brahma|karmāṇi kārayet.
śūdraḥ śuśrūṣaṇaṃ kuryāt triṣu varṇeṣu nityaśaḥ,
vandan'|āyoga|vidhibhir vaitasīṃ vṛttim āsthitaḥ.
vartamānā yathā|śāstraṃ, prāpya c' âpi mahīm imām,
sat kurvanti mahā|bhāgā gurūn, su|viguṇān api.

prāpya dyūtena ko rājyaṃ kṣatriyas toṣṭum arhati,
tathā nṛśaṃsa|rūpo 'yaṃ Dhārtarāṣṭraś ca nirghṛṇaḥ?
tath" âdhigamya vittāni ko vikatthed vicakṣaṇaḥ
nikṛtyā vañcan'|āyogaiś caran vaitaṃsiko yathā?

excellent bowmen, will fight Árjuna with our army drawn up into divisions, like the *dánavas* fighting Indra.

ASHVATTHÁMAN said:

THE CATTLE ARE not yet won. They have not even crossed 50.1
the border of the country, let alone reached Hástina·pura! So why are you boasting, Karna? Even when they have won numerous battles, acquired enormous wealth and defeated enemy armies, real heroes do not say a thing about their manly valor. Fire blazes without speaking and the sun shines silently. The earth itself bears the worlds and the static and active creatures within them without a word.

The tasks of the four castes have been devised by the self-existent Brahma, so that wealth might be amassed by
each as they act without transgression. A brahmin who has 50.5
studied the Vedas should act as priest at sacrifices or perform sacrifices himself. A kshatriya, relying on his bow, should perform sacrifices but not act as a priest at sacrifices. A vaishya, once he has attained wealth, should make sure that the rites in the Vedas are performed for him, but a shudra should always perform dutiful homage to the other three castes. As for the rest, they should make their living, employing adaptability with the rules of activity and worship. But those illustrious men who act in accordance with the scripture have won this whole earth and behave well toward their betters, even if they are very wicked.

Which kshatriya who had won a kingdom through a game of dice ought to be pleased with himself, like this worthless and noxious son of Dhrita·rashtra? Which wise man, who had attained his wealth dishonestly by acting

50.10 katamaṃ dvairathaṃ yuddhaṃ
yatr' âjaiṣīr Dhanañjayam,
Nakulaṃ, Sahadevaṃ vā?
dhanaṃ yeṣāṃ tvayā hṛtam.
Yudhiṣṭhiro jitaḥ kasmin, Bhīmaś ca balināṃ varaḥ?
Indraprasthaṃ tvayā kasmin saṅgrāme nirjitaṃ purā?
tath" âiva katamad yuddhaṃ, yasmin Kṛṣṇā jitā tvayā,
eka|vastrā sabhāṃ nītā, duṣṭa|karman, rajasvalā!
mūlam eṣāṃ mahat kṛttaṃ, sār'|ârthī candanaṃ yathā,
karma kārayithāḥ, sūta, tatra kiṃ Viduro 'bravīt!
yathā|śakti manuṣyāṇāṃ śamam ālakṣayāmahe,
anyeṣām api sattvānām, api kīṭa|pipīlikaiḥ.
Draupadyāḥ saṃparikleśaṃ na kṣantuṃ Pāṇḍavo 'rhati.
50.15 kṣayāya Dhārtarāṣṭrāṇāṃ prādur bhūto Dhanañjayaḥ!
tvaṃ punaḥ paṇḍito bhūtvā vācaṃ vaktum ih' êcchasi;
vair'|ânta|karaṇo Jiṣṇur na naḥ śeṣaṃ kariṣyati?
n' âiṣa devān, na gandharvān, na surān, na ca rākṣasān
bhayād iha na yudhyeta Kuntī|putro Dhanañjayaḥ.
yaṃ yam eṣo 'tisaṃkruddhaḥ saṅgrāme nipatiṣyati,
vṛkṣaṃ Garutmān vegena vinihatya tam eṣyati.
tvatto viśiṣṭaṃ vīryeṇa, dhanuṣy amara|rāṭ|samam,
Vāsudeva|samaṃ yuddhe taṃ Pārthaṃ ko na pūjayet?
50.20 devaṃ daivena yudhyeta, mānuṣeṇa ca mānuṣam
astraṃ hy astreṇa yo hanyāt, ko 'rjunena samaḥ pumān?

through deceitful means, as though he were a common poacher, would boast?

In which single-chariot combat did you defeat Dhanan·jaya, Nákula or Saha·deva? But you did steal their property. 50.10
In which battle was Yudhi·shthira defeated, or Bhima, the greatest of powerful men? In which conflict in days gone by did you conquer Indra·prastha? What about that fight when you defeated Krishná, dragging her to court as she bled, dressed in a single garment, you miscreant! Greedy for gain, you cut the mighty root of the Pándava family tree as though it were sandalwood, and you forced them into your service, *suta*, but remember what Vídura said!

We see forgiveness from men according to their capacity for it, and so with other living creatures such as insects and ants. The son of Pandu, though, ought not to forgive Dráupadi's suffering. Dhanan·jaya has revealed himself to destroy 50.15
the sons of Dhrita·rashtra! Assuming the stance of a wise man, of course you want to make speeches over and over again, but won't Jishnu, the bringer of death to his enemies, just finish us off?

Dhanan·jaya, the son of Kuntí, would not fail to fight out of fear, even if he were facing gods, *gandhárvas*, celestials or *rákshasas*. Whomseover he should attack when enraged in battle he will forcibly strike down just as Gáruda breaks down a tree. He exceeds you in valor, is the king of the gods' equal in bowmanship and is like Vasudéva himself in
battle, so who would not revere Partha? Which man is a 50.20
rival for Árjuna, who matches divine weapons with divine and human weapons with human when he fights? Those who know the sacred law know that it says, "The pupil is

«putrād an|antaraṃ śiṣya, iti» dharma|vido viduḥ.
eten' âpi nimittena priyo Droṇasya Pāṇḍavaḥ.

yathā tvam akaror dyūtam, Indraprasthaṃ yath" âharaḥ,
yath" ānaiṣīḥ sabhāṃ Krsnāṃ, tathā yudhyasva Pāṇḍavam.
ayaṃ te mātulaḥ prājñaḥ, kṣatra|dharmasya kovidaḥ,
dur|dyūta|devī Gāndhāraḥ Śakunir yudhyatām iha!
n' âkṣān kṣipati Gāṇḍīvaṃ, na Kṛtaṃ, Dvāparaṃ na ca.
jvalato niśitān bāṇāṃs tāṃs tān kṣipati Gāṇḍivaṃ

50.25 na hi Gāṇḍīva|nirmuktā gārdhra|pakṣāḥ su|tejanāḥ
n' ântareṣv avatiṣṭhante girīṇām api dāraṇāḥ.
Antakaḥ, Pavano, Mṛtyus, tath" âgnir vaḍavā|mukhaḥ—
kuryur ete kva cic cheṣaṃ; na tu kruddho Dhanañjayaḥ.
yathā sabhāyāṃ dyūtaṃ tvaṃ mātulena sah' âkaroḥ,
tathā yudhyasva saṅgrāme Saubalena su|rakṣitaḥ.

yudhyantāṃ kāmato yodhā;
n' âhaṃ yotsye Dhanañjayam.
Matsyo hy asmābhir āyodhyo,
yady āgacched gavāṃ padam.

BHĪṢMA uvāca:

51.1 SĀDHU PAŚYATI vai Drauṇiḥ, Kṛpaḥ sādhv anupaśyati.
Karṇas tu kṣatra|dharmeṇa kevalaṃ yoddhum icchati.
ācāryo n' âbhivaktavyaḥ puruṣeṇa vijānatā.
deśa|kālau tu saṃprekṣya, «yoddhavyam» iti me matiḥ.

not inferior to the son." And it is for this reason that the son of Pandu is Drona's favorite.

So fight against the son of Pandu in the same way you did with the game of dice and with Indra·prastha and with Krishná in court. Let your wise uncle, the deceitful gambler Shákuni of Gandhára, who is skilled in the duty of a kshatriya, fight here! The Gandíva doesn't throw dice like the Krita or Dva·para. Instead, the Gandíva shoots blazing,
sharpened arrows upon its enemies. The vulture-feathered, 50.25
tearing shafts fired from Gandíva are so energetic that they even penetrate mountains. Yama, Vayu, Death and horse-faced Agni all leave at least something remaining, but not furious Dhanan·jaya. Just as you played dice in the assembly with your uncle, now fight in battle, well protected by the son of Súbala.

Let the warriors fight according to their wishes, but I will not fight Dhanan·jaya. We should fight the King of Matsya if he comes in the tracks of his cattle.

BHISHMA said:

ASHVATTHÁMAN, Drona's son, sees matters correctly, and 51.1
Kripa also observes wisely. And, as for Karna, he wishes to fight purely because of his kshatriya duty. The teacher should not be reproached by a man of wisdom. But, taking the time and place into account, it is my opinion that we should fight this battle.

yasya sūrya|samāḥ pañca sapatnāḥ syuḥ prahāriṇaḥ,
katham abhyudaye teṣāṃ na pramuhyeta paṇḍitaḥ?
sv'|ârthe sarve vimuhyanti ye 'pi dharma|vido janāḥ.
tasmād, rājan, bravīmy eṣa vākyaṃ, te yadi rocate.
51.5 Karṇo hi yad avocat tvāṃ, tejaḥ|saṃjananāya tat.

ācārya|putraḥ kṣamatāṃ, mahat kāryam upasthitam.
n' âyaṃ kālo virodhasya Kaunteye samupasthite.
kṣantavyaṃ bhavatā sarvam, ācāryeṇa, Kṛpeṇa ca.
bhavatāṃ hi kṛt'|âstratvaṃ, yath" āditye prabhā, tathā.
yathā candramaso lakṣmīḥ sarvathā n' âpakṛṣyate,
evaṃ bhavatsu brāhmaṇyam, brahm'|âstram ca pratiṣṭhitam.

catvāra ekato vedāḥ, kṣātram ekatra dṛśyate
n' âitat samastam ubhayaṃ kasmiṃś cid anuśuśruma,
anyatra Bhārat'|ācāryāt sa|putrād, iti me matiḥ,
51.10 Vedāntaś ca, Purāṇāni, itihāsaṃ purātanam.
Jāmadagnyam ṛte, rājan, ko Droṇād adhiko bhavet?
Brahm'|âstraṃ c' âiva, vedāś ca n' âitad|anyatra dṛśyate.
ācārya|putraḥ kṣamatāṃ; n' âyaṃ kālo vibhedane.
sarve saṃhatya yudhyāmaḥ Pākaśāsanim āgatam.
balasya vyasanān' îha yāny uktāni manīṣibhiḥ,
mukhyo bhedo hi teṣāṃ tu pāpiṣṭho viduṣāṃ mataḥ.

How could a shrewd man fail to feel bewildered when
faced with five enemy heroes, as radiant as the sun, as they
are on the brink of success? Even men well versed in sacred
law are bewildered when it comes to their own interests.
That is why, my king, I am telling you these things, regardless of whether they please you. What Karna said to you was 51.5
to raise morale.

May the teacher's son forgive him, for the task at hand
is critical. This is not the time for hostile dispute, since
the son of Kuntí is close. You must forgive everything, as
must the teacher Kripa. Virtuosity of weaponry resides in
you just as certainly as light resides in the sun. Just as total
beauty is never diminished in the moon, so the Vedas and
the Brahma weapon remain firmly within you.

The four Vedas have been seen to exist within one person,
and the traits of a kshatriya in another, but it is unheard of
for both to exist together in any person. That is, of course,
in my opinion, except for the teacher of the Bharata race
and his son. Who could surpass Drona, my king, other 51.10
than Jamad·agni, from among the *Vedántas*, the *Purának*s,
and the ancient histories? Nowhere else can one observe
this coexistence of the Brahma weapon and the Vedas. Let
the teacher's son forgive him, for this is not the time for
division. Let us all, united, fight against this son of Indra,
the punisher of Paka, now that he has come. The principal
disaster that can befall an army, from among those listed by
wise men, and that which is considered the absolute worst,
is division among its leaders.

AŚVATTHĀM" ôvāca:

n' âiva nyāyyam idaṃ vācyam asmākaṃ, puruṣa'|rṣabha.
kiṃ tu roṣa|parītena guruṇā bhāṣitā guṇāḥ?
51.15 śatror api guṇā grāhyā, doṣā vācyā guror api.
sarvathā sarva|yatnena putre śiṣye hitaṃ vadet.

DURYODHANA uvāca:

ācārya eṣa kṣamatām, śāntir atra vidhīyatām.
a|bhidyamāne tu gurau tad vṛttaṃ roṣa|kāritam.

VAIŚAMPĀYANA uvāca:

tato Duryodhano Droṇaṃ kṣamayām āsa, Bhārata,
saha Karṇena, Bhīṣmeṇa, Kṛpeṇa ca mah"|ātamanā.

DROṆA uvāca:

yad etat prathamaṃ vākyaṃ Bhīṣmaḥ Śāntanavo 'bravīt,
ten' âiv' âhaṃ prasanno vai, nītir atra vidhīyatām.
yathā Duryodhanaṃ Pārtho n' ôpsarpati saṅgare
sāhasād, yadi vā mohāt, tathā nītir vidhīyatām.
51.20 vana|vāse hy a|nirvṛtte darśayen na Dhanañjayaḥ.
dhanaṃ c' ālabhamāno 'tra n' âdya tat kṣantum arhati.
yathā n' âyaṃ samāyuñjyād Dhārtarāṣṭrān kathañ cana,
na ca senā parājayyāt, tathā nītir vidhīyatām.
uktaṃ Duryodhanen' âpi purastād vākyam īdṛśam.
tad anusmṛtya, Gāṅgeya, yathāvad vaktum arhasi.

ASHVATTHÁMAN said:

Bull-like man, we do not need to be told this axiom. But what of the qualities mentioned by the teacher who was filled with anger? Even the qualities of an enemy should 51.15
be conceded, and the faults of a teacher should also be mentioned. So one should describe a son's or pupil's good aspects fully and with all possible effort.

DURYÓDHANA said:

Let the teacher be forgiving and let peace be restored. For the fury that flared up will all be in the past when our guru is at peace with us.

VAISHAMPÁYANA said:

Then Duryódhana, Bhárata, suppressed Drona's anger with the help of Karna, Bhishma and the high-souled Kripa.

DRONA said:

I was soothed by the first words that Bhishma, son of Shántanu, spoke. Now we should decide on our tactics so that Partha does not encounter Duryódhana in battle; let arrangements be made to prevent it happening either from rashness or folly. For Dhanan·jaya would not reveal him- 51.20
self if the term of his exile to live in the forest were not yet finished. Nor ought he to forgive us today once he has taken back the wealth of cattle. So let arrangements be made to prevent him from encountering Dhrita·rashtra's son's troops and defeating our army. Duryódhana mentioned the same point earlier on, but bearing his comments about the Pándavas' exile in mind, son of the Ganges, you ought to speak accordingly.

BHĪṢMA uvāca:

52.1 KALĀḤ, KĀṢṬHĀŚ CA yujyante, muhūrtāś ca, dināni ca,
ardha|māsāś ca, māsāś ca, nakṣatrāṇi, grahās tathā,
ṛtavaś c' âpi yujyante, tathā saṃvatsarā api.
evaṃ kāla|vibhāgena kāla|cakraṃ pravartate.
teṣāṃ kāl'|âtirekeṇa, jyotiṣāṃ ca vyatikramāt,
pañcame pañcame varṣe dvau māsāv upajāyataḥ.
eṣām abhyadhikā māsāḥ pañca ca, dvādaśa kṣapāḥ
trayodaśānāṃ varṣāṇām, iti me vartate matiḥ.
52.5 sarvaṃ yathāvac caritaṃ, yad yad ebhiḥ pratiśrutam.
evam etad dhruvaṃ jñātvā tato Bībhatsur āgataḥ.
sarve c' âiva mah"|ātmānaḥ, sarve dharm'|ârtha|kovidāḥ.
yeṣāṃ Yudhiṣṭhiro rājā, kasmād dharme 'parādhnuyuḥ?
a|lubdhāś c' âiva Kaunteyāḥ, kṛtavantaś ca duṣ|karam.
na c' âpi kevalaṃ rājyam iccheyus te 'n|upāyataḥ.
tad" âiva te hi vikrāntum īṣuḥ Kaurava|nandanāḥ.
dharma|paśa|nibaddhās tu na celuḥ kṣatriya|vratāt.
yac c' ân|ṛta iti khyāyād yaḥ, sa gacchet parābhavam.
vṛṇuyur maraṇaṃ Pārthā, n' ân|ṛtatvaṃ kathaṃ cana.
52.10 prāpta|kāle tu prāptavyaṃ n' ôtsṛjeyur nara'|ṛṣabhāḥ,
api Vajra|bhṛtā guptaṃ; tathā|vīryā hi Pāṇḍavāḥ.
pratiyudhyema samare sarva|śastra|bhṛtāṃ varam.
tasmād yad atra kalyāṇaṃ loke sadbhir anuṣṭhitam,
tat saṃvidhīyatāṃ śīghram, mā vo hy artho 'bhyagāt param.

BHISHMA said:

THE TIMES, INSTANTS, moments, days, fortnights, 52.1
months, constellations and planets pass and so the seasons and years also fall away as the wheel of time with its divisions revolves. Owing to their inherent surplus and the passing of the heavenly bodies, two months are added every five years. According to my calculations, that would make it a surplus of five months and twelve nights on the original thirteen
years. So the Pándavas have accomplished everything that 52.5
they promised. Bibhátsu has come in certain knowledge of this.

All of them are high-souled and all are aware of duty and profit. King Yudhi·shthira is with them, so how could they transgress the law? The sons of Kuntí are not avaricious and have achieved a difficult task. They do not desire their kingdom through just any means, or those descendants of Kuru would have shown their strength before now. But, rather, bound by the chains of virtue, they do not stray from the vows of the kshatriya order.

The man who asserts that they are cheating will come to ruin. The sons of Pritha choose death before any dishonesty.
But when the time comes those bull-like men, the sons of 52.10
Pandu, would not forsake what must be won back, even if it were guarded by the wielder of the thunderbolt, since they possess his valor. We will fight the greatest of all weapon-bearers in battle, so let us quickly adopt tactics that the wise have devised for success in this world, to prevent your property from coming into contact with the enemy.

na hi paśyāmi saṅgrāme kadā cid api, Kaurava,
ek'|ânta|siddhiṃ, rāj'|éndra; saṃprāptaś ca Dhanaṃjayaḥ.
saṃpravṛtte tu saṅgrāme bhāv'|âbhāvau, jay'|âyayau,
avaśyam ekaṃ spṛśato dṛṣṭam, etad a|saṃśayam.
tasmād yuddh'|ôcitaṃ karma, karma vā dharma|saṃhitam
kriyatām āśu, rāj'|êndra; saṃprāptaś ca Dhanañjayaḥ.

DURYODHANA uvāca:

52.15 n' âhaṃ rājyaṃ pradāsyāmi Pāṇḍavānāṃ, pitā|maha,
yuddh'|ôpacārikaṃ yat tu, tac chīghraṃ pravidhīyatām.

BHĪṢMA uvāca:

atra yā māmikā buddhiḥ, śrūyatāṃ yadi rocate.
sarvathā hi mayā śreyo vaktavyaṃ, Kuru|nandana.
kṣipraṃ bala|catur|bhāgaṃ gṛhya gaccha puraṃ prati.
tato 'paraś catur|bhāgo gāḥ samādāya gacchatu.
vayaṃ c' ârdhena sainyasya pratiyotsyāma Pāṇḍavam.
ahaṃ, Droṇaś ca, Karṇaś ca, Aśvatthāmā, Kṛpas tathā
pratiyotsyāma Bībhatsum āgataṃ kṛta|niścayam,
Matsyaṃ vā punar āyātam, āgataṃ vā śata|kratum.
aham āvārayiṣyāmi, vel" êva makar'|ālayam.

VAIŚAṂPĀYANA uvāca:

52.20 tad vākyaṃ ruruce teṣāṃ Bhīṣmeṇ' ôktaṃ mah"|ātmanā.
tathā hi kṛtavān rājā Kauravāṇām an|antaram.
Bhīṣmaḥ prasthāpya rājānaṃ, go|dhanaṃ tad an|antaram,
senā|mukhyān vyavasthāpya vyūhituṃ saṃpracakrame.

Káurava, I have never seen any absolute success in battle, but, lord of kings, Dhanan·jaya has arrived. In battle there is life and death, victory and defeat, and without doubt an army inevitably undergoes one of them. Therefore, regardless of whether battle is the proper action or whether it is a suitable act as regards moral law, lord of kings, organize yourself quickly. Dhanan·jaya is coming.

DURYÓDHANA said:

I will not return the Pándavas' kingdom to them, grand- 52.15
father, so let the arrangements for battle be organized swiftly.

BHISHMA said:

Please listen to my plan if it pleases you. Descendant of Kuru, I ought to advise what is completely best for you. Quickly take a quarter of the army and go to the city, and let another quarter go and take back the cattle. We will fight the son of Pandu with half the army. Drona and I, and Karna, Ashvattháman and Kripa, will fight resolutely against Bibhátsu when he comes or the King of Matsya if he approaches, or even Indra, who has performed a hundred sacrifices, should he come. I will ward them off like the shore wards off the ocean, the home of monsters.

VAISHAMPÁYANA said:

The advice given by high-souled Bhishma pleased them 52.20
and so the king of the Kurus immediately acted accordingly. When he had sent off the king and the wealth of cattle, Bhishma arranged the divisions of the army without delay and organized them into ranks.

BHĪṢMA uvāca:

ācārya, madhye tiṣṭha tvam; Aśvatthāmā tu savyataḥ;
Kṛpaḥ Śāradvato dhīmān pārśvaṃ rakṣatu dakṣiṇam;
agrataḥ sūta|putras tu Karṇas tiṣṭhatu daṃśitaḥ.
ahaṃ sarvasya sainyasya paścāt sthāsyāmi pālayan.

BHISHMA said:

Teacher, you stand in the middle, and Ashvattháman, stand to the left. Let the wise Kripa, son of Sharádvata, guard the right flank, and let Karna, the son of a *suta*, stand armed at the front. I will stand at the back of the entire army, protecting it from there.

53–65

BATTLE BEGINS

VAIŚAMPĀYANA uvāca:

53.1 TATHĀ VYŪḌHEṢV anīkeṣu Kauraveyeṣu, Bhārata,
upāyād Arjunas tūrṇaṃ ratha|ghoṣeṇa nādayan.
dadṛśus te dhvaj'|âgraṃ vai, śuśruvuś ca mahā|svanam,
dodhūyamānasya bhṛśaṃ Gāṇḍīvasya ca niḥsvanam.
tatas tu sarvam ālokya Droṇo vacanam abravīt
mahā|ratham anuprāptaṃ dṛṣṭvā Gāṇḍīva|dhanvinam.

DROṆA uvāca:

etad dhvaj'|âgraṃ Pārthasya dūrataḥ saṃprakāśate,
eṣa ghoṣaḥ sa ratha|jo; roravīti ca vānaraḥ.
53.5 eṣa tiṣṭhan ratha|śreṣṭhe rathe ca rathināṃ varaḥ.
utkarṣati dhanuḥ|śreṣṭhaṃ Gāṇḍīvam aśani|svanam.
imau ca bāṇau sahitau pādayor me vyavasthitau,
aparau c' âpy atikrāntau karṇau saṃspṛśya me śarau.
niruṣya hi vane vāsaṃ, kṛtvā karm' âtimānuṣam,
abhivādayate Pārthaḥ, śrotre ca paripṛcchati.
cira|dṛṣṭo 'yam asmābhiḥ prajñāvān, bāndhava|priyaḥ,
atīva jvalito lakṣmyā Pāṇḍu|putro Dhanaṃjayaḥ.
rathī, śarī, cāru|talī, niṣaṅgī,
śaṅkhī, patākī, kavacī, kirīṭī,
khaḍgī ca, dhanvī ca bibhāti Pārthaḥ,
śikhī vṛtaḥ sragbhir iv' ājya|siktaḥ.

ARJUNA uvāca:

53.10 iṣu|pāte ca senāyā hayān saṃyaccha, sārathe.
yāvat samīkṣe sainye 'smin kv' âsau Kuru|kul'|âdhamaḥ.
sarvān etān an|ādṛtya dṛṣṭvā tam ati|māninam
tasya mūrdhni patiṣyāmi; tata ete parājitāḥ.

VAISHAMPÁYANA said:

THEN, BHÁRATA, when the Kuru army was drawn up into divisions, Árjuna advanced quickly, creating a din with the clatter of his chariot. They saw the top of his banner and heard the massive twang of Gandíva shaking violently. Having seen all this, and noticing that the mighty warrior, the Gandíva archer, was coming, Drona spoke these words: 53.1

DRONA said:

That is the top of Partha's banner shining from afar, and that is the rattle of his chariot. That is the monkey screech-
ing and that is the best of warriors standing on an excellent 53.5
chariot. He draws the greatest bow, Gandíva, which booms like thunder. These two arrows have landed together at my feet, and two more arrows only just miss grazing my ears. Now that he has finished his exile in the forest and accomplished superhuman feats, Partha salutes me and speaks in my ears.

Dhanan·jaya, the wise son of Pandu, dear to his relatives, is visible to us now after his long absence, blazing with excessive beauty. Partha, who possesses a chariot, arrows, lovely palm straps, a quiver, conch, flag and armor, a crown, a sword and a bow, gleams like a fire sprinkled with melted butter surrounded with sacrificial ladles.

ÁRJUNA said:

Hold the horses steady, charioteer, at an arrow's distance 53.10
from the army. In the meantime, I will look to see where that vilest member of the Kuru race stands in this host. Ignoring all those men, when I catch sight of that excessively arrogant man I will leap down on his head, and then the others will

eṣa vyavasthito Droṇo, Drauṇiś ca tad an|antaram,
Bhīṣmaḥ, Kṛpaś ca, Karṇaś ca mah"|êṣv|āsāḥ samāgatāḥ.
rājānaṃ n' âtra paśyāmi. gāḥ samādāya gacchati
dakṣiṇaṃ mārgam āsthāya, śaṅke, jīva|parāyaṇaḥ!
utsṛj' âitad rath'|ânīkaṃ, gaccha yatra Suyodhanaḥ.
tatr' âiva yotsye, Vairāṭe, n' âsti yuddhaṃ nirāmiṣam.
taṃ jitvā vinivartiṣye gāḥ samādāya vai punaḥ!

VAIŚAMPĀYANA uvāca:

53.15 evam uktaḥ sa Vairāṭir hayān saṃyamya yatnataḥ,
niyamya ca tato raśmīn yatra te Kuru|puṅgavāḥ.
acodayat tato vāhān yatra Duryodhano gataḥ.
utsṛjya ratha|vaṃśaṃ tu prayāte Śvetavāhane,
abhiprāyaṃ viditvā ca Kṛpo vacanam abravīt,
«n' âiṣo 'ntareṇa rājānaṃ Bībhatsuḥ sthātum icchati!
tasya pārṣṇiṃ grahīṣyāmo javen' âbhiprayāsyataḥ
na hy enam atisaṃkruddham eko yudhyeta saṃyuge
anyo devāt sahasr'|âkṣāt, Kṛṣṇād vā Devakī|sutāt,
ācāryāc ca sa|putrād vā Bhāradvājān mahā|rathāt.
kiṃ no gāvaḥ kariṣyanti, dhanaṃ vā vipulaṃ tathā,
Duryodhanaḥ Pārtha|jale purā naur iva majjati?»

53.20 tath" âiva gatvā Bībhatsur, nāma viśrāvya c' ātmanaḥ,
śalabhair iva tāṃ senāṃ śaraiḥ śīghram avākirat.
kīryamāṇāḥ śar'|âughais tu yodhās te Pārtha|coditaiḥ,
n' âpaśyann āvṛtāṃ bhūmiṃ, n' ântarikṣaṃ ca patribhiḥ.
teṣām āpatatāṃ yuddhe n' âpayāne 'bhavan matiḥ.

be defeated. That is Drona standing there and his son Ashvattháman next to him. Bhishma and Kripa and Karna, the great bowmen, are gathered together. But I do not see the king. He is leaving, taking the cattle with him, going down the southern road, intent on saving his life! Leave this army of chariots and go to where Suyódhana is. There I will fight, son of Viráta, and the battle will not be profitless. For when I have defeated him I will turn back, taking the cattle with me!

VAISHAMPÁYANA said:

Thus addressed, the son of Viráta restrained the horses 53.15
with great effort, then redirected them with his reins away from where those bull-like Kurus were. Then he hastened the horses to the place where Duryódhana had gone. But once Shveta·váhana had left that array of chariots and gone away, Kripa, understanding his purpose, said, "Bibhátsu doesn't want to take his stand on his chariot far from the king! Let us quickly attack his flanks as he goes, for no one can fight him alone in battle when he is so enraged, other than the god of a thousand eyes or Krishna, the son of Dévaki, or the teacher with his son, the great warrior descendant of Bharad·vaja. For what good will cattle or vast wealth do us if Duryódhana sinks like a boat in Partha's swell?"

Meanwhile, Bibhátsu had gone and announced himself 53.20
by name, and swiftly showered the army with arrows like locusts. The warriors, covered with the mass of arrows Partha had cast, could not see a thing. The earth and sky were filled with the feathered shafts. Even those who had been mentally prepared for battle could not escape now that they

śīghratvam eva Pārthasya pūjayanti sma cetasā.
tataḥ śaṅkhaṃ pradadhmau sa dviṣatāṃ loma|harṣaṇam.
visphārya ca dhanuḥ|śreṣṭhaṃ dhvaje bhūtāny acodayat.
tasya śaṅkhasya śabdena, ratha|nemi|svanena ca,
Gāṇḍīvasya ca ghoṣeṇa pṛthivī samakampata,
53.25 a|mānuṣāṇāṃ bhūtānāṃ teṣāṃ ca dhvaja|vāsinām.
ūrdhvaṃ pucchān vidhunvānā, rebhamāṇāḥ samantataḥ,
gāvaḥ pratinyavartanta diśam āsthāya dakṣiṇām.

VAIŚAMPĀYANA uvāca:

54.1 SA ŚATRU|SENĀṂ tarasā praṇudya,
gās tā vijity' âtha dhanur|dhar'|âgryaḥ
Duryodhanāy' âbhimukhaṃ prayāto
bhūyo raṇaṃ so 'bhicikīrṣamāṇaḥ.
goṣu prayātāsu javena Matsyān
Kirīṭinam kṛta|kāryaṃ ca matvā
Duryodhanāy' âbhimukhaṃ prayātaṃ
Kuru|pravīrāḥ sahasā nipetuḥ.
teṣām anīkāni bahūni, gāḍhaṃ
vyūḍhāni dṛṣṭvā, bahula|dhvajāni,
Matsyasya putraṃ dviṣatāṃ nihantā
Vairāṭim āmantrya tato 'bhyuvāca:
«etena tūrṇaṃ pratipāday' êmān
śvetān hayān kāñcana|raśmi|yoktrān.
javena sarveṇa kuru prayatnam;
āsādaye 'haṃ Kuru|siṃha|vṛndam.
54.5 gajo gajen' êva mayā dur|ātmā
yoddhuṃ samākāṅkṣati sūta|putraḥ.
tam eva māṃ prāpaya, rāja|putra,
Duryodhan'|âpāśraya|jāta|darpam!»

had fallen into such misfortune. But in the privacy of their minds they respected Partha's speed.

Then Árjuna blew his conch shell, which made his enemies' hair bristle. Twanging that greatest of bows, he goaded
on the creatures in his flag. At the sound of his conch, the din 53.25
of his chariot wheels, the roar of Gandíva and the screech of the supernatural creatures living on the flag, the earth itself trembled. The cattle shook their raised tails and, mooing together, turned around, taking a southerly course.

VAISHAMPÁYANA said:

ONCE HE HAD quickly scared away the enemy army and 54.1
won back the cattle, that best of archers, once again eager to fight a battle, went back toward Duryódhana. Once the cattle were charging back to the Matsyas at speed, the leading Káurava heroes believed that Kirítin had already achieved his task, so they suddenly flew at Árjuna as he sped toward Duryódhana.

And, observing their tightly ranked numerous forces with huge numbers of flags, that slayer of his enemies addressed the son of Viráta, the King of Matsya, saying: "Hasten these white horses restrained with golden reins down this path, and act with all speed and effort, for I will charge at this
pride of Káurava lions. The wicked-souled *suta*'s son wants 54.5
to do battle with me just as an elephant strives to fight with another. Take me to him, prince! Take me to that man who has become so conceited with Duryódhana as his refuge."

sa tair hayair vāta|javair bṛhadbhiḥ
putro Virāṭasya suvarṇa|kakṣaiḥ
vyadhvaṃsayat tad rathinām anīkaṃ,
tato 'vahat Pāṇḍavam āji|madhye.
taṃ Citraseno viśikhair vipāṭhaiḥ,
Saṅgrāmajic, Chatrusaho, Jayaś ca
pratyudyayur Bhāratam āpatantaṃ
mahā|rathāḥ Karṇam abhīpsamānāḥ.
tataḥ sa teṣāṃ puruṣa|pravīraḥ
śarāsan'|ârciḥ, śara|vega|tāpaḥ
vrātaṃ rathānām adahat sa|manyur,
vanaṃ yath" âgniḥ Kuru|puṅgavānām.
tasmiṇs tu yuddhe tumule pravṛtte
Pārthaṃ Vikarṇo 'tirathaṃ rathena
vipāṭha|varṣeṇa Kuru|pravīro
bhīmena Bhīm'|ânujam āsasāda.
54.10 tato Vikarṇasya dhanur vikṛṣya
jāmbūnad'|âgry'|ôpacitaṃ, dṛḍha|jyam
apātayat taṃ dhvajam asya mathya;
chinna|dhvajaḥ so 'py apayāj javena.
taṃ śātravāṇāṃ gaṇa|bādhitāraṃ,
karmāṇi kurvantam a|mānuṣāṇi,
Śatruṃtapaḥ Pārtham a|mṛṣyamāṇaḥ
samārdayac chara|varṣeṇa Pārtham.
sa tena rājñ" âtirathena viddho,
vigāhamāno dhvajinīṃ Kurūṇām,
Śatruṃtapaṃ pañcabhir āśu viddhvā
tato 'sya Sūtaṃ daśabhir jaghāna.

Viráta's son dispersed the army of chariots with those massive, golden-armored horses, swift as the wind, and conveyed the son of Pandu into the midst of the battlefield. But Chitra·sena, Sangrámajit, Shatru·saha and Jaya, the mighty warriors, wishing to help Karna, headed for Bhárata and charged in, armed with arrows and long missiles. But the infuriated foremost of men, swift as an arrow, burned the multitude of chariots belonging to the Káuravan bulls, like a fire consuming a forest, as he shot flaming arrows from his bow.

While that tumultuous battle continued, Vikárna, a hero among the Kurus, approached Partha on his chariot, attacking Bhima's younger brother, the excellent chariot-warrior, with a terrible shower of long arrows. In reply, Árjuna 54.10
brought his flag down upon Vikárna's strong-stringed bow, the tip of which was abundantly furnished with gold from the river Jambu, and destroyed it. And, seeing his banner slashed, Vikárna speedily ran away.

Then Shatrun·tapa, unable to endure Partha, that oppressor of his enemies, accomplishing inhuman feats, began to torment the son of Pritha with a shower of arrows. Pierced by that excellent royal chariot-warrior, Árjuna, immersed in the bannered army of the Kurus, wounded Shatrun·tapa with five arrows and killed his charioteer with ten.

tataḥ sa viddho Bharata'|rṣabheṇa
bāṇena gātr'|āvaraṇ'|âti|gena
gat'|âsur ājau nipapāta bhūmau,
nago nag'|âgrād iva vāta|rugṇaḥ.
nara'|rṣabhās tena nara'|rṣabheṇa
vīrā raṇe vīratareṇa bhagnāḥ
cakampire, vāta|vaśena kāle
prakampitān' îva mahā|vanāni.

54.15 hatās tu Pārthena nara|pravīrā
gat'|âsav' ôrvyāṃ su|ṣupuḥ su|veṣāḥ
vasu|pradā, Vāsava|tulya|vīryāḥ,
parājitā Vāsava|jena saṅkhye,
suvarṇa|kārṣṇāyasa|varma|naddhā
nāgā yathā haimavatāḥ pravṛddhāḥ.
tathā sa śatrūn samare vinighnan
Gāṇḍīva|dhanvā puruṣa|pravīraḥ
cacāra saṃkhye vidiśo diśaś ca,
dahann iv' âgnir vanam ātap'|ânte.
prakīrṇa|parṇāni yathā vasante
viśātayitvā pavano 'mbudāṃś ca,
tathā sapatnān vikiran Kirīṭī
cacāra saṃkhye 'tiratho rathena.
śoṇ'|âśva|vāhasya hayān nihatya
Vaikartana|bhrātur a|dīna|sattvaḥ
ekena Saṅgrāmajitaḥ śareṇa
śiro jahār' âtha kirīṭa|mālī.

So, struck by that bull-like Bharata with an arrow that passed straight through his shield, he collapsed dead on the battlefield ground, just as a tree is torn from the top of a mountain by the wind. Heroic bull-like men were crushed in battle by too heroic a bull-like man, and they trembled like mighty forests shaking from the force of the wind at the time of all dissolution.

And so those well-dressed leading men, benefactors equal 54.15
to Vásava in heroism, were killed by Partha, and lay dead on the ground, their lives having left them, defeated by the son of Vásava in battle, like fully grown Himálayan elephants covered in armor of black iron and gold. Killing his enemies in battle, that foremost of men, the Gandíva archer, moved about in all directions in the battle, like a fire burning a forest at the end of the summer. Just as the wind disperses clouds and scatters leaves in spring, so Kirítin, the great chariot-warrior, shook his enemies, roving through battle with his car.

Once he had killed the red horses drawing the chariot belonging to Sangrámajit, the sun's nephew, Árjuna, possessed of unimpaired goodness and crowned with a diadem, removed his head with a singe arrow.

tasmin hate bhrātari sūta|putro
Vaikartano vīryam ath' âdadānaḥ
pragṛhya dantāv iva nāga|rājo
maha"|rṣabhaṃ vyāghra iv' âbhyadhāvat.
54.20 sa Pāṇḍavaṃ dvādaśabhiḥ pṛṣatkair
Vaikartanaḥ śīghram atho jaghāna;
vivyādha gātreṣu hayāṃś ca sarvān
Virāṭa|putraṃ ca kare nijaghne.

tam āpatantaṃ sahasā Kirīṭī
Vaikartanaṃ vai taras" âbhipatya
pragṛhya vegaṃ nyapataj javena,
nāgaṃ Garutmān iva citra|pakṣaḥ.
tāv uttamau sarva|dhanur|dharāṇāṃ,
mahā|balau, sarva|sapatna|sāhau.
Karṇasya Pārthasya niśamya yuddhaṃ
didṛkṣamāṇāḥ Kuravo 'bhitasthuḥ.
sa Paṇḍavas tūrṇam udīrṇa|kopaḥ
kṛt'|āgasaṃ Karṇam udīkṣya harṣāt
kṣaṇena s'|âśvaṃ, sa|rathaṃ, sa|sārathim,
antar|dadhe ghora|śar'|âugha|vṛṣṭyā.
tataḥ su|viddhāḥ, sa|rathāḥ, sa|nāgā
yodhā vinedur Bharata'|rṣabhāṇām,
antar|hitā Bhīṣma|mukhāḥ sah'|âśvāḥ
Kirīṭinā kīrṇa|rathāḥ pṛṣatkaiḥ.

When his brother was killed, the son of the sun and a *suta* gathered his strength and rushed at Árjuna like a mighty elephant charges with his tusks out, or like a tiger charges a mighty bull. The son of the sun quickly struck the son 54.20
of Pandu with twelve arrows, swift like spotted deer, and he hit all his horses on their bodies and even struck Viráta's son on his hand.

But Kirítin quickly attacked the sun's son, who was advancing against them violently, and assaulted him forcibly, like Gáruda of multicolored plumage pouncing on a snake. Both of them were fantastic bowmen, very strong and destroyers of their enemies. And so the Kurus, noticing the fight between Karna and Partha, stood still in order to watch. The son of Pandu, whose anger swiftly increased when he saw the offender Karna, acted out of excitement and instantly blocked him from view, along with his chariot, horses and driver, with his shower of innumerable, terrifying arrows. Then the warriors who were pierced and rendered invisible by Kirítin and his arrows with their chariots, elephants and horses, and whose chariot ranks were scattered, began to lament, led by Bhishma.

54.25 sa c' âpi tān Arjuna|bāhu|muktān
śarāñ śar'|âughaiḥ pratihatya vīraḥ
tasthau mah"|ātmā sa|dhanuḥ sa|bāṇaḥ,
sa|visphuliṅgo 'gnir iv' āśu Karṇaḥ.
tatas tv abhūd vai tala|tāla|śabdaḥ
sa|śaṅkha|bherī|paṇava|praṇādaḥ,
prakṣvedita|jyā|tala|niḥsvanaṃ taṃ
Vaikartanaṃ pūjayatāṃ Kurūṇām.
uddhūta|lāṅgūla|mahā|patākaṃ,
dhvaj'|ôttamaṃ s'|ākula|bhīṣaṇ'|ântam,
Gāṇḍīva|nirhrāda|kṛta|praṇādaṃ
Kirīṭinaṃ prekṣya nanāda Karṇaḥ.
sa c' âpi Vaikartanam ardayitvā
s'|âśvaṃ, sa|sūtaṃ, sa|rathaṃ pṛṣatkaiḥ
tam āvavarṣa prasabhaṃ Kirīṭī,
pitā|mahaṃ, Droṇa|Kṛpau ca dṛṣṭvā.
sa c' âpi Pārthaṃ bahubhiḥ pṛṣatkair
Vaikartano megha iv' âbhyavarṣat.
tath" âiva Karṇaṃ ca kirīṭa|mālī
saṃchādayām āsa śitaiḥ pṛṣatkaiḥ.
54.30 tayoḥ su|tīkṣṇān sṛjatoḥ śar'|âughān
mahā|śar'|âugh'|âstra|vivardhane raṇe
rathe vilagnāv iva candra|sūryau
ghan'|ântareṇ' ânudadarśa lokaḥ.
ath' āśu|kāro caturo hayāṃś ca
vivyādha Karṇo niśitaiḥ Kirīṭinaḥ;
tribhiś ca yantāram a|mṛṣyamāṇo
vivyādha tūrṇaṃ; tribhir asya ketum.
tato 'bhividdhaḥ samar'|âvamardī,
prabodhitaḥ siṃha iva prasuptaḥ,

But the hero Karna struck the numerous arrows released by Árjuna with masses of his own missiles, and with his bow and arrows the high-souled man seemed like a swift flickering spark of fire. Then the sound of clapping sprang up with blares of conch shells and booms of kettledrums and cymbals, as the Kurus praised the sun's son, who was himself making a din as his bowstring struck his palms. Karna watched the monkey banner with tail raised, the frightful creature agitated at the top of the flagpole and Kirítin making a racket by twanging Gandíva, and he bellowed. 54.25

So Kirítin, glancing at Drona, Kripa and his grandfather, violently harassed the sun's son, along with his horses, chariot and driver, by raining down swift arrows. But the sun's son, like a cloud, also rained numerous swift arrows on Partha. Árjuna, crowned in his diadem, once again blocked out all light with his sharp arrows. They both shot masses 54.30
of extremely sharp arrows at each other in the battle, which comprised a general hacking with great multitudes of arrows and other weapons. To the spectators, they looked like the sun and the moon caged within thick clouds.

Karna, the swift worker, unable to tolerate it, hit Kirítin's four horses and his charioteer with three sharpened shafts and also quickly hit his flagpole with three more. Now that he had been hit, Jishnu, the Káuravan bull, Gandíva archer and crusher of opponents in battle, kept attacking with his straight shafts, like a lion awakened from sleep. Bombarded with a shower of arrows and weapons, that high-souled

Gāṇḍīva|dhanvā, ṛṣabhaḥ Kurūṇām
a|jihma|gaiḥ Karṇam iyāya Jiṣṇuḥ.
śar'|âstra|vṛṣṭyā nihato mah"|ātmā
prāduś cakār' âtimanuṣya|karma.
prācchādayat Karṇa|rathaṃ pṛṣatkair,
lokān imān sūrya iv' âṃśu|jālaiḥ.
sa hastin" êv' âbhihato gaj'|êndraḥ
pragṛhya bhallān niśitān niṣaṅgāt
ākarṇa|pūrṇaṃ ca dhanur vikṛṣya
vivyādha gātreṣv atha sūta|putram.
54.35 ath' âsya bāh'|ûru|śiro|lalāṭaṃ,
grīvāṃ, var'|âṅgāni par'|âvamardī
śitaiś ca bāṇair yudhi nirbibheda
Gāṇḍīva|muktair aśani|prakāśaiḥ.
sa Pārtha|muktair iṣubhiḥ praṇunno,
gajo gajen' êva jitas, tarasvī
vihāya saṅgrāma|śiraḥ prayāto
Vaikartanaḥ Pāṇḍava|bāṇa|taptaḥ.

VAIŚAMPĀYANA uvāca:

55.1 APAYĀTE TU Rādheye Duryodhana|puro|gamāḥ
anīkena yathā|svena śanair ārcchanta Pāṇḍavam.
bahudhā tasya sainyasya vyūḍhasy' âpatataḥ śaraiḥ
adhārayata vegaṃ sa, vel" êva tu mah"|ôdadheḥ.
tataḥ prahasya Bībhatsuḥ Kaunteyaḥ Śvetavāhanaḥ
divyam astraṃ prakurvāṇaḥ pratyāyād ratha|sattamaḥ.
yathā raśmibhir ādityaḥ pracchādayati medinīm,
tathā Gāṇḍīva|nirmuktaiḥ śaraiḥ Pārtho diśo daśa.
55.5 na rathānāṃ, na c' âśvānāṃ, na gajānāṃ, na varmaṇām
a|nividdhaṃ śitair bāṇair āsīdd hy aṅgulam antaram.

man, the accomplisher of superhuman feats, covered Karna's chariot with swift arrows, just as the sun covers these worlds with his rays.

Like an elephant king being attacked by another tusker, Árjuna took some sharpened arrows from his quiver, drew his bow fully up to his ear and shot the *suta*'s son in his limbs. That crusher of his enemies pierced his arms, thighs, 54.35
head, forehead and neck and many parts of his handsome body with his arrow shafts, shining like lightning as they were released from Gandíva in battle. The son of the sun, scarred by the arrows shot by Partha, and burned by the son of Pandu's shafts, quickly withdrew from the front line of battle and fled, like one elephant defeated by another.

VAISHAMPÁYANA said:

WHEN RADHÉYA fled, then the others, led by Duryódha- 55.1
na along with the army, each in their turn fell upon the son of Pandu with their arrows. He repeatedly endured the force of the army, being attacked by divisions with arrows, just as the shore withstands the great ocean. Then Bibhátsu, the son of Kuntí, who rides white horses, that greatest of chariot-warriors, smiled and advanced, firing his divine weapon. Just as the sun covers the earth with its rays, so Partha covered all directions with the arrows fired from the Gandíva. None of those who fought with chariots, who rode 55.5
elephants or horses, or armed foot soldiers had two fingers' width of space unwounded by his arrows.

divya|yogāc ca Pārthasya, hayānām Uttarasya ca
śikṣā|śilp'|ôpapannatvād, astrāṇāṃ ca parikramāt,
vīryavattvaṃ drutaṃ c' âgryaṃ dṛṣṭvā Jiṣṇor, apūjayan,
kāl'|âgnim iva, Bībhatsuṃ nirdahantam iva prajāḥ.
n' ârayaḥ prekṣituṃ śekur jvalantam iva pāvakam.
tāni grastāny anīkāni rejur Arjuna|mārgaṇaiḥ
śailaṃ prati bal'|âbhrāṇi vyāptān' îv' ârka|raśmibhiḥ,
aśokānāṃ vanān' îva cchannāni bahuśaḥ śubhaiḥ.
rejuḥ Pārtha|śarais tatra tadā sainyāni, Bhārata,
55.10 srajo 'rjuna|śaraiḥ śīrṇaṃ śuṣyat|puṣpaṃ hiraṇ|mayam.
chatrāṇi ca patākāś ca khe dadhāra sadā|gatiḥ.
sva|bala|trāsanāt trastāḥ paripetur diśo daśa
rath'|âṅga|deśān ādāya Pārtha|cchinna|yugā hayāḥ.
karṇa|kakṣa|viṣāṇeṣu, antar'|ôṣṭheṣu c' âiva ha,
marmasv, aṅgeṣu c' âhatya pātayat samare gajān.
Kaurav'|âgra|gajānāṃ tu śarīrair gata|cetasām
kṣaṇena saṃvṛtā bhūmir, meghair iva nabhas|talam.
yug'|ânta|samaye sarvaṃ yathā sthāvara|jaṅgamam
kāla|kṣayam a|śeṣeṇa dahaty agra|śikhaḥ śikhī,
tadvat Pārtho, mahā|rāja, dadāha samare ripūn.
55.15 tataḥ sarv'|âstra|tejobhir, dhanuṣo niḥsvanena ca,
śabden' â|mānuṣāṇāṃ ca bhūtānāṃ dhvaja|vāsinām,
bhairavaṃ śabdam aty|arthaṃ vānarasya ca kurvataḥ,
daivāripāc ca, Bībhatsus tasmin Dauryodhane bale
bhayam utpādayām āsa balavān ari|mardanaḥ.

Because of Partha's use of celestial weapons, the ingenuity and training of his horses and Úttara, and his prowess with missiles, seeing Jishnu's valor and superb dexterity, the people worshipped Bibhátsu as the fire burning at the end of the world. None of the enemy were able to look directly at Árjuna as he blazed like fire.

Those armies afflicted with Árjuna's arrows shone like
armies of clouds on a mountain pervaded by the sun's rays.
Struck with Partha's arrows, they resembled woods of Ashó-
ka trees obscured by masses of beautiful flowers. The armies,
Bhárata, covered with Árjuna's arrows, resembled a golden 55.10
garland, but withered where the flowers were decaying.

The ever-moving wind kept the umbrellas and banners flying in the air. But the horses, whose yokes Partha had severed, rushed in all directions, terrified by the confusion among their own forces, still dragging with them various parts of chariots. Elephants, hit on the ears, sides, tusks, labia, vital organs and limbs, fell down on the battlefield, and so the earth was quickly overcast with the dead bodies of Káuravan elephants, as though it were the surface of the sky overcast with storm clouds.

Like the flame of blazing fire burning all things, static
and mobile, at the end of the *yuga*, with the annihilation
at the end of time, so Partha, my great king, consumed
his enemies in battle. Through the splendid vivacity of all 55.15
his weapons, the twang of his bow and the screech of the
supernatural creatures living in his flag, and the excessively
horrible howl of the monkey, and through use of his conch
shell, Bibhátsu, the mighty crusher of enemies, put terror
into Duryódhana's forces.

ratha|śaktim amitrāṇāṃ prāg eva nipatad bhuvi
s' ôpayāt sahasā paścāt, sāhasāc c' âbhyupeyivān.
śara|vrātaiḥ su|tīkṣṇ'|âgraiḥ samādiṣṭaiḥ khagair iva
Arjunas tu kham āvavre lohita|prāśanaiḥ khagaiḥ.
atra madhye yath" ârkasya raśmayas tigma|tejasaḥ,
diśāsu ca tathā, rājann, a|saṃkhyātāḥ śarās tadā.
55.20 sakṛd ev' ânataṃ śekū ratham abhyasituṃ pare,
alabhyaḥ punar aśvais tu rathāt so 'tiprapādayet.
te śarā dviṭ|śarīreṣu yath" âiva na sasajjire,
dviḍ|anīkeṣu Bībhatsor na sasajje rathas tadā.
sa tad vikṣobhayām āsa hy arāti|balam añjasā,
ananta|bhogo bhuja|gaḥ krīḍann iva mah"|ârṇave.
asyato nityam atyarthaṃ, sarvam ev' âti|gas tathā,
a|śrutaḥ śrūyate bhūtair dhanur|ghoṣaḥ Kirīṭinaḥ.
saṃtatās tatra mātaṅgā bāṇair alp'|ântar'|ântare
saṃvṛtās tena dṛśyante, meghā iva gabhastibhiḥ.
55.25 diśo 'nubhramataḥ sarvāḥ, savya|dakṣiṇam asyataḥ,
satataṃ dṛśyate yuddhe sāyak'|āsana|maṇḍalam.
patanty a|rūpeṣu yathā cakṣūṃṣi na kadā cana,
n' â|lakṣyeṣu śarāḥ petus tathā Gāṇḍīva|dhanvanaḥ.
mārgo gaja|sahasrasya yugapad gacchato vane
yathā bhavet, tathā jajñe ratha|mārgaḥ Kirīṭinaḥ.

Having toppled the staffs of his enemies' chariots to the ground, Árjuna approached the rear at speed, once he had quickly left the flanks, and with his masses of extremely sharp-pointed arrows, like birds of prey directed by handlers, he covered the sky with blood-drinking predators. Just as scorchingly brilliant sunbeams fill the middle of a container and are contracted from lack of space, so, my king, his innumerable arrows barely had sufficient space though they filled all directions.*

The enemy were able to focus on his chariot only once 55.20
before they were taken down with their horses and caused to pass into the next world. Just as his arrows passed unimpeded through his enemies' bodies, so too did Bibhátsu's chariot pass unimpeded through his enemies' forces. He instantly convulsed the enemy force like a snake of infinite coils playing in the ocean. As Kirítin continuously carried on this way, the extraordinary twang of his bow, which eclipsed all else, was so loud that such a noise had never been heard before by living beings.

The crowd of elephants covered with densely packed arrows resembled clouds pierced by shafts of sunlight. Roving 55.25
in all directions, going left and right, his bow was seen to remain constantly circular in battle. Just as eyes never rest on things that are not beautiful, so the arrows belonging to the wielder of Gandíva never landed off target. Just like the path of a thousand elephants traveling together in the forest, so was the path that Kirítin's chariot created.

«nūnaṃ Pārtha|jay'|âiṣitvāc Chakraḥ sarv'|âmaraiḥ saha
hanty asmān, ity» amanyanta Pārthena nihatāḥ pare.
ghnantam atyartham a|hitān Vijayaṃ tatra menire
Kālam Arjuna|rūpeṇa saṃharantam iva prajāḥ.
55.30 Kuru|senā|śarīrāṇi Pārthen' âiv' āhatāṇy api
seduḥ Pārtha|hatān' îva Pārtha|karm'|ânuśāsanāt.
oṣadhīnāṃ śirāṃs' îva dviṣac|chīrṣāṇi so 'nvayāt.
avaneṣuḥ Kurūṇāṃ hi vīryāṇy Arjuna|jād bhayāt.
Arjun'|ânila|bhinnāni vanāny Arjuna|vidviṣām
cakrur lohita|dhārābhir dharaṇīṃ lohit'|ântarām.
lohitena samāyuktaiḥ pāṃsubhiḥ pavan'|ôddhṛtaiḥ
babhūvur lohitās tatra bhṛśam āditya|raśmayaḥ.
s'|ârkaṃ khaṃ tat kṣaṇen' āsīt sandhyāyām iva lohitam.
apy astaṃ prāpya sūryo 'pi nivarteta, na Pāṇḍavaḥ.
55.35 tān sarvān samare śūraḥ pauruṣe samavasthitān
divyair astrair a|cinty'|ātmā sarvān ārcchad dhanur|dharān.
sa tu Droṇaṃ tri|saptatyā kṣura|prāṇāṃ samārpayat,
Duḥsahaṃ daśabhir bāṇair, Drauṇim aṣṭābhir eva ca
Duḥśāsanaṃ dvā|daśabhiḥ, Kṛpaṃ Śāradvataṃ tribhiḥ.
Bhīṣmaṃ Śāntanavaṃ ṣaṣṭyā, rājānaṃ ca śatena ha,
Karṇaṃ ca karṇinā karṇe vivyādha para|vīra|hā.
tasmin viddhe mah"|êṣv|āse Karṇe sarv'|âstra|kovide,
hat'|âśva|sūte, vi|rathe, tato 'nīkam abhajyata.

And when Partha struck them, men thought, "Surely Indra with all the immortals is killing us, because he wishes for Partha's victory." And they considered Víjaya, who was slaughtering his enemies excessively, to be Death, Kala, in the guise of Árjuna, annihilating all living creatures. The 55.30
bodies of the Kuru army, hacked down by Partha, were afflicted in such a way that they could have been killed only by Partha, or according to the direction of Partha's actions.

He hacked off the heads of his enemies as though they were the heads of herbs. The Kurus' bravery evaporated from fear of Árjuna. The forests of Árjuna's enemies, brought down by Árjuna's storm wind, turned the earth itself red with bloody rains. The dust, raised by the wind and mingled with blood, made the rays of the sun bright red. In an instant the sky and sun were so scarlet that it could have been evening. In fact even the sun grants a reprieve when it has set, but not the son of Pandu. That brave man of 55.35
inconceivable character, firm in his manliness, fell upon all those bowmen with his celestial weapons in battle.

He shot Drona with seventy-three sharp-edged arrows, and Dúhsaha with ten arrows and Drona's son, Ashvattháman, with eight, as well as twelve at Duhshásana and three at Kripa, son of Sharádvata. The slayer of enemy heroes hit Bhishma, the son of Shántanu, with six arrows, and King Duryódhana with a hundred, and then he hit Karna in the ear with an arrow. When that expert archer, Karna, who was skilled in every weapon, was hit, his horses and charioteer were killed, and he was without his chariot, the army began to break ranks.

tat prabhagnaṃ balaṃ dṛṣṭvā Pārtham āji|sthitaṃ punaḥ,
abhiprāyaṃ samājñāya Vairāṭir idam abravīt:
55.40 «āsthāya ruciraṃ, Jiṣṇo, rathaṃ sārathinā mayā,
katamaṃ yāsyase 'nīkam? ukto yāsyāmy ahaṃ tvayā.»

ARJUNA uvāca:

«lohit'|âśvam, ariṣṭaṃ yaṃ vaiyāghram anupaśyasi,
nīlāṃ patākām āśritya rathe tiṣṭhantam, Uttara,
Kṛpasy' âitad anīk'|âgryaṃ. prāpayasv' âitad eva mām.
etasya darśayiṣyāmi śīghr'|âstraṃ dṛḍha|dhanvinaḥ.
dhvaje kamaṇḍalur yasya śātakaumbha|mayaḥ śubhaḥ,
ācārya eṣa hi Droṇaḥ sarva|śastra|bhṛtāṃ varaḥ.
sadā mam' âiṣa mānyas tu, sarva|śastra|bhṛtām api.
su|prasannaṃ mahā|vīraṃ kuruṣv' âinaṃ pradakṣiṇam,
55.45 atr' âiva v" âvaroh' âinam; eṣa dharmaḥ sanātanaḥ.
yadi me prathamaṃ Droṇaḥ śarīre prahariṣyati,
tato 'sya prahariṣyāmi, n' âsya kopo bhaved iti.

asy' âvidūre hi dhanur dhvaj'|âgre yasya dṛśyate,
ācāryasy' âiṣa putro vai, Aśvatthāmā mahā|rathaḥ.
sadā mam' âiṣa mānyas tu, sarva|śastra|bhṛtām api.
etasya tvaṃ rathaṃ prāpya nivartethāḥ punaḥ punaḥ.
ya eṣa tu rath'|ânīke suvarṇa|kavac'|āvṛtaḥ
sen'|âgryeṇa tṛtīyena vyāvahāryeṇa tiṣṭhati,
yasya nāgo dhvaj'|âgre, 'sau hema|ketana|saṃvṛtaḥ
Dhṛtarāṣṭr'|ātmajaḥ śrīmān eṣa rājā Suyodhanaḥ.
55.50 etasy' âbhimukhaṃ, vīra, rathaṃ para|rath'|ārujam
prāpayasv' âiṣa rājā hi pramāthī yuddha|dur|madaḥ.

Noticing the troops break apart, Viráta's son addressed Partha, who was standing on the battlefield, in order to know his intention, in the following words: "Jishnu, stand- 55.40
ing on this lovely chariot, with me as your driver, which part of the army shall I go to? For I will go wherever you tell me."

ÁRJUNA said:

"That secure-looking man, Úttara, whom you see with russet horses and a tiger-skin, using a blue flag and standing on his chariot, is Kripa. Take me to the front of his forces. I will show that steady archer my swiftness with weapons. That man who has a beautiful golden water jar on his flag is the teacher Drona, the greatest of all those who bear weapons. I always respect him, and indeed so do all those who wield weapons. So circle that great hero very graciously,
or dismount, for that is the everlasting moral law. If Drona 55.45
should hit my body first, then I will strike him and he will admit there is no sin.

Not far from him is the teacher's son, the great warrior Ashvatthámán, whose flag depicts a bow. I always revere this man as do all who wield weapons. So when you have reached his chariot stop repeatedly. That man who is wearing golden armor, standing in the ranks of chariots surrounded by the third and fresh part of the army, on the top of whose flag there is a golden emblem of an elephant, is the son of Dhri-
ta·rashtra, the illustrious King Suyódhana. Hero, bring this 55.50
chariot, which shatters enemy cars, to face him. This king is a destroyer who lusts for battle. He is considered Drona's first and foremost pupil in swiftness with weapons. But I

eṣa Droṇasya śiṣyāṇāṃ śīghr'|âstre prathamo mataḥ.
etasya darśayiṣyāmi śīghr'|âstraṃ vipulaṃ raṇe.
nāga|kakṣā tu rucirā dhvaj'|âgre yasya tiṣṭhati,
eṣa Vaikartanaḥ Karṇo viditaḥ pūrvam eva te.
etasya ratham āsthāya Rādheyasya dur|ātmanaḥ
yatto bhavethāḥ; saṅgrāme spardhate hi sadā mayā.

yas tu nīl'|ânusāreṇa pañca|tāreṇa ketunā
hast'|āvāpī, bṛhad|dhanvā rathe tiṣṭhati vīryavān;
55.55 yasya tār'|ârka|citro 'sau dhvajo ratha|vare sthitaḥ,
yasy' âitat pāṇḍuraṃ chatraṃ vimalaṃ mūrdhni tiṣṭhati;
mahato ratha|vaṃśasya nānā|dhvaja|patākinaḥ
balāhak'|âgre sūryo vā ya eṣa pramukhe sthitaḥ;
haimaṃ candr'|ârka|saṃkāśaṃ kavacaṃ yasya dṛśyate,
jāta|rūpa|śiras|trāṇaṃ manas tāpayat' îva me,
eṣa Śāṃtanavo Bhīṣmaḥ sarveṣāṃ naḥ pitā|mahaḥ
rāja|śriy" âbhivṛddhaś ca, Suyodhana|vaś'|ânugaḥ.

paścād eṣa prayātavyo, na me vighna|karo bhavet.
etena yudhyamānasya yattaḥ saṃyaccha me hayān.»
55.60 tato 'bhyavahad a|vyagro Vairāṭiḥ Savyasācinam
yatr' âtiṣṭhat Kṛpo rājan yotsyamāno Dhanaṃjayam.

VAIŚAMPĀYANA uvāca:

56.1 TĀNY ANĪKĀNY adṛśyanta Kurūṇām ugra|dhanvinām,
saṃsarpante yathā meghā gharm'|ânte manda|mārutāḥ.
abhyāśe vājinas tasthuḥ, samārūḍhāḥ prahāriṇaḥ,
bhīma|rūpāś ca mātaṅgās tomar'|âṅkuśa|noditāḥ,
mahā|mātraiḥ samārūḍhā, vicitra|kavac'|ôjjvalāḥ.

will show him the extent of my speed in battle. That man, who has a lovely elephant belt depicted on the top of his banner, is the son of the sun, known as Karna, whom you already know. Bring the chariot to a rest in front of black-hearted Radhéya, but be on your guard, because he always challenges me to fight in battle.

That man whose banner is blue with five stars, the mighty man standing on his chariot with an enormous bow in his
hand, whose banner is variegated with stars and the sun, 55.55
and fixed to an excellent chariot, over whose head stands a spotless white parasol; the man who stands at the head of a massive throng of chariots full of various flags and banners, like the sun at the forefront of thunderclouds; the man whose golden armor resembles the brilliance of the sun and the moon, and whose golden helmet torments my mind— that man is Bhishma, the son of Shántanu, and the grandfather of us all. Rendered prosperous by the king's success, he is obedient to Suyódhana's will.

Approach him last, so that he doesn't cause me problems.
Control my horses while I fight with him." So the son of 55.60
Viráta, my king, steadily drove Savya·sachin's chariot to the place where Kripa stood eager to fight with Dhanan·jaya.

VAISHAMPÁYANA said:

THE FORCES OF those formidable Kuru bowmen looked 56.1
like clouds, gliding past with the gentle wind at the end of the hot season. Nearby stood horses and the warriors who rode them, and elephants of terrifying appearance, wearing beautifully shining, variegated armor, and ridden by elephant-drivers, urged on with lances and elephant goads.

tataḥ Śakraḥ sura|gaṇaiḥ, samāruhya su|darśanam,
sah' ôpāyāt tadā, rājan, Viśv'|Âśvi|Marutāṃ gaṇaiḥ.
tad deva|yakṣa|gandharva|mah"|ôraga|samākulam
śuśubhe 'bhra|vinirmuktaṃ grahāṇām iva maṇḍalam.
56.5 astrāṇāṃ ca balaṃ teṣāṃ mānuṣeṣu prayuñjatām,
tac ca bhīmaṃ mahad yuddhaṃ Kṛp'|Ârjuna|samāgame
draṣṭum abhyāgatā devāḥ sva|vimānaiḥ pṛthak pṛthak.
śataṃ śata|sahasrāṇāṃ yatra sthūṇā hiraṇ|mayī,
maṇi|ratna|mayī c' ânyā prāsādaṃ tad adhārayat,
tataḥ kāma|gamaṃ, divyaṃ, sarva|ratna|vibhūṣitam
vimānaṃ deva|rājasya śuśubhe khe|caraṃ tadā.
tatra devās trayastriṃśat tiṣṭhanti saha|Vāsavāḥ,
gandharvā, rākṣasāḥ, sarpāḥ, pitaraś ca maha"|rṣibhiḥ.
tathā rājā Vasumanā, Balākṣaḥ, Supratardanaḥ,
Aṣṭakaś ca, Śibiś c' âiva, Yayātir Nahuṣo, Gayaḥ,
56.10 Manuḥ, Pūrū, Raghur, Bhānuḥ, Kṛśāśvaḥ, Sagaro, Nalaḥ
vimāne deva|rājasya samadṛśyanta su|prabhāḥ.
Agner, Īśasya, Somasya, Varuṇasya, Prajāpateḥ,
tathā Dhātur, Vidhātuś ca, Kuberasya, Yamasya ca,
Alambuṣ"|Ôgrasenānāṃ, gandharvasya ca Tumburoḥ
yathā|mānaṃ yath"|ôddeśaṃ vimānāni cakāśire.
sarva|deva|nikāyāś ca, siddhāś ca, parama'|rṣayaḥ
Arjunasya Kurūṇāṃ ca draṣṭuṃ yuddham upāgatāḥ.

Then Shakra, riding a particularly handsome chariot, accompanied by a host of gods, multitudes of Vishvas, Ashvins and Maruts, came down, my king. The sky, thronged with gods, *yakshas*, *gandhárvas* and mighty snakes, glowed just as the firmament on a cloudless night is luminous with the orbs of the planets. The gods came, each in turn with their 56.5
own car, to test the force of their weapons when used in human conflict and to watch the great and terrible fight when Kripa and Árjuna met.

The celestial, airborne vehicle belonging to the king of the gods, able to go wherever its owner desired, gleamed, furnished as it was with every conceivable jewel, and possessing hundreds of thousands of golden pillars as well as one made from jewels and gems which supported the lofty roof.

And there stood the thirty-three gods with Vásava, and *gandhárvas*, *rákshasas*, *nagas* and ancestors with the sages. Glittering beautifully on the king of the gods' chariot appeared kings, Vásumanas, Baláksha, Supratárdana, Áshtaka and Shibi, as well as Yayáti, Náhusha, Gaya and Ma- 56.10
nu, Puru, Raghu and Bhanu, Krisháshva, Ságara and Nala. There, the cars of Agni, Isha, Soma, Váruna, Praja·pati and the Creator, the Maintainer, Kubéra and Yama, as well as those belonging to Alámbusha, Ugra·sena and the *gandhárva* Túmburu shone, in order and according to their proper place. All the hosts of gods, *siddhas* and most excellent sages came to watch the fight between Árjuna and the Kurus.

divyānāṃ sarva|mālyānāṃ gandhaḥ puṇyo 'tha sarvaśaḥ
prasasāra vasant'|âgre vanānām iva, Bhārata.

56.15 tatra ratnāni devānāṃ samadṛśyanta tiṣṭhatām,
ātapa|trāṇi, vāsāṃsi, srajaś ca, vyajanāni ca.
upāśāmyad rajo bhaumaṃ, sarvaṃ vyāptaṃ marīcibhiḥ.
divya|gandhān upādāya vāyur yodhān asevata.
prabhāsitam iv' ākāśaṃ citra|rūpam, alaṅ|kṛtam
saṃpatadbhiḥ, sthitaiś c' âpi nānā|ratna|vibhāsitaiḥ

vimānair vividhaiś citrair upānītaiḥ sur'|ôttamaiḥ.
Vajra|bhṛc chūśubhe tatra vimāna|sthaiḥ surair vṛtaḥ,
bibhran mālāṃ mahā|tejāḥ padm'|ôtpala|samāyutām.
viprekṣyamāṇo bahubhir n' ātṛpyat su|mah"|āhavam.

VAIŚAṂPĀYANA uvāca:

57.1 DṚṢṬVĀ VYŪḌHĀNY anīkāni Kurūṇāṃ, Kuru|nanadana,
tatra Vairāṭim āmantrya Pārtho vacanam abravīt:
«jāmbūnada|mayī vedī dhvaje yasya pradṛśyate,
tasya dakṣiṇato yāhi, Kṛpaḥ Śāradvato yataḥ.»

Dhanañjaya|vacaḥ śrutvā Vairāṭis tvaritas tataḥ
hayān rajata|saṃkāśān hema|bhāṇḍān acodayat.
ānupūrvyāt tu tat sarvam āsthāya javam utttamam
prāhiṇoc candra|saṃkāśān kupitān iva tān hayān.

57.5 sa gatvā Kuru|senāyāḥ samīpaṃ haya|kovidaḥ
punar āvartayām āsa tān hayān vāta|raṃhasaḥ.
pradakṣiṇam upāvṛtya maṇḍalaṃ, savyam eva ca,

The holy perfume of all those divine garlands wafted everywhere, like the fragrance of forests at the beginning of spring, Bhárata. The parasols, clothes, wreaths and fans of 56.15
the gods who were standing there resembled jewels. The dust disappeared from the ground and everything was pervaded by light. Celestial perfume wafted on the breeze and it soothed the warriors. It was as though the air was illuminated, decorated with beautiful forms of arriving and stationary, diversely decorated chariots, glittering with various jewels, brought by the chief of the gods.

The massively powerful thunderbolt-wielder was dazzling, surrounded by celestials stationed on their chariots, and wearing a garland consisting of lotuses and water lilies. And though he gazed at the great battle, he was not satisfied with his incessant scrutiny.

VAISHAMPÁYANA said:

SEEING THE KURU forces drawn up into battle order, 57.1
descendant of Kuru, Partha addressed Viráta's son, saying these words: "Go to where Kripa, the son of Sharádvata, is going past the southern side of the chariot, which has an altar of the river Jambu gold emblazoned on its flag."

Having heard Dhanan·jaya's words, the son of Viráta quickly urged on those silvery-gleaming horses decked in golden bridles. Climbing to top speed through all paces in order, he drove on those seemingly agitated horses, gleaming the color of the moon. A skilled driver, he went near the 57.5
Kuru army and then turned his horses, swift as the wind, back again. The Prince of Matsya, truly expert in driving,

Kurūn saṃmohayām āsa Matsyo yānena tattva|vit.
Kṛpasya ratham āsthāya Vairāṭir a|kuto|bhayaḥ
pradakṣiṇam upāvṛtya tasthau tasy' âgrato balī.
tato 'rjunaḥ śaṅkha|varaṃ Devadattaṃ mahā|ravam
pradadhmau balam āsthāya, nāma viśrāvya c' ātmanaḥ.
tasya śabdo mahān āsīd dhamyamānasya Jiṣṇunā
tathā vīryavatā saṃkhye, parvatasy' êva dīryataḥ.
57.10 pūjayāñ cakrire śaṅkhaṃ Kuravaḥ saha|sainikāḥ,
Arjunena tathā dhmātaḥ śata|dhā yan na dīryate.
divam āvṛtya śabdas tu nivṛttaḥ śuśruve punaḥ,
sṛṣṭo Maghavatā vajraḥ prapatann iva parvate.
etasminn antare vīro bala|vīrya|samanvitaḥ
Arjunaṃ prati saṃrabdhah Kṛpaḥ parama|durjayaḥ.
a|mṛṣyamāṇas taṃ śabdaṃ Kṛpaḥ Śāradvatas tadā
Arjunaṃ prati saṃrabdho yuddh'|ârthī sa mahā|rathaḥ
mah"|ôdadhi|jam ādāya dadhmau vegena vīryavān.
sa tu śabdena lokāṃs trīn āvṛtya rathināṃ varaḥ
dhanur ādāya su|mahaj jyā|śabdam akarot tadā.
57.15 tau rathau sūrya|saṃkāśau yotsyamānau mahā|balau,
śāradāv iva jīmūtau, vyarocetāṃ vyavasthitau.
tataḥ Śāradvatas tūrṇaṃ Pārthaṃ daśabhir āśu|gaiḥ
vivyādha para|vīra|ghnaṃ niśitair, marma|bhedibhiḥ.
Pārtho 'pi viśrutaṃ loke Gāṇḍīvaṃ param'|āyudham
vikṛṣya cikṣepa bahūn nārācān marma|bhedinaḥ.

turned now to the right, then left, going in circles, and so totally confused the Kurus.

Once Viráta's mighty and fearless son had encircled him, he approached Kripa and stood in front of him. Árjuna, having announced himself by name, blew the loud, fantastic conch shell called Deva·datta. The piercing sound created when it was blown by the valiant Jishnu in battle was like
a mountain splitting. When the conch did not split into a 57.10
hundred pieces as it was blown by Árjuna, the Kurus and their soldiers showed their respect. And when the sound reached heaven it echoed back and resounded as if it were a thunderbolt hurled onto a mountain by Mághavan.

In the meantime, the hero endowed with mighty strength, the near-invincible Kripa, was furious with Árjuna. Kripa, the son of Sharádvata, was unable to bear the sound, so the powerful and valiant warrior, in a fury with Árjuna and eager to fight, picked up his own ocean-born conch shell and blew it with force. That best of charioteers filled the three worlds with the sound. Then he took up his bow and plucked his massive bowstring.

And those two powerful chariot-warriors, splendid as the 57.15
sun, stood determined, conspicuous as a couple of autumnal clouds. Then, suddenly, the son of Sharádvata pierced Partha, the slaughterer of enemy heroes, with ten swift, sharp and organ-splitting arrows. But Partha, too, drew his greatest of weapons, the Gandíva, famed throughout the world, and shot numerous organ-piercing iron arrows.

tān a|prāptāñ śitair bāṇair nārācān rakta|bhojanān
Kṛpaś ciccheda Pārthasya śataśo 'tha sahasraśaḥ.
tataḥ Pārthas tu saṃkruddhaś citrān mārgān pradarśayan,
diśaḥ saṃchādayan bāṇaiḥ, pradiśaś ca mahā|rathaḥ,
eka|cchāyam iv' ākāśam akarot sarvataḥ prabhuḥ;
57.20 prācchādayad a|mey'|ātmā Pārthaḥ śara|śataiḥ Kṛpam.
sa śarair arditaḥ kruddhaḥ śitair agni|śikh'|ôpamaiḥ
tūrṇaṃ daśa|sahasreṇa Pārtham a|pratim'|âujasam
ardayitvā mah"|ātmānaṃ nanarda samare Kṛpaḥ.
tataḥ kanaka|parv'|âgrair vīraḥ sannata|parvabhiḥ
tvaran Gāṇḍīva|nirmuktair Arjunas tasya vājinaḥ
caturbhiś caturas tīkṣṇair avidhyat param'|êṣubhiḥ.
te hayā niśitair bāṇair, jvaladbhir iva panna|gaiḥ,
utpetuḥ sahasā sarve. Kṛpaḥ sthānād ath' âcyavat.
cyutaṃ tu Gautamaṃ sthānāt samīkṣya Kuru|nandanaḥ
n' âvidhyat para|vīraghno rakṣamāṇo 'sya gauravam.
57.25 sa tu labdhvā punaḥ sthānaṃ Gautamaḥ Savyasācinam
vivyādha daśabhir bāṇais tvaritaḥ kaṅka|patribhiḥ.
tataḥ Pārtho dhanus tasya bhallena niśitena ha
ciched' âikena, bhūyaś ca hast'|āvāpam ath' âharat.
ath' âsya kavacaṃ bāṇair niśitair marma|bhedibhiḥ
vyadhaman; na ca Pārtho 'sya śarīram avapīḍayat.
tasya nirmucyamānasya kavacāt kāya ābabhau,
samaye mucyamānasya sarpasy' êva tanur yathā.

Kripa cut Partha's blood-drinking iron arrows into hundreds and thousands of pieces as they approached him with his own sharpened shafts. Then the furious Partha, the mighty chariot-warrior, showed off various tactics and veiled the sky in all directions with his arrows. Powerful Partha, of immeasurable soul, made the entire heavens seem cloaked, and obscured Kripa with his hundreds of arrows. 57.20

But, tormented by those sharp arrows like flames of fire, Kripa became angry, and, having quickly afflicted high-souled Partha of immeasurable energy with ten thousand arrows, he bellowed on the battlefield. Next, the hero Árjuna quickly shot Kripa's four horses with four sharp, excellent, golden-tipped, smooth arrows, fired from Gandíva. All the horses reared up when struck by those sharp arrows like blazing snakes, and so Kripa was dislodged from his place. Seeing that Gáutama had fallen from his position, that descendant of Kuru, the murderer of enemy heroes, did not shoot at him, protecting his dignity.

Then, when he had once again taken his place, Gáutama 57.25
swiftly shot Savya·sachin with ten heron-feathered arrows. In return Partha shot Kripa's bow and severed his finger guard with a single sharpened arrow. Next, Partha also shot off his armor with sharpened, organ-splitting arrows, but did not press upon his body. Freed from his armor, his body resembled the slender form of a snake that has shed its slough in season.

chinne dhanuṣi Pārthena so 'nyad ādāya kārmukam
cakāra Gautamaḥ sa|jyaṃ. tad adbhutam iv' âbhavat.
57.30 sa tad apy asya Kaunteyaś ciccheda nata|parvaṇā.
evam anyāni cāpāni bahūni kṛta|hastavat
Śāradvatasya ciccheda Pāṇḍavaḥ para|vīra|hā.
sa cchinna|dhanur ādāya ratha|śaktiṃ pratāpavān
prāhiṇot Pāṇḍu|putrāya, pradīptām aśanīm iva.

tām Arjunas tad" āyāntīṃ śaktiṃ hema|vibhūṣitām,
viyad|gatāṃ, mah"|ôlk'|ābhāṃ ciccheda daśabhiḥ śaraiḥ.
s" âpatad daśa|dhā chinnā bhūmau Pārthena dhīmatā.
yuga|pac c' âiva bhallais tu tataḥ sa|jya|dhanuḥ Kṛpaḥ
tam āśu niśitaiḥ Pārthaṃ bibheda daśabhiḥ śaraiḥ.

57.35 tataḥ Pārtho mahā|tejā viśikhān agni|tejasaḥ
cikṣepa samare kruddhas trayodaśa śilā|śitān.
ath' âsya yugam ekena, caturbhiś caturo hayān,
ṣaṣṭhena ca śiraḥ kāyāc chareṇa ratha|sāratheḥ,
tribhis tri|veṇuṃ samare, dvābhyām akṣaṃ mahā|rathaḥ,
dvā|daśena tu bhallena cakart' âsya dhvajaṃ tadā.
tato vajra|nikāśena Phālgunaḥ prahasann iva
trayodaśen' Êndra|samaḥ Kṛpaṃ vakṣasy avidhyata.

When his bow was severed by Partha, Gáutama took up another bow, and strung it. It was almost unbelievable,
but Kauntéya severed that one as well with a flat-jointed 57.30
arrow, and so the son of Pandu, the killer of enemy heroes, splintered numerous other bows belonging to the son of Sharádvata, as soon as they were taken in hand. So, having taken up his shattered bow, the majestic Kripa threw his chariot javelin at the son of Pandu, like a blazing bolt of lightning.

But as the javelin came toward him, flashing with gold and flying through the air like a great meteor, Árjuna split it with ten arrows. When the javelin fell to the ground in ten pieces, splintered by cunning Partha, Kripa restrung his bow and seemingly simultaneously fired his arrows. But they were quickly shattered by Partha's ten sharp shafts.

Then Partha, possessing enormous energy and furious in 57.35
battle, shot thirteen arrows, sharpened on stone, like flames of flashing fire. With one he broke Kripa's yoke, with the next four he hit Kripa's four horses, with the sixth arrow he severed the driver's head from his body, and with three that mighty chariot-warrior cut Kripa's triple chariot pole in battle, and with a further two he hit the chariot wheel. With the twelfth arrow he pierced the banner, and then Phálguna, with the appearance of lightning and smirking, a match for Indra himself, struck Kripa in the chest with his thirteenth arrow.

sa cchinna|dhanvā, vi|ratho, hat'|âśvo, hata|sārathiḥ,
gadā|pāṇir avaplutya tūrṇaṃ cikṣepa tāṃ gadām.
57.40 sā ca muktā gadā gurvī Kṛpeṇa su|pariṣkṛtā
Arjunena śarair nunnā pratimārgam ath' āgatam.
taṃ tu yodhāḥ parīpsantaḥ Śāradvatam a|marṣaṇam
sarvataḥ samare Pārthaṃ śara|varṣair avākiran.
tato Virāṭasya suto savyam āvṛtya vājinaḥ
Yamakaṃ maṇḍalaṃ kṛtvā tān yodhān pratyavārayat.
tataḥ Kṛpam upādāya virathaṃ te nara'|rṣabhāḥ
upajahrur mahā|vegāḥ Kuntī|putrād Dhanañjayāt.

VAIŚAMPĀYANA uvāca:

58.1 KṚPE 'PANĪTE Droṇas tu pragṛhya sa|śaraṃ dhanuḥ
anvadravad an|ādhṛṣyaḥ śoṇ'|âśvaḥ Śvetavāhanam.
sa tu rukma|rathaṃ dṛṣṭvā gurum āyāntam antikāt
Arjuno jayatāṃ śreṣṭha Uttaraṃ vākyam abravīt.

ARJUNA uvāca:

yatr' âiṣā kāñcanī vedī dhvaje yasya prakāśate,
ucchritā pravare daṇḍe, patākābhir alaṅ|kṛtā,
atra māṃ vaha, bhadraṃ te, Droṇ'|ânīkāya, sārathe,
aśvāḥ śoṇāḥ prakāśante bṛhantaś, cāru|vāhinaḥ,
snigdha|vidruma|saṃkāśās, tāmr'|āsyāḥ, priya|darśanāḥ,
yuktā ratha|vare yasya sarva|śikṣā|viśāradāḥ.
58.5 dīrgha|bāhur, mahā|tejā, bala|rūpa|samanvitaḥ,
sarva|lokeṣu vikrānto Bhāradvājaḥ pratāpavān,
buddhyā tulyo hy Uśanasā, Bṛhaspati|samo naye.

Since his bow was shattered, his chariot lost, and his horses and driver killed, Kripa jumped down quickly, mace in hand, and threw it at him. But, driven off course by Árju- 57.40
na's arrows, the heavy, beautifully adorned mace, thrown by Kripa, came back along the same trajectory on which it had set out. Then the soldiers, wanting to rescue the angry son of Sharádvata, showered Partha on all sides on the battlefield with downpours of arrows. Next Viráta's son, the charioteer, turned the horses to the left and created the Yámaka circle, and so warded the soldiers off. Those bull-like men took Kripa, bereft of his chariot, and moving swiftly they led him away from Dhanan·jaya Kauntéya.

VAISHAMPÁYANA said:

WHEN KRIPA HAD been led away, Drona, who rode red 58.1
horses, seized his bow and arrow and attacked Árjuna, the white-horsed charioteer, at a run. But noticing his teacher close by, approaching on his golden chariot, Árjuna, the best of victors, spoke to Úttara.

ÁRJUNA said:

Take me, bless you, to the warrior on whose banner gleams a golden altar, lofty and decorated with flags on the excellent flagpole. Take me to Drona's forces and to that charioteer, who has large, beautiful, red gleaming horses, handsome, with glossy, coral coats and copper appearance, and proficient in all training, yoked to his chariot.

Drona, the long-armed descendant of Bharad·vaja, is fan- 58.5
tastically energetic, possesses both strength and beauty, and is famed throughout all worlds for being courageous and powerful. He is comparable to Úshanas in intelligence,

vedās tath" âiva catvāro, brahma|caryaṃ tath" âiva ca,
sa|saṃhārāṇi sarvāṇi divyāny astrāṇi, māriṣa,
dhanur|vedaś ca kārtsnyena yasmin nityaṃ pratiṣṭhitaḥ,
kṣamā, damaś ca, satyaṃ ca, ānṛśaṃsyam, ath' ârjavam—
ete c' ânye ca bahavo yasmin nityaṃ dvije guṇāḥ,
ten' âhaṃ yoddhum icchāmi mahā|bhāgena saṃyuge.
tasmāt taṃ prāpay' ācāryaṃ. kṣipram, Uttara, vāhaya.

VAIŚAṂPĀYANA uvāca:

58.10 Arjunen' âivam uktas tu Vairāṭir hema|bhūṣaṇān
codayām āsa tān aśvān Bhāradvāja|rathaṃ prati.
tam āpatantaṃ vegena Pāṇḍavaṃ rathināṃ varam
Droṇaḥ pratyudyayau Pārthaṃ matto mattam iva dvipam.
tataḥ prādhmāpayac chaṅkhaṃ bherī|śata|ninādinam.
pracukṣubhe balaṃ sarvam uddhūta iva sāgaraḥ.

atha śoṇān sad|aśvāṃs tān haṃsa|varṇair mano|javaiḥ
mikṣitān samare dṛṣṭvā vyasmayanta raṇe narāḥ.
tau rathau vīra|sampannau dṛṣṭvā saṅgrāma|mūrdhani
ācārya|śiṣyāv a|jitau, kṛta|vidyau, manasvinau,
58.15 samāśliṣṭau tad" ânyonyaṃ Droṇa|Pārthau mahā|balau
dṛṣṭvā prākampata muhur Bharatānāṃ mahad balam.

harṣa|yuktas tataḥ Pārthaḥ prahasann iva vīryavān,
rathaṃ rathena Droṇasya samāsādya mahā|rathaḥ,
abhivādya mahā|bāhuḥ sāmawpūrvam idaṃ vacaḥ
uvāca ślakṣṇayā vācā Kaunteyaḥ para|vīra|hā,

equal to Brihas·pati in wise policy, knows the four Vedas and is devoted to his Brahmic duties. My friend, all celestial weapons as well as their restraint and the entire treatise of archery reside eternally in this man. Forgiveness, self-restraint, truth, compassion, correct aim—these and numerous other virtues all abide eternally within this twice-born man. I want to fight this illustrious man in battle. So, Úttara, quickly head for the teacher, and take me there.

VAISHAMPÁYANA said:

Thus addressed by Árjuna, Viráta's son drove the golden- 58.10
bridled horses toward the chariot belonging to Bharad·vaja's son. But Drona also charged toward Partha, the son of Pandu, that best of charioteers, who was flying toward him at speed, like one furious elephant charging another. Then he blew his conch, which boomed like a hundred kettledrums, and the entire army convulsed like the sea being churned up in a storm.

Watching those excellent russet horses mingling in combat with Árjuna's swan-colored horses, as swift as thought, the soldiers in the battle were awestruck. Seeing those two chariot-warriors, both spirited, learned and invincible, master and student, endowed with heroism, powerful Drona 58.15
and Partha, in the lock of combat, at the front of the battle, the mighty force of the Bharatas suddenly began to tremble.

Heroic Partha, the great warrior, joyful and almost laughing, approached Drona's chariot with his own. Once he had saluted him, long-armed Kauntéya, the destroyer of enemy heroes, spoke these friendly and sincere words: "We have lived out our exile in the forest, and we are eager to carry

«uṣitāḥ smo vane vāsaṃ pratikarma cikīrṣavaḥ!
kopaṃ n' ârhasi naḥ kartuṃ, sadā samara|dur|jaya.
ahaṃ tu prahṛte pūrvaṃ prahariṣyāmi te, 'n|agha.
iti me vartate buddhis. tad bhavān kartum arhati.»
58.20 tato 'smai prāhiṇod Droṇaḥ śarān adhika|viṃśatim.
a|prāptāṃś c' âiva tān Pārthaś ciccheda kṛta|hastavat.
tataḥ śara|sahasreṇa rathaṃ Pārthasya vīryavān
avākirat tato Droṇaḥ śīghram astraṃ vidarśayan.
hayāṃś ca rajata|prakhyān kaṅka|patraiḥ śilā|śitaiḥ
avākirad a|mey'|ātmā Pārthaṃ saṃkopayann iva.

evaṃ pravavṛte yuddhaṃ Bhāradvāja|Kirīṭinoḥ,
samaṃ vimuñcatoḥ saṅkhye viśikhān dīpta|tejasaḥ
tāv ubhau khyāta|karmāṇāv, ubhau vāyu|samau jave,
ubhau divy'|âstra|viduṣāv, ubhāv uttama|tejasau
kṣipantau śara|jālāni mohayām āsatur nṛpān.
58.25 vyasmayanta tato yodhā ye tatr' āsan samāgatāḥ.
śarān visṛjatos tūrṇaṃ «sādhu! sādhv! ity» apūjayan.
«Droṇaṃ hi samare ko 'nyo yoddhum arhati Phālgunāt?
raudraḥ kṣatriya|dharmo 'yaṃ, guruṇā yad ayudhyata!»

ity abruvañ janās tatra saṅgrāma|śirasi sthitāḥ.
vīrau tāv abhisaṃrabdhau, saṃnikṛṣṭau, mahā|bhujau
chādayetāṃ śara|vrātair anyonyam a|parājitau.
visphārya su|mahac cāpaṃ hema|pṛṣṭhaṃ dur|āsadam
Bhāradvājo 'tha saṃkruddhaḥ Phālgunaṃ pratyavidhyata.
sa sāyaka|mayair jālair Arjunasya rathaṃ prati

out reprisals! You shouldn't be angry with us, since you are always near unbeatable in battle. I will strike you, sinless man, but only if you strike me first. This is my plan, but you ought to act as you think best."

Drona shot more than twenty arrows at him, but dex- 58.20
trous Partha destroyed them before they even reached him. Then heroic Drona showed off his swiftness with weapons and covered Partha's chariot with a thousand arrows. That man of immeasurable soul, deliberately angering Partha, covered his bright silver horses with heron-feathered arrows sharpened on stone.

And so the battle began between the son of Bharad·vaja and Kirítin, as they matched each other's flame like arrows blazing with energy, both renowned for their exploits, and both swift as the wind. Both men, full of the utmost energy and skilled with celestial weapons, hurled blazing arrows,
and by so doing confounded the kings. By this point, the 58.25
warriors who were gathered together were astounded. They showed their respect for Drona, who was swiftly shooting arrows, shouting, "Bravo! Bravo! Who else other than Phálguna is worthy to fight Drona in battle? The duty of a kshatriya is indeed severe, since Árjuna is fighting with his teacher!"

So the men spoke to each other as they stood on the battlefield. And those two long-armed furious heroes faced one another and covered each other with flocks of arrows, but neither was able to overpower the other. Then the son of Bharad·vaja, full of rage, drew his massive, gold-backed and unparalleled bow, and shot at Phálguna. Shooting at Árjuna's chariot with nets of splendid arrows polished on stone,

bhānumadbhiḥ śilā|dhautair bhānor acchādayat prabhām.
58.30 Pārthaṃ ca su|mahā|bāhur mahā|vegair mahā|rathaḥ
vivyādha niśitair bāṇair, megho vṛṣṭy" êva parvatam.
tath" âiva divyaṃ Gāṇḍīvaṃ dhanur ādāya Pāṇḍavaḥ
śatru|ghnaṃ vegavān hṛṣṭo, bhāra|sādhanam uttamam,
visasarja śarāṃś citrān suvarṇa|vikṛtān bahūn.
nāśayañ śara|varṣāṇi Bhāradvājasya vīryavān
tūrṇaṃ cāpa|vinirmuktais; tad adbhutam iv' âbhavat.
sa rathena caran Pārthaḥ prekṣaṇiyo Dhanañjayaḥ
yugapad dikṣu sarvāsu sarvato 'strāṇy adarśayat.
eka|cchāyam iv' ākāśaṃ bāṇaiś cakre samantatah.
n' âdṛśyata tadā Droṇo nīhāreṇ' êva saṃvṛtaḥ.
58.35 tasy' âbhavat tadā rūpaṃ saṃvṛtasya śar'|āuttamaiḥ
jājvalyamānasya tadā parvatasy' êva sarvataḥ.
dṛṣṭvā tu Pārthasya raṇe śaraiḥ sva|ratham āvṛtam,
sa visphārya dhanuḥ śreṣṭhaṃ, megha|stanita|niḥ|svanam,
agni|cakr'|ôpamaṃ, ghoraṃ vyakarṣat param'|āyudham;
vyaśātayac charāṃs tāṃs tu Droṇaḥ samiti|śobhanaḥ.
mahān abhūt tataḥ śabdo, vaṃśānām iva dahyatām.
Jāmbū|nada|mayaiḥ puṅkhaiś citra|cāpa|vinirgataiḥ
prācchādayad a|mey'|ātmā diśaḥ, sūryasya ca prabhām.
58.40 tataḥ kanaka|puṅkhānāṃ śarāṇāṃ nata|parvaṇām
viyac|carāṇāṃ viyati dṛśyante bahavo vrajāḥ.
Droṇasya puṅkha|saktāś ca prabhavantaḥ śar'|āsanāt
eko dīrgha iv' âdṛśyad ākāśe saṃhataḥ śaraḥ.

he created shade from the glare of the sun. That massive-armed chariot-warrior shot with great violence at Partha with sharp arrows, like a cloud showering a mountain. 58.30

But the forceful son of Pandu joyfully took up the divine bow Gandíva, the slayer of enemies and the greatest accomplisher of mighty feats, and shot a large variety of arrows decorated with gold. The valiant man quickly annihilated the son of Bharad·vaja's showers of arrows with shafts released from his bow, and it was astounding. Then Partha, handsome Dhanan·jaya, moving on his chariot, simultaneously displayed his weapons in all directions. The sky was completely transformed into a single stretch of shade. Drona could not be seen, as though he were veiled by mist, since his appearance was shrouded by excellent arrows on all sides, as though he were a blazing mountain. 58.35

Noticing his own chariot veiled with Partha's arrows in battle, Drona drew his most excellent bow, the sound of which was as booming as thunderclouds, and drawing that frightful and greatest of weapons, like a wheel of fire, Drona, conspicuous in battle, fired his arrows. There followed a tremendous crack, like the sound of burning bamboo.

The man of immeasurable soul created shade from the glare of the sun with his beautiful, golden, feathered arrows as they were released from his bow. The masses of golden-winged, smoothed-down arrows looked like birds in the sky, and the arrows fired from Drona's bow looked as though their wings were touching. They seemed to have formed one long arrow in midair. 58.40

evaṃ tau svarṇa|vikṛtān vimuñcantau mahā|śarān
ākāśaṃ saṃvṛtaṃ vīrāv ulkābhir iva cakratuḥ.
śarās tayos tu vibabhuḥ kaṅka|barhiṇa|vāsasaḥ,
paṅktyaḥ śaradi kha|sthānāṃ haṃsānāṃ caratām iva.
yuddhaṃ samabhavat tatra su|saṃrabdhaṃ mah"|ātmanoḥ
Droṇa|Pāṇḍavayor ghoraṃ, Vṛtra|Vāsavayor iva.
58.45 tau gajāv iva c' āsādya viṣāṇ'|âgraiḥ paras|param,
śaraiḥ pūrṇ'|āyat'|ôtsṛṣṭair anyonyam abhijaghnatuḥ.

tau vyavāharatāṃ yuddhe saṃrabdhau, raṇa|śobhinau,
udīrayantau samare divyāny astrāṇi bhāgaśaḥ.
atha tv ācārya|mukhyena śarān sṛṣṭāñ śilā|śitān
nyavārayac chitair bāṇair Arjuno jayatāṃ varaḥ.
darśayan vīkṣamāṇānām astram ugra|parākramaḥ
iṣubhis tūrṇam ākāśaṃ bahubhiś ca samāvṛṇot.

jighāṃsantaṃ nara|vyāghram Arjunaṃ tigma|tejasam
ācārya|mukhyaḥ samare Droṇaḥ śastra|bhṛtāṃ varaḥ
Arjunena sah' âkrīḍac charaiḥ sannata|parvabhiḥ.
58.50 divyāṇy astrāni varṣantaṃ tasmin vai tumule raṇe
astrair astrāṇi saṃvārya Phālgunaṃ samayodhayat.
tayor āsīt saṃprahāraḥ kruddhayor nara|siṃhayoḥ
a|marṣiṇos tad" ânyonyaṃ deva|dānavayor iva.

Those heroes, shooting their long, golden-decorated arrows, seemed to blanket the sky with meteors, and their arrows, which were furnished with heron and peacock feathers, resembled gaggles of geese flying through the sky in autumn. The furious and terrifying battle that took place between high-souled Drona and the son of Pandu resembled that between Vritra and Vásava. Like a couple of elephants 58.45
charging at each other with the points of their tusks, they attacked one another with arrows fired from their full-drawn bows.

So those enraged ornaments of war fought in combat, each in turn bringing out their celestial weapons in battle. Then Árjuna, the best of victors, warded off the stone-sharpened arrows shot by the foremost of teachers with his own sharp missiles. Revealing the missile to the spectators, that man of fierce prowess quickly filled the sky with his many arrows.

But Drona, the best of those who wield weapons, the foremost of teachers, noticed that Árjuna, the fiercely energetic tiger among men, was trying to strike him, so he toyed with Árjuna, employing his smooth, flat arrows. He fought 58.50
in that tumultuous battle with Phálguna, resisting Árjuna as he rained down celestial weapons, and fought his opponents' weapons with his own. The conflict between those two furious lion-like men, both unable to bear the other, was like the battle between the gods and the *dánavas*.

Aindraṃ, Vāyavyam, Āgneyam astram astreṇa Pāndavaḥ
Droṇena mukta|mātraṃ tu grasati sma punaḥ punaḥ.
evaṃ śūrau mah"|êṣv|āsau visṛjantau śitāñ śarān
eka|cchāyaṃ cakratus tāv ākāśaṃ śara|vṛṣṭibhiḥ.
tatr' Ârjunena muktānāṃ patatāṃ vai śarīreṣu,
parvateṣv iva vajrāṇāṃ, śarāṇāṃ śrūyate svanaḥ.
58.55 tato nāgā, rathāś c' âiva, vājinaś ca, viśāṃ pate,
śoṇit'|âktā vyadṛśyanta, puṣpitā iva kiṃśukāḥ.
bāhubhiś ca sa|keyūrair, vicitraiś ca mahā|rathaiḥ,
suvarṇa|citraiḥ kavacair, dhvajaiś ca vinipātitaiḥ,
yodhaiś ca nihatais tatra Pārtha|bāṇa|prapīḍitaiḥ
balam āsīt samudbhrāntaṃ Droṇ'|Ârjuna|samāgame.
vidhunvānau tu tau tatra dhanuṣī bhāra|sādhane
ācchādayetām anyonyaṃ titakṣantau raṇ' êṣubhiḥ.
tayoḥ samabhavad yuddhaṃ tumulaṃ, Bharata'|rṣabha,
Droṇa|Kaunteyayos tatra Bali|Vāsavayor iva.
58.60 atha pūrṇ'|āyat'|ôtsṛṣṭaiḥ śaraiḥ sannata|parvabhiḥ
vyadārayetām anyonyaṃ prāṇa|dyūte pravartite.
ath' ântarikṣe nādo 'bhūd Droṇaṃ tatra praśaṃsatām,
«duṣ|karaṃ kṛtavān Droṇo, yad Arjunam ayodhayat,
pramāthinaṃ, mahā|vīryaṃ, dṛḍha|muṣṭiṃ, dur|āsadam,
jetāraṃ deva|daityānāṃ, sarveṣāṃ ca mahā|ratham.»
a|vibhramaṃ ca, śikṣāṃ ca, lāghavaṃ, dūra|pātitām
Pārthasya samare dṛṣṭvā Droṇasy' âbhūc ca vismayaḥ.
atha Gāṇḍīvam udyamya divyaṃ dhanur a|marṣaṇaḥ
vicikarṣa raṇe Pārtho bāhubhyāṃ, Bharata'|rṣabha.
58.65 tasya bāṇa|mayaṃ varṣaṃ, śalabhānām iv' āyatim,
dṛṣṭvā te vismitāḥ sarve, «sādhu! sādhv! ity» apūjayan.

Time and again, the son of Pandu stopped the Aindra, Vayávya and Agnéya weapons, all fired by Drona, with his own. So, in this way, those two brave, outstanding archers fired sharp arrows, and by so doing caused the sky to become a single expanse of shade, with their rains of shafts. The din of the arrows Árjuna fired, landing on the soldiers' bodies, sounded like the noise of thunderclaps on mountains.

Elephants and even chariots and horses, my king, smeared 58.55
with blood, looked like *kínshuka* trees in bloom. The scattered braceleted arms, variously decorated warriors, beautiful golden armor and banners, and soldiers killed when Partha's arrows struck them panicked the army during the duel between Drona and Árjuna.

The two men flexed their highly effective bows, blanketed and then hit each other with their arrows. Bull-like Bharata, the fight that occurred between Drona and Kauntéya was
as tumultuous as that between Valin and Vásava. Then, 58.60
gambling with their lives, they began to tear each other open with smooth, flat arrows fired from their fully extended bows. But then came a voice in the sky praising Drona, saying: "Drona has accomplished a tricky task inasmuch as he has fought with Árjuna, the destroyer, a man of great valor, firm grip, the unassailable conqueror of gods and *daityas*, the best chariot-warrior of all."

Seeing Partha's steadiness, skill, speed and massive range in battle, Drona was amazed. Then truculent Partha, o bull-like Bharata, took up his divine bow, Gandíva, and drew
it with both arms. Seeing that rain of arrows, like a flight 58.65
of locusts, everyone was amazed and praised him, saying, "Bravo! Bravo!"

na ca bāṇ'|ântare vāyur asya śaknoti sarpitum,
aniśaṃ saṃdadhānasya, śarān utsṛjatas tathā.
dadarśa n' ântaraṃ kaś cit Pārthasy' âdadato 'pi ca.
tathā śīghr'|âstra|yuddhe tu vartamāne su|dāruṇe
śīghraṃ śīghrataraṃ Pārthaḥ śarān anyān udīrayat.
tataḥ śata|sahasrāṇi śarāṇāṃ nata|parvaṇām
yugapat prāpataṃs tatra Droṇasya ratham antikāt.
58.70 kīryamāṇe tadā Droṇe śarair Gāṇḍīva|dhanvanā
hā|hā|kāro mahān āsīt sainyānāṃ, Bharata'|rṣabha.
Pāṇḍavasya tu śīghr'|âstraṃ Maghavā pratyapūjayat,
gandharv'|âpsarasaś c' âiva, ye ca tatra samāgatāḥ.

tato vṛndena mahatā rathānāṃ ratha|yūtha|paḥ
ācārya|putraḥ sahasā Pāṇḍavaṃ paryavārayat.
Aśvatthāmā tu tat karma hṛdayena mah"|ātmanaḥ
pūjayām āsa Pārthasya, kopaṃ c' âsy' âkarod bhṛśam.
sa manyu|vaśam āpannaḥ Pārtham abhyadravad raṇe,
kirañ chara|sahasrāṇi, parjanya iva vṛṣṭimān.
58.75 āvṛtya tu mahā|bāhur yato Drauṇis, tato hayān,
antaraṃ pradadau Pārtho Droṇasya vyapasarpitum.
sa tu labdhv" ântaraṃ tūrṇam apāyāj javanair hayaiḥ,
chinna|varma|dhvajaḥ, śūro, nikṛttaḥ param'|êṣubhiḥ.

Not even the wind itself was able to pierce the mass of arrows as he incessantly fired those closely packed shafts, and the spectators could not discern any interval between Árjuna's taking up his missiles. While that extremely terrifying battle of swiftly fired weapons was taking place, Partha began to shoot the rest of his arrows more quickly. Then hundreds of thousands of smooth, flat arrows reached Drona's chariot simultaneously.

There was a great cry of "Alas! Oh no!" from the soldiers, 58.70
bull-like Bharata, when Drona was enveloped by the arrows shot by the Gandíva archer. But Mághavan and the *gandhárvas* and *ápsaras*es who were gathered there applauded the son of Pandu's speed with weapons.

Then the teacher's son, the commander of a troop of chariots, quickly hemmed the son of Pandu in with his great multitude of cars. High-souled Ashvattháman respected Partha's feat in his heart, despite being completely furious. But, subject to the power of his anger, he charged at Partha, pouring down thousands of arrows, like a storm cloud full of rain.

So long-armed Partha turned his horses, directing them 58.75
toward the son of Drona, and in this way he gave Drona some space to escape. That brave man was quickly taken up and sped away on swift horses, for his armor and banner were shredded and he was wounded by the excellent arrows.

VAIŚAMPĀYANA uvāca:

59.1 TATO DRAUṆIR, mahā|rāja, prayayāv Arjunaṃ raṇe.
ṭāṃ Pārthaḥ pratijagrāha, vāyu|vegam iv' ôddhatam,
śara|jālena mahatā, varṣamāṇam iv' âmbudam.
tayor dev'|âsura|samaḥ saṃnipāto mahān abhūt
kiratoḥ śara|jālāni, Vṛtra|Vāsavayor iva.
na sma sūryas tadā bhāti, na ca vāti samīraṇaḥ
śara|jāl'|āvṛte vyomni cchāyā|bhūte samantataḥ.
mahāṃś caṭacaṭā|śabdo yodhayor hanyamānayoḥ,
dahyatām iva veṇūnām, āsīt, para|purañ|jaya.
59.5 hayān asy' Ârjunaḥ sarvān kṛtavān alpa|jīvitān;
te, rājan, na prajānanta diśaṃ kāñ cana mohitāḥ.
tato Drauṇir mahā|vīryaḥ Pārthasya vicariṣyataḥ
vivaraṃ sūkṣmam ālokya jyāṃ ciccheda kṣureṇa ha.
tad asy' âpūjayan devāḥ karma dṛṣṭv" âti|mānuṣam.
Droṇo, Bhīṣmaś ca, Karṇaś ca, Kṛpaś c' âiva mahā|rathāḥ,
«sādhu! sādhv! iti» bhāṣanto 'pūjayan karma tasya tat.
tato Drauṇir dhanuḥ śreṣṭham apakṛṣya ratha'|rṣabham
punar ev' âhanat Pārthaṃ hṛdaye kaṅka|patribhiḥ.
tataḥ Pārtho mahā|bāhuḥ prahasya svanavat tadā
yojayām āsa navayā maurvyā Gāṇḍīvam ojasā.
59.10 tato 'rdha|candram āvṛtya tena Pārthaḥ samāgamat,
vāraṇen' êva mattena matto vāraṇa|yūtha|paḥ.

VAISHAMPÁYANA said:

THEN, GREAT KING, the son of Drona made for Árjuna in 59.1
battle, and, as he showered him with shafts like a rain cloud made strong by the force of a gale wind, Partha received him with his own massive downpour of arrows. Flying at each other, scattering showers of shafts, that great encounter was like that between the gods and *ásura*s, or that between Vritra and Vásava. The sun did not shine, and the wind did not blow, for the sky was completely veiled by the downpours of their arrows. As they fought and struck each other, destroyer of enemy cities, the piercing crackling sounds resembled the din of burning bamboo.

My king, Árjuna made all Ashvatthámans horses near 59.5
senseless, so they became confused and did not know which direction to go. But Drona's tremendously heroic son, noticing a tiny opening as Partha was roaming about, cut Árjuna's bowstring with the blade of his arrow. The gods applauded his superhuman feat when they saw it, and Drona, Bhishma, Karna and Kripa, the mighty warriors, all shouted "Bravo! Bravo!" and applauded his accomplishment.

Next, Drona's son drew his most excellent bow and shot Partha, the bull among charioteers, in the chest with his heron-feathered arrows. But long-armed Partha laughed loudly and then attached a new, strong string to Gandíva.
When he had drawn it till it resembled the half-moon, Par- 59.10
tha attacked, just as the furious leader of a herd of elephants attacks another enraged tusker.

tataḥ pravavṛte yuddhaṃ pṛthivyām eka|vīrayoḥ
raṇa|madhye dvayor evaṃ su|mahal, loma|harṣaṇam.
tau vīrau dadṛśuḥ sarve Kuravo vismay'|ânvitāḥ
yudhyamānau mahā|vīryau, yūtha|pāv iva saṃgatau.
tau samājaghnatur vīrāv anyonyaṃ puruṣa'|rṣabhau
śarair āśīviṣ'|ākārair, jvaladbhir iva panna|gaiḥ.

akṣayyāv iṣudhī divyau Pāṇḍavasya mah"|ātmanaḥ,
tena Pārtho raṇe śūras tasthau girir iv' â|calaḥ.
59.15 Aśvatthāmnaḥ punar bāṇāḥ kṣipram abhyasyato raṇe
jagmuḥ parikṣayaṃ tūrṇam; abhūt ten' âdhiko 'rjunaḥ.

tataḥ Karṇo mahā|cāpaṃ vikṛṣy' âbhyadhikaṃ tathā
avākṣipat; tataḥ śabdo hā|hā|kāro mahān abhūt.
tataś cakṣur dadhe Pārtho yatra visphāryate dhanuḥ;
dadarśa tatra Rādheyaṃ; tasya kopo vyavardhata.
sa roṣa|vaśam āpannaḥ Karṇam eva jighāṃsayā
tam aikṣata vivṛttābhyāṃ netrābhyāṃ Kuru|puṅgavaḥ.

tathā tu vimukhe Pārthe Droṇa|putrasya sāyakāt
tvaritāḥ puruṣā, rājann, upājahruḥ sahsraśaḥ.
59.20 utsṛjya ca mahā|bāhur Droṇa|putraṃ Dhanañjayaḥ
abhidudrāva sahasā Karṇam eva sapatna|jit.
tam abhidrutya Kaunteyaḥ krodha|saṃrakta|locanaḥ
kāmayan dvairathaṃ tena yuddham, vacanam abravīt:

The fight between those two heroes, matchless on earth in the middle of battle, was tremendously hair-raising. All the Káuravas, filled with wonder, watched those two extraordinarily powerful men fight like a couple of elephant herd leaders. Those heroes, both bull-like men, attacked each other with arrows like blazing poisonous snakes.

But since the two celestial quivers belonging to the high-souled son of Pandu were inexhaustible, brave Partha could
remain still in battle like an unshakable mountain. But, in 59.15
contrast, Ashvattháman's arrows, because of the speed with which he shot them in battle, quickly came to the end of their supply, and so Árjuna came out on top.

Then Karna, drawing his large bow to its full extension, twanged it and there followed a great cry of "Oh! Amazing!" Partha turned his gaze to where the bow was twanged, and when he saw Radhéya before him his rage increased. Subject to the power of his anger, the bull-like Kuru was eager to kill Karna, and he glared at him with rolling eyes.

When Partha's back was turned to the son of Drona's arrows, those men, my king, quickly shot at him in their thousands. Now that the long-armed Dhanan·jaya, conqueror 59.20
of his enemies, had left Drona's son, he rushed swiftly at Karna. Charging toward him, eyes red from rage, the son of Kuntí, desiring single-chariot combat with Karna, spoke these words:

ARJUNA uvāca:

60.1 KARṆA! YAT TE sabhā|madhye bahu vācā vikatthitam,
«na me yudhi samo 'st' îti,» tad idaṃ samupasthitam!
so 'dya, Karṇa, mayā sārdhaṃ vyavahṛtya mahā|mṛdhe
jñāsyasy a|balam ātmānaṃ, na c' ânyān avamanyase.
avocaḥ paruṣā vāco dharmam utsṛjya kevalam;
idaṃ tu duṣ|karaṃ manye yad idaṃ te cikīrṣitam.
yat tvayā kathitaṃ pūrvaṃ mām an|āsādya kiṃ cana,
tad adya kuru, Rādheya, Kuru|madhye mayā saha.
60.5 yat sabhāyāṃ sa Pāñcālīṃ kliśyamānāṃ dur|ātmabhiḥ
dṛṣṭavān asi, tasy' âdya phalam āpnuhi kevalam.
dharma|pāśa|nibaddhena yan mayā marṣitaṃ purā
tasya, Rādheya, kopasya vijayaṃ paśya me mṛdhe.
vane dvādaśa varṣāṇi yāni soḍhāni, dur|mate,
tasy' âdya pratikopasya phalaṃ prāpnuhi saṃprati!
ehi, Karṇa, mayā sārdhaṃ pratiyudhyasva saṅgare;
prekṣakāḥ Kuravaḥ sarve bhavantu tava sainikāḥ!

KARNA uvāca:

bravīṣi vācā yat, Pārtha, karmaṇā tat samācara.
atiśete hi te vākyaṃ karm' âitat prathitaṃ bhuvi.
60.10 yat tvayā marṣitaṃ pūrvaṃ tad a|śaktena marṣitam!
ito gṛhṇīmahe, Pārtha, tava dṛṣṭvā parākramam!
dharma|pāśa|nibaddhena yat tvayā marṣitaṃ purā,
tath" âiva baddham ātmānam a|baddham iva manyase.
yadi tāvad vane vāso yath" ôktaś caritas tvayā,

ÁRJUNA said:

KARNA! NOW IS the time to back up the outrageous boast 60.1
you made in the midst of court—that you have no equal in battle! Today Karna, fighting me in a great battle, you will know your own weakness and you will no longer treat others with scorn! You put all virtue aside once and for all and spoke harsh words, but I don't believe it will be easy for you to achieve what you want. So, Radhéya, prove what you only boasted in the past, failing to take me into consideration at all, and fight with me now in the midst of the Kurus.

You watched as the Princess of Pancháli was molested in 60.5
court by black-hearted men, and so now you will reap the full consequences of your actions. It is because I was bound by the constraints of virtue that I previously endured it, but now, Radhéya, behold my rage-fueled victory in battle. For twelve years we suffered in the forest, you wicked-minded man, but today—right now—you will reap the fruit of our fury! Come on, then, Karna, fight me in battle, and let all the Káuravan soldiers be our spectators!

KARNA said:

Partha, speak with actions, not words! The whole world
knows that your bark is worse than your bite! You endured 60.10
matters in the past because of your impotence to stop it! We will accept your prowess when we see it, Partha! If you really endured events in the past because you were subject to the will of virtue, then you are still bound despite the fact that you think you are unrestricted. If, as you say, you have lived out your exile in the forest, then you are truly in bad shape

tat tvaṃ, dharm'|ârtha|vit, kliṣṭaḥ sa mayā yoddhum icchasi?
yadi Śakraḥ svayaṃ, Pārtha, yudhyate tava kāraṇāt
tath" âpi na vyathā kā cin mama syād vikramiṣyataḥ.
ayaṃ, Kaunteya, kāmas te na cirāt samupasthitaḥ.
yotsyase hi mayā sārdham, adya drakṣyasi me balam!

ARJUNA uvāca:

60.15 idānīm eva tāvat tvam apayāto raṇān mama;
tena jīvasi, Rādheya, nihatas tv anu|jas tava.
bhrātaraṃ ghātayitvā kas, tyaktvā raṇa|śiraś ca kaḥ
tvad anyaḥ kaḥ pumān satsu brūyād evaṃ vyavasthitaḥ?

VAIŚAMPĀYANA uvāca:

iti Karṇaṃ bruvann eva Bībhatsur a|parājitaḥ
abhyayād visṛjan bāṇān kāy'|āvaraṇa|bhedinaḥ.
pratijagrāha taṃ Karṇaḥ prīyamāṇo mahā|rathaḥ,
mahatā śara|varṣeṇa varṣamāṇam iv' âmbudam.
utpetuḥ śara|jālāni ghora|rūpāṇi sarvaśaḥ;
avidhyad aśvān, bāhvoś ca, hast'|āvāpaṃ pṛthak pṛthak.
60.20 so '|mṛṣyamāṇaḥ Karṇasya niṣaṅgasy' âvalambanam
ciccheda niśit'|âgreṇa śareṇa nata|parvaṇā.
upāsaṅgād upādāya Karṇo bāṇān ath' âparān
vivyādha Pāṇḍavaṃ haste; tasya muṣṭir aśīryata.
tataḥ Pārtho mahā|bāhuḥ Karṇasya dhanur acchinat.
sa śaktiṃ prāhiṇot tasmai. tāṃ Pārtho vyadhamac charaiḥ.

from your study of religious merit, so how can you want to fight with me? Even if Shakra himself were to fight on your behalf, Partha, I would have no fear of wanting to display my power. Kauntéya, your wish will soon be granted. You will fight with me now and you will witness my strength for yourself!

ÁRJUNA said:

The only reason you are alive now, Radhéya, is that you fled from battle with me, but your brother is dead. What other man but you, who had got his brother killed and then abandoned the front line of battle, would boast as you do, while standing in the company of good men? 60.15

VAISHAMPÁYANA said:

Speaking in this way to Karna, Bibhátsu, undefeated by his enemies, charged at him, shooting armor-splitting arrows. But Karna, the great chariot-warrior, cheerfully received Árjuna with a great shower of his own arrows, like a rain cloud pouring down torrents. That terrifying-looking rain of arrows fell everywhere, hitting horses, arms and hand protectors, each in turn.

And Árjuna, unable to endure it, cut the strap of Karna's quiver with a sharp-pointed, smooth, flat arrow. But, taking other arrows from his quiver, Karna shot the son of Pandu on his hand so his grip slackened. Then long-armed Partha shattered Karna's bow, and when he retaliated by throwing a spear at him, Partha shot it down with his arrows. 60.20

tato 'nupetur bahavo Rādheyasya pad'|ânugāḥ;
tāṃś ca Gāṇḍīva|nirmuktaiḥ prāhiṇod Yama|sādanam.
tato 'sy' âśvāñ śarais tīkṣṇair Bībhatsur bhāra|sādhanaiḥ
ākarṇa|muktair abhyaghnaṃs; te hatāḥ prāpatan bhuvi.
60.25 ath' âpareṇa bāṇena jvalitena mah"|âujasā
vivyādha Karṇaṃ Kaunteyas tīkṣṇen' ôrasi vīryavān.
tasya bhittvā tanu|trāṇaṃ kāyam abhyagamac charaḥ.
tataḥ sa tamas" āviṣṭo na sma kiṃ cit prajajñivān,
sa gāḍha|vedano hitvā raṇaṃ prāyād udaṅ|mukhaḥ.
tato 'rjuna udakrośad; Uttaraś ca mahā|rathaḥ.

VAIŚAMPĀYANA uvāca:

61.1 TATO VAIKARTANAṂ jitvā Pārtho Vairāṭim abravīt:
«etan māṃ prāpay' ânīkaṃ, yatra tālo hiraṇ|mayaḥ.
atra Śāntanavo Bhīṣma rathe 'smākaṃ pitā|mahaḥ
kāṅkṣamāṇo mayā yuddhaṃ tiṣṭhaty amara|darśanaḥ.»
atha sainyaṃ mahad dṛṣṭvā ratha|nāga|hay'|ākulam
abravīd Uttaraḥ Pārtham apaviddhaḥ śarair bhṛśam:
«n' âhaṃ śakṣyāmi, vīr', êha niyantuṃ te hay'|ôttamān.
viṣīdanti mama prāṇā, mano vihvalat' îva me.
61.5 astrāṇām iva divyānāṃ prabhāvaḥ saṃprayujyatām,
tvayā ca Kurubhiś c' âiva, dravant' îva diśo daśa;
gandhena mūrchitaś c' âhaṃ vasā|rudhira|medasām;
dvaidhī|bhūtaṃ mano me 'dya tava c' âiva prapaśyataḥ!
a|dṛṣṭa|pūrvaḥ śūrāṇāṃ mayā saṅkhye samāgamaḥ.
gadā|pātena mahatā, śaṅkhānāṃ niḥsvanena ca,
siṃha|nādaiś ca śūrāṇāṃ, gajānāṃ bṛṃhitais tathā,

At this point, Karna's numerous infantry followers flew at him, but he sent them down to Yama's abode with the arrows fired from Gandíva. Bibhátsu killed Karna's horses with his sharp and highly effective arrows, fired from his bow extended right up to his ear, and, dead, they fell to the
ground. Then, with another blazing, fantastically powerful 60.25
sharp arrow, majestic Kauntéya shot Karna in the chest. The arrow split the armor and pierced Karna's body. He was filled with darkness and unaware of anything. But then, afflicted with pain, he left the battle and headed north. Árjuna and Úttara, the mighty chariot-warrior, called after him.

VAISHAMPÁYANA said:

ONCE HE HAD defeated the son of the sun, Partha said to 61.1
the son of Viráta: "Take me to the part of the army where the golden Palmyra tree is. For that is where immortal-looking Bhishma, the son of Shántanu, our grandfather, waits on his chariot hoping to fight me." Then, scanning that mighty army full of chariots, elephants and horses, Úttara, who had been pierced by a great many arrows, said to Partha:

"I am not able to guide your excellent horses, hero. My
energy is sinking and my mind seems unsteady. All ten 61.5
directions seem to be spinning around owing to the power of the celestial weapons that you and the Kurus use. I'm feeling faint from the stench of fat, blood and marrow. My mind feels like it has split in two after all I have seen today! Never before have I seen such a gathering of brave heroes in battle. The great mace-thumps and conch-blares, the lion-roars of the warriors, the trumpeting of elephants, and the

Gāṇḍīva|śabdena bhṛśam aśani|pratimena ca,
śrutiḥ smṛtiś ca me, vīra, pranaṣṭā mūḍha|cetasaḥ!
alāta|cakra|pratimaṃ maṇḍalaṃ satataṃ tvayā
vyākṣipyamāṇaṃ samare, Gāṇḍīvaṃ ca prakarṣatā
dṛṣṭiḥ pracalitā, vīra, hṛdayaṃ dīryat' îva me.
61.10 vapuś c' ôgraṃ tava raṇe, kruddhasy' êva Pinākinaḥ,
vyāyacchatas tava bhujaṃ dṛṣṭvā bhīr me bhavaty api.
n' ādadānaṃ, na saṃdhānaṃ, na muñcantaṃ śar'|ôttamān
tvām ahaṃ saṃprapaśyāmi, paśyann api na cetanaḥ.
avasīdanti me prāṇā, bhūr iyaṃ calat' îva ca.
na ca pratodaṃ raśmīś ca saṃyantuṃ śaktir asti me.»

ARJUNA uvāca:

mā bhaiṣīḥ. stambhay' ātmānaṃ! tvay" âpi, nara|puṅgava,
atyadbhutāni karmāṇi kṛtāni raṇa|mūrdhani!
rāja|putro 'si, bhadraṃ te, kule Matsyasya viśrute!
jātas tvaṃ śatru|damane n' âvasīditum arhasi.
61.15 dhṛtiṃ kṛtvā su|vipulāṃ, rāja|putra, rathe mama
yudhyamānasya samare hayān saṃyaccha, śatru|han!

VAIŚAMPĀYANA uvāca:

evam uktvā mahā|bāhur Vairāṭiṃ nara|sattamaḥ
Arjuno rathināṃ śreṣṭha Uttaraṃ vākyam abravīt:
«sen"|âgram āśu Bhīṣmasya prāpayasv' âitad eva mām.
ācchetsyāmy aham etasya dhanur|jyām api c' āhave!
asyantaṃ divyam astraṃ māṃ citram adya niśāmaya,
śata|hradām iv' āyāntīṃ stanayitnor iv' âmbare.

thundering boom of Gandíva have made my mind muddled and my hearing and memory have been destroyed, hero!

My vision is fuzzy, hero, and my heart is torn, from seeing you stretch the Gandíva in battle, and draw it into a complete circle resembling a wheel of fire. Watching your fero- 61.10
cious form, arm extended in battle, like the raging trident-wielder, I am afraid. I cannot even see as you take out your excellent arrows, or attach them to the bow or fire them; although I am looking I have no perception. My spirits are sinking and the earth itself is moving. I do not have the energy to hold the whip and reins."

ÁRJUNA said:

Don't be afraid. Control yourself! Bull among men, you too have performed amazing feats in the front line of battle! You are a prince, bless you, and born into the renowned lineage of Matsya! You ought not to be disheartened while
punishing your enemies. So take as much courage as pos- 61.15
sible, prince, and guide my horses in battle while I fight, o slayer of your enemies!

VAISHAMPÁYANA said:

Thus the long-armed best of men addressed Viráta's son. Then Árjuna, the best of charioteers, added one more thing, speaking to Úttara: "Take me quickly to the front of Drona's section of the army and I will sever his bowstring in battle! Today behold me and my beautiful celestial weapon shooting forth, like lightning and thunder of a thousand flashes roaring in the clouds

suvarṇa|pṛṣṭhaṃ Gāṇḍīvaṃ drakṣyanti Kuravo mama.
‹dakṣiṇen' âtha vāmena, katareṇa svid asyati?›
61.20 iti māṃ saṅgatāḥ sarve tarkayiṣyanti śatravaḥ.
śoṇit'|ôdāṃ, rath'|āvartāṃ, nāga|nakrāṃ, dur|atyayām
nadīṃ praskandayiṣyāmi para|loka|pravāhinīm.
pāṇi|pāda|śiraḥ|pṛṣṭha|bāhu|śākhā|nirantaram
vanaṃ Kurūṇāṃ chetsyāmi śaraiḥ sannata|parvabhiḥ.
jayataḥ Kauravīṃ senām ekasya mama dhanvinaḥ
śataṃ mārgā bhaviṣyanti pāvakasy' êva kānane.

mayā cakram iv' āviddhaṃ sainyaṃ drakṣyasi kevalam;
iṣv|astre śikṣitaṃ citram ahaṃ darśayit" âsmi te.
a|saṃbhrānto rathe tiṣṭha sameṣu viṣameṣu ca.
divam āvṛtya tiṣṭhantaṃ giriṃ bhindyāṃ sma patribhiḥ.
61.25 aham Indrasya vacanāt saṅgrāme 'bhyahanaṃ purā
Paulomān Kālakhañjāṃś ca sahasrāṇi śatāni ca.
aham Indrād dṛḍhāṃ muṣṭiṃ, Brahmaṇaḥ kṛta|hastatām,
pragāḍhe tumulaṃ citram iti viddhi Prajāpateḥ.
ahaṃ pāre samudrasya Hiraṇyapura|vāsinām
jitvā ṣaṣṭiṃ sahasrāṇi rathināṃ ugra|dhanvinām.

śīryamāṇāni kūlāni pravṛddhen' êva vāriṇā
mayā Kurūṇāṃ vṛndāni pātyamānāni paśya vai.
dhvaja|vṛkṣaṃ, patti|tṛṇaṃ, ratha|siṃha|gaṇ'|āyutam
vanam ādīpayiṣyāmi Kurūṇām astra|tejasā.
61.30 tān ahaṃ ratha|nīḍebhyaḥ śaraiḥ sannata|parvabhiḥ
yattān sarvān, atibalān, yotsyamānān avasthitān

The Kurus will see my golden-backed Gandíva. 'Does he
shoot with his right or left hand?' the enemy will all argue 61.20
when they are gathered together. I will cause a dreadful river to gush forth, taking itself to the other world with waters of blood, and whirlpools of chariots, and elephants instead of crocodiles. I will fell a forest of Kurus, densely packed with hands and feet, heads and backs, and arms as its branches, with my flat, smooth arrows. A hundred paths will open up before me, as in a forest fire, when I defeat the Kuru army single-handedly with my bow.

You will see the army whirling like a wheel at my hand, and I will display my varied training in archery and other weapons to you. Stand firm on the chariot, regardless of whether we travel over level or uneven ground. With my winged arrows I can split the Suméru mountain, which stands reaching to heaven.

A long time ago I annihilated the Paulómas and the Kala· 61.25
khanjas by the hundreds of thousands in battle at Indra's command. I have learned my surety of grasp from Indra, my dexterity from Brahma, and my varied knowledge of tactics in packed tumultuous battle from Praja·pati. On the far side of the ocean I defeated sixty thousand bowmen and fierce charioteers riding on Hiránya·pura.

Watch as I destroy multitudes of Kurus as though they are clusters of flowers being scattered by a violent storm. With the majesty of my weapons I will set fire to the Káuravan forest, with its trees of banners and infantry grasses interspersed
with prides of chariot lions. I will single-handedly fight all 61.30
those mighty warriors to the death, though they battle determinedly, and I will drag them from the inside of their

ekaḥ saṃkālayiṣyāmi, Vajra|pāṇir iv' âsurān.
Raudraṃ Rudrād ahaṃ hy astraṃ,
Vāruṇaṃ Varuṇād api,
astram Āgneyam Agneś ca,
Vāyavyaṃ Mātar|iśvanaḥ,
vajr'|âdīni tath" âstrāṇi
Śakrād aham avāptavān.
Dhārtarāṣṭra|vanaṃ ghoraṃ nara|siṃh'|âbhirakṣitam
aham utpāṭayiṣyāmi, Vairāṭe, vyetu te bhayam.»
evam āśvāsitas tena Vairāṭiḥ Savyasācinā
vyavāgāhad rath'|ânīkaṃ bhīmaṃ Bhīṣm'|âbhirakṣitam.
tam āyāntaṃ mahā|bāhuṃ jigīṣantaṃ raṇe Kurūn
abhyavārayad a|vyagraḥ krūra|karm" āpagā|sutaḥ.
61.35 tasya Jiṣṇur upāvṛtya dhvajaṃ mūlād apātayat,
vikṛṣya kala|dhaut'|âgraiḥ; sa viddhaḥ prāpatad bhuvi.
taṃ citra|māly'|ābharaṇāḥ, kṛta|vidyā, manasvinaḥ
āgacchan bhīma|dhanvānaṃ catvāraś ca mahā|balāḥ,
Duḥśāsano, Vikarṇaś ca, Duḥsaho, 'tha Viviṃśatiḥ.
āgatya bhīma|dhanvānaṃ Bībhatsuṃ paryavārayan.
Duḥśāsanas tu bhallena viddhvā Vairāṭam Uttaram,
dvitīyen' Ârjunaṃ vīraḥ pratyavidhyat stan'|ântare.
tasya Jiṣṇur upāvṛtya pṛthu|dhāreṇa kārmukam
cakarta gārdhra|patreṇa jāta|rūpa|pariṣkṛtam.
61.40 ath' âinaṃ pañcabhiḥ paścāt pratyavidhyat stan'|ântare.

chariots with my smooth, flat arrows, like the thunderbolt-wielder fighting the *ásuras*.

I have obtained the Raudra weapon from Rudra, the Váruna from Váruna, the Agnéya weapon from Agni, the Vayávya from the god of the wind, as well as the thunderbolt and other weapons from Indra. I will uproot Dhartaráshtra's terrifying forest, guarded by lion-like men though it may be, son of Viráta, so abandon your fear."

Viráta's son, encouraged in this way by Savya·sachin, barged his way into the terrifying forces of chariots guarded by Bhishma. But Bhishma, the son of the river Ganges, a man of cruel feats, was unfazed, and kept back long-armed Árjuna, desperate to defeat his enemies in battle. So Jishnu 61.35
turned back toward him and felled Bhishma's banner at its base by firing with his golden-tipped shafts, and the pole fell to the ground.

Then, draped with beautiful garlands, those four spirited, learned and massively powerful warriors, Duhshásana, Vikárna, Dúhsaha and Vivínshati, approached the formidable archer. Coming toward Bibhátsu, the terrifying bowman, they surrounded him. The hero Duhshásana hit Úttara, Viráta's son, with his first arrow, and with his second he shot Árjuna in the chest. But Jishnu turned toward him and shattered his gold-plated bow with a broad-edged, vulture-feathered arrow, and he pierced his chest with five more 61.40
afterward.

so 'payāto raṇaṃ hitvā Pārtha|bāṇa|prapīḍitaḥ.
taṃ Vikarṇah śarais tīkṣṇair, gṛdhra|patrair, a|jihma|gaiḥ
vivyādha para|vīra|ghnam Arjunaṃ Dhṛtarāṣṭra|jaḥ.
tatas tam api Kaunteyaḥ śareṇ' ānata|parvaṇā
lalāṭe 'bhyahanat tūrṇaṃ; sa viddhaḥ prāpatad rathāt.
tataḥ Pārtham abhidrutya Duḥsahaḥ sa|Viviṃśatiḥ
avākirac charais tīkṣṇaiḥ parīpsur bhrātaraṃ raṇe.
tāv ubhau gārdhra|patrābhyāṃ
niśitābhyāṃ Dhanañjayaḥ
viddhvā yugapad a|vyagras
tayor vāhān asūdayat.
61.45 tau hat'|âśvau vibhinn'|âṅgau Dhṛtarāṣṭr'|ātmajāv ubhau
abhipatya rathair anyair apanītau pad'|ânugaiḥ.
sarvā diśaś c' âbhyapatad Bībhatsur a|parājitaḥ
kirīṭa|mālī Kaunteyo labdha|lakṣo, mahā|balaḥ.

VAIŚAṂPĀYANA uvāca:

62.1 ATHA SAṄGAMYA sarve te Kauravāṇāṃ mahā|rathāḥ
Arjunaṃ sahitā yattāḥ pratyayudhyanta, Bhārata.
sa sāyaka|mayair jālaiḥ sarvatas tān mahā|rathān
prācchādayad a|mey'|ātmā, nīhāreṇ' êva parvatān.
nadadbhiś ca mahā|nāgair, hreṣamāṇaiś ca vājibhiḥ,
bherī|śaṅkha|ninādaiś ca sa śabdas tumulo 'bhavat.
nar'|âśva|kāyān nirbhidya, lauhāni kavacāni ca
Pārthasya śara|jālāni viniṣpetuḥ sahasraśaḥ.
62.5 tvaramāṇaḥ śarān asyan Pāṇḍavaḥ prababhau raṇe
madhyan|dina|gato 'rciṣmāñ śarad' îva divākaraḥ.

Hit and pained by Partha's arrows, Duhshásana fled from battle. But Vikárna, Dhrita·rashtra's son, struck Árjuna, the murderer of enemy heroes, with his sharp and straight, vulture-feathered arrows. Kauntéya hit him in return on the forehead with a flat arrow, and, once shot, Vikárna quickly fell headlong from his chariot. Next, Dúhsaha and Viví-nshati charged Partha, showering him with sharp arrows, desperate to retrieve their brother in the battle.

But Dhanan·jaya, unperturbed, shot both of them at the same time with two sharpened vulture-feathered shafts, and
killed their horses. With both their horses now dead and 61.45
their limbs mangled, the two sons of Dhrita·rashtra fled and were led away with other chariots, brought by the infantry who had followed them. Then powerful Kauntéya, Bibhátsu, crowned with a diadem, undefeated by his enemies and skilled with missiles, attacked all directions.

VAISHAMPÁYANA said:

THEN ALL THE great Kuru warriors came together and 62.1
rushed at Árjuna in one go and attacked him, Bhárata. But the immeasurable-souled man enveloped all those mighty warriors with arrowy showers, just as mist covers mountains. There was a clashing roar from the trumpeting elephants and neighing horses and piercing sounds from the conches and kettledrums. Partha's arrowy showers fell in their thousands, piercing the bodies of men and horses as well as steel
armor. The son of Pandu, shooting his arrows, shone in bat- 62.5
tle as though he were the autumn sun firing his resplendent rays at midday.

upaplavanti vitrastā rathebhyo rathinas tathā,
sādinaś c' âśva|pṛṣṭhebhyo, bhūmau c' âiva padātayaḥ.
śaraiḥ saṃchidyamānānāṃ kavacānāṃ mah"|ātmanām
tāmra|rājata|lauhānām prādur āsīn mahā|svanaḥ.
channam āyodhanaṃ sarvaṃ śarīrair gata|cetasām
gaj'|âśva|sādināṃ tatra śita|bāṇ'|ātta|jīvitaih.
rath'|ôpasth'|âbhipatitair āstṛtā mānavair mahī.
pranṛtyat' îva saṅgrāme cāpa|hasto Dhanañjayaḥ.
62.10 śrutvā Gāṇḍīva|nirghoṣaṃ, visphūrjitam iv' âśaneḥ,
trastāni sarva|sainyāni vyapāgacchan mah"|āhavāt.
kuṇḍal'|ôṣṇīṣa|dhārīṇi, jāta|rūpa|srajas tathā
patitāni sma dṛśyante śirāṃsi raṇa|mūrdhani.
viśikh'|ônmathitair gātrair bāhubhiś ca sa|kārmukaiḥ
sa|hast'|ābharaṇaiś c' ânyaiḥ pracchannā bhāti medinī.
śirasāṃ pātyamānānām antarā niśitaiḥ śaraiḥ
aśma|vṛṣṭir iv' ākāśād abhavad, Bharata'|rṣabha.
darśayitvā tath" ātmānaṃ raudraṃ rudra|parākramaḥ,
avaruddho 'carat Pārtho varṣāṇi tridaśāni ca,
krodh'|âgnim utsṛjan vīro Dhārtaraṣṭreṣu Pāṇḍavaḥ.
62.15 tasya tad dahataḥ sainyaṃ dṛṣṭvā c' âiva parākramam
sarve śānti|parā yodhā Dhārtarāṣṭrasya paśyataḥ.
vitrāsayitvā tat sainyaṃ, drāvayitvā mahā|rathān,
Arjuno jayatāṃ śreṣṭhaḥ paryavartata, Bhārata.
prāvartayan nadīṃ ghorāṃ śoṇit'|ôdāṃ, taraṅgiṇīm,
asthi|śaivāla|sambādhāṃ, yug'|ânte kāla|nirmitām,
śara|cāpa|plavāṃ, ghorāṃ, keśa|śaivala|śādvalām,

Terrified charioteers plummeted from their cars, cavalry leaped from their horses' backs to the ground and the infantry, too, fell about. A great din arose from high-souled warriors as their copper, silver and steel armor clashed together. The entire battlefield was covered with the lifeless corpses of dead horse and elephant cavalry, killed by the sharp arrows. The ground was scattered with men who had fallen from the driving box of their chariots. It seemed as if Dhanan·jaya, bow in hand, was dancing on the battlefield.
Upon hearing the Gandíva's twang, booming like thunder, 62.10
entire trembling forces retreated from the great battle.

Severed fallen heads could be seen on the front line still wearing their earrings, turbans and golden wreaths. But the earth glistened with beauty, scattered with arrow-torn limbs, arms still clutching their bows, and hands still wearing their decorations, as well as other parts. Bull-like Bharata, while heads were falling, severed by sharpened arrows, it seemed as though it were a rain of stones.

The terrifyingly strong hero Partha then displayed his fierce soul, and the son of Pandu, who had been restrained for thirteen years, wandered about and poured the fire of
his rage onto Dhartaráshtra's troops, until all the warriors 62.15
stopped fighting, once they saw his power as he scorched the army, although they were in sight of Duryódhana.

Once he had made the army tremble before him, and routed great warriors, Árjuna, the greatest of victors, wandered about, Bhárata. He created a terrifying river with waves of blood-red waters, like that made by time at the end of the *yuga*: full of bones instead of moss, with bows and arrows as its boats, horrifying with hair instead of grassy

tanutr'|ôṣṇīṣa|sambādhāṃ, nāga|kūrma|mahādvipām,
medo|vas"|âsṛk|pravahāṃ, mahā|bhaya|vivardhinīm,
raudra|rūpāṃ, mahā|bhīmāṃ, śvāpadair abhināditām,
62.20 tīkṣṇa|śastra|mahā|grāhāṃ, kravyāda|gaṇa|sevitām,
muktā|hār'|ōrmi|kalilāṃ, citr'|âlaṅkāra|budbudām,
śara|saṅgha|mah"|āvartāṃ, nāga|nakrāṃ, dur|atyayām,
mahā|ratha|mahā|dvīpāṃ, śaṅkha|dundubhi|niḥsvanām
cakāra ca tadā Pārtho nadīṃ dus|tara|śoṇitām.
ādadānasya hi śarān, sandhāya ca vimuñcataḥ,
vikarṣataś ca Gāṇḍīvaṃ na kaś cid dadṛśe janaḥ.

VAIŚAMPĀYANA uvāca:

63.1 TATO DURYODHANAḤ, Karṇo, Duḥśāsana|Viviṃśatī,
Droṇaś ca saha putreṇa, Kṛpaś c' âpi mahā|rathaḥ
punar yayuś ca saṃrabdhā Dhanañjaya|jighāṃsavaḥ,
visphārayantaś cāpāni balavanti dṛḍhāni ca.
tān vikīrṇa|patākena rathen' āditya|varcasā
pratyudyayau, mahā|rāja, samantād vānara|dhvajaḥ.

tataḥ Kṛpaś ca, Karṇaś ca, Droṇaś ca rathināṃ varaḥ
taṃ mah"|âstrair mahā|vīryaṃ parivārya Dhanañjayam,
63.5 śar'|âughān samyag asyanto, jīmūtā iva vārṣikāḥ,
vavarṣuḥ śara|varṣāṇi pātayanto Dhanañjayam.
iṣubhir bahubhis tūrṇaṃ samare loma|vāhibhiḥ
a|dūrāt paryavasthāpya pūrayām āsur ādṛtāḥ.
tathā tair avakīrṇasya divyair astraiḥ samantataḥ
na tasya dvy|aṅgulam api vivṛtaṃ sampradṛśyate.

moss, full of armor and turbans, with huge elephants for turtles and snakes, with fat and marrow as the currents of the flow. It is an augmenter of great fear, horrendous in appearance and terrifying. It roars with beasts of prey, has 62.20
sharp weapons instead of great sharks, and is heaving with hordes of cannibals. It is filled with waves of pearl necklaces, bubbles of beautiful ornaments, and whirlpools of masses of arrows. It is insurmountable with its elephants for crocodiles, and, packed with warriors and elephants, it resounds with drums and conches. The bloody river that Partha made was invincible. The men watching could not discern any pause between him taking up the arrows, attaching them and releasing them when he drew Gandíva.

VAISHAMPÁYANA said:

THEN DURYÓDHANA, Karna, Duhshásana, Vivínshati 63.1
and Drona, along with his son, and also the great warrior Kripa, charged again, furious and eager to kill Dhanan·jaya. Those powerful men drew their solid bows fully and shot. In return, monkey-flagged Árjuna, great king, attacked them with his bannered chariot as splendid as the sun.

But Kripa, Karna and Drona, the best of charioteers, hemmed the great hero Dhanan·jaya in with their mighty weapons. Pouring their masses of arrows as if they were tor- 63.5
rential rain clouds, they showered Dhanan·jaya with floods of arrows, attempting to topple him. Intent and zealous, they soon covered the nearby area in battle with their numerous feathered arrows. Veiled with divine weapons on all sides as he was, not even two fingers' width of space appeared to be uncovered.

tataḥ prahasya Bībhatsur divyam Aindraṃ mahā|rathaḥ
astram āditya|saṅkāśaṃ Gāṇḍīve samayojayat.
śara|raśmir iv' ādityaḥ pratasthe samare balī
kirīṭa|mālī Kaunteyaḥ; sarvān prācchādayat Kurūn.

63.10 yathā balāhake vidyut, pāvako vā śil"|ôccaye,
tathā Gāṇḍīvam abhavad, Indr'|āyudham iv' ānatam.
yathā varṣati parjanye vidyud vibhrājate divi,
dyotayantī diśaḥ sarvāḥ, pṛthivīṃ ca samantataḥ,

tathā daśa diśaḥ sarvā patad Gāṇḍīvam āvṛṇot.
nāgāś ca rathinaḥ sarve mumuhus tatra, Bhārata.
sarve śānti|parā yodhāḥ sva|cittāni na lebhire,
saṅgrāme vimukhāḥ sarve yodhās te hata|cetasaḥ.
evaṃ sarvāṇi sainyāni bhagnāni, Bharata'|rṣabha,
vyadravanta diśaḥ sarvā, nirāśāni sva|jīvite.

VAIŚAMPĀYANA UVĀCA:

64.1 TATAḤ ŚĀNTANAVO Bhīṣmo Bharatānāṃ pitā|mahaḥ
vadhyamāneṣu yodheṣu Dhanañjayam upādravat.
pragṛhya kārmuka|śreṣṭhaṃ jata|rūpa|pariṣkṛtam,
śarān ādāya tīkṣṇ'|âgrān, marma|bhedān, pramāthinaḥ,
pāṇḍureṇ' ātapa|treṇa dhriyamāṇena mūrdhani
śuśubhe sa nara|vyāghro giriḥ sūry'|ôdaye yathā.
pradhmāya śaṅkhaṃ Gāṅgeyo Dhārtarāṣṭrān praharṣayan
pradakṣiṇam upāvṛtya Bībhatsuṃ samavārayat.

64.5 tam udīkṣya samāyāntaṃ Kaunteyaḥ para|vīra|hā
pratyagṛhṇāt prahṛṣṭ'|ātmā dhārā|dharam iv' âcalaḥ.

But Bibhátsu, the mighty warrior, laughed and attached Indra's divine weapon, which shone like the sun to Gandíva, and powerful Kauntéya, crowned with a diadem, rose in battle like the sun but with arrows as his rays, and enveloped all the Kurus. The Gandíva was curved like Indra's rainbow, 63.10
like lightning in a cloud or fire on a mountain. Just as lightning flashes in the sky in a rain cloud, so all the directions and the entire earth were illuminated.

The flying Gandíva concealed all ten directions, and the elephants and charioteers were left stupefied, Bhárata. All the warriors stopped fighting, unable to order their own thoughts other than to flee from battle, now that they had lost their minds. So, bull-like Bharata, all the ranks of the army were broken and everyone fled in all directions without a hope for survival.

VAISHAMPÁYANA said:

BHISHMA, SHÁNTANU's son and the grandfather of all the 64.1
Bharatas, charged at Dhanan·jaya while the soldiers were being destroyed. Taking his greatest gold-embellished bow, and his sharp-pointed, organ-piercing, destructive arrows, while his white parasol was being held over his head, that tiger among men shone like a mountain at sunrise. The son of the Ganges blew his conch and cheered Dhrita·rashtra's troops, then came up on Bibhátsu's right, and held him back. But Kauntéya, the murderer of enemy heroes, noticed 64.5
him approaching and was pleased at heart to receive him, just as a mountain receives a cloud.

tato Bhīṣmaḥ śarān aṣṭau dhvaje Pārthasya vīryavān
samārpayan mahā|vegān, śvasamānān iv' ôragān.
te dhvajaṃ Pāṇḍu|putrasya samāsādya patatriṇaḥ
jvalantaṃ kapim ājaghnur, dhvaj'|âgra|nilayāṃś ca tān.
tato bhallena mahatā pṛthu|dhāreṇa Pāṇḍavaḥ
chatraṃ ciccheda Bhīṣmasya; tūrṇaṃ tad apatad bhuvi.
dhvajaṃ c' âiv' âsya Kaunteyaḥ śarair abhyahanad bhṛśam
śīghra|kṛd, ratha|vāhāṃś ca, tath" ôbhau pārṣṇi|sārathī.
64.10 a|mṛṣyamāṇas tad Bhīṣmo jānann api sa Pāṇḍavam
divyen' âstreṇa mahatā Dhanañjayam avākirat.
tath" âiva Pāṇḍavo Bhīṣme divyam astram udīrayan
pratyagṛhṇād a|mey'|ātmā, mahā|megham iv' â|calaḥ.
tayos tad abhavad yuddhaṃ tumulaṃ loma|harṣaṇam
Bhīṣmasya saha Pārthena Bali|Vāsavayor iva.
praikṣanta Kuravaḥ sarve yodhāś ca saha|sainikāḥ.
bhallair bhallāḥ samāgamya Bhīṣma|Pāṇḍavayor yudhi
antarikṣe vyarājanta kha|dyotāḥ prāvṛṣ' îva hi.

agni|cakram iv' āviddhaṃ savya|dakṣiṇam asyataḥ
Gāṇḍīvam abhavad, rājan, Pārthasya sṛjataḥ śarān.
64.15 tataḥ saṃchādayām āsa Bhīṣmaṃ śara|śataiḥ śitaiḥ,
parvataṃ vāri|dhārābhiś chādayann iva toyadaḥ.
tāṃ sa velām iv' ôdbhūtāṃ śara|vṛṣṭiṃ samutthitām
vyadhamat sāyakair Bhīṣmaḥ, Pāṇḍavaṃ samavārayat.
tatas tāni nikṛttāni śara|jālāni bhāgaśaḥ
samare ca vyaśīryanta Phālgunasya rathaṃ prati.

The majestic Bhishma shot eight arrows, hissing like snakes, at Partha's banner, and reaching the Pándava's flying flag, and the blazing monkey, he struck those creatures who had settled at the top of the banner. In response, the son of Pandu split Bhishma's umbrella with his massive broad-edged javelin and it quickly fell to the ground. Swift-acting Kauntéya also struck his banner with numerous arrows and then his chariot and horses as well as both the flank charioteers.

Bhishma couldn't tolerate this, and, knowing the son 64.10
of Pandu, he covered Dhanan·jaya with a great celestial weapon. The Pándava also hurled a celestial weapon at Bhishma, and that man of immeasurable soul received that first weapon like a mountain receives a huge cloud. Then a hair-raising tumultuous battle broke out between that pair. The fight between Bhishma and Partha was like that of Valin and Vásava. All the Kuru warriors and their army soldiers were watching the fight between Bhishma and Pandu's son, as javelins came clashing into javelins, like fireflies shining in the air in the rainy season.

The Gandíva seemed like an unbroken ring of fire, my king, as Partha shot his arrows now with the left hand, and
now the right. Árjuna enveloped Bhishma with a hundred 64.15
sharp arrows, like a cloud covering a mountain with rain downpours. Bhishma dispersed the shower of arrows with his own shafts just as the shore resists the surge of the sea, and covered Pandu's son in return. And the men who had been shredded by the showers of arrows crumbled in battle by Phálguna's chariot.

tataḥ kanaka|puṅkhānāṃ śara|vṛṣṭiṃ samutthitām
Pāṇḍavasya rathāt tūrṇaṃ, śalabhānām iv' āyatim,
vyadhamat tāṃ punas tasya Bhīṣmaḥ śara|śataiḥ śitaiḥ.
tatas te Kuravaḥ sarve, «sādhu! sādhv! iti» c' âbruvan.
«duṣ|karaṃ kṛtavān Bhīṣmo, yad Arjunam ayodhayat.
64.20 balavāṃs, taruṇo, dakṣaḥ, kṣipra|kārī Dhanañjayaḥ.
ko 'nyaḥ samarthaḥ Pārthasya vegaṃ dhārayituṃ raṇe,
ṛte Śāntanavād Bhīṣmāt, Kṛṣṇād vā Devakī|sutāt,
ācārya|pravarād v" âpi Bhāradvājān mahā|balāt?»
astrair astrāṇi saṃvārya krīḍantau Bharata'|rṣabhau
cakṣūṃṣi sarva|bhūtānāṃ mohayantau mahā|balau,
Prājāpatyaṃ, tath" âiv' Āindram,
Āgneyaṃ, Raudra|dāruṇam,
Kauberaṃ, Vāruṇaṃ c' âiva,
Yāmyaṃ, Vāyavyam eva ca
prayuñjānau mah"|ātmānau
samare tau viceratuḥ.
vismitāny atha bhūtāni tau dṛṣṭvā saṃyuge tadā,
«sādhu Pārtha mahā|bāho! sādhu Bhīṣm'! êti» c' âbruvan.
64.25 «n' âyaṃ yukto manuṣyeṣu, yo 'yaṃ saṃdṛśyate mahān
mah"|âstrāṇāṃ saṃprayogaḥ samare Bhīṣma|Pārthayoḥ.»

Then a swift shower of golden-winged arrows rose from the son of Pandu's chariot like a flight of locusts. Bhishma once again dispersed that attack with a hundred sharp arrows. Then all the Kurus shouted, "Bravo! Bravo! Bhishma is accomplishing a tricky task by fighting with Árjuna. For 64.20
Dhanan·jaya is strong, young and dextrous, and he moves fast. Who else is able to endure Partha's force in battle, bar Bhishma, the son of Shántanu, or Krishna, the son of Dévaki, or mighty Bharad·vaja, the greatest of teachers?"

Repelling weapons with weapons, those two massively powerful bull-like Bharatas amused themselves with battle and mesmerized the eyes of all living creatures. Those two high-souled men roamed around in battle, employing the divine weapons from Praja·pati, Indra, Agni and the ferocious Rudra, as well as Kubéra's, Váruna's, Yama's and Vayu's. Watching those two in combat, all creatures were astonished. "Bravo, long-armed Partha! Bravo, Bhishma!" they shouted. "The great technique that Bhishma and Par- 64.25
tha are using in battle is not seen among humans."

evaṃ sarv'|âstra|viduṣor astra|yuddham avartata.
astra|yuddhe tu nirvṛtte śara|yuddham avartata.
atha Jiṣṇur upāvṛtya kṣura|dhāreṇa kārmukam
cakarta Bhīṣmasya tadā jāta|rūpa|pariṣkṛtam.
nimeṣ'|ântara|mātreṇa Bhīṣmo 'nyat kārmukaṃ raṇe
samādāya mahā|bāhuḥ sa|jyaṃ cakre mahā|rathaḥ.
śarāṃś ca su|bahūn kruddho mumoc' āśu Dhanañjaye.
Arjuno 'pi śarāṃs tīkṣṇān Bhīṣmāya niśitān bahūn
cikṣepa su|mahā|tejās, tathā Bhīṣmaś ca Pāṇḍave.
64.30 tayor divy'|âstra|viduṣor asyator niśitāñ śarān
na viśeṣas tadā, rājan, lakṣyate sma mah"|ātmanoḥ.

ath' âvṛṇod daśa diśaḥ śarair ati|rathas tadā
kirīṭa|mālī Kaunteyaḥ, śūraḥ Śāntanavas tathā.
atīva Pāṇḍavo Bhīṣmaṃ, Bhīṣmaś c' âtīva Pāṇḍavam.
babhūva tasmin saṅgrāme, rājaṃl, loke tad adbhutam.
Pāṇḍavena hatāḥ śūrā Bhīṣmasya ratha|rakṣiṇaḥ
śerate sma tadā, rājan, Kaunteyasy' âbhito ratham.
tato Gāṇḍīva|nirmuktā niramitraṃ cikīrṣavaḥ
āgacchan puṅkha|saṃśliṣṭāḥ Śvetavāhana|patriṇaḥ.
64.35 niṣpatanto rathāt tasya dhautā hairaṇya|vāsasaḥ
ākāśe samadṛśyanta haṃsānām iva paṅktayaḥ.
tasya tad divyam astraṃ hi vigāḍhaṃ citram asyataḥ
prekṣante sm' ântarikṣa|sthāḥ sarve devāḥ sa|Vāsavāḥ.
taṃ dṛṣṭvā parama|prīto gandharvaś citram adbhutam
śaśaṃsa deva|rājāya Citrasenaḥ pratāpavān:

So in this manner the fight with missiles continued between those two men, both well versed in all weaponry. When the battle with weapons was over, then came the battle of arrows. Jishnu advanced and shattered Bhishma's gold-embellished bow with a razor-sharp arrow. But, within the blink of an eye, Bhishma, the long-armed chariot-warrior, had taken up another bow in battle and strung it. Full of rage, he quickly fired numerous arrows at Dhanan·jaya. The enormously energetic Árjuna shot plenty of sharpened, pointed arrows at Bhishma, who returned the favor to the son of Pandu. But since both of them were well versed in 64.30
all weapons, no distinction could be made between those high-souled men firing arrows at each other, my king.

The mighty crowned chariot-warrior Kauntéya and Shántanu's brave son cloaked all ten directions with their arrows. The Pándava viciously attacked Bhishma and Bhishma viciously attacked the Pándava in turn. My king, the duel was a wonder of this world. Bhishma's brave chariot guards were killed by Pandu's son, my king, and they fell in front of Kauntéya's chariot. Shveta·váhana's winged and feathered arrows, which he shot from Gandíva, went scattering everything and obliterated the entire enemy.

As they flew from his chariot, the hordes of golden- 64.35
winged arrows in the sky resembled skeins of geese. All the gods in the sky, led by Indra, watched the beautiful, celestial weapon in motion. As they gazed at the amazing and magnificent weapon, the splendid *gandhárva*, Chitra·sena, said to the king of the gods:

«paśy' êmān Pārtha|nirmuktān saṃsaktān iva gacchataḥ!
citra|rūpam idaṃ Jiṣṇor divyam astram udīryataḥ!
n' êdaṃ manuṣyāḥ saṃdadhyur, na h' îdaṃ teṣu vidyate.
paurāṇānāṃ mah"|âstrāṇāṃ vicitro 'yaṃ samāgamaḥ!
64.40 ādadānasya hi śarān, saṃdhāya ca vimuñcataḥ,
vikarṣataś ca Gāṇḍīvaṃ n' ântaraṃ samadṛśyata!
madhyan|dina|gataṃ sūryaṃ pratapantam iv' âmbare
n' âśaknuvanta sainyāni Pāṇḍavaṃ prativīkṣitum.
tath" âiva Bhīṣmaṃ Gāṅgeyaṃ draṣṭuṃ n' ôtsahate janaḥ.
ubhau viśruta|karmāṇāv, ubhau tīvra|parākramau,
ubhau sadṛśa|karmāṇāv, ubhau yudhi su|durjayau.»

ity ukto deva|rājas tu Pārtha|Bhīṣma|samāgamam
pūjayām āsa divyena puṣpa|varṣeṇa, Bhārata.
64.45 tataḥ Śāntanavo Bhīṣmo vāmaṃ pārśvam atāḍayat
paśyataḥ pratisaṃdhāya vidhyataḥ Savyasācinaḥ.
tataḥ prahasya Bībhatsuḥ pṛthu|dhāreṇa kārmukam
ciccheda gārdhra|patreṇa Bhīṣmasy' āditya|tejasaḥ.
ath' âinaṃ daśabhir bāṇaiḥ pratyavidhyat stan'|ântare
yatamānaṃ parākrāntaṃ Kuntī|putro Dhanañjayaḥ.
sa pīḍito mahā|bāhur gṛhītvā ratha|kūbaram
Gāṅgeyo yuddha|dur|dharṣas tasthau dīrgham iv' ântaram.
taṃ visaṃjñam apovāha saṃyantā ratha|vājinām
upadeśam anusmṛtya, rakṣamāṇo mahā|ratham.

"Look how the arrows Partha has fired travel as though attached! The technique Jishnu has developed with this celestial weapon is wonderful! Humans cannot use this technique, for it is not found among them. This blend of great weaponry from ages past makes for great entertainment! No 64.40
pause can be discerned between his taking up the arrows, attaching them and firing them by drawing the Gandíva! The troops cannot even look at the Pándava as he blazes like the noonday sun in the sky. Nor do the men dare to look at Bhishma, the son of the Ganges. Both men are notorious for their feats, both are excessively powerful, both have similar accomplishments, and both are near invincible in battle."

Thus addressed, Bhárata, the king of the gods honored the encounter between Partha and Bhishma with a divine rain of flowers. Bhishma, Shántanu's son, attacked on the 64.45
left-hand side while Savya·sachin watched and adjusted his arrow to hit him. Then, laughing, Bibhátsu, radiant as the sun, split Bhishma's bow with a broad-edged, vulture-feathered arrow. Dhanan·jaya, the son of Kuntí, hit Bhishma in the chest with ten arrows, despite the fact that he was fighting at full strength. Once the long-armed son of the Ganges, who was near unconquerable in battle, was injured, he clung to his chariot pole for a long while. So his chariot-driver, remembering his training and protecting the great warrior, whisked the unconscious man away.

VAIŚAMPĀYANA UVĀCA:

65.1 BHĪṢME TU saṅgrāma|śiro vihāya
palāyamāne Dhṛtarāṣṭra|putraḥ
utsṛjya ketuṃ vinadan mah"|ātmā
dhanur vigṛhy' Ârjunam āsasāda.
sa bhīma|dhanvānam udagra|vīryaṃ
Dhanañjayaṃ śatru|gaṇe carantam
ākarṇa|pūrṇ'|āyata|coditena
vivyādha bhallena lalāṭa|madhye.

sa tena bāṇena samarpitena,
jāmbū|nad'|âgreṇa, su|saṃhitena
rarāja, rājan, mahanīya|karmā,
yath" âika|parvā rucir'|âika|śṛṅgaḥ.
ath' âsya bāṇena vidāritasya
prādur babhūv' âsṛg ajasram uṣṇam
sa tasya jāmbūnada|puṅkha|citro
bhittvā lalāṭaṃ su|virājate sma.

65.5 Duryodhanaś c' âpi tam ugra|tejāḥ,
Pārthaś ca Duryodhanam eka|vīraḥ,
anyonyam ājau puruṣa|pravīrau
samau samājagmatur Ājamīḍhau.

tataḥ prabhinnena mahā|gajena
mahī|dhar'|ābhena punar Vikarṇaḥ
rathaiś caturbhir gaja|pāda|rakṣaiḥ
Kuntī|sutaṃ Jiṣṇum ath' âbhyadhāvat.
tam āpatantaṃ tvaritaṃ gaj'|êndraṃ
Dhanañjayaḥ kumbha|vibhāga|madhye
ākarṇa|pūrṇena mah"|āyasena
bāṇena vivyādha mahā|javena.
Pārthena sṛṣṭaḥ sa tu gārdhra|patra

VAISHAMPÁYANA said:

WHEN BHISHMA HAD fled, abandoning the front line of battle, Dhrita·rashtra's high-souled son, raising his flag and roaring, took hold of his bow and advanced toward Árjuna. He hit Dhanan·jaya, that terrifying bowman of intense prowess, in the middle of the forehead, as he moved about among the throngs of his enemies, with a shaft shot from a bow fully extended to the ear. 65.1

And that man, made famous by his achievements, my king, shone with the well-joined and fixed golden-tipped arrow, like a charming mountain with a single peak. Cut open by the arrow, warm blood flowed continuously from his split forehead, and he glistened beautifully like a garland
of golden flowers. The fiercely energetic Duryódhana struck 65.5
him, and Partha, that preeminent hero, struck Duryódhana, and so those heroes, both born in the race of Ajamídha, attacked each other.

Then Vikárna again attacked Jishnu Kauntéya with a huge elephant in rut, resembling a mountain, and with four chariots to protect the elephant's feet. But Dhanan·jaya, noticing that lord of elephants quickly rushing toward him, shot it in the middle of its temple with his swift, iron-pointed arrow, fired from his bow, fully drawn to his ear. Once fired by Partha, that vulture-feathered arrow pierced the elephant all the way to the feathers and tore the enormous mountain-like elephant open, as when Indra hurls lightning at a lofty peak. Tormented by the arrow, the elephant king's limbs trembled in pain inside himself, and he

ā puṅkha|deśāt praviveśa nāgam,
vidārya śaila|pravaraṃ prakāśaṃ
yath" âśaniḥ parvatam Indra|sṛṣṭaḥ.
śara|prataptaḥ sa tu nāga|rājaḥ
pravepit'|âṅgo, vyathit'|ântar'|ātmā,
saṃsīdamāno nipapāta mahyāṃ
vajr'|āhataṃ śṛṅgam iv' â|calasya.
65.10 nipātite danti|vare pṛthivyāṃ
trāsād Vikarṇaḥ sahas" âvatīrya
tūrṇaṃ padāny aṣṭa|śatāni gatvā
Viviṃśateḥ syandanam āruroha.
nihatya nāgaṃ tu śareṇa tena
vajr'|ôpamen' âdrivar'|âmbud'|ābham
tathā|vidhen' âiva śareṇa Pārtho
Duryodhanaṃ vakṣasi nirbibheda.
tato gaje rājati c' âiva bhinne,
bhagne Vikarṇe ca sa|pāda|rakṣe,
Gāṇḍīva|muktair viśikhaiḥ praṇunnās
te yodha|mukhyāḥ sahas" âpajagmuḥ.
dṛṣṭv" âiva Pārthena hataṃ ca nāgaṃ,
yodhāṃś ca sarvān dravato niśamya,
rathaṃ samāvṛtya Kuru|pravīro
raṇāt pradudrāva yato na Pārthaḥ.
taṃ bhīma|rūpaṃ tvaritaṃ dravantaṃ
Duryodhanaṃ śatru|saho 'bhiṣaṅgāt
prāsphoṭayad yoddhu|manāḥ Kirīṭī
bāṇena viddhaṃ rudhiraṃ vamantam.

ARJUNA uvāca:

65.15 vihāya kīrtiṃ, vipulaṃ yaśaś ca

collapsed and fell to the ground, like the peak of a mountain struck by a thunderbolt.

And when that excellent tusker fell to the ground, Vi- 65.10
kárna suddenly leaped off, trembling with fear, and quickly retreated eight hundred paces before climbing onto Vivínshati's chariot. Once he had killed the elephant, which resembled a cloud on a mountain, with his thunderbolt-like arrow, Partha pierced Duryódhana in the chest with the same kind of shaft. Since both the king and the elephant were wounded and Vikárna had broken ranks along with the chariot guards, the warriors left facing the front, who were being repelled by the sharp arrows fired from Gandíva, quickly fled.

When he saw Partha kill the elephant and noticed that his warriors were all running away, Duryódhana, the foremost Káuravan hero, turned his chariot around and fled from battle to wherever Partha was not. But as Duryódhana was swiftly escaping, a picture of terror, hit by an arrow and vomiting blood, Kirítin, bursting for battle and able to endure any enemy, shouted in anger.

ÁRJUNA said:

Why are you running away and turning your back on 65.15
the battle, relinquishing your wide fame and glory? Why

yuddhāt parāvṛtya palāyase kim?
na te 'dya tūryāṇi samāhatāni
tath" âiva rājyād avaropitasya?
Yudhiṣṭhirasy' âsmi nideśa|kārī
Pārthas tṛtīyo yudhi saṃsthito 'smi.
tad artham āvṛtya mukhaṃ prayaccha,
nar'|êndra, vṛttaṃ smara, Dhārtarāṣṭra!
moghaṃ tav' êdaṃ bhuvi nāma|dheyaṃ
«Duryodhan'» êt' îha kṛtaṃ purastāt.
na h' îha duryodhanatā tav' âsti
palāyamānasya raṇaṃ vihāya!
na te purastād atha pṛṣṭhato vā
paśyāmi, Duryodhana, rakṣitāram.
apehi yuddhāt, puruṣa|pravīra,
prāṇān priyān Pāṇḍavato 'dya rakṣa!

are the drums not being beaten now as they were when you set out from your kingdom? I am the obedient executor of Yudhi·shthira's orders, and I stand here in battle as Pritha's third son. For that reason, turn back and show me your face, lord of kings and son of Dhrita·rashtra, and remember your duty!

Your name, Duryódhana—"invincible"—which was given to you in the past, has been proved fruitless! There is nothing invincible about running away during the battle and abandoning the fight! I don't see your bodyguard, Duryódhana, either behind or in front, so flee from the fight today, foremost hero among men, and save your precious life from the son of Pandu!

66–69
THE KÁURAVAS' HUMILIATING DEFEAT AND ÚTTARA'S TRIUMPHANT RETURN

VAIŚAMPĀYANA UVĀCA:

66.1 ĀHŪYAMĀNAŚ CA sa tena saṅkhye
mah"|ātmanā vai Dhṛtarāṣṭra|putraḥ
nivartitas tasya gir'|âṅkuśena,
mahā|gajo matta iv' âṅkuśena.
so '|mṛṣyamāṇo vacas" âbhimṛṣṭo
mahā|rathen' âti|rathas tarasvī
paryāvavart' âtha rathena vīro,
bhogī yathā pāda|tal'|âbhimṛṣṭaḥ.
tam prekṣya Karṇaḥ parivartamānam,
nivartya saṃstabhya ca viddha|gātram,
Duryodhanasy' uttarato 'bhyagacchat
Pārthaṃ nṛvīro yudhi hema|mālī.
Bhīṣmas tataḥ Śāntanavo vivṛtya
hiraṇya|kakṣas tvaray" âbhiṣaṅgī
Duryodhanaṃ paścimato 'bhyarakṣat
Pārthān mahā|bāhur adhijya|dhanvā.
66.5 Droṇaḥ, Kṛpaś c' âiva, Viviṃśatiś ca,
Duḥśāsanaś c' âiva vivṛtya śīghram
sarve purastād vitat'|ôru|cāpā
Duryodhan'|ârthaṃ tvarit" âbhyupeyuḥ.
sa tāny anīkāni nivartamānāny
ālokya pūrṇ'|âugha|nibhāni Pārthaḥ,
haṃso yathā megham iv' āpatantaṃ,
Dhanañjayaḥ pratyatapat tarasvī.
te sarvataḥ saṃparivārya Pārtham
astrāṇi divyāni samādadānāḥ
vavarṣur abhyetya śaraiḥ samantān,
meghā yathā bhū|dharam ambu|vargaiḥ.
tato 'stram astreṇa nivārya teṣāṃ

VAISHAMPÁYANA said:

PROVOKED BY THAT high-souled hero into fighting, Dhrita·rashtra's son turned back, angered by his goading words, like a mighty rutting elephant beaten by the driver's hook. Unable to endure those taunts, stung by that mighty chariot-warrior, the swift, powerful and brave warrior turned back with his chariot as though he were a snake crushed under the soles of feet. 66.1

Karna spotted him turning around and so he himself headed back, and, having encouraged the wounded man, the golden-crowned hero advanced against Partha in battle, going just north of Duryódhana's chariot. Shántanu's son, Bhishma, was humiliated and so quickly turned back his own horses decked with golden bridles. The long-armed man, with his strung bow in hand, defended Duryódhana from Partha from behind him. Drona, Kripa, Vivínshati 66.5
and Duhshásana all speedily turned as well, and swiftly flew back from behind, with their long-stringed bows drawn for Duryódhana's sake.

When Partha Dhanan·jaya saw these forces all returning like swelling floods, he quickly rushed at them just as a goose flies at a cloud. They surrounded Partha on all sides and, taking hold of their divine weapons, they advanced raining down arrows in all directions, like clouds pouring torrents of rain on a mountain. But, dispelling the weapons belonging to those Káuravan bull-like men with his own, the wielder of the Gandíva, the son of Indra, who could endure any enemy, formed in full view another weapon called Sammóhana, the missile of delusion; an impossible weapon to beat.

Gāṇḍīva|dhanvā Kuru|puṅgavānām
Saṃmohanaṃ śatru|saho 'nyad astraṃ
prāduś cakār' Āindrir a|pāraṇīyam.
tato diśaś c' ânudiśo vivṛtya
śaraiḥ su|dhārair, niśitaiḥ, su|patraiḥ,
Gāṇḍīva|ghoṣeṇa manāṃsi teṣāṃ
mahā|balaḥ pravyathayāñ cakāra.
66.10 tataḥ punar bhīma|ravaṃ pragṛhya
dorbhyāṃ mahā|śaṅkham, udāra|ghoṣam,
vyanādayat sa pradiśo, diśaḥ, khaṃ,
bhuvaṃ ca Pārtho dviṣatāṃ nihantā.
te śaṅkha|nādena Kuru|pravīrāḥ
saṃmohitāḥ Pārtha|samīritena,
utsṛjya cāpāṇi dur|āsadāni
sarve tadā śānti|parā babhuvuḥ.
tathā visaṃjñeṣu ca teṣu Pārthaḥ
smṛtvā ca vākyāni tath" Ôttarāyāḥ,
«niryāhi madhyād,» iti Matsya|putram
uvāca, «yāvat Kuravo visaṃjñāḥ.
ācārya|Śāradvatayoḥ su|śukle,
Karṇasya pītaṃ ruciraṃ ca vastram,
Drauṇeś ca rājñaś ca tath" âiva nīle
vastre samādatsva, nara|pravīra.
Bhīṣmasya saṃjñā tu tath" âiva manye
jānāti so 'stra|pratighātam eṣaḥ.
etasya vāhān kuru saṃyatas tvam;
evaṃ hi yātavyam a|mūḍha|saṃjñaiḥ.»

The mighty hero covered all directions and quarters with his sharp, well-pointed and beautifully feathered arrows, and with the twang of Gandíva he made their minds tremble. Then, having picked up his massive, horrifyingly howl- 66.10
ing and enormously loud conch in both hands once more, Partha, the destroyer of his enemies, made it roar; filling the quarters and directions, sky and earth. The leading Kuru heroes were rendered senseless by the noise of the conch when Partha blew it. They all became motionless and dropped their usually dangerous bows.

And when they were all stupefied Partha remembered Uttará's request, and spoke to the Prince of Matsya, saying: "Go out from the middle while the Kurus are still senseless, hero among men, and take the teacher's bright white clothing as well as Sharádvata's son's, Karna's lovely yellow clothing, Drona's son's and the king's blue garments. I reckon Bhishma is fully concious, since he knows how to counteract the weapon. So keep his horses to your left, for we will be attacked by those who have regained consciousness when they are no longer transfixed."

66.15 raśmīn samutsṛjya tato mah"|ātmā
rathād avaplutya Virāṭa|putraḥ
vastrāṇy upādāya mahā|rathānāṃ
tūrṇaṃ punaḥ svaṃ ratham āruroha.
tato 'nvaśāsac caturaḥ sad|aśvān
putro Virāṭasya hiraṇya|kakṣān.
te tad vyatīyur dhvajinām anīkaṃ
śvetā vahanto 'rjunam āji|madhyāt.
tath" ânuyāntaṃ puruṣa|pravīraṃ
Bhīṣmaḥ śarair abhyahanat tarasvī.
sa c' âpi Bhīṣmasya hayān nihatya
vivyādha Pārtho daśabhiḥ pṛṣatkaiḥ.
tato 'rjuno Bhīṣmam apāsya yuddhe
viddhv" âsya yantāram a|riṣṭa|dhanvā
tasthau vimukto ratha|vṛnda|madhyān
meghaṃ vidāry' êva sahasra|raśmiḥ.
labdhvā hi saṃjñāṃ tu Kuru|pravīrāḥ,
Pārthaṃ nirīkṣy' âtha sur'|Êndra|kalpam,
raṇe vimuktaṃ sthitam ekam ājau
sa Dhārtarāṣṭras tvaritaṃ babhāṣe,
66.20 «ayaṃ kathaṃ vai bhavato vimuktas?
tathā pramathnīta, yathā na mucyet!»
tam abravīc Chāntanavaḥ prahasya
«kva te gatā buddhir abhūt, kva vīryam,
śāntiṃ parāṃ prāpya yadā sthito 'bhūr
utsṛjya bāṇāṃś ca dhanur vicitram?
na tv eṣa Bībhatsur alaṃ nṛśaṃsaṃ
kartuṃ, na pāpe 'sya mano viśiṣṭam.
trailokya|hetor na jahet sva|dharmaṃ.
sarve na tasmān nihatā raṇe 'smin.

So Viráta's high-souled son let go of the reins and jumped down from the chariot. Once he had gathered the warriors' clothes, he quickly climbed back into his car. Then Viráta's son urged on the four pure-white horses, decked with golden bridles, and those massive white horses went past the banner-filled army and whisked Árjuna away from the midst of the battlefield. But Bhishma swiftly fired arrows at him as that greatest hero of men was leaving. 66.15

Partha killed Bhishma's horses, then shot him with ten shafts. But, once he had shot his driver, Árjuna left Bhishma behind on the battlefield. The wielder of the undamaged bow burst out from the midst of the divisions of chariots, like the thousand-rayed sun bursting through a cloud. When the leading men of the Kurus recovered their senses and saw Partha standing alone and free on the battlefield, like Indra among the celestials, Dhrita·rashtra's son quickly
said, "How did this man escape you? Attack him so that he 66.20
cannot get away!"

Shántanu's son laughed and said to him: "Where did your sense and prowess go when you stood in a trance, dropping your arrows and splendid bow? Bibhátsu is not capable of committing malicious deeds. Nor is his mind characteristically wicked. He would not compromise his own duty even for the sake of all three worlds. This is the reason that we have not all been killed. So quickly, foremost Káuravan hero, go back to the Kurus, and let Partha return now that he has won back the cattle. Don't throw away your own advantage because of folly. One should rather do what brings good fortune."

kṣipraṃ Kurūn yāhi, Kuru|pravīra,
vijitya gāś ca pratiyātu Pārthaḥ.
mā te svako 'rtho nipateta mohāt.
tat saṃvidhātavyam a|riṣṭa|bandham.»
Duryodhanas tasya tu tan niśamya
pitā|mahasy' ātma|hitaṃ vaco 'tha
atīta|kāmo yudhi so 'tyamarṣī
rājā viniḥśvasya babhūva tūṣṇīm.
tad Bhīṣma|vākyaṃ hitam īkṣya sarve,
Dhanañjay'|âgniṃ ca vivardhamānam,
nivartanāy' âiva mano nidadhyur
Duryodhanaṃ te parirakṣamāṇāḥ.
66.25 tān prasthitān prītamanāḥ sa Pārtho
Dhanañjayaḥ prekṣya Kuru|pravīrān,
a|bhāṣamāṇo 'nunayaṃ muhūrtaṃ
vaco 'bravīt samparihṛtya bhūyaḥ.
pitā|mahaṃ, Śāntanavaṃ ca vṛddhaṃ,
Droṇaṃ guruṃ ca praṇipatya mūrdhnā,
Drauṇiṃ, Kṛpaṃ c' âiva, Kurūṃś ca māṇyāñ,
charair vicitrair abhivādya c' âiva.
Duryodhanasy' ôttama|ratna|citraṃ
ciccheda Pārtho mukuṭaṃ śareṇa.
āmantrya vīrāṃś ca tath" âiva mānyān,
Gāṇḍīva|ghoṣeṇa vinādya lokān.
sa Devadattaṃ sahasā vinādya,
vidārya vīro dviṣatāṃ manāṃsi,
dhvajena sarvān abhibhūya śatrūn
sa|hema|mālena virājamānaḥ.
dṛṣṭvā prayātāṃs tu Kurūn Kirīṭī
hṛṣṭo 'bravīt tatra sa Matsya|putram:

Impatient King Duryódhana was calmed by his grandfather's words, which were to his benefit, and since his desire for battle had subsided, he sighed and became silent. Everyone else, noting that Bhishma's advice was indeed beneficial, and observing that the fire of Dhanan·jaya had grown, resolved in their minds to return to protect Duryódhana.

Dhanan·jaya Partha watched those leading Káurava 66.25
heroes setting off and was glad in his heart. He saluted them and paid his respects for a little while, and then spoke to them and turned back again. When he had bowed his head before the aged son of Shántanu, his grandfather, and his guru Drona, he saluted Drona's son, Kripa, and Kurus worthy of honor with beautiful arrows. But then Partha shattered Duryódhana's crown, fashioned from various highly precious jewels, with an arrow.

Once he had paid his respects to the venerable heroes in this manner, he made the worlds reverberate with the twang of Gandíva. Suddenly he blew Deva·datta, his conch, and by so doing that hero unnerved his enemies' minds. As he humiliated all his enemies with their defeat, he shone with his golden garland and banner. Kirítin was happy as he watched the Kurus leaving and he said to the Prince of Matsya: "Turn the horses back, for the cattle have been won and the enemy
is going home, so go back to the city in cheerful spirits." And 66.30
the gods, having watched that astounding battle between

«āvartay' âśvān, paśavo jitās te,
yātāḥ pare; yāhi puraṃ prahṛṣṭaḥ.»
66.30 devās tu dṛṣṭvā mahad adbutaṃ tad
yuddhaṃ Kurūṇāṃ saha Phālgunena
jagmur yathā|svaṃ bhavanaṃ pratītāḥ
Pārthasya karmāṇi vicintayantaḥ.

VAIŚAMPĀYANA uvāca:

67.1 TATO VIJITYA saṅgrāme Kurūn sa vṛṣabh'|ēkṣaṇaḥ,
samānayām āsa tadā Virāṭasya dhanaṃ mahat.
gateṣu ca prabhagneṣu Dhārtarāṣṭreṣu sarvataḥ,
vanān niṣkramya gahanād bahavaḥ Kuru|sainikāḥ
bhayāt saṃtrasta|manasaḥ samājagmus tatas tataḥ,
mukta|keśās tv adṛśyanta sthitāḥ prāñjalyas tadā.
kṣut|pipāsā|pariśrāntā, videśa|sthā, vicetasaḥ,
ūcuḥ praṇamya sambhrāntāḥ, «Pārtha, kiṃ karavāma te.»

ARJUNA uvāca:

67.5 svasti vrajata, vo bhadraṃ. na bhetavyaṃ kathañ cana.
n' âham ārtān jighāṃsāmi. bhṛśam āśvāsayāmi vaḥ.

VAIŚAMPĀYANA uvāca:

tasya tām a|bhayāṃ vācaṃ śrutvā yodhāḥ samāgatāḥ
āyuḥ|kīrti|yaśo|dābhis tam āśīrbhir anandayan.
tato 'rjunaṃ nāgam iva prabhinnam
utsṛjya śatrūn vinivartamānam
Virāṭa|rāṣṭr'|âbhimukhaṃ prayāntaṃ
n' â|śaknuvaṃs taṃ Kuravo 'bhiyātum.
tataḥ sa tan megham iv' āpatantaṃ
vidrāvya Pārthaḥ Kuru|megha|sainyam
Matsyasya putraṃ dviṣatāṃ nihantā
vaco 'bravīt saṃparirabhya bhūyaḥ:

the Kurus and Phálguna, went back to their own homes, delighted, thinking back on Partha's achievements.

VAISHAMPÁYANA said:

So, HAVING DEFEATED the Kurus in combat, that bull-eyed man led back Viráta's great wealth of cattle. While Dhrita·rashtra's routed troops were going in all directions, numerous Kuru soldiers came out of the dense forest. Their minds trembled from fear, so they gathered together and appeared standing with their hair disheveled, joining their hands out of respect. Hungry and thirsty, exhausted in a foreign land, bewildered and confused, they bowed before him and said, "Partha, let us do something for you." 67.1

ÁRJUNA said:

Good luck, bless you, now go. You have nothing to fear. I will not kill the tormented. I will comfort you as much as possible. 67.5

VAISHAMPÁYANA said:

When they had heard his words promising safety, the warriors gathered and rejoiced with blessings conferring fame, renown and long life upon him. The Kurus were unable to attack Árjuna as he went toward Viráta's kingdom, having scattered his routed enemies like an elephant with torn temples.

After he had made the army of masses of Kurus flee, like the wind scattering clouds, Partha, the destroyer of his enemies, addressed the Prince of Matsya, when he had embraced him once more, saying: "You alone know that all the sons of Pritha are living in your father's vicinity, my

«pituḥ sakāśe tava, tāta, sarve
vasanti Pārthā viditaṃ tav' âiva.
tān mā praśaṃser nagaraṃ praviśya;
bhītaḥ praṇaśyedd hi sa Matsya|rājaḥ.
67.10 ‹mayā jitā sā dhvajinī Kurūṇāṃ,
mayā ca gāvo vijitā dviṣadbhyaḥ.›
pituḥ sakāśaṃ nagaraṃ praviśya
tvam ātmanaḥ karma kṛtaṃ bravīhi.»

UTTARA uvāca:

yat te kṛtaṃ karma na pāraṇīyaṃ,
tat karma kartuṃ mama n' âsti śaktiḥ.
na tvāṃ pravakṣyāmi pituḥ sakāśe
yāvan na māṃ vakṣyasi, Savyasācin.

VAIŚAMPĀYANA uvāca:

sa śatru|senām avajitya Jiṣṇur
ācchidya sarvaṃ ca dhanaṃ Kurubhyaḥ
śmaśānam āgatya punaḥ śamīṃ tām
abhyetya tasthau śara|vikṣat'|âṅgaḥ.
tataḥ sa vahni|pratimo mahā|kapiḥ
sah' âiva bhūtair divam utpapāta.
tath" âiva māyā vihita babhūva
dhvajaṃ ca saiṃhaṃ yuyje rathe punaḥ.
vidhāya tac c' āyudham āji|vardhanaṃ,
Kur'|ûttamānām iṣudhīḥ, śarāṃs tathā,
prāyāt sa Matsyo nagaraṃ prahṛṣṭaḥ
Kirīṭinā sārathinā mah"|ātmanā.
67.15 Pārthas tu kṛtvā param'|ârya|karma,
nihatya śatrūn, dviṣatāṃ nihantā
cakāra veṇīṃ ca tath" âiva bhūyo,

friend. So don't praise them once you've entered the city, or the King of Matsya will be alarmed and vanish. Once you have entered the city, say, 'I defeated the banner-bearing 67.10
Káurava army, and I won back the cattle from our enemies,' in your father's presence, and tell people that you yourself accomplished the feat."

ÚTTARA said:

The feat you have accomplished is not one that I could have done, for it is not within my power to achieve such a task. But I will not give you away in my father's presence for as long as you tell me, Savya·sachin.

VAISHAMPÁYANA said:

So, once he had defeated the enemy army and snatched the wealth of cattle from the Kurus, Jishnu once again came to the cemetery. When he came to the *shami* tree, he rested there, his body scarred by arrows. The mighty monkey, the chariot's symbol, flew up into the sky with the other creatures. So, the illusion that had been produced was lost, and the lion flag was attached to the chariot again.

Once he had replaced the weapon that augments the battlefield, as well as the quivers and arrows belonging to the greatest men of the Kurus, the Matsyan prince went back to the city, happy, with the high-souled Kirítin as his charioteer. Now that he had achieved an excellently worthy feat, 67.15
insofar as that killer of his enemies had indeed killed his enemies, Partha plaited his hair again and took the reins from Úttara once more. The high-souled hero happily entered the city, having adopted the disguise of Brihan·nala the charioteer.

jagrāha raśmīn punar Uttarasya.
viveśa hṛṣṭo nagaraṃ mahā|manā
Bṛhannalā|rūpam upetya sārathiḥ.
tato nivṛttāḥ Kuravaḥ prabhagnā vaśam āsthitāḥ
Hāstināpuram uddiśya sarve dīnā yayus tadā.
panthānam upasaṅgamya Phālguno vākyam abravīt:
«rāja|putra, pratyavekṣya samānītāni sarvaśaḥ
go|kulāni, mahā|bāho vīra, go|pālakaiḥ saha,
tato 'par'|âhṇe yāsyāmo Virāṭa|nagaraṃ prati,
āśvāsya, pāyayitvā ca, pariplāvya ca vājinaḥ.
67.20 gacchantu tvaritāś c' ême go|pālāḥ preṣitās tvayā
nagare priyam ākhyātuṃ; ghoṣayantu ca te jayam.»
ath' Ôttaras tvaramāṇaḥ sa dūtān
ājñāpayad vacanāt Phālgunasya,
«ācakṣadhvaṃ vijayaṃ pārthivasya.
bhagnāḥ pare, vijitāś c' âpi gāvaḥ.»
ity evaṃ tau Bhārata|Matsya|vīrau
saṃmantrya, saṅgamya tataḥ śamīṃ tām
abhyetya bhūyo vijayena tṛptāv,
utsṛṣṭam āropayatāṃ sva|bhāṇḍam.
sa śatru|senām abhibhūya sarvām,
ācchidya sarvaṃ ca dhanaṃ Kurubhyaḥ
Vairāṭir āyān nagaraṃ pratīto
Bṛhannalā|sārathinā pravīraḥ.

VAIŚAṂPĀYANA uvāca:

68.1 DHANAṂ C' ÂPI vijity' āśu Virāṭo vāhinī|patiḥ
viveśa nagaraṃ hṛṣṭaś caturbhiḥ Pāṇḍavaiḥ saha.
jitvā Trigartān saṅgrāme, gāś c' âiv' ādāya sarvaśaḥ
aśobhata mahā|rāja saha|Pārthaḥ śriyā vṛtaḥ.
tam āsana|gataṃ vīraṃ, suhṛdāṃ harṣa|vardhanam,

As the routed and defeated Kurus turned back, all going miserably toward Hástina·pura, Phálguna, on his way home, said to Úttara as he was going along: "Prince, wait till the cattle have been gathered together from all over with their cowherds and we will enter Viráta's city in the afternoon, once we have soothed the horses and given them a drink and a wash. Let these cowherds go quickly, sent on 67.20
ahead, to announce the good news in the city, and let them shout about your victory."

Úttara swiftly ordered the messengers according to Phálguna's advice, saying, "Announce the king's victory. The enemy are routed and the cattle have been won back." Then those two Matsyan and Bháratan heroes consulted together and went back to the *shami* tree satisfied with their victory, and they climbed up to retrieve their property, which they had left there. Now that he had overpowered the entire enemy army and snatched back the full wealth of cattle from the Kurus, Viráta's hero son happily returned back to the city with Brihan·nala as his charioteer.

VAISHAMPÁYANA said:

MEANWHILE, VIRÁTA, the lord of his army, who had 68.1
quickly won back his wealth, entered his city joyfully with the four sons of Pandu. With the Tri·gartas defeated in battle and his cattle completely retrieved, the mighty king shone along with the Parthas, surrounded by splendor. Once the heroic augmenter of his friends' happiness had sat on his

upāsāñ cakrire sarve saha Pārthaiḥ paran|tapāḥ.
upatasthuḥ prakṛtayaḥ samastā brāhmaṇaiḥ saha;
sabhājitaḥ sa|sainyas tu pratinandy' âtha Matsya|rāṭ
68.5 visarjayām āsa tadā dvijāṃś ca prakṛtīs tathā.
tathā sa rājā Matsyānāṃ Virāṭo vāhinī|patiḥ
Uttaraṃ paripapraccha, «kva yāta?» iti c' âbravīt.
ācakhyus tasya tat sarvaṃ striyaḥ kanyāś ca veśmani,
antaḥ|pura|carāś c' âiva, «Kurubhir go|dhanaṃ hṛtam.
vijetum abhisaṃrabdha eka ev' âti|sāhasāt
Bṛhannalā|sahāyaś ca nirgataḥ pṛthivīñ|jayaḥ,
upayātān ati|rathān Bhīṣmaṃ,
Śāntanavaṃ, Kṛpam,
Karṇaṃ, Duryodhanaṃ, Droṇaṃ,
Droṇa|putraṃ ca ṣaḍ|rathān.»
rājā Virāṭo 'tha bhṛś'|âbhitaptaḥ
śrutvā sutaṃ tv eka|rathena yātam
Bṛhannalā|sārathim āji|vardhanaṃ,
provāca sarvān atha mantri|mukhyān:
68.10 «sarvathā Kuravas te hi, ye c' ânye vasudh'|âdhipāḥ,
Trigartān niḥsṛtāñ śrutvā na sthāsyanti kadā cana.
tasmād gacchantu me yodhā balena mahatā vṛtāḥ
Uttarasya parīps'|ârthaṃ, ye Trigartair a|vikṣatāḥ.»

throne, all the scorchers of the foe made their approach, as did the Parthas. All the ministers stood nearby with the brahmins, and as he was worshipped with his army the King of Matsya saluted them and then dismissed the brahmins 68.5
and his citizens.

Viráta, king of the Matsyas, the leader of his army, inquired about his son, saying, "Where has Úttara gone?" The women and girls who lived in the inner apartments in the palace told him the whole story: that the wealth of cattle had been seized by the Kurus, and that, furious, the earth-conqueror had instantly gone with Brihan·nala as his companion to defeat the six fantastic warriors who had come: Bhishma, son of Shántanu, Kripa, Karna, Duryódhana, Drona and his son, Ashvattháman.

King Viráta was greatly distressed when he heard that his son, the augmenter of battle, had gone out with a single chariot and Brihan·nala as his charioteer, and spoke to all his leading ministers, saying: "The Kurus and those other lords 68.10
of the treasure-bearing earth will never stay when they hear that the Tri·gartas were defeated. Therefore let the warriors who have not been wounded by the Tri·gartas, together with a massive force, set out in order to get Úttara back."

hayāṃś ca, nāgāṃś ca, rathāṃś ca śīghraṃ,
padāti|saṅghāṃś ca tataḥ pravīrān
prasthāpayām āsa sutasya hetor
vicitra|śastr'|ābharaṇ'|ôpapannān.
evaṃ sa rājā MatsyānāṃVirāṭo vāhinī|patiḥ
vyādideś' âtha tāṃ kṣipraṃ vāhinīṃ catur|aṅgiṇīm,
«kumāram āśu jānīta, yadi jīvati vā na vā.
yasya yantā gataḥ ṣaṇḍho, manye 'haṃ sa na jīvati!»

68.15 tam abravīd dharma|rājo vihasya
Virāṭa|rājaṃ tu bhṛś'|âbhitaptam:
«Bṛhannalā sārathiś cen, nar'|êndra,
pare na neṣyanti tav' âdya gās tāḥ.
sarvān mahī|pān sahitān, Kurūṃś ca,
tath" âiva dev'|âsura|siddha|yakṣān
alaṃ vijetuṃ samare sutas te
sv|anuṣṭhitaḥ sārathinā hi tena!»

ath' Ôttareṇa prahitā dūtās te śīghra|gāminaḥ
Virāṭa|nagaraṃ prāpya vijayaṃ samavedayan.
rājñas tat sarvam ācakhyau mantrī vijayam uttamam,
parājayaṃ Kurūṇāṃ c' âpy, upāyāntaṃ tath" Ôttaram,
«sarvā vinirjitā gāvaḥ, Kuravaś ca parājitāḥ!
Uttaraḥ saha sūtena kuśalī ca paran|tapaḥ!»

YUDHIṢṬHIRA uvāca:

68.20 diṣṭyā vinirjitā gāvaḥ, Kuravaś ca palāyitāḥ!
n' âdbhutaṃ tv eva manye 'haṃ yat te putro 'jayat Kurūn.
dhruva eva jayas tasya yasya yantā Bṛhannalā!

He quickly sent out horses, elephants, chariots and divisions of heroic infantry, furnished with various decorations and weapons, for the sake of his son. So it was that King Viráta of the Matsyas, the lord of his army, quickly dispatched his fourfold force of troops, saying, "Swiftly find out whether or not the prince is alive. I do not believe a man who has a eunuch as his driver can be alive!"

But Yudhi·shthira, the king of righteousness, smiled and 68.15
said to terribly distressed King Viráta: "If Brihan·nala is his charioteer, lord of men, then the enemy will not manage to lead away your cattle today. With that excellent worker as his charioteer, your son will be able to completely annihilate all the gathered Káuravan earth-lords, or even the gods, *ásura*s, *siddha*s and *yaksha*s!"

Just then, the swift-traveling messengers dispatched by Úttara reached Viráta's city and were making the victory known. The first minister informed the king of everything: the victory over the Kuru enemy and also Úttara's return, saying, "All the cattle have been won back and the Kurus are defeated! Úttara, the scorcher of the enemy, along with his charioteer, is safe and well!"

YUDHI·SHTHIRA said:

Congratulations on the retrieval of your cattle, and on 68.20
the flight of the Kurus! I do not think it is so astounding that your son triumphed over the Kurus. Victory is assured for the man whose charioteer is Brihan·nala!

VAIŚAMPĀYANA uvāca:

tato Virāṭo nṛpatiḥ saṃprahṛṣṭa|tanū|ruhaḥ
śrutvā sa vijayaṃ tasya kumārasy' â|mit'|âujasaḥ,
ācchādayitvā dūtāṃs tān mantriṇaṃ so 'bhyacodayat:
«rāja|mārgāḥ kriyantāṃ me patākābhir alaṅ|kṛtāḥ,
puṣp'|ôpahārair arcyantāṃ devatāś c' âpi sarvaśaḥ!
kumārā yodha|mukhyāś ca, gaṇikāś ca sv|alaṅ|kṛtāḥ,
vāditrāṇi ca sarvāṇi pratyudyāntu sutaṃ mama!
68.25 ghaṇṭāvān mānavaḥ śīghraṃ mattam āruhya vāraṇam
śṛṅgāṭakeṣu sarveṣu ākhyātu vijayaṃ mama.
Uttarā ca kumārībhir bahvībhiḥ parivāritā
śṛṅgāra|veṣ'|ābharaṇā pratyudyātu sutaṃ mama!»
śrutvā c' êdaṃ vacanaṃ pārthivasya
sarvaṃ puraṃ svastika|pāṇi|bhūtam,
bheryaś ca, tūryāṇi ca, vārijāś ca,
veṣaiḥ par'|ârdhyaiḥ pramadāḥ śubhāś ca,
tath" âiva sūtaiḥ saha māgadhaiś ca,
nāndī|vādyāḥ, paṇavās, tūrya|vādyāḥ
purād Virāṭasya mahā|balasya
pratyudyayuḥ putram ananta|vīryam.
prasthāpya senāṃ, kanyāś ca, gaṇikāś ca sv|alaṅ|kṛtāḥ,
Matsya|rājo mahā|prājñaḥ prahṛṣṭa idam abravīt,
68.30 «akṣān āhara, sairandhrī! Kaṅka, dyūtaṃ pravartatām.»
taṃ tathā|vādinaṃ dṛṣṭvā Pāṇḍavaḥ pratyabhāṣata,
«‹na devitavyaṃ hṛṣṭena kitaven', êti› naḥ śrutam.
taṃ tvām adya mudā yuktaṃ n' âhaṃ devitum utsahe.
priyaṃ tu te cikīrṣāmi. vartatāṃ yadi manyase!»

VAISHAMPÁYANA said:

When he heard of the boundlessly energetic prince's victory, King Viráta was so thrilled that he got goose pimples all over his body. Once he had given new clothes to the messengers, he gave orders to his ministers, saying: "Decorate the royal roads with flags, and let the gods and goddesses be worshipped everywhere with gifts of flowers! And let the young noblemen, leading warriors and courtesans, all beautifully decorated, go out to welcome my son with all kinds of musical instruments! Let the bell-carrying town crier quickly 68.25
climb onto a furious elephant and announce my victory at all the crossroads. Let Uttará, gorgeously dressed and ornamented, accompanied by numerous young noblewomen, go out to welcome my son!"

Having heard the king's speech, the entire city, swastika in hand, with drums, musical instruments, and water-borne conch shells, all came out from mighty Viráta's city to meet his son, endowed with infinite prowess. Beautiful young women in the most exquisite attire also came, as did encomiasts, panegyrists, heralds, musicians and drummers.

Once he had dispatched the army, the girls and the beautifully ornamented courtesans, the wise King of Matsya happily said, "*Sairándhri*, fetch the dice! Kanka, let the game 68.30
begin." When the son of Pandu noticed him addressing him in this fashion, he replied, "We have heard it said that a cheerful man should not play a game of dice with a professional gambler. So I do not dare to gamble with you today when you are so filled with joy. I only want to act in your advantage. But, if you have made your decision, then let the game begin!"

VIRĀṬA uvāca:

striyo, gāvo, hiraṇyaṃ ca, yac c' ânyad vasu kiñ cana,
na me kiñ cit tu rakṣyaṃ te, antareṇ' âpi devitum!

KAṄKA uvāca:

kiṃ te dyūtena, rāj'|êndra, bahu|doṣeṇa mānada?
devane bahavo doṣāḥ; tasmāt tat parivarjayet.
śrutas te yadi vā dṛṣṭaḥ Pāṇḍaveyo Yudhiṣṭhiraḥ.
sa rāṣṭraṃ su|mahat sphītaṃ, bhrātṝṃś ca tridaś'|ôpamān,
68.35 rājyaṃ hāritavān sarvaṃ. tasmād dyūtaṃ na rocaye.
athavā manyase, rājan, dīvyāma, yadi rocate.

VAIŚAṂPĀYANA uvāca:

pravartamāne dyūte tu Matsyaḥ Pāṇḍavam abravīt:
«paśya, putreṇa me yuddhe tādṛśāḥ Kuravo jitāḥ!»
tato 'bravīn mah"|ātmā sa enaṃ rājā Yudhiṣṭhiraḥ,
«Bṛhannalā yasya yantā, kathaṃ sa na jayed yudhi?»
ity uktaḥ kupito rājā Matsyaḥ Pāṇḍavam abravīt:
«samaṃ putreṇa me ṣaṇḍhaṃ, brahma|bandho, praśaṃsasi!
vācy'|â|vācyaṃ na jānīṣe, nūnaṃ mām avamanyase!
Bhīṣma|Droṇa|mukhān sarvān kasmān na sa vijeṣyati?
68.40 vayasyatvāt tu te, brahmann, aparādham imaṃ kṣame.
n' êdṛśaṃ tu punar vācyaṃ yadi jīvitum icchasi!»

VIRÁTA said:

You can't protect any of my wealth: women, cattle, gold or any other wealth I have, even if I do something other than gambling!

KANKA said:

Lord of kings, what business of yours is gambling, an idea full of evils? There are many sins involved in gambling and so one should avoid it. You may have seen or heard of Yudhi·shthira, the son of Pandu. He lost his massive, flourishing kingdom as well as his godlike brothers—he lost all his 68.35
sovereignty—so I do not take pleasure in gambling. But, irrespective of this, if you have made your decision and are pleased with it, my king, then let us play.

VAISHAMPÁYANA said:

While they were playing a game of dice, the King of Matsya said to the son of Pandu: "Look, my son has defeated men such as the Kurus in battle!" The high-souled King Yudhi·shthira replied, "How could he fail to be victorious, when he had Brihan·nala as his charioteer?"

Being spoken to in this manner, the Matsyan king became angry and said to the son of Pandu: "You contemptible brahmin! How dare you praise a eunuch as though he were my son's equal! You have no idea of what one should and shouldn't say, and you are certainly treating me with contempt! Why wouldn't he defeat all those warriors with Bhishma and Drona leading them? I forgive your offense, brah- 68.40
min, only for the sake of friendship. But don't say something like that again if you want to live!"

YUDHIṢṬHIRA uvāca:

yatra Droṇas, tathā Bhīṣmo,
Drauṇir, Vaikartanaḥ, Kṛpaḥ,
Duryodhanaś ca rāj'|êndras,
tath" ânye ca mahā|rathāḥ,
marud|raṇaiḥ parivṛtaḥ sākṣād api marut|patiḥ
ko 'nyo Bṛhannalāyās tān pratiyudhyeta saṅgatān?
yasya bāhu|bale tulyo na bhūto, na bhaviṣyati,
atīva samaraṃ dṛṣṭvā harṣo yasy' ôpajāyate,
yo 'jayat saṅgatān sarvān sa|sur'|âsura|mānavān,
tādṛśena sahāyena kasmāt sa na vijeṣyate?

VIRĀṬA uvāca:

68.45 bahuśaḥ pratiṣiddho 'si, na ca vācaṃ niyacchasi!
niyantā cen na vidyeta, na kaś cid dharmam ācaret!

VAIŚAṂPĀYANA uvāca:

tataḥ prakupito rājā tam akṣeṇ' āhanad bhṛśam
mukhe Yudhiṣṭhire kopān, «n' âivam, ity» eva bhartsayan.
balavat pratividdhasya nastaḥ śoṇitam āvahat;
tad a|prāptaṃ mahīṃ Pārthaḥ pāṇibhyāṃ pratyagṛhṇata.
avaikṣata sa dharm'|ātmā Draupadīṃ pārśvataḥ sthitām.
sā jñātvā tam abhiprāyaṃ, bhartuś citta|vaś'|ânugā,
pātraṃ gṛhītvā sauvarṇaṃ jala|pūrṇam a|ninditā
tac choṇitaṃ pratyagṛhṇād yat prasusrāva nastataḥ.

YUDHI·SHTHIRA said:

Where Drona, Bhishma, Drona's son, Ashvattháman, the son of the sun and Kripa, as well as Duryódhana, the king of kings, and other great warriors, are assembled, or even where Indra himself, lord of the Maruts in person, stands surrounded by hordes of Maruts, who else but Brihan·nala could fight against them all together? No one has ever been nor will anyone ever be his equal in strength of arms. He is a man who is completely overcome with excitement upon seeing a battle, and it is he who defeated all the congregated gods, *ásuras* and men. With such a companion as this, why indeed should your son not be victorious?

VIRÁTA said:

You have been repeatedly prohibited, but you will not 68.45
hold your tongue! If there were no one to punish, then no one would practice virtue!

VAISHAMPÁYANA said:

Inflamed with rage, the king struck Yudhi·shthira hard in the face with his die and threatened him, shouting, "Don't do it again!" Violently hit, blood ran out of his nose, but the son of Pritha caught it in his hands so it didn't fall to the ground. The virtuous-souled man glanced askance at Dráupadi, who was standing to one side, and, obedient to her husband's will, she understood his wish. The faultless lady took a golden cup full of water, and caught the blood flowing from his nose.

68.50 ath' Ôttaraḥ śubhair gandhair, mālyaiś ca vividhais tathā
avakīryamāṇaḥ saṃhṛṣṭo nagaraṃ svairam āgataḥ,
sabhājyamānaḥ pauraiś ca, strībhir, jāna|padais tathā.
āsādya bhavana|dvāraṃ pitre saṃpratyavedayat.
tato dvāḥ|sthaḥ praviśy' âiva Virāṭam idam abravīt:
«Bṛhannalā|sahāyaś ca putro dvāry Uttaraḥ sthitaḥ.»

tato hṛṣṭo Matsya|rājaḥ kṣattāram idam abravīt:
«praveśyatām ubhau tūrṇaṃ, darśan'|ēpsur ahaṃ tayoḥ.»
kṣattāraṃ Kuru|rājas tu śanaiḥ karṇam upājapat,
«Uttaraḥ praviśatv eko. na praveśyā Bṛhannalā.
68.55 etasya hi mahā|bāhor vratam etat samāhitam,
yo mam' âṅge vraṇaṃ kuryāc, choṇitaṃ v" âpi darśayet,
anyatra saṅgrāma|gatān na sa jīvet kathañ cana.
na mṛṣyād bhṛśa|saṃkruddho māṃ dṛṣṭvā tu sa|śoṇitam
Virāṭam iha s'|âmātyaṃ hanyāt sa|bala|vāhanam!»

tato rājñaḥ suto jyeṣṭhaḥ prāviśat Pṛthivīñjayaḥ.
so 'bhivādya pituḥ pādau Kaṅkaṃ c' âpy upatiṣṭhata.
tato rudhira|saṃyuktam, an|ek'|âgram, an|āgasam,
bhūmāv āsīnam ek'|ânte sairandhryā pratyupasthitam,
tataḥ papraccha pitaraṃ tvaramāṇa iv' Ôttaraḥ:
«ken' âyaṃ tāḍito, rājan, kena pāpam idaṃ kṛtam?»

VIRĀṬA uvāca:

68.60 may" âyaṃ tāḍito jihmo; na c' âpy etāvad arhati!
praśasyamāne yac, chūre, tvayi, ṣaṇḍhaṃ praśaṃsati!

Meanwhile, Úttara, being strewn with charming per- 68.50
fumes and beautiful garlands, happily entered the city at a slow pace, being honored by the citizens, women and people from the provinces. When he reached the door of the palace, he had himself announced to his father. So the doorman entered and said to Viráta: "Your son Úttara is waiting at the door with Brihan·nala."

The King of Matsya was delighted and replied to the doorkeeper: "Let them both enter immediately, for I am eager to see them both." But Yudhi·shthira, the king of the Kurus, gently whispered in the doorman's ear, "Let Úttara
enter on his own. Brihan·nala mustn't enter. For that long- 68.55
armed man has taken a vow that whoever wounds my body so that I bleed will not live unless it occurs in battle. He will not endure seeing me bleeding. Instead, he will become excessively angry and kill Viráta right here with his ministers and powerful army!"

Then the king's eldest son, Príthivin·jaya, entered and, once he had paid his respects at his father's feet, he also stood before Kanka. But as he saw that sinless man busily covered in blood, sitting on the ground at the back, being attended by the *sairándhri*, Úttara immediately asked his father: "Who has beaten this man, king? Who committed this sin?"

VIRÁTA said:

I beat this morally crooked man and it's less than he 68.60
deserves! When I was praising you, my brave son, he was praising that eunuch!

UTTARA uvāca:

a|kāryaṃ te kṛtaṃ, rājan. kṣipram eva prasādyatām
mā tvāṃ brahma|viṣaṃ ghoraṃ sa|mūlam iha nirdahet.

VAIŚAMPĀYANA uvāca:

sa putrasya vacaḥ śrutvā Virāṭo rāṣṭra|vardhanaḥ
kṣamayām āsa Kaunteyaṃ, bhasma cchannam iv' ânalam.
kṣamayantaṃ tu rājānaṃ Pāṇḍavaḥ pratyabhāṣata:
«ciraṃ kṣāntam idaṃ, rājan, na manyur vidyate mama.
yadi hy etat pated bhūmau rudhiraṃ mama nastataḥ,
sa|rāṣṭras tvaṃ, mahā|rāja, vinaśyethā, na saṃśayaḥ.
68.65 na dūṣayāmi te, rājan, yad vai hanyād a|dūṣakam;
balavantaṃ prabhuṃ, rājan, kṣipraṃ dāruṇam āpnuyāt.»
śoṇite tu vyatikrānte praviveśa Bṛhannalā.
abhivādya Virāṭaṃ tu Kaṅkaṃ c' âpy upatiṣṭhata.
kṣāmayitvā tu Kauravyaṃ raṇāḍ Uttaram āgatam
praśaśaṃsa tato Matsyaḥ śṛṇvataḥ Savyasācinaḥ,
«tvayā dāyādavān asmi, Kaikeyī|nandi|vardhana.
tvayā me sadṛśaḥ putro na bhūto, na bhaviṣyati.
padaṃ pada|sahasreṇa yaś caran n' âparādhnuyāt,
tena Karṇena te, tāta, katham āsīt samāgamaḥ?
68.70 manuṣya|loke sakale yasya tulyo na vidyate,
tena Bhīṣmeṇa te, tāta, katham āsīt samāgamaḥ?
ācāryo Vṛṣṇi|vīrāṇāṃ, Kauravāṇāṃ ca yo dvijaḥ,
sarva|kṣatrasya c' ācāryaḥ, sarva|śastra|bhṛtāṃ varaḥ,

ÚTTARA said:

King, you have done something that should never be done. Quickly appease him so that terrible brahminical poison does not scorch you to the roots.

VAISHAMPÁYANA said:

Having heard his son's words, Viráta, the augmenter of his kingdom, begged Kauntéya, who was like a fire hidden by ashes, for forgiveness. The Pándava answered the king when he entreated him for forgiveness: "King, it was forgiven a long time ago, and there is no anger in me. If the blood from my nose had fallen to the ground, then, great king, you would doubtless have been destroyed along with
your kingdom. But I do not blame you, king, for hitting 68.65
an innocent person, since as a general rule, my lord, the powerful quickly resort to violence."

When the bleeding was stemmed, Brihan·nala entered, and, once he had saluted Viráta and Kanka, he waited. The King of Matsya, who had gained forgiveness from the chief of the Kurus, then praised Úttara, who had returned from the battle, within earshot of Savya·sachin, saying, "O enhancer of Kaikéyi's joy, I have a true heir in you. I have never had, nor will I ever have, a son to match you.

How could you have fought with Karna, who does not
miss one step in a thousand, my boy, and how could you 68.70
have fought against Bhishma, who has no equal in the entire world of men, son? How could you have fought with Drona, the twice-born teacher of the Vrishni and Kuru heroes, that best of all wielders of weapons, who is the teacher of all kshatriyas, my lad? How could there have been a battle

tena Droṇena te, tāta, katham āsīt samāgamaḥ?
ācārya|putro yaḥ śūraḥ sarva|śastra|bhṛtām api,
Aśvatthām" êti vikhyātas, ten' āsīt saṅgaraḥ katham?
raṇe yaṃ prekṣya sīdanti hṛta|svā vaṇijo yathā,
Kṛpeṇa tena te, tāta, katham āsīt samāgamaḥ?
parvataṃ yo 'bhividhyeta rāja|putro mah"|êṣubhiḥ,
Duryodhanena te, tāta, katham āsīt samāgamaḥ?
68.75 avagāḍhā dviṣanto me, sukho vāto 'bhivāti mām,
yas tvaṃ dhanam ath' âjaiṣīḥ Kurubhir grastam āhave
teṣāṃ bhay'|âbhipannānāṃ sarveṣāṃ bala|śālinām!
nūnaṃ prakālya tān sarvāṃs tvayā yudhi, nara'|rṣabha,
ācchinnaṃ go|dhanaṃ sarvaṃ, śārdūlen' āmiṣaṃ yathā.»

UTTARA uvāca:

69.1 NA MAYĀ NIRJITĀ gāvo, na mayā nirjitāḥ pare.
kṛtaṃ tat sakalaṃ tena deva|putreṇa kena cit.
sa hi bhītaṃ dravantaṃ māṃ deva|putro nyavartayat.
sa c' âtiṣṭhad rath'|ôpasthe vajra|sannahano yuvā.
tena tā nirjitā gāvaḥ, Kuravaś ca parajitāḥ.
tasya tat karma vīrasya. na mayā, tāta, tat kṛtam.
sa hi Śāradvataṃ, Droṇaṃ, Droṇa|putraṃ ca vīryavān,
sūta|putraṃ ca, Bhīṣmaṃ ca cakāra vimukhāñ śaraiḥ.
69.5 Duryodhanaṃ, Vikarṇaṃ ca sa|nāgam iva yūtha|pam
prabhagnam abravīd bhītaṃ rāja|putraṃ mahā|balaḥ:
‹na Hāstinapure trāṇaṃ tava paśyāmi kiñ cana.
vyāyāmena parīpsasva jīvitaṃ, Kaurav'|ātmaja.

between you and the renowned Ashvattháman, the teacher's son, who is also a hero among all weapon-bearers? How could you have encountered Kripa, my son, upon sight of whom men sink down into despair like merchants who are robbed? How could you have fought against Duryódhana, the prince who can pierce a mountain with his powerful arrows, my lad?

My enemies have vanished, and a pleasant breeze blows 68.75
around me. Since you retrieved the wealth that the Kurus seized in battle, all those strong men are filled with terror! You have surely driven them all off in battle, you bull among men, and took my entire wealth of cattle away from them like tigers snatching meat."

ÚTTARA said:

I DID NOT RECOVER the cattle, nor was it me who defeated 69.1
the enemy. The entire feat was accomplished by some son of a god. In fact, that divine prince, a youth who could strike like lightning, made me turn back as I ran away in terror, and took his stand on the chariot. It was that man who won back the cattle and vanquished the Kurus. The achievement belongs entirely to that hero. It wasn't me who did it, father.

He made the son of Sharádvata, Drona, Drona's mighty
son, the *suta*'s son and Bhishma flee with his arrows. Then 69.5
the mighty man spoke to the terrified and defeated Prince Duryódhana and Vikárna like the leader of a herd of elephants, saying: "I do not see any protection for you in Hástina·pura. Try to save your life in combat, Kuru-born prince. You will not escape by running away, king, so make

na mokṣyase palāyaṃs tvaṃ, rājan, yuddhe manaḥ kuru.
pṛthivīṃ bhokṣyase jitvā, hato vā svargam āpsyasi!›
sa nivṛtto nara|vyāghro muñcan vajra|nibhāñ śarān
sacivaiḥ saṃvṛto rājā, rathe nāga iva śvasan.
tam dṛṣṭvā roma|harṣo 'bhūd, ūru|kampaś ca, māriṣa.
sa tatra siṃha|saṅkāśam anīkaṃ vyadhamac charaiḥ.
69.10 tat praṇudya rath'|ânīkaṃ siṃha|saṃhanano yuvā
Kurūṃs tān prahasan, rājan, saṃsthitān hṛta|vāsasaḥ.
ekena tena vīreṇa ṣaḍ|rathāḥ parinirjitāḥ,
śārdūlen' êva mattena yathā vana|varā mṛgā.

VIRĀṬA uvāca:

kva sa vīro mahā|bāhur deva|putro mahā|yaśāḥ,
yo me dhanam ath' âjaiṣīt Kurubhir grastam āhave?
icchāmi tam ahaṃ draṣṭum, arcituṃ ca mahā|balam,
yena me tvaṃ ca gāvaś ca rakṣitā deva|sūnunā.

UTTARA uvāca:

antar|dhānaṃ gatas tatra deva|putro mahā|balaḥ
sa tu śvo vā para|śvo vā, manye, prādur bhaviṣyati.

VAIŚAṂPĀYANA uvāca:

69.15 evam ākhyāyamānaṃ tu cchannaṃ satreṇa Pāṇḍavam
vasantaṃ tatra n' â|jñāsīd Virāṭo vāhinī|patiḥ.
tataḥ Pārtho 'bhyanujñāto Virāṭena mah"|ātmanā
pradadau tāni vāsāṃsi Virāṭa|duhituḥ svayam.
Uttarā tu mah"|ârhāṇi vividhāni navāni ca
pratigṛhy' âbhavat prītā tāni vāsāṃsi bhāminī.

up your mind for battle. If you win, you will enjoy the whole world, but if you are killed then you will have heaven itself!" That tiger-like king hissed like a snake on his chariot as he turned back, firing arrows like thunderbolts, surrounded by his counselors.

As I watched, my hair stood on end and my thighs trembled, sir, but the youth shot the army of lion-like men with
his arrows. Then, when that man with lion-like strength had 69.10
driven away the army of chariots, he laughed at the Kurus, my lord, and left them standing there once he'd taken their clothes. The six chariot-warriors were beaten by that single hero like forest-roaming deer by a lone exhilarated tiger.

VIRÁTA said:

Where is this long-armed hero, the highly famed son of a god, who recovered my wealth that the Kurus seized in battle? I want to see this man and pay honor to the mighty divine-born man who protected both you and my cattle!

ÚTTARA said:

That mighty son of a god disappeared right there and then, but I reckon he will make himself visible either tomorrow or the following day.

VAISHAMPÁYANA said:

Viráta, the lord of his army, was unaware that it was 69.15
the son of Pandu who was being described in this manner and indeed that he was living in disguise right there. Then, when given permission by high-souled Viráta, Partha gave the clothes to Viráta's daughter himself. Beautiful Uttará took the very costly, exquisite new clothes, and was

mantrayitvā tu Kaunteya Uttareṇa mah"|ātmanā
iti|kartavyatāṃ sarvāṃ, rājan, Pārtha|Yudhiṣṭhire,
tatas tathā tad vyadadhād yathāvat, puruṣa'|ṛṣabha,
saha putreṇa Matsyasya prahṛṣṭā Bharata'|ṛṣabhāḥ.

delighted. Kauntéya concocted a plan with high-souled Úttara, concerning everything that needed to be arranged for King Yudhi·shthira, the son of Pritha, my king. So, bull-like man, that bull of the Bharata race cheerfully carried it out accordingly with the Matsyan prince.

70–72
THE END OF THE PÁNDAVAS' EXILE

VAIŚAMPĀYANA uvāca:

70.1 TATAS TṚTĪYE divase bhrātaraḥ pañca Pāṇḍavāḥ
snātāḥ, śukl'|âmbara|dharāḥ, samaye carita|vratāḥ
Yudhiṣṭhiraṃ puras|kṛtya sarv'|ābharaṇa|bhūṣitāḥ
dvāri mattā yathā nāgā bhrājamānā mahā|rathāḥ,
Virāṭasya sabhāṃ gatvā bhūmi|pāl'|āsaneṣv atha
niṣeduḥ pāvaka|prakhyāḥ sarve, dhiṣṇyeṣv iv' âgrayaḥ.
teṣu tatr' ôpaviṣeṣṭeṣu Virāṭaḥ pṛthivī|patiḥ
ājagāma sabhāṃ kartuṃ, rāja|kāryāṇi sarvaśaḥ.
70.5 śrīmataḥ Pāṇḍavān dṛṣṭvā jvalataḥ pāvakān iva,
muhūrtam iva ca dhyātvā, sa|roṣaḥ pṛthivī|patiḥ
atha Matsyo 'bravīt Kaṅkaṃ deva|rūpam iva sthitam,
Marud|gaṇair upāsīnaṃ tri|daśānām iv' ēśvaram:
«sa kil' âkṣ'|âtivāpas tvaṃ sabhā|stāro mayā vṛtaḥ.
atha rāj'|āsane kasmād upaviṣṭas tv alaṅ|kṛtaḥ?»
parihās'|ēpsayā vākyaṃ Virāṭasya niśamya tat
smayamāno 'rjuno, rājann, idaṃ vacanam abravīt.

ARJUNA uvāca:

Indrasy'|ârdh'|āsanaṃ, rajann, ayam āroḍhum arhati,
brahmaṇyaḥ, śrutavāṃs, tyāgī, yajña|śīlo, dṛḍha|vrataḥ.
70.10 eṣa vigrahavān Dharma, eṣa vīryavatāṃ varaḥ.
eṣa buddhy" âdhiko loke, tapasāṃ ca parāyaṇam.
eṣo 'straṃ vividhaṃ vetti trailokye sa|car'|âcare,
na c' âiv' ânyaḥ pumān vetti, na vetsyati kadā cana,
na devā, n' âsurāḥ ke cin, na manuṣyā, na rākṣasāḥ,
gandharva|yakṣa|pravarāḥ sa|kiṃnara|mah"|ôragāḥ.

VAISHAMPÁYANA said:

AND ON THE third day, with their vow fulfilled, washed 70.1
and dressed in white clothes, the five Pándava brothers, the great warriors, gleaming with all their decorations, led by Yudhi·shthira, sparkled like intoxicated elephants at the door. Once they entered Viráta's assembly they sat on the thrones for kings and they all seemed like bright fires on altars.

And when they were sitting there, Viráta, the lord of earth, came to hold his assembly and to do all royal tasks,
and saw the glorious Pándavas like blazing fires. After a 70.5
moment's thought, the King of Matsya grew furious and said to the divinely handsome Kanka, who was sitting there like the king of the gods surrounded by hordes of Maruts: "I employed you as the gambling superintendent and a courtier! So why are you all dressed up and sitting on the royal throne?"

Having heard Viráta's words, but wanting to tease him, Árjuna smiled and said these words, my king.

ÁRJUNA said:

This man deserves to mount Indra's throne and share it with him, king. Devoted to the brahmins and learned in the Vedas, he rejects worldly concerns. He is constantly
engaged in sacrifice and firm in his vows. This man is the 70.10
best of the strong, and virtue incarnate. He is the foremost of wise men in this world, and his end will be asceticism. No other person in the three worlds of mobile and immobile creatures knows, or ever will know, what he knows of varied

dīrgha|darśī, mahā|tejāḥ, paura|jānapada|priyaḥ.
Pāṇḍavānāṃ ati|ratho, yajña|dharma|paro, vaśī.
maha"|ṛṣi|kalpo rāja'|ṛṣiḥ sarva|lokeṣu viśrutaḥ.
balavān, dhṛtimān, dakṣaḥ, satya|vādī, jit'|êndriyaḥ.
dhanaiś ca sañcayaiś c' âiva Śakra|Vaiśravaṇ'|ôpamaḥ.
70.15 yathā Manur mahā|tejā lokānāṃ parirakṣitā,
evam eṣa mahā|tejāḥ praj'|ânugraha|kārakaḥ.

ayaṃ Kurūṇām ṛṣabho dharma|rājo Yudhiṣṭhiraḥ.
asya kīrtiḥ sthitā loke sūryasy' êv' ôdyataḥ prabhā
saṃsaranti diśaḥ sarvā yaśaso 'sya iv' âṃśavaḥ,
uditasy' êva sūryasya tejaso 'nu gabhastayaḥ
enaṃ daśa|sahasrāṇi kuñjarāṇāṃ tarasvinām
anvayuḥ pṛṣṭhato, rājan, yāvad adhyāvasat Kurūn.
triṃśad evaṃ sahasrāṇi rathāḥ kāñcana|mālinaḥ
sad|aśvair upasampannāḥ pṛṣṭhato 'nuyayus tadā.
70.20 enam aṣṭaśatāḥ sūtāḥ su|mṛṣṭa|maṇi|kuṇḍalāḥ
abruvan māgadhaiḥ sārdhaṃ, purā Śakram iva ṛṣayaḥ.

enaṃ nityam upāsanta Kuravaḥ kiṅ|karā yathā,
sarve ca, rājan, rājāno dhan'|ēśvaram iv' âmarāḥ.
eṣa sarvān mahī|pālān kara|dān samakārayat,
vaiśyān iva mahā|bhāgo vivaśān sva|vaśān api.
aṣṭ'|âśīti|sahasrāṇi snātakānāṃ mah"|ātmanām

weapons. Neither the gods, nor *ásuras*, nor any men, *rákshasas*, *gandhárvas*, *yaksha* leaders, *kínnaras* or mighty snakes are like him.

He has the gift of foresight and great energy, and is dear to citizens and provincials alike. He is the greatest chariot-warrior of the Pándavas. He is intent on virtue and sacrifice and he is restrained. This royal sage is famed throughout all worlds as being like a mighty seer. He is strong, wise, intelligent, truthful and in control of his senses. He is like Indra in wealth and Kubéra in accumulation. He is a defender 70.15
of worlds like Manu with his outstanding prowess. He is indeed a man of enormous energy who treats all creatures with kindness.

He is the bull of the Kurus, Yudhi·shthira, the king of righteousness. His fame in this world has been elevated to the splendor of the sun, and his glory passes through all directions like its beams. Just as the rays of sunlight follow the dazzling risen sun, so when he lived among the Kurus ten thousand swift elephants followed behind him, king. Thirty thousand chariots wreathed in gold, furnished with excellent horses, followed behind him in those days. Just as 70.20
sages praise Indra, eight hundred heralds decked in earrings of beautifully sparkling jewels, along with panegyrists, sang his praises in the old days.

The Kurus, o king, and all kings waited upon him like slaves, just like the celestials upon Kubéra, lord of wealth. This illustrious man made all kings pay tribute as though they were subject vaishyas, despite the fact that they were free. Eighty thousand *snátakas* took their livelihood from this king, who is an excellent practitioner of vows. This king

upajīvanti rājānam enaṃ su|carita|vratam.
eṣa vṛddhān, a|nāthāṃś ca, paṅgūn, andhāṃś ca mānavān
putravat pālayām āsa prajā dharmeṇa vai vibhuḥ.
70.25 eṣa dharme, dame c' âiva, krodhe c' âpi jita|vrataḥ.
mahā|prasādo, brahmaṇyaḥ, satya|vādī ca pārthivaḥ.
śīghraṃ tāpena c' âitasya tapyate sa Suyodhanaḥ
sa|gaṇaḥ, saha Karṇena, Saubalen' âpi vā vibhuḥ.
na śakyante hy asya guṇāḥ prasaṅkhyātuṃ, nar'|ēṣvara.
eṣa dharma|paro nityam, ānṛśaṃsyaś ca Pāṇḍavaḥ.
evaṃ|yukto mahā|rājaḥ Pāṇḍavaḥ pārthiva'|ṛṣabhaḥ
kathaṃ n' ârhati rāj'|ârham āsanaṃ, pṛthivī|pate?

VIRĀṬA uvāca:

71.1 YADY EṢA RĀJĀ Kauravyaḥ Kuntī|putro Yudhiṣṭhiraḥ,
katamo 'sy' Ârjuno bhrātā, Bhīmaś ca katamo balī?
Nakulaḥ, Sahadevo vā, Draupadī vā yaśasvinī?
yadā dyūta|jitāḥ Pārthā, na prājñāyanta te kva cit.

ARJUNA uvāca:

ya eṣa Ballavo brūte sūdas tava, nar'|âdhipa,
eṣa Bhīmo, mahā|rāja, bhīma|vega|parākramaḥ.
eṣa krodha|vaśān hatvā parvate Gandhamādane
saugandhikāni divyāni Kṛṣṇ"|ârthe samupāharat.
71.5 gandharva eṣa vai hantā Kīcakānāṃ dur|ātmanām,
vyāghrān, ṛkṣān, varāhāṃś ca hatavān strī|pure tava.

protected the old, the helpless, the crippled and the blind like sons, and defended his people with justice. This king 70.25
has completed his vows in virtue, self-restraint and anger. He is exceedingly gracious to brahmins, and he is truthful.

King Suyódhana and his followers, such as Karna and Súbala's son, were quickly stung with pain on account of this man. But his virtues are not able to be calculated, lord of men. This son of Pandu is intent on virtue and always merciful. So, possessed of such things, how is it that this great king, the son of Pandu, a bull among kings, does not deserve a seat worthy of a king, lord of earth?

VIRÁTA said:

IF THIS IS THE Kuru king Yudhi·shthira, the son of Kuntí, 71.1
then which one is Árjuna, his brother, and which is mighty Bhima? Or Nákula, Saha·deva or the renowned Dráupadi? Since they were defeated at dice, the sons of Pritha have not be known of anywhere.

ÁRJUNA said:

This man whom you call Bállava, and is your cook, king, this man is Bhima, great king, of excellent prowess and terrifying force. This is the man who killed those *rákshasas*, enslaved to their fury, on the Gandha·mádana mountain, and took beautifully fragranced celestial flowers for Krishná's sake. This is the *gandhárva* who killed the wicked- 71.5
souled Kíchakas, and who killed tigers, bears and boars in your inner women's apartments.

yaś c' āsīd aśva|bandhas te, Nakulo 'yaṃ paran|tapaḥ;
go|saṅkhyaḥ Sahadevaś ca Mādrī|putrau mahā|rathau,
śṛṅgāra|veṣ'|ābharaṇau, rūpavantau, yaśasvinau,
mahā|ratha|sahasrāṇāṃ samarthau Bharata'|rṣabhau.
eṣā padma|palāś'|âkṣī su|madhyā cāru|hāsinī
sairandhrī Draupadī, rājan, yasy' ârthe Kīcakā hatāḥ.
Arjuno 'haṃ, mahā|rāja, vyaktaṃ te śrotram āgataḥ,
Bhīmād avara|jaḥ Pārtho, yamābhyāṃ c' âpi pūrva|jaḥ.
71.10 uṣitāḥ smo, mahā|rāja, sukhaṃ tava niveśane,
a|jñāta|vāsam uṣitā garbha|vāsa iva prajāḥ.

VAIŚAMPĀYANA uvāca:

yad" Ârjunena te vīrāḥ kathitāḥ pañca Pāṇḍavāḥ,
tad" Ârjunasya Vairāṭiḥ kathayām āsa vikramam
punar eva ca tān Pārthān darśayām āsa c' Ôttaraḥ.

UTTARA uvāca:

ya eṣa jāmbūnada|śuddha|gaura-
tanur, mahān siṃha iva pravṛddhaḥ,
pracaṇḍa|ghoṇaḥ, pṛthu|dīrgha|netras,
tāmr'|āyat'|âkṣaḥ, Kuru|rāja eṣaḥ.
ayaṃ punar matta|gaj'|êndra|gāmī,
pratapta|cāmīkara|śuddha|gauraḥ,
pṛthv|āyat'|âṃso, guru|dīrgha|bāhur
Vṛkodaraḥ. paśyata, paśyat' âinaṃ!
71.15 yas tv eva pārṣve 'sya mahā|dhanuṣmān,
śyāmo, yuvā, vāraṇa|yūthap'|ôpamaḥ,
siṃh'|ônnat'|âṃso, gaja|rāja|gāmī,
padm'|āyat'|âkṣo, 'rjuna eṣa vīraḥ.

The man who was in charge of your horses is Nákula, the scorcher of the enemy, and this is Saha·deva, your cowherd. Together they are the two great warrior sons of Madri. Both these beautifully dressed, ornamented, handsome and renowned bull-like Bharatas are a match for a thousand warriors.

This slender-waisted sweet-smiling lady with lotus-petal eyes, the *sairándhri*, is in fact Dráupadi, o king, for whose sake the Kíchakas were killed. I am Árjuna, great king, news of whom has clearly reached your ears as being the son of Pritha, the younger brother of Bhima, but elder brother of
the twins. We have lived happily in your home, great king, 71.10
living out our exile of secrecy like fetuses living in the womb.

VAISHAMPÁYANA said:

When those five Pándava heroes were revealed by Árjuna, Viráta's son told of Árjuna's prowess, and Úttara pointed out the Parthas once again.

ÚTTARA said:

This man whose body is bright as pure gold, like a massive fully grown lion, the one with the prominent nose, wide, large eyes and a long coppery face; this is the king of the Kurus. Next, look at this man with the stride of a furious king among elephants, who is bright as heated pure gold, with broad shoulders, and whose arms are long and heavy;
this is Vrikódara—look at him! And this man at his side is 71.15
the mighty archer, the dark-skinned youth, like the leader of a herd of elephants, whose shoulders are wide like those of a lion, whose stride is like a king among elephants, and whose eyes are large like lotuses—this man is the hero Árjuna.

rājñaḥ samīpe puruṣ'|ôttamau tu
yamāv imau Viṣṇu|Mahendra|kalpau.
manuṣya|loke sakale samo 'sti
yayor na rūpe, na bale, na śīle.
ābhyāṃ tu pārśve kanak'|ôttam'|âṅgī
y" âiṣa prabhā mūrtimat" îva gaurī,
nīl'|ôtpal'|ābhā, sura|devat" êva,
Kṛṣṇā sthitā mūrtimat" îva Lakṣmīḥ.

VAIŚAMPĀYANA uvāca:

evaṃ nivedya tān Pārthān Pāṇḍavān pañca bhū|pateḥ
tato 'rjunasya Vairāṭiḥ kathayām āsa vikramam.

UTTARA uvāca:

ayaṃ sa dviṣatāṃ hantā, mṛgāṇām iva kesarī.
acarad ratha|vṛndeṣu nighnaṃs tāṃs tān varān rathān.
71.20 anena viddho mātaṅgo mahān, ek'|êṣuṇā hataḥ,
su|varṇa|kakṣaḥ saṅgrāme dantābhyām agaman mahīm.
anena vijitā gāvo, jitāś ca Kuravo yudhi.
asya śaṅkha|praṇādena karṇau me badhirī|kṛtau.

VAIŚAMPĀYANA uvāca:

tasya tad|vacanaṃ śrutvā Matsya|rājaḥ pratāpavān
Uttaraṃ pratyuvāc' êdam abhipanno Yudhiṣṭhire:
«prasādanaṃ Pāṇḍavasya prāpta|kālaṃ hi rocate.
Uttarāṃ ca prayacchāmi Pārthāya, yadi manyase.»

Near the king are those most excellent men the twins, like Vishnu and great Indra. They have no equal throughout the whole world in beauty, strength and disposition. At their side stands Krishná, whose limbs are the purest gold, the ultimate incarnation of dazzling light, whose complexion is that of a midnight-blue lotus, like a goddess, the living embodiment of Lakshmi.

VAISHAMPÁYANA said:

Once he had introduced those five Pándava sons of Pritha to the king, Viráta's son then related Árjuna's prowess.

ÚTTARA said:

This is the man who annihilated our enemies like a lion among deer. He roamed among the hordes of chariots killing their best chariot-warriors. This man shot and 71.20
killed a huge elephant with a single arrow, and the beast, whose flanks were furnished with gold, fell hitting the earth with his tusks. It was this man who won back the cattle and defeated the Kurus in battle. My ears were deafened by the blare of his conch.

VAISHAMPÁYANA said:

Having heard his words, the powerful King of Matsya turned to Yudhi·shthira in supplication, and said to Úttara: "It seems clear that the time has come to beg for the Pándavas' mercy, and if you approve then I will give my daughter Uttará to Árjuna, the son of Pritha, in marriage."

UTTARA uvāca:

āryāḥ, pūjyāś ca, mānyāś ca, prāpta|kālaṃ ca me matam.
pūjyantāṃ pūjan'|ârhāś ca mahā|bhāgāś ca Pāṇḍavāḥ.

VIRĀṬA uvāca:

71.25 ahaṃ khalv api saṅgrāme śatrūṇāṃ vaśam āgataḥ;
mokṣito Bhīmasenena, gāvaś c' âpi jitās tathā.
eteṣāṃ bāhu|vīryeṇa asmākaṃ vijayo mṛdhe.
evaṃ sarve sah' âmātyāḥ Kuntī|putraṃ Yudhiṣṭhiram
prasādayāmo, bhadraṃ te, s'|ânujaṃ Pāṇḍava'|rṣabham.
yad asmābhir a|jānadbhiḥ kiñ cid ukto nar'|âdhipaḥ,
kṣantum arhati tat sarvaṃ. dharm'|ātmā hy eṣa Pāṇḍavaḥ.

VAIŚAMPĀYANA uvāca:

tato Virāṭaḥ param'|âbhituṣṭaḥ
sametya rājā samayaṃ cakāra.
rājyaṃ ca sarvaṃ visasarja tasmai,
sa|daṇḍa|kośaṃ, sa|puraṃ mah"|ātmā.
Pāṇḍavāṃś ca tataḥ sarvān Matsya|rājaḥ pratāpavān
Dhanañjayaṃ puras|kṛtya «diṣṭyā, diṣṭy"!» êti c' âbravīt.
71.30 samupāghrāya mūrdhānaṃ, saṃśliṣya ca punaḥ punaḥ
Yudhiṣṭhiraṃ ca, Bhīmaṃ ca, Mādrī|putrau ca Pāṇḍavau,
n' âtṛpyad darśane teṣāṃ Virāṭo vāhinī|patiḥ.
sa prīyamāṇo rājānaṃ Yudhiṣṭhiram ath' âbravīt:
«diṣṭyā bhavantaḥ samprāptāḥ sarve kuśalino vanāt!
diṣṭyā sampālitaṃ kṛcchram a|jñātaṃ vai dur|ātmabhiḥ!
idaṃ ca rājyaṃ Pārthāya, yac c' ânyad api kiñ cana;
pratigṛhṇantu tat sarvaṃ Pāṇḍavā a|viśaṅkayā.

ÚTTARA said:

I think the time has come for these noble, venerable, honorable and illustrious Pándavas to be worshipped by us, as they deserve no less.

VIRÁTA said:

Indeed, when I was under my enemies' control in battle 71.25
Bhima·sena rescued me, and my cattle have also been saved. It is through their strength of arms that we have been victorious in war. So we will all propitiate Yudhi·shthira, the son of Kuntí, along with our ministers. Bless you and your brothers, bull-like Pándava. You ought to forgive whatever we may have said out of ignorance, lord of men. The son of Pandu is certainly virtuous in his very soul.

VAISHAMPÁYANA said:

Then high-souled King Viráta was extremely pleased and, approaching him, formed an alliance, relinquishing to him his entire kingdom, along with his scepter, treasury and city. Next, the majestic King of Matsya addressed all the Pándavas, saying, "Thank heaven for this stroke of luck!,"
but first and foremost he spoke to Dhanan·jaya. Though 71.30
he repeatedly embraced Yudhi·shthira, Bhima and the twin sons of Madri and Pandu, and kissed their heads, Viráta, the lord of his army, was not satisfied with looking at them.

Delighted, he then said to King Yudhi·shthira: "Thank heavens you all reached me safely from the forest. Thank heaven you have overcome your wretched exile undiscovered by those wicked-souled men! This kingdom and whatever else I own is for the Parthas, so may the Pándavas accept

Uttarāṃ pratigṛhṇātu Savyasācī Dhanañjayaḥ;
ayaṃ hy aupayiko bhartā tasyāḥ puruṣa|sattamaḥ.»
71.35 evam ukto dharma|rājaḥ Pārtham aikṣad Dhanañjayam;
īkṣitaś c' Ârjuno bhrātrā Matsyaṃ vacanam abravīt:
«pratigṛhṇāmy ahaṃ, rājan, snuṣāṃ duhitaraṃ tava.
yuktaś c' âvāṃ hi sambandho, Matsya|Bhāratayor api!»

VIRĀṬA uvāca:

72.1 KIM ARTHAM, Pāṇḍava|śreṣṭha,
bhāryāṃ duhitaraṃ mama
pratigrahītuṃ n' êmāṃ tvaṃ
mayā dattām ih' êcchasi?

ARJUNA uvāca:

antaḥ|pure 'ham uṣitaḥ sadā paśyan sutāṃ tava,
rahasyaṃ ca prakāśaṃ ca, viśvastāṃ pitṛvan mayi.
priyo bahu|mataś c' âhaṃ nartako gīta|kovidaḥ;
ācāryavac ca māṃ nityaṃ manyate duhitā tava.
vayaḥ|sthayā taya, rajan, saha saṃvatsar'|ôṣitaḥ;
atiśaṅkā bhavet sthāne tava, lokasya vā, vibho.
72.5 tasmān nimantraye 'yaṃ duhitāṃ, manuj'|âdhipa,
śuddho, jit'|êndriyo, dāntas; tasyāḥ śuddhiḥ kṛtā mayā.
snuṣāyāṃ duhitur v" âpi, putre c' ātmani vā punaḥ
atra śaṅkāṃ na paśyāmi; tena śuddhir bhaviṣyati.
abhiśāpād ahaṃ bhīto, mithyā|vādāt, paraṃ|tapa.
snuṣ"|ârtham Uttarāṃ, rājan, pratigṛhṇāmi te sutām.

everything without hesitation. May ambidextrous Dhanan·jaya accept my daughter Uttará, for this best of men would make a suitable husband for her."

Thus addressed, the just King Yudhi·shthira glanced at 71.35
Dhanan·jaya, the son of Pritha, and Árjuna, being watched by his brother, said to the King of Matsya: "I will accept your daughter, king, as my daughter-in-law. It is indeed favorable for an alliance to be formed between the Matsyas and the Bharatas!"

VIRÁTA said:

WHY, BEST OF the Pándavas, do you not want to accept 72.1
my daughter, whom I am giving to you, as your wife?

ÁRJUNA said:

When I lived in the inner apartments I saw your daughter all the time, and she treated me as nothing but a father, both in private and in public. Since I was skilled in singing and dancing I was dear to her and she held me in high regard. Your daughter always thought of me as a teacher. King, I lived with her as a fully grown female companion for a whole year, and so a man in your position or, for that matter, the
entire world may well have false suspicions, lord. Therefore, 72.5
since I am pure and have full control of my senses, I invite your daughter to be my daughter-in-law, king, and by giving her away in marriage I thereby prove her purity.

I do not see any distinction between a daughter-in-law and a daughter, nor for that matter between a son and one's own self, so through this she will be proved to be chaste. I am afraid of false accusations and slander, scorcher of the enemy. So I accept your daughter Uttará as a daughter-in-

svasrīyo Vāsudevasya, sākṣād deva|śiśur yathā,
dayitaś cakra|hastasya, sarv'|âstreṣu ca kovidaḥ,
Abhimanyur mahā|bāhuḥ putro mama, viśām pate.
jāmātā tava yukto vai, bhartā ca duhitus tava.

VIRĀṬA uvāca:

72.10 upapannaṃ Kuru|śreṣṭhe Kuntī|putre Dhanañjaye,
ya evaṃ dharma|nityaś ca, jāta|jñānaś ca Pāṇḍavaḥ.
yat kṛtyaṃ manyase, Pārtha, kriyatāṃ tad an|antaram.
sarve kāmāḥ samṛddhā me, sambandhī yasya me 'rjunaḥ.

VAIŚAṂPĀYANA uvāca:

evaṃ bruvati rāj'|êndre Kuntī|putro Yudhiṣṭhiraḥ
anvaśāsat sa saṃyogaṃ samaye Matsya|Pārthayoḥ.
tato mitreṣu sarveṣu, Vāsudevaṃ ca, Bhārata,
preṣayām āsa Kaunteyo Virāṭaś ca mahī|patiḥ.
tatas trayodaśe varṣe nivṛtte pañca Pāṇḍavāḥ
Upaplavyaṃ Virāṭasya samapadyanta sarvaśaḥ.
72.15 Abhimanyuṃ ca Bībhatsur ānināya, Janārdanam
Ānartebhyo 'pi, Dāśārhān ānayām āsa Pāṇḍavaḥ.
Kāśi|rājaś ca, Śaibyaś ca prīyamāṇau Yudhiṣṭhire
akṣauhiṇībhyāṃ sahitāv āgatau pṛthivī|patī.
akṣauhiṇyā ca sahito Yajñaseno mahā|balaḥ,
Draupadyāś ca sutā vīrāḥ, Śikhaṇḍī c' â|parājitaḥ.
Dhṛṣṭadyumnaś ca durdharṣaḥ sarva|śastra|bhṛtāṃ varaḥ.
samast'|âkṣauhiṇī|pālā, yajvāno, bhūri|dakṣiṇāḥ,
ved'|âvabhṛtha|saṃpannāḥ, sarve śūrās tanu|tyajaḥ.
tān āgatān abhiprekṣya Matsyo dharma|bhṛtāṃ varaḥ

law, king. The beloved nephew of discus-bearing Vasudéva resembles a divine youth in his appearance and is skilled in all weaponry. He is my long-armed son Abhimányu, and he is fit to be your son-in-law and husband to your daughter.

VIRÁTA said:

How appropriately well spoken by the best of the Kurus, 72.10
Dhanan·jaya, the son of Kuntí and Pandu, who is always virtuous and is wise. Partha, may whatever you think should be done, be done immediately. For the man who has Árjuna for his relative has all his wishes granted.

VAISHAMPÁYANA said:

When the king of kings had spoken in this manner, Yudhi·shthira Kauntéya approved the agreement made by the King of Matsya and the son of Pritha. So, Bhárata, the son of Kuntí sent invitations to all his friends and Vasudéva, and Viráta the earth-lord did the same. Then, once the thirteenth year had come to an end, those five Pándavas prospered in every way at Viráta's city of Upaplávya. Bi- 72.15
bhátsu, the son of Pandu, brought over Abhimányu and Janárdana from Anárta, and also fetched the Dashárhas.

The King of Kashi and the earth-lord of Shaibya, friends of Yudhi·shthira, both arrived there with battalions. Mighty Yajña·sena also came with a battalion and the heroic sons of Dráupadi came, as well as Shikhándin, unbeaten by his enemies. The terrifying Dhrishta·dyumna, the best of those who wield weapons, also turned up. All those battalion lords were performers of sacrifices, liberal with gifts, informed in the Vedas and ritual purification, as well as brave and willing to die. When the King of Matsya, the best of those who wield

pūjayām āsa vidhivat sa|bhṛtya|bala|vāhanān.
72.20 prīto 'bhavad duhitaraṃ dattvā tām Abhimanyave.

tataḥ pratyupayāteṣu pārthiveṣu tatas tataḥ
tatr' āgamad Vāsudevo vana|mālī, Halāyudhaḥ,
Kṛtavarmā ca Hārdikyo, Yuyudhānaś ca Sātyakiḥ.
Anādhṛṣṭis tath" Âkrūraḥ, Sāmbo, Niśaṭha eva ca
Abhimanyum upādāya saha mātrā paraṇ|tapāḥ.
Indrasen'|ādayaś c' âiva rathais taiḥ su|samāhitaiḥ
āyayuḥ sahitāḥ sarve parisaṃvatsar'|ôṣitāḥ.

daśa nāga|sahasrāṇi, hayānāṃ ca daś' âyutam,
rathānām arbudaṃ pūrṇaṃ, nikharvaṃ ca padātinām,
72.25 Vṛṣṇy|Andhakāś ca bahavo, Bhojāś ca param'|âujasaḥ
anvayur Vṛṣṇi|śārdūlaṃ Vāsudevaṃ mahā|dyutim.
pāribarhaṃ dadau Kṛṣṇaḥ Pāṇḍavānāṃ mah"|ātmanām,
striyo, ratnāni, vāsāṃsi pṛthak pṛthag an|ekaśaḥ.
tato vivāho vidhivad vavṛdhe Matsya|Pārthayoḥ.

tataḥ śaṅkhāś ca, bheryaś ca, gomukh'|āḍambarās tathā
Pārthaiḥ saṃyujyamānasya nedur Matsyasya veśmani.
ucc'|âvacān mṛgān jaghnur, medhyāṃś ca śataśaḥ paśūn.
surā|maireya|pānāni prabhūtāny abhyahārayan.
gāyan'|ākhyāna|śīlāś ca naṭa|vaitālikās tathā
stuvantas tān upātiṣṭhan, sūtāś ca saha māgadhaiḥ.

weapons, saw all those men coming with their servants and forces and transport, he honored them, being well aware of his duty. Then he happily gave away his daughter to 72.20
Abhimányu.

Then, when all those kings had come from all around, Vasudéva arrived, garlanded with forest flowers, along with Haláyudha, as well as Krita·varman, the son of Hrídika and Yuyudhána, the son of Sátyaki. Those scorchers of the enemy Anádhrishti, Akrúra, Samba andNíshatha also came, bringing Abhimányu with his mother. Then Indra·sena came with well-built chariots, leading all the others who had lived together for a whole year.

Ten thousand elephants and a hundred thousand horses came with ten million chariots and a billion infantry soldiers, as well as numerous Vrishnis and Ándhakas and su- 72.25
perbly energetic Bhoja warriors following the glorious Vasudéva, a tiger among Vrishnis. Krishna gave wealth consisting of many women, jewels and clothing to each of the high-souled Pándavas in turn. Then the marriage between the Matsya and Partha families got under way, according to custom.

Conches and drums, trumpets and tambourines were all decided upon by the sons of Pritha and they resounded in the Matsyan king's palace. Various deer and other sacrificial beasts were slaughtered in their hundreds. Considerable amounts of wine and intoxicating drinks were fetched, and actors, bards, heralds and panegyrists, practiced in singing and storytelling, waited upon them reciting their eulogies.

72.30 Sudeṣṇāṃ ca puras|kṛtya Matsyānāṃ ca vara|striyaḥ
ājagmuś cāru|sarv'|âṅgyaḥ, su|mṛṣṭa|maṇi|kuṇḍalāḥ.
varṇ'|ôpapannās tā nāryo rūpavatyaḥ, sv|alaṅ|kṛtāḥ;
sarvāś c' âbhyabhavat Kṛṣṇā rūpeṇa yaśasā śriyā.
parivāry' Ôttarāṃ tās tu rāja|putrīm alaṅ|kṛtām,
sutām iva Mahendrasya puras|kṛty' ôpatasthire.

tāṃ pratyagṛhṇāt Kaunteyaḥ sutasy' ârthe Dhanañjayaḥ,
Saubhadrasy' ân|avady'|âṅgīṃ Virāṭa|tanayāṃ tadā.
tatr' âtiṣṭhan mahā|rājo rūpam Indrasya dhārayan.
snuṣāṃ tāṃ pratijagrāha Kuntī|putro Yudhiṣṭhiraḥ.
72.35 pratigṛhya ca tāṃ Pārthaḥ, puras|kṛtya Janārdanam,
vivāhaṃ kārayām āsa Saubhadrasya mah"|ātmanaḥ.

tasmai sapta sahasrāṇi hayānāṃ vāta|raṃhasām,
dve ca nāga|śate mukhye prādād, bahu dhanaṃ tadā.
hutvā samyak samiddh'|âgnim, arcayitvā dvi|janmanaḥ,
rājyaṃ balaṃ ca kośaṃ ca sarvam ātmānam eva ca.

kṛte vivāhe tu tadā Dharma|putro Yudhiṣṭhiraḥ
brāhmaṇebhyo dadau vittaṃ yad upāharad Acyutaḥ.
go|sahasrāṇi, ratnāni, vastrāṇi vividhāni ca,
bhūṣaṇāni ca mukhyāni, yānāni, śayanāni ca,
72.40 bhojanāni ca hṛdyāni, pānāni vividhāni ca.
tan mah"|ôtsava|saṃkāśaṃ hṛṣṭa|puṣṭa|jan'|āyutam
nagaraṃ Matsya|rājasya śuśubhe, Bharata'|ṛṣabha.

Next came the preeminent Matsyan women, with perfect 72.30
figures, decked in earrings of dazzling jewels, with Sudéshna at their head. But Krishná surpassed all those beautiful
women, with their charming complexions and lovely ornaments, in terms of beauty, fame and splendor. They formed
Uttará's retinue and led the ornamented princess, who resembled great Indra's daughter, forward.

Dhanan·jaya Kauntéya accepted Viráta's daughter of
faultless limbs, on behalf of his son by Subhádra. Then great
King Yudhi·shthira, son of Kuntí, as handsome as Indra,
took his place there and also accepted her as his daughter-
in-law. Once he had accepted her, the son of Pritha, with 72.35
Janárdana in front of him, got Subhádra's high-souled son's
marriage ceremony under way.

Viráta gave him seven thousand horses, fleet as the wind, two hundred superb elephants and a great deal of wealth besides. Once he had poured the oblation and fuel onto the fire and worshipped the twice-born, Viráta offered his kingdom, army, treasury and his entire self to the Pándavas.

After the marriage was over, Yudhi·shthira, the son of
Dharma, gave the wealth that imperishable Krishna had
brought to the brahmins. He gave away thousands of cattle,
jewels, beautiful robes, excellent ornaments, chariots and
beds, food and various lovely drinks. The Matsyan king's 72.40
capital, o bull-like Bharata, brimming with joyful, well-fed
people, sparkled like a great festival.

NOTES

Bold *references are to the English text;* ***bold italic*** *references are to the Sanskrit text. An asterisk (*) in the body of the text marks the word or passage being annotated.*

1.15 The god Dharma granted the Pándavas a boon ('The Forest' (*Vana/parvan*) MBh III.298.16) to ensure that they would not be recognized in this thirteenth year of exile.

1.24 The name **Kanka** means heron. Yudhi·shthira's father, the god Dharma, appeared to the Pándavas at the end of 'The Forest' (*Vana/parvan*, MBh III.297.11) in the form of a *yakṣa* heron, promising them that they would remain unrecognized during their year in disguise.

2.32 The story of Nala's period of living in disguise begins in 'The Forest' (*Vana/parvan*), MBh III.13.

3.18 Technically, a **sairándhri** is a mixed-caste servant or artisan who takes residence in an employer's home, often with a specific skill, such as, in this instance, hairdressing. They had more freedom than some servants and could travel to find employment, like contract workers. Elsewhere in the book I will leave *sairándhri* untranslated in the English, for there is no suitable English translation.

5.23 'The Great Hall' (*Sabhā/parvan*), MBh II.56.

5.24 'The Great Hall' (*Sabhā/parvan*), MBh II.29.

5.25 Notice here how the text shows the derivation of **Nákula**'s name: *na kule* from ***kule n' âsti***.

5.26 'The Great Hall' (*Sabhā/parvan*), MBh II.28.

7.1 Viráta's city is situated in the modern district of Jaipur, in Rajasthan.

14.34 **Suta** can mean charioteer or herald. When the context is specific, I have translated it accordingly, but when used as a patronymic of Kíchaka, as here, or Karna, I have left it in transliteration to try to enforce the sense of the word as a title of rank or position in court.

18.2 In 'The Great Hall' (*Sabhā/parvan*), MBh II.60, Duryódhana sends a servant to drag Dráupadi to court. However, he is hesitant to do so, and so it is Duhshásana who drags her to court.

22.82 Shiva was excluded from his father-in-law's great sacrifice, and, being insulted, he destroyed Daksha's sacrifice.

39.10 Hánuman the monkey king is the emblem upon Árjuna's flag. Hánuman is the enemy of Rávana, the king of Lanka.

39.10 This title refers to the fact that Árjuna has the same name as a tree.

39.10 This is a reference to Indra, the enemy of the mountains. It was Indra who removed the mountains' wings and forced them to remain motionless. The only exception to this being Máinaka, son of Mount Himálaya.

49.12 Literally, this means "should be given a remedy," but I have tried to leave it idiomatic.

55.19 The translation of this *śloka* uses the commentary of Nila·kantha, and so readers may find it is not exactly literal.

PROPER NAMES AND EPITHETS

ÁDITYAS Collection of gods whose chief was Váruna

AGÁSTI Sage and husband of Lopa·mudra. Agásti is the reputed author of several hymns in the 'Rig Veda'

AGNI Fire and the fire god. Agni is a chief god in the Vedic pantheon

AIRÁVATA Indra's elephant

AJÁTA·SHATRU Name of Yudhi·shthira

AKRÚRA Krishna's paternal uncle

ALÁMBUSHA Name of an *ápsaras*

ALÁMBUSHA A *rákshasa* whom Ghatótkacha kills

ANADHRÍSHTI Pándavan ally

ANÁRTA Name of a country

ÁNDHAKA Name of tribe descended originally from Yadu

ÁPSARAS Celestial nymphs; companions of the *gandhárva*s

ARÍSHTA·NEMI Name Saha·deva adopts when in disguise

ÁRJUNA Third of the Pándava bothers. His ten names include Dhanan·jaya, Partha, Phálguna, Savya·sachin, Jishnu, Bibhátsu, Kirítin, Shveta·váhana, Víjaya and Krishna

ÁSHTAKA Legendary King

ASHVA·TTHAMAN Son of Drona and Kripi. Also a great warrior and a follower of the sons of Dhrita·rashtra

ASHVINS Divine Twins and fathers of Nákula and Saha·deva

ÁSURA Demon

AVÁNTI Name of a country and its people

BALÁHAKA One of Krishna's horses

BALÁKSHA Legendary King

BÁHLIKA King of the Báhlikas; allied to the sons of Dhrita·rashtra

BALI Name of a Demon

BÁLLAVA Name adopted by Bhima when in disguise

BHANU Legendary King

BHARAD·VAJA Patronymic of Drona

BHÁRATA Descendent of Bharata

BHARATA Son of Dasha·ratha and Kaikéyi; younger brother of Rama

BHIMA Second of the Pándava brothers also known as Bhima·sena, Vrikódara and Partha

BHISHMA Son of king Shántanu and Gangá; renowned for his wisdom and fidelity; follower of the sons of Dhrita·rashtra. Also known as Gangeya and Shántanava

BHOJA Name of a people descended from Maha·bhoja

BHRIGU Sage descendant of a line of men

BHUTI Prosperity personified

BRIHAN·NALA Name that Árjuna adopts when in disguise

CHEDI Name of a country in modern Chandail and Boglekhand and the name of a people

CHITRA·SENA Son of Dhrita·rashtra

CHYÁVANA Sage and husband of Sukánya

DÁNAVA One of a group of anti-gods

DÁRUKA Vasudéva's charioteer

DASHÁRNA Name of a people and a country

DEVA·DATTA Name of Árjuna's conch shell

DÉVAKI Krishna's mother

DHARMA The divine personification of the Law (*dharma*) and Yudhi·shthira's father

DHAUMYA Family priest of the Pándavas

DHRISTHA·DYUMNA Son of Drúpada

DHRITA·RASHTRA The blind Kuru king; father of the hundred Káuravas, including Duryódhana

DRÁUPADI Wife of the five Pándava brothers; Drúpada' daughter. Also known as Krishná and Pancháli

DRONA Brahmin warrior and teacher of the Káuravas and Pándavas;

father of Ashva·tthaman

DRÚPADA King of Panchála; father of Dhrishta·dyumna, Shikhándin and Dráupadi

DÚHSAHA Son of Dhrita·rashtra

DÚHSHALA Son of Dhrita·rashtra

DUHSHÁSANA Son of Dhrita·rashtra

DURGA Goddess also known as Uma or Párvati, the wife of Shiva

DÚRMUKHA Son of Dhrita·rashtra

DURYÓDHANA Eldest son of of Dhrita·rashtra and king of the Káuravas. Also known as Suyódhana and Dharta·rashtra

DVAITA·VANA Name of a forest

DVÁRAVATI Krishna's capital city, in modern day Gujarat. One of the seven sacred cities

DYUMAT·SENA Prince of Shalva; father of Sátyavat

GANDHÁRVA Celestial beings; companions of the *ápsaras*

GANDHÁRVI Female celestial being; companions of the *ápsaras*

GÁRUDA A bird deity; Vishnu-Krishna's vehicle; son of Káshyapa and Vínata

GÁUTAMA Kripa

GAYA Royal sage

GO·PALA Cowherd: Name of Saha·deva when in disguise

GRAHA Planets

GRÁNTHIKA Name that Nákula adopts when in disguise

GUDA·KESHA Árjuna

HALÁYUDHA Name of Bala·rama, Krishna's elder brother

HIDÍMBA Giant *rákshasa* killed by Bhima·sena

HRI Modesty personified

HRÍDIKA Father of Krita·varman

INDRA King of the gods and father of Árjuna. Also known as Shakra,

Vásava and Mághavan

INDRA·PRASTHA City of the Pandu princes. Known in modern day as Delhi

INDRA·SENA Ally of the Pándavas

ISHA Name of Shiva as lord of the North-east quarter

JAMAD·AGNI Sage descended from Bhrigu

JÁNAKA Father of Sita

JANAM·ÉJAYA A king who is the direct descendent of the Pándavas. The 'Maha·bhárata' is recited to him by Vaishampáyana

JATÁSURA A *rákshasa* killed by Bhima·sena

JAYA Yudhi·shthira's secret name at Viráta's court

JAYAD·BALA Saha·deva's secret name at Viráta's court

JAYAD·RATHA Sindhu-Sauvíra king who fights for the Káuravas

JAYÁNTA Bhima's secret name at Viráta's court

JAYAT·SENA Nákula's secret name at Viráta's court

JIMÚTA Wrestler whom Bhima defeats in Viráta's city

KAIKÉYI Descendent of Kékaya and wife of Viráta. Also known as Sudéshna

KALA·KHANJA Race of *ásuras*

KALI A form of the goddess Durga

KANKA Name that Yudhi·shthira adopts when in disguise

KANSA Krishna's cousin and enemy

KANTI Loveliness personified

KARNA Ally of Duryódhana; the Pándavas' older half brother; son of Kuntí and the Sun; foster son of Ádhiratha and Radha. Also known as Radhéya, Vrisha and Vasu·shena

KASHI Name of a people and country

KÉSHAVA Krishna

KÍCHAKA General of Viráta's army; brother of Queen Sudéshna of Matsya

KÍNNARA Celestial chorister

KÍNNARI Female celestial chorister

KIRTI Renown personified

KRIPA Son of sage Sharádvat who was raised by king Shántanu. A follower of the sons of Dhrita·rashtra also known as Sháradvata or Gáutama

KRISHÁSHVA Legendary King

KRISHNA Avatar of the god Vishnu; allied to the Pándavas

KRITA·VARMAN Ally of the Pándavas; Son of Hrídika

KUBÉRA Lord of riches and leader of the *yakshas* and demons. Also known as Vaishrávana

KUNTÍ Wife of Pandu; mother of the three eldest Pándava brothers, and, by the Sun, of Karna

KURUS Descendents of Kuru. The name can refer to the Káuravas and Pándavas, but more often it refers only to the sons of Dhrita·rashtra and their followers

LOPA·MUDRA Wife of Agásti

MÁDHAVA Krishna

MADIRÁKSHA Brother of Shataníka and Viráta

MADRI Pandu's second wife; mother of the Pándava twins Nákula and Saha·deva

MÁGHAVAN Indra

MÁLINI Celestial maiden

MÁLINI Name Dráupadi adopts when in disguise

MALLA Name of a people and a country

MANU First man and progenitor of the human race; archetypal sage

MARUT Storm Gods

MÁTALI Indra's charioteer

MATSYA Name of Viráta's kingdom.

MEGHA·PUSHPA One of Krishna's horses

MISHRA·KESHI Name of an *ápsaras*

NAGA Serpent demons

NÁHUSHA Legendary king and heavenly sage who was the father of Yayáti, and who was at one time installed as King of the Gods

NÁKULA One of the Pándava twins (brother of Saha·deva), and son of Madri and the Ashvins

NALA Name of a constellation

NANDA Husband of Yashóda and foster-father of Krishna

NARA The Primeval Man or eternal Spirit prevading the universe, always associated with Naráyana. Also associated with Árjuna

NARÁYANA Son of the Primeval Man, always associated with Nara. Also associated with Krishna

NÍSHATHA Son of Bala·rama and Révati

NIVÁTA·KÁVACHA *dánavas*

PAKA *daitya* killed by Indra

PANCHÁLA Name of a country and a people. Drúpada is king of the Panchálas and Dráupadi is their princess.

PÁNDAVA Son of Pandu

PANDU Heir to the Lunar Dynasty and brother of Dhrita·rashtra; legal father of the Pándavas; husband of Kuntí and Madri

PANDU Son of Vyasa and brother of Dhrita·rashtra and Vídura

PATÁCCHARA Name of a people.

PAULÓMA Class of Demon

PÁVAKA Agni

PINÁKA Rudra-Shiva's staff

PRAJA·PATI The secondary creator or demiurge

PUNDARÍKA Name of an *ápsaras*

PURU Son of Yayáti and King of the Lunar dynasty

RADHÉYA Karna

RAGHU Ancient King and ancestor of Rama

RÁKSHASA Demon

RÁKSHASI Female Demon

RAMA Avatar of Vishnu

RÓHINI Name of a constellation, personified as the Moon's favourite wife

RUDRA Vedic storm god and later Shiva

SÁGARA Ancient King of the Solar dynasty

SAHA·DEVA One of the Pándava twins (bother of Nákula) and son of Madri and the Ashvins

SÁINDHAVA "Coming from the country of Sindhu". Used as a title for Jayad·ratha

SAIRÁNDHRI Female servant often of mixed caste. Disguise which Dráupadi adopts

SAMBA Son of Krishna and Jámbavati

SANGRÁMAJIT Káurava warrior

SANKÁRSHANA Name of Bala·rama, Krishna's elder brother

SARÁSVATI Goddess of speech

SATYA·BHAMA One of Krishna's eight wives

SÁTYAVAT Son of Dyumat·sena and husband of Sávitri

SÁVITRI Wife of Sátyavat

SHAIBYA One of Krishna's horses; also name of a country.

SHÁKUNI King of Gandhára and son of Súbala; brother in law of Dhrita·rashtra and uncle of Duryódhana, for whom he wins the rigged dicing match against Yudhi·shthira. He is also known as Sáubala

SHALVA Name of a country

SHANKHA Viráta's eldest son

SHÁNTANU Father of Bhishma

SHARÁDVATA Patronymic of Kripa

SHATANÍKA Brother of Madiráksha and Viráta

SHATRU·SAHA Káurava warrior

SHIBI Legendary King who saved Agni from Indra

SHIKHÁNDIN Son of Drúpada born as a man to kill Bhishma

SHIVA Name of the destroying and reproducing deity

SHRI Glory personified

SHURA·SENA Name of a country around Máthura

SITA Wife of Rama and daughter of Jánaka; princess of Vidéha also known as Jánaki

SOMA Personified libation derived from the Soma plant and Vedic god

SOMA·DATTA King allied to the sons of Dhrita·rashtra

SUDÁKSHINA Uttará

SUDÉSHNA Queen of Matsya and wife of Viráta

SUGRÍVA Monkey king

SUGRÍVA One of Krishna's horses

SUKÁNYA Wife of the sage Chyávana and daughter of Sharyáta

SUPRATÁRDANA Legendary king

SURÁSHTRA Name of a country

SURYA God of the sun

SURYA·DATTA Matsyan Royalty

SUSHÁRMAN King of the Trigártas

SUTA Title of a charioteer or herald

TANTI·PALA Name that Saha·deva adopts when in disguise

TRINA·BINDU An ancient sage and prince

TÚMBURU A *gandhárva* who had previously been condemned to be a *rákshasa* by Kubéra

TVASHTRI The divine artisan, sometimes hostile to Indra, and father of the Tríshiras.

UGRA·SENA Legendary king of Máthura who was deposed by Kansa but later restored to his throne by Krishna

UPAPLÁVYA City in the kingdom of Matsya

ÚRAGA *Naga*

ÚTTARA Prince of Matsya; Viráta's son; Árjuna's charioteer; brother of Uttará; also called Bhumin·jaya and Príthivin·jaya

UTTARÁ Princess of Matsya, daughter of Viráta and sister of Úttara. Also known as Sudákshina

VAISHAMPÁYANA Pupil of Vyasa (seer and "author" of the epic). The character who recites the 'Maha·bhárata' to Janam·éjaya

VAISHRÁVANA Kubéra

VALA Demonic being defeated by Indra

VALI A daitya

VALIN Brother of monkey king Sugríva

VÁRUNA Major god of the Vedic pantheon; in later mythology god of the ocean

VÁSAVA Indra

VASU Class of gods

VASUDÉVA Patronymic of Krishna

VÁSUKI Serpent king

VÁSUMANAS Legendary King

VAYU god of the wind

VÍDURA Uncle of both sets of cousins (the Kurus and the Pándavas), and brother of Dhrita·rashtra and Pandu

VIDYA·DHARI Female supernatural being who serves Shiva

VÍJAYA Árjuna's secret name at Viráta's court, and also one of his ten names

VIKÁRNA Son of Dhrita·rashtra

VIRÁTA King of Matsya

VISHALÁKSHA Matsyan hero

VISHVA Class of Gods

VISHVA·KARMAN Divine Creative Architect either identified as the son of Brahma or with Tvashtri

Vivímshati Son of Dhrita·rashtra

Vrishni Name of a tribe of people from whom Krishna is descended

Vritra Vedic demon, the instigator of a universal drought who was killed by Indra

Yádavas Descendents of Yadu

Yajñaséni Dráupadi

Yakril·loma Name of a people

yaksha Tree spirit, able to assume any shape

yakshi Female tree spirit, able to assume any shape

Yama The God of the spirits of the dead

Yashóda Wife of the cowherd Nanda and Krishna's foster-mother

Yayáti Legendary King of the Lunar dynasty and son of King Náhusha

Yudhi·shthira Eldest of the Pándavas. Son of the god Dharma. Also known as Bhárata, Partha, best of the Kurus, Dharma·raja, and Ajáta·shatru

Yugan·dhara Name of a country

Yuyudhána Son of Sátyaka, also known as Sátyaki

INDEX

Sanskrit words are given in the English alphabetical order, according to the accented CSL pronunciation aid. They are followed by the conventional diacritics in brackets.

Permitted finals:							(Except āḥ/aḥ)			
k	ṭ	t	p	ṅ	n	m	ḥ/r	āḥ	aḥ	Initial letters:
k	ṭ	t	p	ṅ	n	ṃ	ḥ	āḥ	aḥ	k/kh
g	ḍ	d	b	ṅ	n	ṃ	r	ā	o	g/gh
k	ṭ	c	p	ṅ	ṃś	ṃ	ś	āś	aś	c/ch
g	ḍ	j	b	ṅ	ñ	ṃ	r	ā	o	j/jh
k	ṭ	ṭ	p	ṅ	ṃṣ	ṃ	ṣ	āṣ	aṣ	ṭ/ṭh
g	ḍ	ḍ	b	ṅ	ṇ	ṃ	r	ā	o	ḍ/ḍh
k	ṭ	t	p	ṅ	ṃs	ṃ	s	ās	as	t/th
g	ḍ	d	b	ṅ	n	ṃ	r	ā	o	d/dh
k	ṭ	t	p	ṅ	n	ṃ	ḥ	ā	aḥ	p/ph
g	ḍ	d	b	ṅ	n	ṃ	r	ā	o	b/bh
ṅ	ṇ	n	m	ṅ	n	ṃ	r	ā	o	*nasals* (n/m)
g	ḍ	d	b	ṅ	n	ṃ	r	ā	o	y/v
g	ḍ	d	b	ṅ	n	ṃ	*zero*[1]	ā	o	r
g	ḍ	l	b	ṅ	l̃[2]	ṃ	r	ā	o	l
k	ṭ	c ch	p	ṅ	ñ ś/ch	ṃ	ḥ	āḥ	aḥ	ś
k	ṭ	t	p	ṅ	n	ṃ	ḥ	āḥ	aḥ	ṣ/s
gg h	ḍḍ h	dd h	bb h	ṅ	n	ṃ	r	ā	o	h
g	ḍ	d	b	ṅ/ṅṅ[3]	n/nn[3]	m	r	ā	a[4]	*vowels*
k	ṭ	t	p	ṅ	n	m	ḥ	āḥ	aḥ	*zero*

[1]ḥ or r disappears, and if a/i/u precedes, this lengthens to ā/ī/ū. [2]e.g. tān+lokān=tāl̃ lokān.
[3]The doubling occurs if the preceding vowel is short. [4]Except: aḥ+a=o '.

Final vowels:

a	ā	i	ī	u	ū	ṛ	e	ai	o	au	*Initial vowels:*
' â	" â	y a	y a	v a	v a	r a	e '	ā a	o '	āv a	a
' ā	" ā	y ā	y ā	v ā	v ā	r ā	a ā	ā ā	a ā	āv ā	ā
' ê	" ê	' î	" î	v i	v i	r i	a i	ā i	a i	āv i	i
' ē	" ē	' ī	" ī	v ī	v ī	r ī	a ī	ā ī	a ī	āv ī	ī
' ô	" ô	y u	y u	' û	" û	r u	a u	ā u	a u	āv u	u
' ō	" ō	y ū	y ū	' ū	" ū	r ū	a ū	ā ū	a ū	āv ū	ū
a' r	a" r	y ṛ	y ṛ	v ṛ	v ṛ	' ṛ̂	a ṛ	ā ṛ	a ṛ	āv ṛ	ṛ
' âi	" âi	y e	y e	v e	v e	r e	a e	ā e	a e	āv e	e
' āi	" āi	y ai	y ai	v ai	v ai	r ai	a ai	ā ai	a ai	āv ai	ai
' âu	" âu	y o	y o	v o	v o	r o	a o	ā o	a o	āv o	o
' āu	" āu	y au	y au	v au	v au	r au	a au	ā au	a au	āv au	au